THE COUNTERFEIT HEIRESS

ALSO BY TASHA ALEXANDER

And Only to Deceive

A Poisoned Season

A Fatal Waltz

Tears of Pearl

Dangerous to Know

A Crimson Warning

Death in the Floating City

Behind the Shattered Glass

The Adventuress

A Terrible Beauty

Death in St. Petersburg

Elizabeth: The Golden Age

THE COUNTERFEIT HEIRESS

A

LADY EMILY

MYSTERY

Tasha Alexander

Minotaur Books New York

In memory of Barbara Mertz, who brought me countless hours of reading pleasure

This is a work of fiction. All of the characters, organizations, and events portrayed in this novel are either products of the author's imagination or are used fictitiously.

www.minotaurbooks.com

The Library of Congress has cataloged the hardcover edition as follows:

Alexander, Tasha, 1969–
The counterfeit heiress : a Lady Emily mystery / Tasha Alexander. — First edition.
p. cm. — (A Lady Emily mystery)
ISBN 978-1-250-02469-5 (hardcover)
ISBN 978-1-250-02468-8 (ebook)
1. Upper class—England—Fiction. 2. Impostors and imposture—Fiction. 3. Heiresses—Fiction. 4. Murder—Investigation—Fiction. 5. London (England)—Fiction. 6. Paris (France)—Fiction. 7. Historical fiction. I. Title.
PS3601.L3565C68 2014
813'.6—dc23

2014019882

ISBN 978-1-250-06743-2 (trade paperback)
ISBN 978-1-250-17515-1 (Minotaur Signature Edition)

Our books may be purchased in bulk for promotional, educational, or business use. Please contact your local bookseller or the Macmillan Corporate and Premium Sales Department at 1-800-221-7945, extension 5442, or by email at MacmillanSpecialMarkets@macmillan.com.

First Minotaur Signature Edition: March 2018

10 9 8 7 6 5 4 3 2 1

ACKNOWLEDGMENTS

Myriad thanks to . . .

Charlie Spicer, Andy Martin, Sarah Melnyk, April Osborn, Tom Robinson, and Anne Hawkins. I'm certain there is no better team in publishing.

Ann Mah, a wonderful writer whose knowledge of Paris is inspiring. I have never eaten so well as when I followed her advice. Wish we were at Ambassade de Bourgogne right now.

Jon Clinch, whose spectacular manuscript inspired me to have Estella read Belzoni.

Linda Kimmel, a fellow fan of Elizabeth Peters, who won the right to name a character in this book. We will be seeing much more of Christabel Peabody next year. . . .

As always, my writer pals and dear friends, whom I cannot do without: Brett Battles, Rob Browne, Bill Cameron, Christina Chen, Kristy Kiernan, Elizabeth Letts, Carrie Medders, Kelly O'Connor McNees, Deanna Raybourn, Missy Rightley, Renee Rosen, and Lauren Willig.

Xander Tyska, the best-ever research assistant. You will make an outstanding historian.

My parents, who are simply fantastic.

Andrew, always.

Tend me to-night:
May be it is the period of your duty:
Haply, you shall not see me more; or if,
A mangled shadow: perchance to-morrow
You'll serve another master.

—WILLIAM SHAKESPEARE, *ANTONY AND CLEOPATRA*

2 July 1897
Devonshire House, London

1

I raised the long, curved bow and with two fingers pulled back its string, all the while resisting the urge to remove one of the silver-shafted arrows nestled in the quiver slung over my shoulder.

"It would be so easy," I said, a sigh escaping my lips as I gazed across the ballroom.

"Too easy." My husband, his dark eyes sparkling, lowered my weapon with a single finger. "It would be beneath you, Emily."

"It is not often one is permitted to arm oneself at a ball," I said. "Fancy dress is a marvelous thing, and as such, my taking full advantage of the situation is nothing short of strict necessity. Without seeing an arrow, my prey may not realize she has been made a target."

"My dear girl, were you actually planning to shoot the dreadful woman, I would hand the arrows to you myself. As things stand, however, she is far too thick to understand that, by raising your bow, you are putting her on notice." Colin Hargreaves had no patience for gossips, and I had set my sights on one of society's worst, the lady whose lack of discretion had caused all of society to learn that Colin had refused the queen's offer of a dukedom some six months ago. The awkwardness of the incident had been compounded by the fact that my mother had encouraged Her Majesty to dangle the prize before him, and now both she and the queen were embarrassed, put out, and displeased. Not with my husband, however. So far as the two of them were concerned, he was incapable of any wrongdoing. They were convinced that I must have motivated his inexplicable refusal, and forgave him for indulging his wife, although the queen did make some quiet comments to him about how even she had, on occasion, bowed to the will of her dear Albert. My mother was less forgiving. She refused to see me for three months. I bore the loss with what I hope appeared more like reasonable equanimity than obvious relief.

"I am not certain one ought to take military advice from Beau Brummell," I said. I could not deny that Regency fashion, with its snug trousers, well-cut coats, and tall, gleaming boots, suited my husband's athletic form well. Nonetheless, Colin and I had argued about his choice of costume. "You should have dressed as an Homeric hero—"

"Hector, I assume?"

"You were perfectly free to go as Achilles if that better suited you," I said. "All I did was remind you that such a choice would necessitate your sleeping at your club instead of at home. I understand some husbands prefer that sort of arrangement."

He put his arm around my waist and pulled me close. "I shall never be one of those husbands. I am, however, stung that you could suggest I choose Achilles over Hector. You know me too well to make such a monumental error. Did we not cover this ground thoroughly before we were married?"

"Of course we did," I said. "I should never have considered your proposal if your views on the subject were not first utterly clear to me. Tonight, though, our hostess instructed us to dress in costumes allegorical or historical—"

"Dating before 1815," Colin interrupted. "Yes, I am well aware of the fact. It is why I specifically tied my cravat in a fashion favored by

Mr. Brummell prior to that year. My entire ensemble is an exercise in historical dress."

"So far as satisfying the technical details of our instructions, yes, but I stand by my belief that you are violating the spirit of the duchess's request."

"Riddle me, my sweet love, what matters to society more than fashion? And who mattered more to gentlemen's fashion than Beau Brummell? I argue that my choice of costume is of the greatest historical significance to the current gathering."

"You are impossible," I said, standing on my tiptoes to give him a quick kiss on the cheek.

"Be careful not to take your role as Artemis too seriously, Emily. I have plans for you later that do not include still finding ourselves in this wretched house at dawn. I see Bainbridge making eyes at you from across the room. He looks rather like a sheep, so I shall leave you to deal with it. I am long overdue for a cigar. Make sure to promise no one but me your last waltzes."

"I am not about to let you hide out until then," I said. He took my hand, raised it to his lips, lingering over it too long, just as he had in the days of our courtship, and my body, just as it had then, tingled from the tips of my toes to the top of my head.

Jeremy Sheffield, Duke of Bainbridge, and one of my dearest childhood friends, had not been making eyes at me from across the room or anywhere else. Jeremy thoroughly enjoyed the freedom provided by his status as bachelor duke as much as he thoroughly dreaded the confines of marriage. I might be carrying the bow of the goddess of the hunt tonight, but Jeremy kept himself armed daily with what he viewed as weapons in his fight against matrimony. I was one of them, the girl he could never wed, a semipermanent distraction that half the mothers in London were convinced kept him from proposing to their extremely eligible—and willing—

daughters. They believed I had once spurned him, and that his heart had not yet recovered. The old dragons might sympathize with him now, so long as they believed it could enhance their daughters' chances with him later, but pining forever would not be allowed. This fit nicely with my friend's own plans, as Jeremy had no intention of leaving his dukedom forever without an heir. He was simply too committed at present to his love of debauchery and irresponsibility to settle down. Only once he had achieved his oft-stated goal of being recognized as the most useless man in England would he agree to find a wife.

I waved my bow at him as he started to cross the room in my direction. Devonshire House was crammed full that night, none of the beau monde wanting to miss the masquerade ball Louisa, the Duchess of Devonshire, had planned in honor of the queen's Diamond Jubilee. Seven hundred of London's best had received invitations, and I could well believe that number, if not more, had heaved through the entrance gates to the house, eager to show off the elaborate costumes they had ordered for the occasion. It was as if we all had been dropped into a book of the best sort of historical fiction. Napoleon and Josephine sipped champagne while King Arthur and one of the myriad Valkyries (I had counted at least six so far) took a turn on the dance floor. Two Cleopatras did their best to avoid standing too near each other. Petrarch wooed Desdemona, Lord Nelson was in a heated political discussion with a seventeenth-century baron, and the Furies delighted the room with torches illuminated by electric lights.

Jeremy had made very little progress through the crowd to me, but a gentleman dressed as an ancient Greek from the time of Pericles stepped forward, his face hidden by a theatrical mask depicting tragedy, his flowing robes gathered over one arm. His eyes moved up and down my costume, but when he scrutinized my face, he tilted his head to the side, looked around, and sighed.

"*Sleep, delicious and profound* . . ." He let his voice trail.

"*The very counterfeit of death,*" I finished for him, delighted to have found someone at the ball who shared my love of the ancient poet. I had, some years ago, translated Homer's *Odyssey* from the original Greek and was often criticized by my mother for quoting all things Homerian. "What a surprise to—"

He grabbed my arm, wrenched it, and stood too close to me, his eyes flashing. "You are not at all as advertised, madam. I believe my requirements were quite clear. This will not do in the least." He turned on his heel and tore away from me. No sooner had he departed than Jeremy was at my side.

"My darling Em, have you scared off another suitor?"

"I am a married woman, your grace, I do not have suitors."

"Except me," he said, kissing my hand and grinning. "Frightful old bloke, wasn't he? Was he supposed to be Julius Caesar? Pity I don't have any knives. Or fellow conspirators."

"He was Greek, not Roman."

"Never could tell the difference."

"I cannot say that shocks me," I said. "It was very odd, him approaching me like that. He seemed to expect someone else. There must be another Artemis at the ball."

"There could be a thousand and yet none could so much as hope to catch the silvery beauty of the moon like you do, Em."

I rolled my eyes. "Really, Jeremy. There's no need to talk like that when you don't have an audience to witness your flirting. Who are you meant to be?" I asked.

"Robert Dudley, first Earl of Leicester, another gentleman in love with an unattainable lady. I am quite bent on bringing back Elizabethan fashion. It shows off my fine legs, don't you think?"

"I am not the proper person to answer such a question, but I see Cécile. She will no doubt have a firm opinion on the matter." Cécile du Lac, one of my closest friends, had come from Paris just for the Devonshires' ball.

"The duke is in need of a firm opinion?" Cécile asked as she joined us.

"Thinking about it, more like a firm hand," I said.

"I am incapable of giving him either at the moment," Cécile said. "I have just learned that Estella Lamar is in attendance this evening. Are you acquainted with her?"

"The same Estella Lamar who is always climbing pyramids and exploring India?" Jeremy asked. "One can hardly open a newspaper without seeing a picture of her somewhere exotic. I am a tremendous admirer of her exploits. Capital lady."

"She is the very one," Cécile said. "I have not seen her in more years than I care to admit and am bent on finding her. Will you help me? She is dressed rather like you, Kallista." Almost from the moment we had met, Cécile had refused to use my given name. She did not like it and much preferred the nickname bestowed on me by my first husband—a nickname he had never used in my presence and, hence, one I had not learned of until after his death. Cécile felt no compunction in usurping it as her own, but then, Cécile never felt compunction in usurpation when she believed it necessary to her own edification.

"Madame du Lac!" Jeremy took a step back and gasped. "Or should I say *Your Majesty*? What a wonderful thing to see Marie Antoinette with her head back where it ought to be."

"I have always wanted to have a boat in my hair," Cécile said. "It is irrational, I know, but I was taken with the notion as a child and thought this the perfect opportunity to play out the fantasy. Now help me find my friend." The House of Worth had made Cécile's costume, a fine confection of eighteenth-century fashion, replete with an enormous powdered wig fitted with a delicate model ship. Her silk satin gown, with its wide panier hoop, measured nearly six feet, and the stomacher that peeked through her overgown was covered with embroidered flowers shot through with golden thread.

We combed the ballroom first and then retreated to the garden at the suggestion of a young lady dressed as Dante's Beatrice, who informed us she had just seen Miss Lamar headed in that direction. Cécile explained, as we made our way, that Estella, upon inheriting an enormous fortune after her parents died within days of each other, had embarked on a life of adventure and exploration. As a result, she had not seen much of her friends in the following years and had proved a terrible correspondent. She and Cécile were of an age, and as young ladies in Paris society had been inseparable. Cécile had very much missed her in the subsequent years.

Cardinal Mazarin, engaged in a lively conversation with the Lady of the Lake, paused long enough to tell us Miss Lamar had just exited the supper tent, and we soon found her speaking with our host, the duke, who was dressed as the Emperor Charles V. Estella was in a costume so similar to mine that from a distance, we might have been twins. The folds of our Grecian robes fell with the same grace, though hers skewed to pale green while mine were icy blue. Her headdress had on it a crescent moon lit by electricity. Mine, though not a showcase of our rapidly advancing age, was still lovely, its mother-of-pearl moon surrounded by sparkling diamonds.

Cécile called out to her friend as we came upon her from behind. Miss Lamar turned, a smile on her face, and gave a hearty wave in our direction. Cécile stopped dead.

"You are not Estella Lamar." She marched toward the woman, her eyes flashing. "What is the meaning of this?"

The Duke of Devonshire, perplexed and embarrassed, did his best to placate his guests. "Madame du Lac, I assure you this is indeed Miss Estella Lamar. She took a break from her exploration of the Nile just to be at our little party."

"I do not think much else could have induced me to leave Egypt," Miss Lamar said. Her face did not betray her travels. It was lined, as one would expect for someone her age, but there was not so much as a hint of color from desert sun. My mother would have been most impressed.

"I have not the slightest interest in where you claim to have been or why you might want to be here," Cécile said, "but I would very much like to know what has induced you to pose as one of the dearest friends of my youth. I knew Estella almost as well as I know myself. You look nothing like her—your eyes aren't even the right color. Estella's are emerald green and quite unmistakable. Furthermore, she was a good four inches shorter than I. Am I to believe that exploration causes fully grown adults to add inches to their height? Or do your golden sandals have heels of six or seven inches?"

Miss Lamar—or whoever she was—blanched. Her eyes darted nervously and her lips trembled. Cécile moved closer to her and without the slightest hesitation the other woman pushed her away, flinging her roughly to the ground, and started to run. I lunged forward, wanting to make sure my friend, who had whacked her head on the base of a decorative column, was all right.

"This is but a trifle," Cécile said, blotting the blood on her forehead with a lace handkerchief. "You must apprehend her at once."

Estella

Truth be told, Estella had never much liked going out. Not even when she was a small girl, and her nurse had taken her through the narrow streets of Paris, before Baron Haussmann had torn them up to make way for his grand boulevards, to the private gardens outside the Tuileries Palace, where the emperor invited selected children to play with his son, the Prince Imperial. Estella was far too old to play with the prince, and she had never understood the fascination some people had for gardens. She did not like the way the flowers moved in the wind, as if they were alive, nor could she abide the teeming insects flitting in and out around them. As she grew older, this lack of understanding expanded from gardens to society in general. Why an otherwise rational being would choose to spend the evening in a crowded ballroom or at a tedious dinner party mystified her. All those voices, talking at once, were impossible to understand. She despised it.

Estella's father, one of the richest men in France, had spoiled her from the beginning, but with complete disregard for her interests and passions. He was older than her friends' fathers by almost a generation, and had married her mother after the death of his much-loved first wife. Estella's half siblings, all four of them, resented their stepmother, but had long since left home and started their own families, making no effort to contact Estella until their father's will had stunned them into wanting to know her better.

One might easily imagine that a gentleman in Monsieur Lamar's position had chosen his second wife with little regard for love. Having been made a widower once, he must be forgiven for refusing to risk his heart another time. He was, as he often said, excessively fond of the new Madame Lamar. She was a pretty little thing, petite and curvy, with a quick wit and generous nature, and it could not be denied that her husband felt a passionate attraction to her, at least until the ravages of time began to erode the youthful beauty that he had once found so appealing. He still treated her with care and respect, but Madame Lamar, so many years younger than he, craved adoration, and as her husband could not provide her with that, she insisted on having it from her daughter.

Estella needed no convincing. Her mother was a vision of loveliness and told the most exciting stories. Nurse was boring as anything, so Estella took to hiding in a nursery cupboard as often as possible. Monsieur Lamar might have found this odd had it ever been brought to his attention, but as he never ventured to the nursery and didn't speak to the nurse when she brought Estella down for her daily quarter of an hour visit with her parents, his daughter's peculiar habits were wholly unknown to him. Madame Lamar thought Estella's cupboard charming, and ordered the nurse to fit it out for the child so that it might be a more comfortable hiding place. Nurse removed the lowest shelf, covered the small floor with a soft bit of carpet, and placed a child-sized stool in the corner. In the opposite corner, Estella stored a little silver box covered with engraved flowers, given to her by her mother to house treasures. When Madame Lamar inquired as to why the box remained empty more than a year after she had presented it to her daughter, Estella explained that as she was unable to capture the stories her mother told her, there was nothing precious enough to go inside. Madame Lamar could not have been more charmed and suggested that Estella start telling stories of her own to the dolls Monsieur Lamar gave to the child every month.

Until then, Estella had never taken particular notice of the dolls with their porcelain faces and elaborate dresses. Now that her mother had anointed them as *Worthwhile,* Estella looked at them from an entirely new point of view. She chose the ones she liked the best, preferring ones with eyes the same hue of emerald as her own, and allowed these favorites to sit in her cupboard with her. Her mother had erred in only one way, by suggesting Estella could invent wonderful stories. Why would Estella even try when she already knew by heart the best ones? She told her mother's stories to the dolls, over and over. They proved a good audience.

Madame Lamar happily indulged the child until she reached an age when moving in society became necessary. When Estella resisted attending parties and dances, her mother offered no sympathy. Madame Lamar wanted to be adored in public, and if her husband was not up to the job, she believed her daughter ought to rise to the occasion. Estella had no wish to disappoint her mother, and when she realized what it was her mother required, she did her best to satisfy her, but the girl proved too awkward to be of much use. Madame Lamar longed for her to shine socially, to be a belle, to have the brightest and best men in France vying for her affections, all the while noticing that the young lady standing before them could never have been so remarkable if it were not for her extraordinary mother. Estella was to be Madame Lamar's crowning glory.

This, alas, was not to be. Estella rarely made eye contact with anyone other than her mother. She never knew what to say to men when they attempted a flirtation. Once, at a ball, she started to tell one of her mother's stories, one Estella had repeated often to her dolls, and was crushed when the group around her burst into laughter. Cécile du Lac, a young lady her age, whom Estella's mother had coaxed her time and time again to befriend, stepped forward and scolded the group.

"If you ingrates are incapable of realizing Mademoiselle Lamar is telling you something of great importance to her, you do not deserve her company." With that, Cécile took Estella by the arm and marched her out of the room and into the grand hall of the house. "They are reprehensible, the lot of them. Is your mother insisting that you, too, marry? I hate the very idea of marriage, but can no longer avoid it. You must come to my wedding next month. I can promise you copious amounts of champagne."

That had cemented their friendship, although Estella had never quite managed to admit to Cécile that marriage wasn't the only thing she wanted to avoid. Cécile had taken her up, and for now that would suffice to satisfy her mother. When, soon after the wedding, Cécile's husband died, Estella used her friend's grief to persuade her mother that after witnessing such a tragedy she should be allowed to wait a little longer before entering into an engagement of her own. Her mother never need know Cécile did not miss her husband in the least, and by the time Estella would have had to start taking seriously her parents' efforts to see her married, the issue had become moot. Typhoid took them both from her in the span of a single week.

2

I left Cécile in the very capable hands of the Duke of Devonshire, grabbed Jeremy by the arm, and shoved him in front of me so that he might clear a path through the crowd as we searched for the woman we now believed to be an ersatz Estella. We saw her go up the garden stairs and back into the house, but could not reach her before she had disappeared into the ballroom. I caught a glimpse of her as she slipped out of the room and did my best to catch her, but was unable to get close enough.

"She's gone," Jeremy said. I had sent him running ahead to the front of the house to inquire if she had been witnessed leaving. "The servants say she went on foot, but it's entirely possible her carriage is waiting outside in the crush. The street is all but blocked."

"Then we need to search every carriage," I said. I felt a hand on my back and turned to see my husband.

"What trouble are the two of you causing?" he asked, his countenance growing serious as he listened to my story and shook his head. "The carriages are unlikely to prove of any use. Even if one of them belongs to her, it would not be able to move and she would have had no choice but to continue on foot if escape was her goal. No doubt she is already in a hansom cab headed no one knows where."

I might have objected to Colin's dismissal of my idea that we search the carriages were he not the most skilled and trusted agent at the Crown's disposal. The queen quite depended on him whenever pesky matters cropped up requiring a discreet sort of investigation, and although there were few things about which Her Majesty and I agreed, Colin's talents were one of them. "Quite," I said. "What do you suggest?"

"Nothing," he said. "A woman comes into a costume ball pretending to be someone she is not. What is the crime? If anything, she has admirably stuck to the spirit of the evening."

"She is pretending to be someone invited as a guest," I said. "That is a far cry from turning up in an ironic costume."

"Devonshire thought it was a coup to lure the mysterious Estella Lamar to his party," Jeremy said. "I can't imagine he would have welcomed an imposter into his home."

Colin frowned. "The duchess may have thought it was a coup. I can assure you it was of no significance to Devonshire. I should not be shocked to learn that the duchess planned the whole thing as a nice bit of theater for her party. Do you really think someone like Estella Lamar, who busies herself exploring the world, would have the slightest interest in a fancy dress ball?"

I sighed. "Perhaps you are right."

"I never thought I would agree with any of your deductions, Hargreaves," Jeremy said. "It always astonishes me when you prove useful."

"Is that so?" Colin asked. "Then astonish me by proving your own self useful, Bainbridge. Dance with my wife. I've never been able to tolerate a quadrille."

"Cécile may never forgive you," I said as my husband untied the long ribbon, embroidered with the Greek key, that crossed the bodice of my dress and wrapped around my waist.

"I rushed straight to her side, offered to spirit her home and call for a doctor. How have I not taken adequate care of her? She chose to stay at the party. If anything, I may find it difficult to forgive her for barring us from making an early exit. I told you I had no desire to stay until dawn."

"She is worried about her friend," I said, placing over the back of a chair the delicate silver ivy that had hung from my waist. Colin removed my headdress. "She did not need anything further from you regarding her own self, but she does want us to look into the matter of the woman impersonating Estella Lamar."

"I do not wish to speak of it." He fiddled with the pins in my hair, causing it to spill in masses of unruly waves over my shoulders. "Come to think of it, there is nothing of which I wish to speak at the moment." He bent over and kissed my neck and I knew distracting him from his purpose would be folly. Deciding this purpose was far more interesting than any conversation, I tugged at his cravat, and was silently cursing Beau Brummell for adopting such complicated knots, when a sharp knock on the door brought us both to attention.

"Mr. Hargreaves, sir, Davis here." Our butler never opened my bedroom door without first announcing himself. "A footman has come from the Duke of Devonshire. His Grace requires you most urgently. I am afraid a guest at his party has turned up dead. Murdered, sir. I assume I need say nothing more."

We were out the door almost at once. Rosy-fingered dawn had already begun to streak the sky as we returned to Devonshire House, where the duke, after a brief and private chat with my husband, thanked me for not being angry at our having been disturbed at such an antisocial hour and then left us to our work. He showed no surprise that I had accompanied my husband. My reputation had preceded me, and he knew full well I would have my piece of the investigation; I had proved myself too many times in the past for it to be any other way.

Colin explained the situation to me as soon as we were free from our host, who, despite accepting my having a role, had not felt personally comfortable discussing murder with a lady. The body of a middle-aged woman had been found, not in his grounds, but more than a mile away, her clothing, or rather, her costume, giving her away as a guest of the duke's. The police had come to Devonshire House in the hope of identifying her, but here the duke had failed them. All he could tell them was that he had believed her to be Estella Lamar until Cécile du Lac had corrected his error. He had thought it best to summon Colin at once. The family, he had explained, did not desire any part in a scandal. Neither he nor the duchess had the slightest idea as to the truth about their mysterious guest, and they were eager to have the matter separated from them and their home as quickly as possible.

Colin directed our carriage to Lambeth Bridge, where members of Scotland Yard met us. They frowned when they saw me but kept their thoughts silent as they led us to a sad scene near the grounds of St. Mary's School. The body, still dressed in the robes of Artemis so similar to my own, lay crumpled in a heap underneath a tree.

"This rather changes the situation," I said. "Perhaps Cécile is right to be concerned about her friend." We inspected the poor woman's remains—she had been stabbed in the neck—and then I left Colin to examine the rest of the scene while I went straight back home to wake up Cécile. Ordinarily, she insisted on sleeping until at least eleven, but when I arrived in Park Lane a bit before nine, she was already up, dressed, and breakfasted. Cécile had never been the sort of lady who put on airs or needed coddling. She took the news of the death of Estella's would-be doppelgänger without so much as a Gallic shrug, called for the carriage, and demanded that we go to her friend's house at once.

"Estella Lamar lives in London?" I asked as the carriage crossed through Mayfair toward Belgravia. "Wouldn't it have been simpler to call on her there than to wait to see her at a ball?"

"Estella has never liked uninvited callers," Cécile said. "Furthermore, it seems unlikely that she spends much time in residence here, given her proclivity for travel. I had no reason to think it possible to find her in London until I learned last night she was supposed to be at the ball."

The Lamar mansion—for it could be called nothing short of that—covered the better part of a block not far from Belgrave Square. An ornate gilded iron gate blocked from the street the imposing edifice, a masterpiece of Georgian architecture, and we were admitted to the house by a liveried servant without having to wait. Once inside, the butler seemed almost too eager to assist us.

"I am terribly sorry," he said, "but Mademoiselle Lamar is not at home."

"Not at home because she is not in residence or not at home because she is not seeing visitors?" I asked. "Please do not trifle with me—"

"Milady, I would be most distraught if you thought I would dare trifle with you. Mademoiselle Lamar is not in residence, nor has she been for some time. Are you closely acquainted with her?"

"You are impertinent for a butler," Cécile said, narrowing her eyes and nodding. "I find it surprisingly endearing."

"I beg your forgiveness, milady." He bowed, twice. "I only meant to inquire in the hopes that you might have knowledge of our mistress's plans. Her lengthy absence has left all of us below stairs a bit rusty, I suppose. If you are close to her, you might know when she will grace this house once again with her presence."

"When was she last here?" I asked.

"Oh, milady, I could hardly say."

"Try," Cécile said.

"I mean no disrespect," he said, bowing again. "It was . . . let me see . . . old Monsieur Lamar and his wife died in 1875. Mademoiselle was here only briefly while she was in mourning, so I suppose we haven't seen her more than that one time since she took possession of the house."

"She has not been here in more than twenty years?" I asked.

"That is correct, milady."

"Yet she means to keep the house?"

"So far as we can tell, milady."

Cécile and I exchanged confused glances. "The house does not appear to be shut up," I said. "Are all the rooms open?"

"Yes, Mademoiselle Lamar gave clear directions when she inherited that the house was to be fully staffed and ready for her arrival at all times."

"You are not working with a skeleton staff?" I asked.

"No, milady."

"And you have been in this mode for two decades without anyone living above stairs?" To call this situation unusual would be to grossly underestimate it. Families often spent long periods of time away from their town homes—although two decades was an extreme absence—but they always had the servants close up the houses when they were away. Furniture and paintings were covered, curtains drawn, and only the barest staff left on board wages to ensure nothing dire happened while their masters were away.

"That is correct."

"Does she keep in contact with you?" I asked.

"Oh, yes, she has always been a conscientious mistress," the butler said. "She sends a letter from nearly every stop in her travels. We had one from Siam not two months ago."

"Siam?" Cécile asked. "May I be so bold as to ask to see this letter? I have known Mademoiselle Lamar since my youth and am most interested."

"Then you no doubt are all too aware of her concerns about King

Chulalongkorn's interactions with the west. She does not want the Siamese to lose any bit of their native culture."

"Is that so?" Cécile asked. "How very like Mademoiselle Lamar."

"If you would allow me to lead you to a sitting room, I shall gladly share the letter with you."

Once he had left us alone in a pretty—if dated—room covered in William Morris paper and furnished in comfortable and attractive fashion, Cécile and I scrutinized Estella's letter. She did indeed mention concerns about the Siamese king's relationship with western powers, and she gave a wonderfully newsy account of her arrival in the country, more newsy than one would expect a lady to write to her butler. Furthermore, she gave almost no direction regarding her wishes for the keeping of the house.

"Estella was never like that," Cécile said. "Inappropriately friendly with servants?"

"It is highly unusual," I said. "Do you recognize her handwriting?"

"So far as I can remember, yes," Cécile said. "I have had letters from her, but not more than one or two every year."

"Do you write back to her?" I asked.

"Yes, although I suspect she does not always receive my replies as she rarely responds to anything in them. Travel can make that sort of thing difficult. One often misses one's post, and Estella might not have always left a forwarding address."

"Quite." I rang for the butler. "Were you aware that your mistress had responded to an invitation from the Duke and Duchess of Devonshire? Apparently she intended to appear at their ball last night."

"Why, we have heard nothing, milady," he said. "That letter is the last we have had and you can see for yourself she made no mention of such a plan. Surely she didn't come to London and not stay in the house?"

"No, that seems unlikely," I said. "However, someone else, an imposter, came to the ball claiming to be Miss Lamar. Have you had any contact with such a person?"

"I can assure you not," he said, pulling himself up straight. "None of us in the house would ever stand for a pretender. We are all so very fond of Mademoiselle Lamar, you see."

"How long have you been in her employ?" I asked.

"Her father hired me when he married the second Madame Lamar."

"So you knew Estella as a child?" Cécile asked.

"Yes, milady. That is why we all feel so, well, if I may speak freely?"

"Please do," I said.

"We feel protective of her, milady. She never had an easy time of it."

"How so?" I asked.

"I couldn't explain it precisely, but she didn't seem like other young ladies. Never much liked being around people her own age. Always preferred being alone or with her mother, and of course her mother was not much at home, so she often seemed lonely."

"Was there tension between Miss Lamar and her parents?" I asked.

"No, milady. Her father spoiled her and her mother coddled her."

"Did they spend much time in London?" I asked.

"They came three times a year without exception until their deaths and always brought their daughter."

"Would you object to our taking a look around the house?" I asked. Estella may not have been in it for years, but I held out hope that its furnishings and her possessions might give us some insight into why the murdered woman had chosen to impersonate her. The butler hesitated, but in the end acquiesced, leaving us to explore. Two hours later, Cécile and I emerged without having found any hint of clarity. The house, though beautifully furnished, was void of all personality save for its owner's large collection of porcelain dolls, which were displayed, their glass eyes staring, in a dim and crowded room off the nursery. I was all too happy to close the door on them.

Estella

ii

Despite being of an age when most young ladies were married and settled, Estella identified herself an orphan. She missed her parents dreadfully, or so she said, over and over, primarily to her dolls. It was true her mother had stopped telling her stories years ago, and that she had rarely seen her father, although he had continued to present dolls to her on occasion, which should have suggested to her just how little he knew about his daughter. Jewelry would have been more appropriate at this stage in her life. Furthermore, Estella could not deny the fact that her parents' deaths had come with an unexpected benefit—now that they were gone, no one expected her to move in society, at least not for a while. This was a revelation. Estella could stay holed up at home without anyone pressuring her to go out. Instead, she was lauded for her daughterly devotion and for taking so seriously the period of mourning intended to honor her mother and father.

The family solicitor, also the executor of her parents' estate, took practical matters in hand for her. Estella was past the age that would have required a guardian, but Monsieur Pinard had been able to tell almost at once that she would need a great deal of assistance when it came to managing her inheritance, particularly as her father's will had caused deep consternation among her half siblings. The inheritance law, *droit de succession,* required that an estate be divided into two parts: the *réserve légale,* which must be split equally among the deceased's children, and the *quotité disponible,* which could be disposed of without limitations..

Estella and her four siblings shared the *réserve légale,* each of them receiving an equal portion of seventy-five percent of the enormous fortune their father had amassed in his lifetime. The remaining twenty-five percent he gave in its entirety to Estella. Compounding the matter was the fact that his wife, the dreaded stepmother, had been given in her marriage settlement all of the family's material possessions: the houses in London and Paris, the villa in the south of France, jewelry, art, and furnishings. As Estella was her mother's only child, she had inherited it all, much to the consternation of her half brothers and half sisters.

Monsieur Pinard could offer no explanation to the frustrated and angry heirs as to why their father had not given them a portion beyond what the law required; Monsieur Lamar had not given him one. The will was sound, and despite their best attempts, the children of the first Lamar marriage could not break it. Once forced to accept this, they turned their attention to their much younger half sister. Surely Estella could be persuaded to share.

They descended upon her a month after the courts ruled against them, smothering her with compliments and treats and invitations, not understanding that Estella could not bear such overtures. She used mourning as an excuse to put off receiving them and began to isolate herself more and more in the house in Paris. Only her dear friend, Cécile du Lac, was allowed to call, and then only when the visit was prearranged.

Cécile, newly out of mourning for her not-lamented husband, refused to let Estella remove herself from the world. Instead, she brought her books to read, primarily accounts of travel and exploration, believing they might kindle in Estella an interest in the world. She persuaded Estella, gently at first, and then with some force, to become part of the society Cécile had started carving out for herself, introducing her to artists and writers, dancers and composers. Much to her surprise, Estella found comfort in their presence. Like her, they seemed to keep parts of themselves private, although unlike her, they revealed bits in their creative endeavors. Estella had no creative endeavors to share.

As time passed, all of her siblings save one left her more or less alone. Their inheritances, though not as large as they might have liked, gave them enough capital to provide an exceedingly generous annual income. For three years, François, older than Estella by more than a dozen years, never let a month go by without appearing at her house, insisting that he wanted nothing more than to know better his baby sister. Estella never trusted his intentions, but eventually did allow him to dine with her on occasion. He did not object to hearing her tell those old stories of her mother's, and for that she was grateful, whatever his motives.

Estella's world might have continued like this for the remainder of her life had she not met someone different from the rest. This individual needed her in a way she had not previously considered. Romance had never interested her, but as she listened to the laments of her bohemian friends, she became increasingly fascinated by commerce and finance, two things that seemed to constantly plague them. She had more money than she could spend in a lifetime, and she wanted to do something with it. Not simply charity, but business. She wanted to invest, but not the way her father had. Her friends would not let her buy shares in their work—such a thing was anathema to artists and their ilk. Cécile's compatriots could barely tolerate the old idea of patrons. So Estella turned her head in another direction, and asked Monsieur Pinard for assistance.

For six months, the stalwart solicitor sent myriad investment options to his client. None met her satisfaction. Estella did not want to merely own a piece of a company, she wanted to feel as if she were helping to create a world, but it did not seem that businessmen understood what she meant by that until the day a businessman turned up on her doorstep, confident that he could change the world and become rich by Christmas. He knew without doubt that no one else could offer what Estella Lamar had.

He had spotted Estella in a café, where she was dining with an extremely elegant lady and several ragtag artists. Although she laughed when it was more or less appropriate and smiled when circumstances merited it, he could tell she was an outsider, not wholly comfortable. Her clothing, though unfashionable, was of the finest fabrics, and her jewelry suggested she was in possession of a not inconsiderable fortune. All this combined with her lack of ease with her friends told him she was vulnerable. He followed her home that night, and stood outside a mansion that surpassed his every hope. Estella Lamar could change his world in an instant, and she hardly need notice she was doing it.

3

Colin was not yet home when Cécile and I returned from the Lamar residence, so we had time to visit the boys in the nursery before rendezvousing with him and catching each other up on all we had learned. Our twins, Henry and Richard, were toddling about now, chasing after Tom, our ward, who was a bit older than they. Tom had come to us soon after his birth, his mother a young woman I had considered a friend until I discovered she had committed the heinous crime of murder—a murder that, up until then, I had believed she was helping me to investigate. The sensational nature of the case had caused a stir throughout the Continent and worked its way back to England, and we knew we could not hide the details, particularly as some of the individuals involved (I refer to my erstwhile nemesis, Emma Callum) insisted on revealing the identity of the child's mother. The subsequent newspaper coverage destroyed any chance of keeping the story quiet. As a result, Colin and I had decided to face the challenge head-on, and refused to let anyone disparage Tom. My husband, upon hearing disapproving murmurs in his club, let it be known he was not opposed to the idea of a duel to defend the honor of his adopted son. He is an excellent shot; all whispers ceased at once. I, being no stranger to staring down the dragons of Mayfair, had no problem keeping the ladies of society politely in line. No one ought to blame a child for his parent's sins. Furthermore, his share of our fortune would ensure he would have no difficulty gaining the approval of any mother hoping to see her daughter well settled when the time came.

Our boys challenged two of Cécile's long-held official positions. First, that she believed no man alive could prove interesting before age forty. Second, that she found children sticky and generally reprehensible. She had avoided her own nieces and nephews with deft skill until they turned twenty, insisting to her sister, their mother, that no one could be depended upon to be rational before then and that she had no inclination for dealing with anyone so lacking in mental capacity.

Cécile did not visit when the boys were babies. Infants, she said, were not to be borne. Now, though, she had succumbed to her desire to see me, or at least to lay eyes upon my husband, whom she considered (rightly) to be the most handsome man on earth, and was forced to deal with the presence of the children in the house. She had traveled with her two small dogs, Brutus and Caesar, upon whom she doted. I resisted the temptation to point out their similarities to small children. Cécile had always favored Caesar, considering this a way of making up for the historical injustices suffered by his namesake at Brutus's instigation. When we first had Nanny bring the boys down to meet her, they ignored Cécile and went straight for the dogs. While Tom and Richard adored Brutus, Henry pounced on Caesar at once. Despite her best intentions, Cécile was unable to view this as anything less than proof of Henry's superior intelligence. She wanted to hire a Latin tutor for him on the spot. I did not allow this, of course, not because of his age, but because I believe children ought to have a firm grip on Greek before moving on to the study of Latin. Cécile only shrugged and abandoned the scheme. Before long, she was taken with all three of the boys and considered herself their second mother.

"It is unforgiveable, Kallista, that you should have offspring who insist on being so charming," Cécile said as we returned to the library so that Nanny might put the boys down for a nap. "I do not need this sort of distraction."

"Enjoy them while you can," I said. "They'll be off to school before you know it."

"They are not yet two years old."

"They are barely past one, but their father registered them at Eton almost the moment they were born. You have twelve years to enjoy them if he doesn't change his mind about leaving their early education to tutors."

"I do not like your English boarding schools," Cécile said.

"I should have thought you want them sent away at eight, not to be seen again until they're finished with university."

"I shall not respond to such a statement."

I suppressed a smile and rang for Davis, requesting tea for me and champagne for Cécile, who refused to drink anything else. Colin returned just as the butler did with our libations, and opened the wine himself, his face grim.

"No one has come forward to identify the body," he said, filling Cécile's glass, "and there are as yet no missing persons reports that match her description."

"Perhaps she has no family," I said. "Surely someone will miss her eventually?"

"One would hope so," Colin said, taking the cup of tea I poured for him. "The weather was quite warm last night, and that has a tendency to bring out the worst sort of violence in people. It's entirely possible she was nothing more than a random victim."

"I noticed her headdress wasn't missing," I said, "but I don't recall if she was wearing any other jewelry."

"Her bow and arrows were gone. There was one jewel-encrusted golden cuff on her left wrist, none on the other."

I closed my eyes and tried to remember seeing her at the ball. "I am certain she had them on both arms."

"Kallista is correct," Cécile said. "I took note of them when I confronted her. She also wore a matching choker. I do not think, however, that any of them was genuine. The stones looked like paste."

"You are certain?" Colin asked.

Cécile shrugged. "I am no jeweler, but am confident in what I saw. Surely your police friends can draw a conclusion from the remaining bracelet?"

"Yes," I said. "Regardless, a random thief would have taken them and tried to pawn them. He wouldn't necessarily know their value."

"He may have left the second bracelet for any number of reasons," Colin said. "I presume he intended to take everything she had that might prove valuable, but he may have heard someone approaching and decided to run."

"Why was she pretending to be Estella?" Cécile asked. "There must be some clue in her clothing or the location where she was killed."

"I am afraid not, Cécile," Colin said. "There is no evidence at this point to make us think this was anything other than a robbery gone wrong."

"Why would a woman dressed like that run all the way to the river?" I asked. "She knew her guise was up at the party, but if she had gone as a lark, she needn't have run so far. The Duke of Devonshire certainly wasn't going to rush after her."

"Until we know who she is, I am afraid there's nothing to connect her to Miss Lamar," Colin said. "We must consider the possibility that Miss Lamar herself hired her as a joke. I have already sent a cable to her last known hotel."

"I shouldn't expect a reply," I said. "Forgive me, Cécile, but your friend is a strange woman. I am all for adventurous travel, but Miss Lamar seems to have taken it to an extreme."

"Emily, that is hardly charitable," Colin said. "Her parents are dead, she's estranged from her siblings, and she has no husband. Why shouldn't she travel the world?"

"I do not object to that in the least. What I find odd is that her house in London is left fully staffed and open, despite the fact that she hasn't set foot in it for more than twenty years. That, my dear husband, strikes me as exceedingly bizarre and has made me consider the idea of her travels in a different light. It is almost as if she is running away from something."

"She has little to keep her in Paris," Cécile said. "I should very much like to know the state of her home there. Is it fully staffed and ready at all times for her imminent arrival?"

"We should go to Paris and see," I said.

"No." Colin crossed his arms. "Absolutely not. We shall remain here and investigate the only case we have before us. Estella Lamar may be disturbed, eccentric, or on the run, but so far as we know she has broken no laws and is in no need of assistance. I suggest, Cécile, that you contact her solicitor if you are worried about her. I telephoned him this morning to find out his client's whereabouts, and while he was in possession of only limited information, he did not seem concerned in the slightest about her."

"You are right of course, Monsieur Hargreaves," Cécile said, "as a man of your ethereal beauty ought to be. Estella's travels have long disturbed me, in part, I believe, because I consider myself responsible for them. It was I who filled her head with thoughts of exotic locales and adventure. She was so bleak after her parents died, and I wanted to draw her back out into the world. When she left for Egypt, I felt guilty, knowing that she had until then preferred to be at home and alone. I worried that I pressured her to do something she was not entirely comfortable with."

"She was comfortable enough to continue traveling for two

decades," Colin said. "If anything, she owes you profound thanks for having rescued her from what sounds like a rather depressing life."

"And I am certain she is not alone, Cécile," I said. "She must have companions with her. I remember the picture of her in the papers when she was standing in front of the Taj Mahal. There was another lady with her, as well as two native guides."

"You were not worried about her before last night," Colin said. "It is understandable that you are a bit unnerved now, but there is no reason to think the murder is connected to your friend. Should I learn anything to the contrary, I promise you will be the first to know."

"After Kallista, I hope," Cécile said, her eyes sparkling. "You must always tell her first. To do otherwise is a disaster in marriage."

Colin laughed. "Are you an expert, Cécile? I thought you were opposed to the whole institution."

"In theory I am. I like to believe, however, that the two of you are a worthy exception."

A few hours later, Davis interrupted us to announce a man from Scotland Yard to see Colin. A landlord had come forward and identified the body found near Lambeth Bridge as his tenant, Mary Darby. He had gone to the police after having read a description in the newspaper of the murdered woman.

Colin and I immediately set off to interview the man. His building, in a decent middle-class neighborhood, was clean and neat, lacking altogether in charm, but serviceable. Mary's rooms were on the top floor, up four flights of steep and narrow stairs, with a satisfying view of London's rooftops out two small windows.

"You do not live in the building?" Colin asked, after the man had unlocked the door for us.

"No, sir, my wife and I have a house in St. John's Wood."

I left them to talk while I looked over every inch of Mary Darby's bedroom. There was hardly a speck of dust on any of the surfaces, and the floor was so clean it shined; a poignant reminder of how recently the flat's occupant had tended to her housekeeping. All of her possessions were well organized and neat. I dropped onto my hands and knees to look under the bed and pulled from beneath it a large box.

"I *knew* Worth designed that costume," I said, pulling out the box and opening it, searching for the invoice that would be inside. "It was shipped to this address fewer than four weeks ago. I shall contact Worth and see if she placed the order herself. It seems unlikely. I don't think she could have afforded it."

"Maybe that's why she didn't pay her rent last week," the landlord said. "Ladies and their fancy outfits. Can't blame them for wanting lovely things, can you? Still, it's no excuse for shirking one's responsibilities, and she had never been late before." I forced a smile for him and nodded, not seeing the need to inform him that one Worth gown would cost more than the rent on these rooms for a year. The revelation made me cringe, particularly when I considered how many of them could be found in my wardrobes at home.

Our search of Mary Darby's now vacant flat breathed life into the tragic form I had seen near the river. On one shelf, she had a surprisingly extensive collection of texts, mostly plays, including the complete works of Shakespeare. Many of them were marked up with stage directions scrawled in handwriting identical to that on a letter she had started to write and left on her desk. The letter was dated two days earlier. On the other side of the room, in a walnut chest, we found a leather bag full of medical supplies and several treatises on midwifery.

"She had a decent reputation as a midwife," the landlord said. "I wasn't keen on letting her have the rooms because I had understood she was once an actress, but she had a friend, a doctor, who wrote a right glowing reference about her. I figured she was respectable now, even if she hadn't been always. Thought I should give her the chance to continue on that path."

"You say she never paid late until recently?" Colin asked.

"That's right, sir."

"You wouldn't object to our speaking to your other tenants?" Colin asked.

"Of course not," he said. "I feel awful about what happened to her. She was a good woman."

"Are you still in possession of the details of the doctor who had given the reference?" I asked.

He nodded vigorously. "I will send it over to you the moment I am back in my study. I kept his letter."

Colin gave him a card so that he might do as he said, and we finished cataloging Mary's belongings, knowing that something among them that did not appear significant now might prove worthwhile later. Once the task was complete, we turned our attention to the building's other dwellers. No one had anything but kind words about Mary. She had proven herself a good neighbor over and over, always willing to help with a remedy for a chill or supper when one was down on one's luck. She had delivered all three children belonging to the family on the second floor, and they spoke of her as if she were a saint.

"There was no one kinder," Mrs. McDermott said, dabbing tears with a handkerchief as she spoke. "I can't believe she is gone. I had warned her, you know, to be careful. A lady alone at night, going off wherever she was needed. It's dangerous work, midwifery, and not wholly suitable if you ask me. Noble, yes, but she ought to have had an assistant, a male assistant, who could have protected her if nothing else. She always scoffed at the idea."

"Were you concerned about her safety in general, or was there a more specific threat?" Colin asked.

"Threat?" Mrs. McDermott's eyes flew open wide. "I never said there was a threat, only that she could have been more careful."

"I apologize if I misunderstood," Colin said. "Did she ever have trouble from any of her patients?"

"Never, at least not so far as I knew. She was good as gold, Mary Darby. Worth her weight in it as well."

"Surely some of her patients had less than favorable outcomes? We ladies know how difficult the childbed can be," I said, shooting Colin a look I knew he would recognize at once. He pulled out his notebook and pretended to busy himself with it. I lowered my voice. "When one loses a baby, as so often happens, one may lash out."

"Oh, Mary had her share of that," Mrs. McDermott said, "but she knew how to handle it well enough. Although now that you mention it, I do remember one woman who took it particularly bad. I don't know her name. Mary was always careful about not giving details about her patients. She came to the house once or twice, though, and stood outside across the street wailing and keening, begging Mary to come out and bring the baby. It was a pathetic sight, tragic really. Out there in the pouring rain thinking a midwife had her child instead of the good Lord."

"When was this?" I asked.

"Best I can remember two months ago or so. Spring was so rainy the weeks run together for me, but I know it was well before the Queen's Jubilee."

"May, do you think? Or earlier?" I asked.

Mrs. McDermott pursed her lips and pulled her eyebrows together. "April, I would guess. Don't hold me to it, though."

"Of course not," I said. "Did you ever speak to the woman?"

"Heavens, no! I complained to our landlord first and it was he who told me, after he had looked into the matter, that she was Mary's patient. Poor deranged thing. I do wonder if she's improved by now."

Mrs. McDermott had nothing further to offer, so we thanked her and took our leave. "Mary Darby is more complicated than I had expected," I said.

"Is that so?" Colin asked. "I had anticipated as much."

I raised an eyebrow. "Due, no doubt, to your prolonged experience investigating such matters."

"Yes, if you must know." His wry smile could always melt my heart. "You should appreciate me better."

"You know perfectly well I appreciate you to the point of near blasphemy."

"Good girl." I could see a hint of color in his face and his eyes danced; he was pleased. "A woman willing to pull the stunt Mary Darby did at Devonshire House is not the sort of person looking for a quiet life. Neither is a woman who defies convention and becomes an actress, even a not very successful one."

"And while being a midwife is certainly respectable, it is hardly ordinary," I said, "and suggests a personality open to a great deal of personal disruption. Babies rarely come at convenient times."

"What do you suggest we do next?" he asked.

"You are deferring to me?"

He gave me a neat bow. "I have great faith in your abilities."

Estella

He did not go through Monsieur Pinard to reach her, knowing all too well that no one in the solicitor's office would approve of his scheme. This was his frustration, this was what had held him back at every turn. He was not to blame for the succession of failures that followed in his wake. The trouble was the establishment, people too entrenched in their own views of the world to take him seriously. The trouble now was that he had nothing left, and the creditors were hot after him. This would be no problem if he could only fund this last idea, the one he knew without doubt would bring him back. All he needed were investors, but there were none to be found.

Until he met Estella Lamar. Estella, as he begged her to let him call her during their second meeting, understood him. When he explained to her the benefits of the formula he had purchased from Dr. Maynard, her eyes brightened. She knew the perils of nerves, knew how they could paralyze a person. He had drawn up a plan, illustrating the formula's benefits and the incredible number of people to whom he was confident he could sell it, if only he could secure the funding to finance production. He promised her she could expect to triple her investment in six months, and Estella seemed mildly impressed. Money, she said, concerned her less than anything in the world. She was happy to help him, so long as Dr. Maynard's Patented Formula gave reliable results.

For six long weeks, he brought her testimonials, sample labels, and the details of advertising schemes. He shared with her every bit of work he had done, and Estella appeared in all ways highly motivated to become his partner. She even asked him to draw up an agreement, which he did in rapid order, elated to at last be so close to his goal. Before she signed, however, she wanted to meet Dr. Maynard.

This proved problematic as the doctor, so far as anyone could tell, had disappeared soon after the sale of his formula. He had shuttered his office and vacated his lodgings, leaving no forwarding address. The landlady believed him to have gone to America. When Estella learned this, she began for the first time to show signs of hesitation. Dr. Maynard's Formula, she said, was beginning to appear less and less like a sound investment. Her would-be partner did everything in his limited power to reassure her, even as he grew increasingly desperate, worried that his scheme would fall apart without her, and knowing that his creditors were daily lamenting the demise of debtors' prisons even as they threatened him with increasing violence.

Estella decided that she could go no further without trying Dr. Maynard's Formula herself. Her partner hesitated, not because he doubted the efficacy of the tincture, but because he was not convinced Estella needed it. That she was eccentric could not be doubted, but she did not appear in any way plagued with nerves, despite her insistence that she understood the disorder all too well, and he worried that if she took the formula and noticed no marked effect, she would refuse to enter into a partnership with him. Estella would not be put off, and in the end, he relented. He promised to bring her a sample bottle the next morning.

In his dingy rooms that night, he paced, wondering what he

should do. He had taken a dose himself more than once and felt nothing, but had not been concerned as his nerves had never bothered him in the slightest. Certainly he became agitated on occasion, but that was simply due to his unfortunate financial circumstances. He drummed his fingers on his rickety table and pondered his options until a violent knocking on the door disturbed his concentration. He opened it, knowing full well whom he would find. There was no avoiding them any longer.

One week, they told him. That was all he could have. If his debt was not settled in that time, he could expect to find himself at the bottom of the Seine. A swift punch to his jaw dislodged two of his back teeth. The man in the black coat who smiled while his thug did his ugly work said it would serve to remind him not to dawdle. They left him there, bleeding on the floor, kicking him in the gut on their way out.

Estella's money was his only hope. Her investment in Dr. Maynard's Formula would pay them off and fund his new enterprise. He dragged himself to his feet, washed the blood from his face, and headed for the nearest apothecary.

4

Scotland Yard reported to us that they had found no sign of any of Mary Darby's jewelry having been pawned, but we could not determine whether this was due to the murderer realizing it was fake gold and paste, as confirmed upon examination of the bracelet left on her arm, or because the murderer had taken the jewelry in an attempt to make his crime appear to have been a robbery gone horribly wrong. I had taken with me from Mary's rooms the notebooks and files in which she kept her patients' medical records, and was studying them in the library, searching for the name of the disturbed woman Mrs. McDermott had seen.

"The Duke of Bainbridge, madam." Davis bowed as he announced Jeremy, who clapped my butler on the back as he walked past him.

"You're a good chap, Davis," Jeremy said. Davis flinched.

"Will there be anything else, madam?" Davis had grown accustomed to ignoring Jeremy over the years.

"No, Davis, thank you," I said. "Jeremy, you are a beast, tormenting my butler."

He flopped into the chair nearest me. "I adore Davis. Is it my fault if he does not approve of the high esteem in which I hold him? I have not come only to see you, darling girl. Cécile has summoned me. It appears you are rather letting down the side on this Estella Lamar business and she wants me to assist her."

"You?" I made no attempt to contain either my surprise or my laughter.

"Make light of it if you will," he said. "I am well aware that you have no concern for my feelings. I did prove myself to be of some use when you were investigating Michael Dillman's murder."

"True enough," I said. Jeremy had offered his assistance during that case, three years ago, in which a disturbed gentleman had terrorized London society by exposing long-hidden secrets and committing murder. "I was grateful to you."

"Madame du Lac, it seems, was even more impressed. She has asked me to accompany her to Paris, where together we will attempt to find her missing friend."

"There is no evidence that Estella Lamar is missing. Her travels abroad have been well documented in the press and nothing in any account of her adventures has suggested she is being forced to do anything against her will."

"Don't be a spoilsport, Em," he said. "I wouldn't do this for anyone else, you know. It borders too closely on being useful. But I am mad about Cécile. She is a capital lady and a great deal of fun, and I find myself excessively bored in London. This season is rubbish and I am sick to death of the Jubilee. Paris will provide a nice respite. We leave this evening."

"So soon? Cécile has not mentioned it."

"I wanted to be the one to tell you before I collected her on my way to the station," he said, a wicked grin on his face. "I hoped you might be just a little heartbroken to see me go. With whom will you dance the quadrille? We both know the illustrious Mr. Hargreaves despises it."

"I have always preferred the waltz, so I am afraid I shan't miss you in the slightest." I leaned forward. "And you know my husband will be delighted to see you go."

Jeremy laughed. "Of course. I almost refused Cécile, just to spite him, but decided to do as she asked, as I am certain my absence will cause you to miss me. Madly, I hope."

"London will be the poorer without you," I said as Cécile opened the door.

"Has Bainbridge told you of our plan?" she asked.

"Indeed, although I am sorry to report that I am not nearly so heartbroken as he might like."

"He is a fool," Cécile said, "but we must take consolation in the fact that he knows this better than any of us."

"Truer words were never spoken, my dear Madame du Lac," Jeremy said. Cécile stood next to him, holding out her hand to be kissed. "If I were half so handsome as Hargreaves I am certain I could convince you to marry me."

"Not even the divine Monsieur Hargreaves himself could convince me to marry again," Cécile said. "You, Bainbridge, amusing though you are, have no chance at all."

"Then I shall have no choice, upon my return from Paris, but to resume my attentions to Emily, whether she likes it or not."

I suppressed a sigh. "Cécile, do you really believe something has happened to Estella?"

"It is irrational, *bien sûr,* but I feel compelled to look into the matter. I have been a poor friend to not have done a better job reaching out to her over the years. I could at least have met her once during her travels."

"Did she ever invite you?" I asked.

"*Non,* but that was never her style. At any rate, I have had enough of London and long to return home."

"You, Cécile, I shall miss."

Jeremy smiled and blew me a kiss.

There was no time to dawdle with them. I returned to my work, leaving my friends to plan their Parisian adventure. As soon as I had uncovered the identity of the patient who had recently lost her baby, I collected Colin from the billiards room and set off to find the unfortunate woman. She lived in a neatly furnished house in Maida Vale with her husband. They had no children. The baby lost to them in the spring had been their fifth disappointment. My own past experience informed the way I planned to approach her, as I was all too keenly aware of the pain of losing a child.

Mrs. Hopwood received us in a dark sitting room, the curtains pulled tight, and a mirror above the mantel draped with black crêpe. A side table held a silver carriage clock whose hands had been stopped at 8:36. This must have been the time of the baby's demise. Colin squeezed my hand as he sat next to me on the settee, and gave me a subtle nod of encouragement.

"It is good of you to see us, Mrs. Hopwood," I began. "I am conscious of what a difficult time this is for you, but I am afraid we must ask you some questions about Mary Darby, whom I understand delivered your daughter this spring."

"Delivered her and then took her," Mrs. Hopwood said. "She denies this, of course, but I know the child was not dead. I heard her cries."

"I am so terribly sorry," I said. We had made inquiries at Scotland Yard before coming, and Colin's colleagues there had told us that Mrs. Hopwood had gone to the police to accuse her midwife of kidnapping, but her husband had come forward, quietly, and explained to the detectives that his wife was speaking out of an unmanageable grief, and the matter had never merited investigation. I did not want to draw attention to this, but neither did I want to insult her. "I can only imagine the pain you feel. When did you last see Mary Darby?"

"I have seen her nearly every day since my little one was taken from me."

"Every day?" I asked.

"She haunts my dreams."

"I see. Have you spoken to her in person?" I asked.

"Would you not do everything in your power to see your child returned to you?"

"Of course I would. Did Miss Darby—"

"Mrs. Darby. She was a widow."

"Did Mrs. Darby offer you any assistance in the matter when you confronted her?"

"She was sweet as anything the day my little one was born." Mrs. Hopwood's voice was reedy, almost breathless. "Told me she understood my pain, and that there would be other chances, but she knew that wasn't true. She showed me the child, you know, after I'd heard her cries, and tried to tell me she was dead. I knew she wasn't. She didn't look like the others."

"It must have been awful," Colin said, leaning forward. "I am most grievously sorry for your pain."

"There needn't have been any," Mrs. Hopwood said. "I heard the child cry, but Mary insisted she had to take her away, to keep her from me. She didn't leave her with us and she would have if the child had been dead, wouldn't she? She would have left her for us to deal with."

Not knowing the details of what had happened on that sad occasion, and not wanting to further agitate the woman, I changed direction. "Did you see Mrs. Darby after that day?"

"I visited her, over and over, but she refused to see me. Wouldn't offer so much as a word of comfort, because she knew she couldn't. She knew she was the instrument of my pain."

"How often did you try to see her?" Colin asked.

"It is so very difficult to remember." Tears pooled in Mrs. Hopwood's already red-rimmed eyes. "She spoke to me only once, and tried to give me something to help me sleep, as if that would take away the memory of what she had done."

"So you did speak to her?" I asked. "Was this here or at her rooms?"

"She would not help me, so what choice did I have?"

I looked to Colin, not sure what to do. "You had to take matters into your own hands, Mrs. Hopwood, didn't you?" he asked.

"I did. I followed her every chance I could, hoping she would lead me to my baby."

"And when you saw her leave Devonshire House last night?" he asked.

"Devonshire House? I can't say she's ever been there, Mr. Hargreaves. She's not nearly that fine a lady. No, no Devonshire House for her."

"But you found her near the river?" Colin pressed.

"No, she was most often at that theater in the West End. I never saw her near the river."

"Which theater, Mrs. Hopwood?" I asked.

"The one not far from St. Martin-in-the-Fields," she said. "They are putting on a production of *A Midsummer Night's Dream*. I think she may have got the idea to steal my baby from being part of something so concerned with fairies and magic and all sorts of evil things."

"Did you ever see her with the baby?" I asked.

"No. I would have taken her back if I had. You must believe me," she said. "I would not leave my little one abandoned. Why will no one help me find her? Will you help me?"

Colin rose to his feet. "I assure you, Mrs. Hopwood, I will personally do everything I can to assist you through this dreadful time. If I may be so bold, I should like to send my private physician to attend to you. He is a man of great intelligence and skill and will be able to help you learn what happened to your daughter."

"I don't want something to make me sleep."

"No, of course not," Colin said, his voice gentle and soothing. "I shall tell him as much."

We took our leave from her and were met by a servant in the corridor near the front door. "Sir, I sent for Mr. Hopwood the moment you arrived. He is outside, hoping to speak to you. He didn't want to disturb my mistress, you see." She opened the door. "He is there, just across the street."

"Please walk with me," Mr. Hopwood said as we approached him. His gray hair and lined face suggested he was considerably older than his wife. "Mrs. Hopwood does not often look out the window, but I do not want to take the chance of alarming her in case she does. No doubt you have ascertained that she is greatly disturbed?"

"Yes, I am afraid so," Colin said.

"There is no question of kidnapping here, sir," Mr. Hopwood said. "Our daughter died within moments of being born."

"Your wife heard her cry?" I asked.

"She did, but it was only once. I held the child myself. There was no life in her."

"I am so sorry," I said.

"We have suffered a series of disappointments, as so many do, but my wife, I am afraid, has come undone from it. She blames the midwife, though there was no indication the woman had done anything wrong. She took it into her head that she spirited the baby off, when in fact I had asked her to do so in order that my wife might be spared having to face another dead infant in the house waiting for burial."

"Did you have a funeral?" Colin asked.

"We did, but Mrs. Hopwood was in no condition to attend. She took, shortly thereafter, to following Mrs. Darby, harassing her. It's rather an embarrassment, and I do not know what to do to stop her. She has refused medical attention and I fear may require institutionalization."

"She has agreed to let my physician see her," Colin said, "but the matter is more serious than you may know. Mary Darby was murdered last night."

"Dear Lord," Mr. Hopwood said. "You don't think—"

"At the moment we are gathering all information pertinent to the investigation," Colin said. "Is it possible your wife attacked her?"

"I should like to say no, but her behavior has been so erratic of late . . ."

"Were you home last night, Mr. Hopwood?" I asked.

"I was not. I have taken to spending several nights a week at my club. In the circumstances it seemed the best thing."

"Quite," Colin said. "Which club?"

"The In and Out. I had a commission in the navy before taking a position in the City. I am employed as a banker now."

"Do you know if Mrs. Hopwood was at home all last night?" I asked.

"She had no plans to go out, but I cannot say with confidence what she did. You are welcome to speak to our servants, but I would request that you allow me to send them down to meet you at the public house two streets over. It is best if Mrs. Hopwood is not further agitated."

"Of course," Colin said, and took from him the details of the establishment in question. Soon we were settled at a table there. Colin ordered a pint of ale for himself and half a pint for me.

"This is rather exciting," I said, sipping the bitter drink. "I've never before been in a public house. Is this what they are all like?" The walls were paneled in dark wood, and a surly barman had handed our beverages to Colin so that he might bring them to our table. The pleasant scent of meat pies filled the premises, and I was about to suggest ordering some when one of Mr. Hopwood's servants approached us.

"My master has sent me to you," he said. "My name is Will Mundy, and I have worked for the Hopwoods these eleven years. We've not a large staff, there are only the three of us, but we take good care of the family."

"I do not doubt it," I said. "We understand the situation has been difficult these past few months, particularly for Mrs. Hopwood."

"Her heart is right broken, madam."

"Do you know if she was home last night?" Colin asked.

"She was most of the evening," he said. "Nearly all of it, in fact. Cook had gone to bed and Molly and me, we was reading the evening paper belowstairs. Mr. Hopwood lets us have it when he stays at his club."

"And you saw Mrs. Hopwood?" I asked.

"She had gone to bed, you see, hours before, but then we heard a commotion on the stairs, and I went to take a look. It was the mistress, still in her nightdress. I asked her if she wanted a cup of warm milk to calm her nerves, but it was like she didn't even see me. She walked straight past me to the front door."

"Did she go outside?" Colin asked.

"I blocked her way, sir," he said. "I meant nothing improper, of course, but I couldn't let her leave the house like that. Not in her nightdress."

"No, you could not," Colin said. "So she remained inside?"

"I turned her round and put her in the direction of going back upstairs and waited until I heard a door close. I figured she had gone back to her room."

"Had she?" I asked.

"I don't rightly know, madam. I thought she had, and I went back downstairs. But then, must have been about ten minutes later, we heard a clatter on the servants' stairs, and she rushed down right past us and out the door before I had the chance to even try to stop her."

"Was she still in her nightdress?" I asked.

"She had put on a cloak, but I could not tell you what she wore beneath it."

"Did you follow her?" Colin asked.

"As quickly as I could, but got no farther than seeing her get into a hansom cab. I have no idea where she went after that."

"What time was this?"

"Round about midnight, best as I can say."

"Did you notify Mr. Hopwood?" Colin asked.

"I know we should have at once, sir, but we couldn't get the telephone to work, and we thought she would come back quickly."

"Did she?"

"No," Will said. "So around two o'clock in the morning, I went to find the master and left a message for him at his club."

"Did he come home?" Colin asked.

"Not until the morning."

"Was the message delivered before then?" I asked.

"I told them at the club it was urgent."

"When did Mrs. Hopwood return home?" Colin asked.

"Just after dawn, sir. She was in a state, her hair wild and her cloak torn."

"Do you have any idea where she had been?" Colin asked.

"None. I'm sorry not to be of more use. Cook said to tell you she has nothing to add. She slept through all the excitement."

"Thank you, Will," Colin said. "Will you send Molly to us straightaway?"

Molly had nothing to contribute beyond corroborating Will's story. She was nervous and upset, afraid she might lose her position if she did not get back to the house quickly enough. We reassured her as best we could before sending her on her way.

"You don't know what it's like," she said before scurrying out the door, "living in a house like that. I fear we'll all be mad before Christmas."

"Well?" I asked my husband once she had gone.

"Mr. Hopwood, I presume?" he asked. "Clearly he has been somewhat less than forthright."

iv

"I am afraid you have taken me for a fool, sir," Estella said to her caller, the man she had let herself come to trust, whom she had believed valued her for the previously unbeknownst-to-her business acumen he insisted she possessed. "I have taken Dr. Maynard's Formula, and found it to be nothing more than worse-than-usual-tasting laudanum. I have no interest in investing in such a thing."

He felt as if the world were crashing down around him. He had added laudanum to the mixture in an attempt to assuage his fear that she would feel no effect when she sampled the tincture. It was a mistake he would long regret. She ordered him to leave the house at once and to never call again. A burly servant bustled him out the back door. Always before he had used the front.

Estella cringed to think of it after he was gone. She had been so foolish, so trusting, so stupid. Monsieur Pinard would have identified this man as a charlatan in an instant, she knew, and she wished she had had the sense to consult with him in the matter. Fortunately none of her friends knew of the now spoiled business arrangement. She had mentioned it once, to Cécile, but only in passing, and her friend was unlikely to remember the conversation. Estella would suffer no more mortification because of it, except in her own head.

For two days after the incident, Estella did not leave her house. She retreated one afternoon to the cupboard in the nursery where she still kept her favorite dolls. It was too cramped for her to sit in comfortably now that she was full grown, but she folded herself into it nonetheless, wrapping her arms around her knees and pulling them to her chin, bending her neck so that her head fit beneath the shelf. She confessed everything to her dolls and saw in their green eyes no mocking laughter, the sort she was certain she would find in her friends' if she told them what she had almost done. She had never before told the dolls a story that had not first belonged to her mother, and now that she had, she felt a release unlike any she had known before. These were her friends, her true friends.

Something tugged at her heart, and she thought of Cécile. Cécile would not laugh at her. Cécile would give her a glass of champagne and tell her this all proved that she was too good and too trusting for most of this world, and that she should be proud to have discovered the fraud before she made her investment. Estella decided to go to the place Saint-Germain-des-Prés, to her friend's house, and confide in her. She drew herself out of the cupboard and threw a cloak around her shoulders before stepping outside into the crisp autumn sunshine. The day was so bright she had to squint to see. The walk to Cécile's was not a short one, but still she did not bother to take her parasol. Instead she tipped her head back, feeling the warmth of the sun on her face.

She turned onto rue du Dragon and had not taken more than three steps when she felt strong arms grab her from behind. A rough cloth covered her face, and when she breathed, the air tasted too sweet. She grew tired, so very tired.

And then the world went black.

5

We returned to the Hopwood residence after finishing with the family's servants, but Mr. Hopwood had not gone there after speaking to us, so we sought him at his place of employment in the City. He looked rather shamefaced when he saw us, and ushered us into a room furnished with a large desk and three uncomfortable chairs. "I should have told you what happened last night," he said, the moment we had sat down.

"Quite an understatement," Colin said. "Please do enlighten us now. First, I want to know precisely what happened. Second, I want to know why you did not tell us earlier."

"I had gone to my club, just as I said, but when I went to bed, I gave strict orders that I was not to be disturbed."

"Why?" I asked.

"You have met my wife. Living with her has become something of a trial, and more often than not she sets off on nocturnal adventures."

"This happens frequently?" Colin asked.

"Not in the extreme," Mr. Hopwood said, "but she has with some regularity ventured out of the house. In the beginning, I followed her in a panic, only to find that she did nothing more than wander for a few blocks before sitting on the pavement, wailing for some time, and then going home."

"This did not make you think she was in dire need of medical attention?" Colin asked. "I can assure you that if my wife were in such a state, I would not dream of abandoning her to her madness."

"Madness? Is that what you think it is? I understand why you would believe that, but it does not adequately address her condition. She is not completely unhinged, and I have no desire to see her locked up in some awful place and treated like she has no reason left at all. She is mad, but for a very specific reason, and one that I am certain will pass in time. This is a temporary setback. A serious one, I agree, but not all-consuming."

"She is a danger to herself wandering around in such a state," Colin said.

"Yes, yes, I suppose so." Mr. Hopwood dropped his face into his hands. "It has become so very difficult, all of it. I am grieving, too, you know, though she does not see it. Grieving without a wife to offer any meaningful support. She is too lost in her own pain to care about anyone else's."

"So you are content to let her wander the streets at night?" I asked. "One almost wonders if you hope she comes to harm."

"No, that is absolutely untrue. I swear it." He rubbed his forehead, his eyes dull. "I realize how dreadful it sounds, that you must think me a monster, but have you ever dealt with a situation like this? At first it consumes you, and you are desperate to fix things. In time, however, you start to realize you have almost no power whatsoever, and you begin to find yourself inured to it. Your helplessness becomes callousness, and before long you hardly remember having emotions at all."

I wanted to lift him from his seat and give him a stern reprimand followed by a lecture on how one ought to treat one's spouse if one has even the barest respect for the marital state, but decided, on balance, the current situation did not merit such actions. They would be neither welcome nor helpful. "No one is arguing these are not the most difficult of times," I said instead.

"It is your duty to look after your wife properly, Hopwood," Colin said, "and I insist that you start to do it at once. Furthermore, I will call at your club to corroborate your version of last night's events. Knowing this, is there anything you wish to add to your narrative?"

"No, there is nothing," he said. "I have given serious thought to what you said to me earlier, Hargreaves, and I cannot believe my wife would hurt anyone, even Mary Darby. Somewhere inside her she knows there is no one to blame for our daughter's death. She may rail against the midwife, she may be upset with her, but she would not strike out physically against her. Of that I am certain."

I cannot say that I shared his confidence.

"Disgraceful man," Colin said as we left. "To allow his wife to carry on in such a manner is unconscionable."

"I have never believed the primary role of a husband is to control his wife," I said. "Quite the contrary."

"You know, my dear, that we agree on this point, but there are times when human decency requires intervention. This is one of them." He ran a hand through his dark hair. "I feel fortunate to have a most rational wife."

"You are extremely fortunate. So fortunate, in fact, that I may even deserve an award of thanks."

"I shall see to that in the most thorough manner possible later this evening. For now, however—"

"The In and Out," I said. "Where I, of course, am not welcome."

"I am certain the navy shall one day come to see the error of their ways."

"It is unlikely I shall live long enough to see it. There is something that has been nagging at me, however, and I would like to pursue it while you explore the hallowed halls of Mr. Hopwood's club. Would you collect me at Devonshire House when you are finished?"

"Let's meet in Green Park instead," he said. "It's too fine a day to spend more time inside than necessary."

Devonshire House and Mr. Hopwood's club could not have been more conveniently located to each other, being only a few blocks apart on Piccadilly, across from Green Park. We had the carriage leave us both at the In and Out (so called because those words were painted, one on each of the two pillars flanking the double doors) and sent it back to Park Lane so that we could walk home. Colin was right: the day was fine and I reveled in the cool breeze that drifted from the park to the pavement. As I approached the London seat of the Duke of Devonshire, I felt, as I always did, a spate of disappointment, for although the house could be counted among the most grand in town when one considered its interior, the exterior gave no hint of what lay inside.

A tall brick wall, devoid of all ornamentation, lined the perimeter of the property, blocking the house from the street. Once inside the gate, the visitor would see that the façade had little more to offer than the wall. It was plain and austere, but the moment one stepped through the portico and into the entrance hall, one was firmly surrounded by luxury. The butler led me up the grand staircase to the first floor, where the duchess received me in a splendid drawing room done up in crimson silk.

"What a success your party was," I said, as she embraced me and we kissed on both cheeks. "A triumph that will not soon be forgot."

"I must admit to being pleased," she said, smoothing her skirts and sitting. "My husband is of no use in planning such things, you know. I have always said he would choose a pig over a party any day of the week, but at least he has the sense not to hold me back." Lady Louisa Cavendish, the Duchess of Devonshire, had earned the reputation as one of—if not the—best hostesses in society, a rank that could prove as much of a burden as an honor, as one continually felt the need to top one's previous accomplishments. She had been married once before, to the Duke of Manchester, who died two years before she decided, at the age of sixty, to wed again. Rumor had it the second duke to earn her affections had been in love with her for years, but she had remained faithful to Manchester until his death. "There was a duel, did you know?"

"I missed that entirely," I said. "Do tell."

"Gentlemen coming to blows in the garden over a lady. Fortunately their weapons were limited by their costumes, so there was no question of firearms at twenty paces. The crusader's sword easily beat his opponent's rapier. Louis XV's courtiers weren't meant for combat, and I am afraid his silk stockings suffered violently."

"Oh dear." I laughed. "I am almost sorry not to have seen it."

"You are here, I presume, not simply to discuss the pleasures of the evening—I am glad, though, that you enjoyed yourself."

"I did, very much so, thank you," I said. "You are correct that I must address another subject, one far less pleasant. We have identified the woman murdered after she left here. I am certain she was not among those who received an invitation, at least not in her legal name."

"No, I had never heard of Mary Darby until your husband sent her name over today. Furthermore, I did not invite Estella Lamar to the ball. It never would have occurred to me to have done so as she is rarely in London. When she appeared without an invitation, I thought that the Jubilee and its festivities must have tempted her to come to England, and I told my butler to admit her at once. It is wretchedly embarrassing to have been so taken in by a charlatan."

"You had no way of knowing she was not who she claimed."

"Unfortunately not," she said. "Have you any notion why this other woman came in her place? I feel as if I've been wound up, and I can't say I much like the joke."

"At the moment we've not the slightest idea. We are trying to reach Miss Lamar, but have as yet been unable to make contact with anyone but her solicitor. He believes her to have recently been in Siam, which suggests it would have been most difficult for her to organize the scheme, if that's what it was."

"I am aware that my husband has communicated as much to your own dear spouse, but I must implore you to please keep this matter as quiet as possible. I do not want our ball in the queen's honor to be overshadowed by scandal and death." She snapped open a lace fan and waved it quickly in front of her face. "Do not think me callous, Lady Emily. I am most grieved that this Darby woman has been killed, but at the same time I am indecently relieved that it did not happen in the confines of my home."

"Of course you are. That is nothing of which to be ashamed."

"I'm afraid I have nothing else that could be of use to you," she said. "I must, however, compliment you on your costume. You made a lovely Artemis."

"You are very kind, Lady Cavendish," I said. "The House of Worth has never let me down. I would be nothing without them."

"Yes, the sons are doing an admirable job continuing the work of their father, aren't they?"

"Quite. They made yours as well, did they not?" The duchess had presided over her party with supreme regality, dressed as Zenobia, Queen of Palmyra, and had entered the ballroom on a litter carried by servants dressed as slaves, each of them with an enormous fan. "I can't think when I've seen any garment so spectacular."

"The dreadful thing weighed a ton, but it was worth it," she said. "I only wish I could wear it again."

"Speaking of costumes puts me in mind of the other topic I hoped to discuss with you. During the ball, an auburn-haired gentleman dressed as an ancient Greek approached me and addressed me with half a line of Homer. At the time I had assumed this was because of my own choice of costume, but when I answered him back, he balked, and scolded me fiercely for not being at all what I had claimed to be. It was exceedingly odd, and I can't help but think he expected, because of my costume, that I was Mary Darby. He had on a mask— one of those theatrical ones, representing tragedy. Have you any idea who he was?"

"Greek . . ." She looked up at the ceiling, closed one eye, and chewed on her bottom lip. "There were so many guests, I'm afraid I cannot recall what each of them wore. His, I am sorry to say, did not make an impression on me. He sounds a horrible man! Have you tried the photographer?"

"I was hoping you could tell me how best to reach him." The duchess had organized for a photographer to set up a makeshift studio in the garden so that he might capture the guests in their spectacular costumes.

She crossed to a table, pulled out a sheet of paper, and scribbled on it. "The Lafayette Studio. Here are the details. I do not believe everyone sat for a picture, but many did. I do hope your mysterious Greek was one of them, as I believe Mr. Lafayette was quite thorough about recording the details of each sitter."

I took the paper from her. "I am most grateful, Lady Cavendish."

"It is good to see you, Lady Emily. Your mother is well, I hope?"

"Always," I said. "It grieved her to miss your party, but my father insisted on traveling abroad this summer. He felt the Jubilee rather more festivity than he could tolerate with equanimity."

She smiled. "How like the earl. He is a dear man. Do send my best to them both."

Leaving the duchess, I made my way to Green Park, where Colin was already waiting, leaning against a tree, reading the *Times*. He folded the paper the moment he saw me, pulled me close, and gave me a kiss.

"Do you think anyone is still scandalized by seeing a husband kiss his wife in public?" he asked, taking my arm in his as we started to walk. "Or has society become so corrupt that nothing shocks it?"

"Fear not," I said, "you are as scandalous as ever. Just look at that lady, there, rushing away from us. She has all but covered her daughter's eyes."

"If you do not slow down you are going to remove my arm from its socket. I can tell you are on fire with purpose and eager to get wherever it is you think necessary," he said. "I shall endeavor to follow your lead, though perhaps at a somewhat more reasonable pace."

I told him our destination, and then took him out of the park and back along Piccadilly, turning into Bond Street. Lafayette Studio had a stellar reputation, partly because its proprietor produced excellent work and partly because he was a favorite not only of the Prince and Princess of Wales, but of Queen Victoria herself. Mr. Lafayette had studios in Glasgow and Manchester, and now one on Bond Street, an expansion he felt necessary due to the number of commissions he received timed to coincide with the Queen's Jubilee. The studio was on the top floor, up three flights of steps, a climb that would have been exhausting for anyone coming to be photographed in heavy court dress, and a disaster on a hot day. One would be drenched with sweat; hardly an ideal look when having one's image immortalized.

"A moment, please!" a voice called as we pushed open the door at the top of the stairs. "Close the door behind you at once, and please do be quick about it."

We followed his directions and then sat in two of the chairs lined up against the wall next to the door. It was a pleasant enough space, genteelly furnished and a comfortable place to wait. A great deal of rustling was coming from the far side of the room through a second door, where I presumed the studio could be found. I peeked in far enough to confirm my suspicion, and was impressed with what I saw. Light flooded in through large skylights in the ceiling, and shelves full of props lined the walls.

"Forgive me," a gentleman said, coming to us and offering Colin his hand. "I am James Lafayette. I am afraid I did not realize I had an appointment booked for this afternoon. Is this the clothing you wanted to wear in your picture?" He looked us up and down, and although my walking suit was fashionable, I could tell he did not think it appropriate for what he believed was the occasion.

"It is I who must apologize. We are not here to have our picture taken," Colin said, introducing us and giving Mr. Lafayette the required background on the reason for our visit.

"That is something of a relief, I confess," Mr. Lafayette said. "My fog-clearing machine has been giving a bit of trouble today, and I have only just now managed to get it nearly to cooperate."

"Fog-clearing machine?" I asked.

"Essential, Lady Emily, if one is to work with electric lights in a fog-ridden city. Glasgow is the worst, if you must know. London is nothing compared to it. There now, I'm rambling, and you are here on official business. How can I help?"

"Among the photographs of guests you took at the Devonshire

House ball, do you recall a gentleman in ancient Greek dress wearing a theatrical mask?" I asked.

"Comedy or tragedy?"

"Tragedy."

"Alas, I do not," he said. "The truth is, however, that I had so many sitters it would be virtually impossible to recall them all. Many came here, to the studio, before the night of the party, as they did not want to be rushed by a crush of others while they were posing." He went to a box on the desk that stood near the door, opened its lid, and started flipping through the photographs inside. "I have developed many of those portraits already, but it will be some weeks before I have finished with the ones taken at the ball."

I stood next to him, peering over his shoulder as he searched. There were dozens of prints, each the same size, each depicting costumed individuals against backgrounds that quite well mimicked Devonshire House's lawn and gardens with their lovely statuary. Periodically, he came to one where the false exterior had been swapped for a suitable indoor location.

"I carried the backgrounds with me to the party as well," he said. "Did I photograph the two of you?"

"No, I am afraid not," Colin said.

"You shall have to make an appointment and return to me with your costumes," he said.

"That would be great fun!" I exclaimed. Colin frowned.

"You were set up in the garden, were you not, Mr. Lafayette?"

"Yes," the photographer replied. "My tent was brightly lit, and the duchess's guests could choose whether to pose inside or out, if you will. I had Turkish carpets and a variety of pieces of furniture and walls we could use to create the right scene for each." He continued going through the box of pictures until he reached the end. "I am afraid there are no masked Greeks here."

"Not many people wore masks that night," I said. "Do you remember anyone hiding his face?"

Mr. Lafayette was a decent-looking man, tall enough and well put together. He pulled his eyebrows close as he considered my question. "I cannot say that I do. Most likely, if someone wearing a mask had come to me, I would have suggested that he take it off for his photograph. I would display it in the picture, of course, but it is best to see one's subject's face."

"I suspect that our Greek came to the ball without a proper invitation," I said. "If that was the case, it is not surprising he would not have sat for a photograph in advance. Are any of the pictures taken on the evening itself finished?"

"A small number, but I have only just finished with them and can assure you they do not include your Greek tragedian," Mr. Lafayette said. "If you will come with me, we can look at the negatives from which I have not yet made prints." He led us through his studio into a room with blacked-out windows. Electric lights shrouded in red glass illuminated the space. Stacks of photographic plates were carefully arranged on tables. "It is a tedious task, but you are welcome to look through them all, so long as you are careful."

He showed us how to handle the plates and how best to look at them. Mr. Lafayette was nothing if not honest: the work was tedious, but fascinating as well. Each image was presented as a negative of how it looked in life: black became white and vice versa, making the individuals photographed appear more like creatures out of classical mythology than London's high society. For nearly two hours we held plates up one at a time until, at last, I found that for which I had searched.

"It is he!"

Estella

V

When Estella woke up, for a moment she thought she was in her cupboard at home. The darkness was lovely, no light fighting to turn her closed lids red, and the surface on which she lay was hard. Too hard, though, she thought, and too rough to be the carpet Nurse had placed on the floor for her all those years ago. She opened her eyes, but the movement had no discernible effect on her senses. Wherever she was, it was pitch-black, so dark that her eyes could not adjust to it, no matter how long she waited.

And she did wait. What else was there to do? As the time passed, her breath grew ragged and fear began to creep through her. She was fully awake now, and only just beginning to realize she had not been dreaming. She felt around her, her hands meeting stone in every direction, and determined that she was on some sort of raised surface. Sitting up, she slowly and with great care moved her legs until they dangled off the edge. The edge of what?

Panic bloomed. What if she fell? How far was the drop to the ground below her? She could see nothing. Swallowing bile, she methodically moved her hands along the edge of what she suspected was a slab of some sort, until she had a general idea of its dimensions. It was long enough for her to lie flat, and wide enough that she need not worry she would roll off it and plunge to her death. She pooled saliva in her mouth, as much as she could, and spat over the side, listening to hear how long it took before hitting the ground. There was no sound of impact. Fear gripped her chest, and she clung to both sides of what she now considered her lifeboat.

As she did this, she realized—stupid that she hadn't noticed at once—that her reticule was still hanging from her wrist. It felt heavier than she remembered. Slowly, she sat up again and opened it. Inside, she could feel her handkerchief and her coin purse, but there were two other objects that had not been there when she left home: something long and smooth and waxy and a small box that rattled when she shook it. A candle and matches! Her hands were trembling so forcefully she nearly dropped the box, so she did her best to still herself, to calm the terror bubbling in her, and to steady her nerves. Perhaps Dr. Maynard's Formula would have come in handy after all, she thought, not appreciating the irony.

With great deliberation, she pulled a breath in for a full count of ten, then released it at the same pace. She did this, over and over, until she began to relax, at least physically. Confident that she could proceed, she picked up the box from her lap and slid it open, feeling her way to the slim wooden sticks inside. She pulled one out, felt for the bulge on its tip and then for the strip on the side of the box. Lifting her hands, she struck the match, three times before she managed to get it lit.

The small flame did little to illuminate the space around her. Without thinking, she put the box back in her lap and tried to grab the candle. Before she could do so, however, the match's flame nipped at her finger and she dropped it, plunging herself again into darkness.

This failure, and the three that followed it, caused her hands to shake again, but at last she managed to light the candle. Relief flooded her. First, she looked down and laughed, almost maniacally, when she realized she had never been more than a few feet above the stone floor. She slipped down from her seat, stood, and in the span of a few heartbeats went from feeling relief to being swallowed by a sensation so awful she could not name it.

She was in a room, a small room, no more than ten feet by eight. Its walls and floor were stone, as she had suspected in the dark, and the ceiling, also stone, hung low. There were no windows, which, to a girl accustomed to hiding in a cupboard, did not in itself prove worrisome. The trouble came from something else.

There was no door.

6

The image captured by Mr. Lafayette's negative was not so clear as I would have liked. As the photographer had suspected, he had not taken the shot with the mask covering the man's face. The subject held it in front of his chest, albeit at an awkward angle, but unfortunately for us, his visage was not clear. He had moved before the photographer was done, and his features were blurred. I called for Mr. Lafayette, who had left us searching the photographic plates in the darkroom while he attended to business in his office, and he came at once, reminding us to keep the black curtain that hung not far from the door in place so that no light would damage his undeveloped plates. I handed him the negative in question.

"Do you have a record of who this is?" I asked.

"Yes," he said. "I kept track of everyone. This is plate 632. Let us see what we have."

Colin and I followed him out of the room and back into the bright studio, our eyes smarting. The photographer opened a thick notebook. For each numbered plate, he had entered the name of the person sitting, the role his costume was meant to represent, and whether the portrait had been taken in his studio or on site at Devonshire House.

"Here we are." He turned the book so we might see the entry.

"Abel Magwitch." My mouth hung open. "Is this meant to be a joke?"

"I am afraid, Lady Emily, that I am not acquainted with Mr. Magwitch." Mr. Lafayette bent over the book. "He was meant to be portraying the poet Homer."

"Homer would not have been wearing the mask of a tragic actor, but Mr. Magwitch's inability to satisfy even the barest requirements of historical accuracy is the least of my concerns." I sighed, frustrated. "I suppose it was foolish to think he would have used his real name."

"How do you know this is false?" Mr. Lafayette asked.

"Abel Magwitch is a character in Mr. Dickens's *Great Expectations,*" I said. "He secretly financed Pip's advancement. I cannot imagine there is any true person in possession of the same name."

"It is not altogether meaningless, perhaps," Colin said. "First, would it be possible for you to make us a print of the photograph, Mr. Lafayette, and have it sent straight over to our house in Park Lane?"

"Of course, sir, it would be my pleasure."

My husband turned to me. "Now, Emily, think about the novel. Who is Magwitch? A criminal, yes? An escaped convict, but a man who is trying to do something good, at least once he meets Pip."

"Yes," I said. "So our Mr. Magwitch, although he is perpetrating a fraud of some sort, means to suggest he is not all bad?"

"I think we have our first glimpse of insight into his character," Colin said.

Mr. Lafayette scowled. "I am more sorry than I can say that the image is not clearer. I do remember the gentleman now. It was nearly as difficult to get him to stand still as it had been to convince him to lower his mask. I feel foolish for not recalling the incident sooner."

"There can be little doubt his movement was deliberate," Colin said. "He did not want to leave a recognizable image of himself."

"I wonder that he had his picture taken at all," I said. "Although, thinking about it, we all initially entered the garden near Mr. Lafayette's marquee. Mr. Magwitch might have caught unwelcome attention if he had made a point of avoiding being photographed. Easier to have a picture made and make sure it's blurry than to act in a way that might have seemed odd to one of his fellow guests."

Colin grunted. "No one commented when I refused to be photographed."

"Yes, my dear, but everyone in the vicinity is bound to have the incident carved vividly into his memory. You were rather insistent on the subject."

"Was that you, Mr. Hargreaves? Dressed as Beau Brummell?" Mr. Lafayette asked.

"Indeed," my husband said. "I do not like fancy dress and have no interest in recording myself in such a state for all posterity to see."

"Then, you, Lady Emily, were the divine Artemis," Mr. Lafayette said. "Come back to me when you can, with your costume. Your husband need not be photographed, but it would be a crime for your ethereal loveliness not to be captured. The goddess herself would be pleased with your representation of her."

I admit to very much enjoying Mr. Lafayette's flattery.

Our visit to the studio having proven a success, we decided to now continue our search for further information about Mary Darby. Mrs. McDermott had mentioned a theater near St. Martin-in-the-Fields, so we made our way back to Piccadilly and followed it past Fortnum and Mason (where I was severely tempted to stop in for a cup of tea—investigation is of critical importance, but so too is keeping oneself well fueled and alert), past the Royal Academy, until we reached the Circus, where we turned into Regent Street. After cutting down Pall Mall and through Trafalgar Square in front of the National Gallery, we paused to determine the best course of action.

"We could try Charing Cross Road to Shaftesbury," Colin said, "but I wouldn't describe that as being near St. Martin-in-the-Fields."

"No," I said. "I remember now. It's the New Adelpi Theater on the Strand that we want. I saw an advertisement in the *Times*. It included a rather horrifying drawing of Bottom fawning over Titania. Put me off the production entirely." We followed the Strand several blocks until the theater came into view. "There it is. Have you ever seen a more unfortunate poster?"

Bottom, portrayed as an extremely vile-looking long-haired donkey, had placed two hooved feet over the shoulders of a seated Titania, who was looking up at him as if she might swallow him whole. Artistically, it was a disaster, and as a means of enticing people passing by to part with any amount of their hard-earned money for a seat in the audience it could have been nothing short of an abject failure. This suspicion was confirmed when we approached the box office, where the clerk, who appeared to have drifted off to sleep leaning on his hand, startled awake when Colin tapped his walking stick on the glass in front of him.

"Oh good heavens! Do forgive me," the clerk said, pushing back into place the spectacles that had slid down his thin nose. He spoke with a breathtaking rapidity. "I was not expecting anyone. Foot traffic has been awfully slow of late, which is unfortunate as this is such a magnificent production of one of Shakespeare's best-loved plays. You, though, you are in for a treat. Would you like tickets for this evening, or for tomorrow's matinee?"

I felt the need to draw breath when he finished.

"I am afraid we are not here to buy tickets. Can you tell us if any of the cast or crew is here?" Colin asked. "I am on official business from Buckingham Palace."

This shook any remaining vestiges of sleep from the clerk. "The palace?" His eyes widened. "Of course. Let me see whom I can rustle up. The director was here earlier. Could you wait just a moment while I inquire?"

"You should have told him we have not come to order the Royal Box prepared," I said. "I do so hate to be an instrument of disappointment."

The clerk returned to the lobby from a door to the stalls accompanied by a tall, broad man with a ruddy complexion, who crossed to us and shook Colin's hand with admirable vigor. "I am Nigel Seton-Williams, the director of this production, and I can assure you that whether it has caught the imagination of Her Majesty or the Prince of Wales, the royal party will find themselves delighted by our play."

"I'm afraid that is not why we are here, although my wife is quite desperate to see the show." Colin knew better than to look at me as he said this. "I do a certain amount of work for Her Majesty, and have been asked to look into the matter of the death of a woman—Mary Darby—who was murdered in the early morning hours of 3 July. Are you familiar with the case?"

"No," Mr. Seton-Williams said. "Mary is dead?"

"Yes. I am very sorry. You knew Mrs. Darby?" I asked. "We understand she had aspirations of being an actress."

"Plentiful aspirations, yes, but sadly not quite so much talent as one would hope. It strikes me to the core to think of her coming to such a tragic end."

"I understand she spent a great deal of time with your company at this theater," Colin said.

"That is true, but also misleading," he said, mopping the beads of sweat that had appeared on his brow. "I had always liked Mary, you see. Mrs. Darby as you called her—not quite the right name. She never was married, but styled herself as a widow."

"Why did she do that?" I asked.

"She felt it afforded her a measure of respectability that *spinster* did not."

"Quite right," I said.

"Mary came to me when I posted a call for auditions. She had always wanted to play Hippolyta in *A Midsummer Night's Dream,* and begged me for the chance. I saw no harm in letting her read, but did not think for a moment that she would be a good choice for the part. Imagine my surprise when she delivered what I can only describe as the performance of a lifetime."

"But you did not cast her?" I asked.

"I wanted to, very much," Mr. Seton-Williams said, "but in her callbacks she was never again able to read so well. I gave her chance after chance. Eventually, I had no choice but to offer the role to someone else. It was more appropriate, really. Mary is—was—quite a bit older than one wants Hippolyta to be."

"How did Mary react to losing the role?" I asked.

"Very badly, I'm afraid. She turned up at our first read-through and caused a bit of a scene. I managed to calm her down and convinced her to return home that day, but she turned up at rehearsals over and over."

"Was she disruptive?" Colin asked.

"No, not after that first time," Mr. Seton-Williams said. "She sat in the back of the theater and watched in silence. After the cast had cleared out, she always made a point of complimenting me on the production."

"Was she continuing her pursuit of theatrical success?" I asked. "Did she mention other auditions?"

"No," he said. "She did, however, tell me that she had found a way to use her admittedly limited talents. A gentleman had hired her to take on the role of a lady of means, but not in a theatrical production. It was to be a bit of a lark, she said, great fun."

"Have you any idea who the gentleman was?" Colin asked.

"None, I'm afraid. All I know about him was that he had a great deal of money. He fitted her up with a wardrobe from Paris. I confess this concerned me—I suspected he might be looking for a lark, but not the kind Mary thought she was to give him."

"Did she mention any impropriety in this man's behavior?" I asked.

"No, and I did ask her about that, especially when she told me about the clothes. I'm no expert when it comes to ladies' dress, but bespoke clothing from one of those famous blokes in France doesn't come cheap, and in my experience, when a gent is dressing a lady—please do excuse me for being crass, madam—he's looking for a mistress."

"How did Mrs. Darby react when you suggested this to her?" Colin asked.

"She laughed," Mr. Seton-Williams said, "and told me that such a thought would never have crossed my mind had I ever read a single letter penned by her employer. I took that to mean that, well, I don't like to say in front of your wife, sir, but I think you know."

"Did Mrs. Darby confirm your suspicions?" Colin asked.

"I never broached the subject with her. Mary was a generally sensible woman, and I trusted her judgment."

"Did she tell you anything else about this role of hers?" I asked.

"Only that she thought this was the sort of acting at which she could be successful," he said. "She had come to accept that the stage was not for her, but that didn't mean she had lost the desire to play a character. She was a bit lonely, I think, and sometimes that makes a person long to be someone else."

"Is there anything else you can tell us, Mr. Seton-Williams?" I asked. "It is quite possible that this role of Mrs. Darby's led directly to her death. Please think carefully. Did Mrs. Darby ever come to the theater during rehearsals with someone? Did you see her meet up with anyone outside?"

"I'm afraid there's nothing else I can add," he said, "but please be assured that should that change, I shall inform you at once."

"Is there anyone else on the premises at the moment to whom we may speak?" Colin asked.

"I don't expect the cast until six. The crew arrives a tad earlier."

I crossed back to the box office where the sleepy-eyed clerk was nodding over a penny dreadful. "Were you working while the play was in rehearsals?" I asked.

"Only the last two weeks before we opened, madam," he said, snapping to attention.

"There was a woman who slipped into the back of the theater quite often to watch the cast rehearse. Do you recall seeing her?"

"Yes, of course. Mrs. Darby. She brought me soup on a particularly damp day after she had heard me coughing the previous afternoon. A very kind lady. She's a midwife, you know, when she's not working as an actress. If, that is, one could say she works as an actress."

"I am sorry to tell you that she has been murdered," I said, "and if we are to find her killer, it is imperative that you tell us anything you can about her. Was she always alone?"

He pulled his spectacles from his face. "I hardly know what to say. This is too dreadful. Yes, she was always on her own."

"Did she talk to you at all about her work?"

"No."

"Did anyone ever come to the theater looking for her?" I asked.

"Only once, but that was just her brother, Mr. Magwitch."

"When was this?" Colin asked.

"No more than two or three days ago. I don't remember precisely. He asked if I knew where to find her. He'd been abroad, he said, and knew his sister was a member of the company here."

"What did you tell him?"

"There was very little to say. I had the impression that she had written to him that she was achieving some measure of success as an actress. It was rather awkward. I did not want to disabuse him of the notion, but I could not pretend she was in the play."

"Had he believed her to be?"

"So far as I could tell. I said she was certainly connected to the company"—he glanced at Mr. Seton-Williams—"I do hope that is all right. She was around quite a bit. I may have let him think she was an understudy." He cringed as he said this.

"An understudy?" I asked.

"There didn't seem to be any harm in it, and she had been kind to me."

"What did Mr. Magwitch say?" Colin asked.

"He thanked me and left."

"Did he seem surprised?" I asked.

"More frustrated, I would say. I had the impression that he had been supporting her, and that she had perhaps overstated her success in the theater as a means of keeping him on board."

"Can you recall any details of his appearance?" I asked.

"I'm afraid not."

"Did he say anything else?"

"Only that if I saw his sister would I please have her send word to the inn at which he was staying."

"How fortunate for us," I said. "Which inn?"

"The George in Southwark. I remember it on account of it being so near where Mr. Shakespeare's own theater once stood." The clerk perked up as he spoke and turned to Mr. Seton-Williams. "I am quite devoted to all things theatrical, sir. I do so hope you can find something for me outside of the box office in your next production."

"Yes, yes," the director said, his lack of enthusiasm cutting.

I looked at my husband. "Proximity to the site of the Globe aside, I remember the George having been mentioned in Mr. Dickens's *Little Dorrit*."

"Depressing novel," Colin said.

"Hardly the point, my dear. Our Magwitch is leaving more clues about himself." We thanked the clerk and Mr. Seton-Williams and exited the theater, but not before the director had implored us to come to his show as his guests. We could hardly refuse the gesture, and agreed to come as soon as we had solved the case at hand.

"It might not be so bad," Colin said, as he hailed a hansom cab to take us to Southwark. "Seton-Williams seems like a sensible enough man, and a bad poster alone ought not condemn a play."

"You are right," I said. "Perhaps it will prove a production worthy of the Bard. At the moment, however, the thought of it is making me hope it takes ages to identify Mary's murderer, and I feel quite awful about that."

"I am confident that even your dread of the play will not compromise your integrity, my love. I can think of no one better able to find justice for Mary Darby."

Estella

VI

Estella's heart was pounding with such force that she was convinced she could hear it, and half believed the sound was echoing off the hard walls of the chamber in which she now found herself entombed. Tears came, and with them ragged sobs that ravaged the back of her throat until it felt raw. She screamed, over and over, begging someone to help her, but when she stopped, she heard nothing but what had been there before: the continued thumping of her own heart and the rush of blood in her ears. There was no sound from outside. Panic and desperation fueling her, she flung herself with all her weight against the hard walls of the chamber, but was unable to so much as budge the stone blocks, so she tried to move them another way, by digging at the mortar around them. Soon her fingers were bleeding and for no purpose. She had not managed to make any impact on the hard substance holding the blocks of the wall in place.

The candle, which she had steadied upright on the slab by securing it in a pool of its own wax, was burning bright, so she knew air was entering the room from somewhere. She studied the ceiling and noticed one section of it looked different from the rest. The stone was a paler shade of gray, and there was no mortar around it. Instead it was surrounded by an open space, about an inch wide. Estella stood directly beneath it and was convinced she could feel movement in the air. She stretched her arms above her, as high as she could, but even on tiptoe was not tall enough to reach it, and as it was on the opposite side of the space from the elevated slab, there was no help to be found. She tried to climb up the wall, but her bloodied fingers could not hold her weight, so she crumpled to the ground, shaking and crying, desperate in a way she had not previously thought possible.

Scared and now in a not inconsiderable amount of pain, Estella retreated to a corner of the room, wedging her body between the wall and the side of the slab, closing herself in even more than she had been before. She hugged her knees to her chest and wept until she had no more tears. Then, an even more unnerving sensation seized her: numbness. She rocked forward and back, keeping an even rhythm, gripping her hands more tightly around her legs. The candle, which she had moved to sit on the floor directly in front of her, flickered, and Estella wondered if she ought to blow it out, in order to conserve it. Conserve it for what? She stopped rocking, and leaned back against the wall just as a sound invaded the space around her. Scraping and the hint of a squeak, the sort made by hinges recently oiled, but not quite enough.

The stone that did not match on the ceiling was upright now, forming a trapdoor through which a ladder appeared. Estella leaped to her feet, then crouched back down. Was this a portent of rescue or something direr? She swallowed hard, buried her face in her hands, and steeled her nerves before forcing herself to stand again. This might be her only chance at escape. She readied herself to charge the person whose feet had just appeared at the top of the ladder.

7

The hansom cab took us past St. Paul's and across London Bridge to Southwark, where the seventeenth-century building that served as the current incarnation of the George Inn stood in Borough High Street. Colin paid our fare and we entered the building, asking to see the man in charge. Mr. Blakely, who introduced himself as such, was everything one would hope to find in an innkeeper. His countenance was jolly and welcoming, and his happily rotund figure made one hope the food at his establishment was better than average. He complimented me on my hat—a jaunty little thing of which I was rather fond—and thanked Colin for having chosen to visit what he promised was the last authentic galleried inn in all of London. He leaned forward to me, confiding that Shakespeare himself had been a great admirer of the ale at the old inn, which stood on the same spot until it was destroyed by fire.

"I fear we are here on Crown business rather than pleasure," Colin said, explaining his position and some brief details about the case at hand, including the information that had led us to him. "Is Mr. Magwitch still here?"

"Magwitch!" The innkeeper gave a hearty guffaw. "Mr. Dickens. He was here as well as Shakespeare, before he wrote us into *Little Dorrit.* Liked our coffee very much. I get a right lot of names out of

Dickens among my guests. There is a fair share of individuals who prefer to register for a room under a *nom de guerre,* most often to hide a romantic indiscretion, which is not to say, madam, that we encourage that sort of behavior at the George. We quite frown upon it. Still, one doesn't always know what is happening beneath one's roof. Thinking on it, I don't believe that we have had a Magwitch before."

"It doesn't lend itself particularly well to romance," I said.

"Too right," Mr. Blakely replied. "If you come with me, I will look up the gentleman's details." We followed him through a labyrinth of low-ceilinged rooms—Colin had to duck his head more than once to avoid the beams—to the side of the building opposite the area that functioned as tavern and restaurant. Here we came to a tall counter, behind which stood a row of wooden filing cabinets. He consulted a large register on the counter and then pulled open a drawer, riffled through it, and pushed it shut.

"Mr. Magwitch is still here, sir. Hasn't yet checked out."

"Could you take us to him?" Colin asked.

"It would be a pleasure."

I need hardly tell the educated reader that Mr. Magwitch was, in fact, not in his room, that he had failed to appear for breakfast that morning, or that he had left the entire balance due the owner of the George unpaid. I had predicted these eventualities almost from the moment the innkeeper had located his erstwhile guest's name in the register. Fortunately for us, the ire of the innkeeper made it unnecessary to encourage him to allow us to search Mr. Magwitch's room; he offered to unlock the door before we had even asked.

"Can't trust these theater people, can you?" he said, leading us into the room.

"Is that how he presented himself?" Colin asked.

"He listed in my register his occupation as theatrical producer," Mr. Blakely said. "I was not at the desk when he arrived."

"Would it be possible to speak with whoever was?" I asked.

"That would be my daughter," he said. "I will run and fetch her now. Look around as long as you like."

The state of Magwitch's room suggested that his departure had not been planned. Two shirts of middling quality still hung in the wardrobe, as did a nightshirt. A razor, shaving brush, and mug sat in front of the mirror next to a pitcher and basin, and a clutter of books and papers were heaped on the table next to the bed.

"A two-day-old edition of the *Daily Yell,*" I said, holding the tabloid up for my husband to see. "A Roman Catholic catechism, a copy of *David Copperfield,* and a used ticket from the boat train, Paris to London."

Colin took the ticket from my hand. "He arrived three days before the ball at Devonshire House."

"He had to have hired Mary before then," I said, "or the costume couldn't have been shipped to her from Worth."

"Yes." Colin handed the ticket back to me and lifted the mattress from the bed. "Nothing here."

"Wait." I reached into the last drawer he had opened.

"Really, Emily, I must draw the line at you inspecting the undergarments of male persons wholly unknown to you."

This did not merit the dignity of a reply. I returned the offending garments, closed the drawer, and returned to the wardrobe. "All of his clothing was made in France. His books and his newspaper are English. I draw no conclusions from the paper. A French tourist might easily peruse the local news, but would be unlikely to choose something in a foreign language for his leisure reading. Furthermore, although Mr. Dickens's fame is widely considered to be international, I find it hard to believe that a Frenchman would be leaving clues to his character based on things found in English novels. We did not think to ask the box office clerk if the man to whom he spoke was a foreigner, but I believe we can comfortably draw the conclusion that he is not."

"I agree he is most likely English," Colin said.

"So why was he in France before he came here?"

"To order clothing from the House of Worth to forward his scheme?"

"Perhaps, but he need not have stayed there until so close to the day of the ball if that were his only purpose abroad," I said. "Furthermore, how many Englishmen would think to consult Worth in such circumstances? Would it not be easier to hire a London-based designer?"

"Magwitch is not traveling in a manner that suggests he can afford Worth." Colin picked up the train ticket from the table. "Second class, and charming though the George is, a gentleman of means would more likely stay at Brown's Hotel."

"Estella Lamar can afford Worth."

"Estella Lamar is in Siam," Colin said.

"Is she?" I asked. "Are you quite sure?"

"You raise an excellent point, my dear. We are in possession of no evidence that proves the fact. The letter her butler showed us purported to have been written by his mistress could have been a forgery. We are in no position to recognize Miss Lamar's handwriting."

"Cécile is. We need to see if there is some connection between Estella and Mary Darby," I said. "Perhaps there is a reason Estella would have wanted Mary dead. She might have had an illegitimate child, delivered by Mary—"

"Estella Lamar is unmarried and of an age with our own dear Cécile. Do you really mean to suggest—"

"No, no, you are correct. It's unlikely, although the fact that she is unmarried has no bearing on the subject. If anything, it would point to her willingness to take the most extreme measures to hide all evidence of the child."

"We do, Emily, agree that there is not a child, correct?" Colin smiled. "I love when you warm to a subject—you are well aware of that—but this, my dear, is one of those flights of fancy far better suited—"

"Yes, yes, to fiction, I know." I pursed my lips. "Someday I shall write an extremely sensational novel and read all three volumes aloud just to torment you. In the meantime, though, I think we should turn our attention to Estella's staff, and not only in London. There may be something afoot at her house in Paris."

"Bainbridge will never let me hear the end of it if you follow him to France, so I suppose there's nothing to be done other than accompany you." He sighed. "I don't imagine you could convince Cécile to send him back to London?"

"Tease however much you like," I said, "but I know you and Jeremy are exceedingly fond of one another, even if you are both too proud to own up to it."

"I have certainly met worse individuals."

"Refrain from telling him that, please. If we are ever to see him married off, it will not be before he is convinced there is nowhere lower for him to sink."

We spoke to Mr. Blakely's daughter before we left the George, but she had very little to say about Mr. Magwitch. He had made almost no impression on the girl. This, coupled with the fact that a sort of brawl had broken out in the bar shortly after he had checked in, had left her with no details to share with us. We hailed a hansom cab outside the inn and paid another visit to Estella's London house, where we questioned each and every member of the staff, none of them giving away the slightest hint that they might have passed news of the Duchess of Devonshire's ball to Mr. Magwitch, let alone that they had been involved in the crime against Mary Darby. They were under instructions to forward all of their mistress's mail to her solicitor in Paris.

Back in Park Lane, Colin gave his valet instructions on what to pack for our trip to Paris while I went to the nursery to speak to Nanny and say good-bye to the boys. My heart twinged as I cuddled them each in turn and kissed their chubby cheeks.

Nanny gave me a little pat on my shoulder. "There, there, Lady Emily, it's always hard the first time you leave them, but you know they are in good hands. My Colin wouldn't stand for anything less, and as I took care of him from the day he was born, they're bound to turn out nearly as well as he."

"We could never do without you." I passed Richard to her and squeezed her hand as she balanced him on her hip. Tom and Henry had been building a tower out of blocks, and were more than happy to be allowed back to their task. I started to miss them before I had reached the bottom of the nursery stairs.

First thing the next morning, we were on our way to the station. Meg had packed my trunks with no direction from me. She knew better than I what to bring on any trip. Colin had left his valet at home, but I could not do without my maid. Cécile had a more than competent staff, but the truth was there was not a soul on earth capable of taming my hair half so well as Meg. I thought back to the days when she had balked at my love of travel, wishing we would stay always in England. Now she was more likely to badger me into going abroad. It pleased me no end that I had affected such a change in her.

I have always been a good traveler, ready to face whatever difficulties might be thrown at me, untroubled by the logistics of the journey itself, but the Channel on that day would have strained the nerves of Admiral Nelson himself; never had I seen the water so rough. By the time we had stepped off the boat, my complexion had taken on an unpleasant hue of green. I slept on the train, and felt partially revitalized by the time we pulled into the Gare du Nord. Cécile had sent a carriage for us, and as we turned onto rue Halévy and passed the magnificent Palais Garnier, home of the Paris Opéra, my spirits began to soar, reaching a crescendo as the Louvre appeared on our left just before we crossed the Seine. Colin leaned close to me.

"We shall have to visit the Pont Neuf while we are here."

The Pont Neuf had become my favorite bridge in all of Paris after Colin had kissed me for the first time while we were standing on it, nearly seven years ago (now is not the time to discuss the fact that I slapped him after the kiss; I do believe my actions were justified in the moment). "Not until we have identified Mary Darby's killer," I said. "It is far too easy to be tempted to give oneself over entirely to romance when in Paris, and we cannot do so in good conscience before the ruthless brute has been captured."

"Has been captured?" Colin's eyebrows shot up. "Did you choose so passive a phrase to deliberately suggest that you do not plan to reel him in yourself?"

I patted his hand. "I thought you might consider it a bit of fun if I left it to you this time."

"Your generous nature never ceases to amaze me."

The carriage turned onto boulevard Saint-Germain, and I fell back against the cushions with a sigh as I looked out the window. Paris had an elegance that could not be found in any other city. Even the manner in which the sunlight glowed against the walls of buildings suggested a keen sense of fashion. Cécile's house was only a little past Café de Flore, in the place Saint-Germain-des-Prés, just off the grand boulevard itself and across from the famous church. It was situated to give one a view of the city that was exactly what one imagines Paris ought to be. Tall buildings with graceful curves, refined details, and iron-railed balconies rose over the traffic-filled street. The bustle of carriages and pedestrians and the accompanying noise was not an irritant, instead it gave everyone in its wake a burst of energy. It was as if the world was converging on this lovely spot, eager to leave all ugliness behind.

Cécile and Jeremy stood at the front door when we arrived, waiting to press glasses of cold champagne into our hands while Caesar and Brutus nipped at our heels. Colin did his best to ignore them—he considered dogs that small beneath his notice—but I bent over to stroke each of them as we entered Cécile's favorite sitting room. Deep azure paint trimmed cream-colored double panels on the walls. Above each pair, a pale plaster frieze depicting the story of the birth of Athena danced in front of its blue background. Two enormous mirrors hung on walls opposite each other, one above a marble mantelpiece, and the other over Cécile's desk. The desk, along with most of the rest of the furniture, was eighteenth century, delicate and gilded, the chairs upholstered in sky-blue silk a few shades lighter than the color on the walls. A large golden harp—which I had never known Cécile to play—stood in front of the fireplace. My favorite object in the room was a table, a *rafraîchissoir.* The top was quite deep—deep enough to have sunk into it two ice buckets for chilling wine, in front of which there was a smooth marble slab, white-veined gray, where one could put glasses waiting to be filled. The rest of the table was fashioned from rich acajou wood, polished until it shone. As always, both of the *rafraîchissoir*'s buckets were full, a bottle of champagne in each.

On each of the room's wall panels Cécile had caused to be hung an Impressionist painting. She counted the artists Renoir, Monet, and Sisley among her dearest friends, and supported them by buying as many of their paintings as they would allow her. Even in their lean days, they did not like to accept charity from her, so she insisted on paying exorbitant prices for their work. She refused to own things that were cheap, she had explained to them, and never doubted that her excellent taste should act as a catalyst for others. As a result, she viewed driving up the prices of Impressionist works to be nothing short of a moral imperative and would not allow the artists to take from her less than what she considered to be a fair price.

"You did not have this one when I was here last." I was standing in front of a Monet. "The way he has captured the sunlight is painfully beautiful."

"It is of Giverny. Do you recognize it, Kallista? It is the path that wanders around the lily pond near the willows."

"I do, very well." I had been to Monet's house there only once, four years ago, when I had taken a friend—and, it must be admitted, a thief—there so that the artist might confront him about a stolen painting. This was far from an unpleasant task, as the thief in question possessed more charm and wit than most gentlemen, and his criminal activities were often limited to ones he viewed as correcting injustices. On that occasion, he claimed to have stolen the painting in question so that he might bestow it upon a more appreciative person. His motives, though suspect, had the shreds of a sense of moral order.

Jeremy had abandoned his usual habit of sinking into the most comfortable chair as soon as he entered a room and was pacing. "Have you come because you do not trust me to handle Cécile's needs? I must say I am quite put out, Hargreaves."

"Believe me, old chap, there is nothing I would prefer than to leave Estella Lamar to you," Colin said. "It appears, however, that there may be some sort of connection between her and Mary Darby."

"So when I identify the murderer before you, will I become indispensible to the queen?" Jeremy asked.

"You might," Colin said, "so consider carefully your actions. If your desire is to be sent all over the Continent and the empire in pursuit of serious work, by all means beat me at my own game. I could use a bit of a holiday. It's been far too long since Emily and I have been to Greece."

"Why do I feel as if I am being played for a fool?" Jeremy asked.

"I know you have not been here much longer than us, but have you called at Estella's house?" I asked.

"Non," Cécile said. "Your telegram was delivered before we had finished overseeing the unpacking of our trunks, so I decided it would be best to wait for you. I did not think so slight a delay would make much of a difference."

"A sound decision," Colin said.

"It is my dearest wish to please you, Monsieur Hargreaves. Your smile is all the reward a lady could ever want."

"You flatter me," Colin said.

"Always." Cécile reclined elegantly on a chaise longue. "I have put together for you on that desk all the letters I have received from Estella since she started to travel. I hope they will prove useful. In addition, I have a book full with numerous clippings of photographs of her that have appeared in the papers. Most are from the early days of her adventures, when I thought she might enjoy seeing them upon her return. As the years have passed, I have stopped collecting them. You can see by the quantity I have that I would have required a library of albums had I continued, as the pictures appeared frequently as ever over the years."

I crossed to the desk and picked up the leather-bound volume. On the first page was an article that featured a daguerreotype of Estella, when she was approximately twenty years old, taken in a studio. The story mentioned only that Mademoiselle Lamar, after a lengthy period of mourning for her parents, had decided to visit Egypt. The tone of the piece suggested it had been written for the society pages, as if it was a not-too-subtle notice to eligible bachelors that the lady traveler would welcome their attentions abroad.

"Did Estella want to get married?" I asked.

"*Non,*" Cécile said. "In all the years I knew her, she never had a gentleman admirer. Estella is no beauty and always moved in an awkward manner one would expect to see in an adolescent. It was almost as if she was not French! I jest, of course, but until she inherited her fortune, she was of no interest to society."

"And when she did inherit?" Colin asked. "Did a pack of fortune hunters descend?"

"Not so many as you might expect." Cécile lifted her glass so that Jeremy might refill it. "Estella did not move much in society, and she rarely welcomed callers to her home. She never entertained and refused nearly every invitation she received. Only the most dedicated gentleman could have attempted to woo her."

"You were close with her, though," I said.

"*Oui,* she was an oddity and I enjoyed her. I thought she might fit in better among artists and creative people than she did in society, and I did all that I could to introduce her to that world, much as I did with you, Kallista. You took to it in a way Estella never did. She came out with me on occasion, and did enjoy her new friends, but she kept them at a distance, never revealing much of herself to anyone."

Jeremy picked up the second bottle of champagne from the *rafraîchissoir.* "I think we ought not open it." Colin rose to his feet. "We have dawdled—most pleasantly, Cécile—long enough. Will you take us to Miss Lamar's, please?"

Estella

Estella waited until the man's booted feet reached the ground before lowering her head and charging at him; she had not wanted to risk damaging the ladder. Her weight, alas, proved insufficient to make much of an impact. His arms encircled her and she struggled against them. Then she heard his voice.

"There, now, fighting me won't help."

It was him, her almost partner, the gentleman—no, she no longer could consider him that—the *man* who had wanted her to invest in Dr. Maynard's Formula. "You!" Her voice sputtered.

"Please, Mademoiselle Lamar, I do not want to hurt you." He kept hold of her with one arm and with the other raised the ladder until it was barely visible. A leather strap hung down from the bottom rung. Estella shoved him as hard as she could, managing to free herself, and jumped at the strap, but it was beyond her reach. "I have brought you some food, wine, and some other supplies."

"What have you done? Why am I here?"

"I'm afraid I am in dire need of your money," he said. "My situation has become rather desperate, you see, and I've no one left to whom I can turn. I had hoped we could come to an agreement about our business arrangement, but when you turned me out of your house, I knew there was no chance of that."

"So you kidnapped me?"

"Forgive me, it is awful, I am well aware of that. It is unconscionable. You would not, though, leave me to the pack of wolves who are prepared to kill me if I cannot repay the loans they gave me?"

"If I had my own pack of wolves I would set them on you without hesitation." Tears smarted in Estella's eyes. Her captor removed a handkerchief from his pocket and gave it to her.

"I am more sorry than you can know to have done this, and I promise I will do everything in my power to keep you as comfortable as possible. All I need is you to write a cheque, Mademoiselle Lamar. I will keep you here only so long as necessary. Once the cash is in my hands, and my debt is paid, I will release you unharmed."

"Do you think me foolish enough to believe that?" She crossed her arms over her chest. "You must know I would march directly to the gendarmes and have you arrested, so why on earth would you release me?"

"I will have already left the country before you could set the police after me."

"So who will rescue me?" This man, Estella thought, was either a simpleton or a fool.

"I have a letter here." He removed the leather satchel that had been slung over his shoulder, unfastened it and pulled from it a sealed envelope. "It is addressed to your steward and gives precise details on how you can be found. I will mail it before I embark on my journey."

"So how will you know I have been rescued? What if the letter is misdirected? What if my steward despises me and laughs at the contents of your letter?"

"I—I could send it to someone else if you would prefer."

"I would prefer that you lower that ladder and let me go."

"I cannot do that. Do you see the bruises on my face?" He opened his mouth wide. "These missing teeth? They are but a hint of what is in store for me if I do not pay these men. You alone have the power to save me, Mademoiselle Lamar, and you will do it."

"I will not."

"Then I will leave you here. Starvation, I am told, is not a pleasant way to die."

Estella flung herself at him again, hitting him and pulling his hair, scratching his face and kicking his shins. He stood his ground, but did not fight back. When she stopped, exhausted and sobbing, she sank to the floor.

"I am thoroughly ashamed of myself, Mademoiselle Lamar. I know what I am doing is diabolical, but the instinct to survive is strong in me. Sign the cheque, let me leave you well supplied, and know that you will return to your ordinary life in a matter of days." He went back to the satchel, which he had placed on the slab. "I have bread and cheese, fruit, an exceptionally nice pâté, a bottle of wine, several of water, and more candles."

"Even if I wanted to write a cheque I could not. Do you think I carry them with me?"

"I removed one from your desk last night. Your house was surprisingly easy to enter under the cover of darkness. When you return home, you must do something about this."

Estella's head throbbed. Her body ached and she felt a deep pain in her soul, a pain she feared would never leave her. She looked around the little stone room and felt fear closing in around her again. The door in the ceiling could be closed so easily. She would never be able to overpower her captor. If there existed another way out of this hideous situation, Estella had no inkling as to what it was.

"Give me a pen." She wrote the cheque, following his precise directions.

"You are better than I deserve." He waved the cheque until the ink had dried, then folded it and put it in his jacket pocket before handing her a blank sheet of paper. "Now I need one other thing. Write a note to your steward, telling him you are taking a trip or staying with a friend, whatever you prefer, just so long as it serves to make him and the rest of your servants know not to expect you home."

"A trip?" Estella balked. "I thought you said I would not be here long."

"I meant an excursion, to Versailles or Fontainebleau, or some such place. You take my meaning. Write."

She did as she was told. What choice did she have?

He read the letter and put it in an envelope. "I shall return tomorrow with more sustenance. You will want this as well, but might prefer not to open it until I have gone." He took a wrapped item out of the satchel and put it on the floor in the corner opposite the slab.

Estella did not reply.

He reached for the leather strap. "Do not attempt to climb the ladder behind me, Miss Lamar. I am stronger than you. You cannot best me physically and I have no desire to hurt you. Let me go and I promise I will return and take good care of you."

What could Estella do but acquiesce? She watched him go, cringing as he returned the trapdoor to its closed position and plunged her into the darkness against which her candle struggled in vain. She lit three more and unwrapped the package he had left behind.

A chamber pot.

Estella could not help herself. She began to laugh.

8

Estella's house was in the place des Vosges, on the right bank of the Seine, and therefore a fair distance from Cécile's. Henri IV had dreamed up this square in the Marais, called place Royale until the Revolution, and had insisted on a high standard of architecture for the buildings surrounding it. No timber frames for so lofty a space! Overzealous revolutionaries had destroyed much of the public sculpture in the city—one could hardly blame them for not wanting to face the haughty stare of a monarch at every turn—and melted down many in order that their metal could be used to make cannons. In 1829, an equestrian statue of Louis XIII had been erected in the square to replace its lost bronze predecessor, which had been commissioned by no one less than Cardinal de Richelieu. In his new incarnation, the king was depicted with a seventeenth-century beard and mustache, but clothed as a Roman emperor, his typically French flowing locks crowned with a laurel wreath. Perhaps as a precaution against the need for future armaments, the new sculpture was fashioned from marble.

The Lamar residence, which had been in the family for countless generations—all the way back to the place's fashionable days—occupied a large portion of the side of the square opposite Louis XIII, and, like its neighbors, was constructed from red brick and stone, its steep slate roof rising high above the neatly manicured park, its entrance housed beneath an arched arcade. A servant admitted us the barest instant after Colin knocked, and we stepped into a grand hall with a staircase that swept to the floor above in a graceful curve. Family portraits hung on the walls, and in the center of the black-and-white tiled floor stood a round table upon which rested a large urn all but overflowing with fresh flowers.

Cécile identified herself to the man who had opened the door, explaining that she was a close friend of Estella's, and inquired whether the mistress of the house was in residence. We knew his answer before he gave it.

"This gentleman, Monsieur Hargreaves, has come from London on the order of Queen Victoria." Cécile's voice dropped a register and she leaned in close to the servant, a severe look on her face. "Her Majesty would be most displeased if we did not assist him in every way possible. We have reason to believe Mademoiselle Lamar is in a great deal of danger."

Colin raised his hand and opened his mouth to speak. Cécile silenced him with a glance.

"This is most terrible." The servant wrung his hands and the look of panic on his face fell only just short of caricature. "Has she left Siam?"

"Is that where you believe her to be?" I asked. "Have you had a letter from her?"

"Not myself, madame, but if you will allow me to fetch the steward, he will be better able to assist you."

He put us in a grand salon, where enormous tapestries covered three of the walls. Above the center of each hung the arms of France and Navarre within the collars of the Order of the Holy Spirit and the Order of Saint Michael. A heavy crystal chandelier illuminated the space, although it was hardly necessary; sunlight poured through four large windows in the outside wall.

"I cannot count the number of times I implored Estella to either move the tapestries or draw the curtains." Cécile marched to the wall hanging nearest her and stood so close her nose nearly touched it. "The light is bound to fade the colors."

I lowered myself into a chair near a wide marble fireplace edged with a simple gilt band fashioned in the shape of the Greek key. "Has the house changed from when you were last here?"

"The basics of what I have seen so far are unaltered, although I do not recall such a great profusion of flowers." Nearly every flat surface held a vase, their sizes as varied as the blooms they held. "The smell of lilies is all but overpowering. What can she be thinking?"

The steward entered, pulling the door to the entrance hall closed behind him. Colin crossed to him before Cécile could interfere, gave his standard introduction, and began to interrogate the man at once.

"We have not seen Mademoiselle Lamar in ages, monsieur." The steward stood very straight and was nearly as tall as my husband. "She departed for Egypt some fifteen-odd years ago and has not returned since."

"Has she, in all that time, sent for any of her belongings?" I asked.

"Not once, madame, but that is hardly surprising. Mademoiselle took nothing with her when she left—she said her clothing was wholly inappropriate for her journey and had new items packed directly into trunks as the seamstresses completed them."

"Who made the clothes? Worth?" Colin asked.

"*Non, monsieur.* Mademoiselle had not the desire for fashion shared by so many ladies. She preferred simpler things. You may speak to her maid if you like. She will know much more about this than I."

"Her maid is here?" I asked.

"*Oui, madame.* Mademoiselle asked that we all remain here and at the ready so that she can arrive unannounced whenever she so desires."

"I should like very much to speak to the maid."

"Bien sûr." He opened the door, poked out his head, and called for the servant stationed in the hall, speaking to him in a low voice before retuning his attention to us. As we questioned him further, it quickly became apparent that the situation here mirrored what we had found in Belgravia. The house, fully staffed, operated as if its mistress had gone across town and would be back for dinner, not that she was gallivanting across continents with no evidence of a plan to return.

While Colin and Jeremy explored the rest of the house, Cécile and I remained in the salon to see the maid. Jeanne was of petite stature, wiry rather than round, and must have been approaching her sixtieth birthday. I wondered that she was still working, but then reminded myself that her duties, such as they were with her mistress away, could not have been taxing in the least.

"Was Mademoiselle Lamar eagerly anticipating her departure?" I asked. "I know it was ages ago, but surely you remember."

"I remember precisely, madame, because she never spoke to me of it. Mademoiselle is not what one could describe as gregarious."

"But she must have mentioned it, if only to tell you she was leaving you here rather than having you accompany her?"

"She did nothing of the sort. I have served the Lamar family for more than thirty years. Mademoiselle's mother asked me to tend to her daughter when she started to go out in society, and I have been with her ever since. Mademoiselle did not much like society, and after her parents' death, went out very little. When she did venture into the wilds of Paris, as she called it, she rarely gave me details. I never knew if I was dressing her for the opera or a ball. As you are her friend, Madame du Lac, you know that she paid no attention to what others thought she should wear."

"That is true." Cécile turned to me to explain. "Estella had two types of gowns: those with long sleeves and those with short sleeves. The weather determined what she wore on any given day."

"Yet we are to believe she ordered a costume from Worth for the Duchess of Devonshire's ball?" I asked.

"*Non, non, non.*" Jeanne stifled a laugh. "Do please forgive me, I mean no disrespect, but Mademoiselle would never have hired Monsieur Worth. She had a seamstress who worked exclusively for her. It was not a simple feat to find someone interested in dressing someone so disinterested in fashion."

I made note of the name of the seamstress. Jeanne was unsure of her current address, but gave me the one she knew from her last dealings with the woman. "Did your mistress take any of her personal possessions when she left?" I asked.

"She took nothing."

"And this did not strike you as odd?" I asked.

The maid threw her hands in the air. "Madame, I do not think you understand what it is to work for her. Mademoiselle Lamar is most uncommunicative. She went out one afternoon, dressed in a long-sleeved gown and a cloak. She sent word to us that evening that she had decided to go to Versailles for several days. Soon thereafter, she wrote to inform the steward that she was leaving for a prolonged trip abroad, and that her seamstress, from whom she had new traveling clothes, was sending them directly to her. Mademoiselle had no firm date by which she planned to return, so she asked that we all remain as we were until she told us otherwise."

"So years go by—*years*—and you all stay here, doing next to nothing, but continuing to draw your salaries." This did not sit well with me.

"What else are we to do?" the maid exclaimed. "Mademoiselle Lamar's orders left no room for doubt and were confirmed for us many times over by her solicitor, Monsieur Pinard. It is all very well to accuse us of taking advantage, but I can assure you that is not the case. I tried three times to give my notice and Monsieur Pinard would not hear of it. Mademoiselle Lamar is adamant about wanting nothing in the house different when she returns."

"I am directing a great deal of displeasure in Monsieur Pinard's direction," Cécile said. "You may go, Jeanne, unless there is anything further you have to tell us."

"What else is there to say?" the maid asked. "Why are you asking all these questions? Has something happened to my mistress?"

"That is what we are trying to determine," I said. "The entire circumstance of this situation is suspicious."

"It is easy for you to say that, coming upon us like this, so many years after Mademoiselle Lamar's departure, but it was not so for us. Her manner of leaving may seem odd to you, but it did not appear out of character to those in her household. You, Madame du Lac, know her well. Were you shocked at the time?"

"I own to having felt a certain amount of surprise," Cécile said. "I had never expected Estella to embark on a journey of any scale. She was loath to leave her house."

"Mademoiselle had very little to say to me," Jeanne said, "but she always read while I tended to her hair, always books about travel and exotic places. Perhaps they fired her imagination."

"They must have." Cécile dismissed the maid, leaned against the back of her chair in that elegant way exclusive to Parisian ladies, and tapped her closed fan against the palm of her left hand. "Estella was so very obsessed with her reading at times, and I do admit that I was not wholly taken aback at the note she sent me when she left. It was an odd way to announce her departure, but her manners had always left much to be desired. She paid little regard to what society expected in terms of ordinary behavior. If I invited her to dinner and managed to convince her to come, I knew to expect that she might leave before dessert had finished. She meant no offense by her actions, but did not stay on when she wanted to go home."

"It appears that neither did she stay home when she wanted to depart." I frowned. "It is most curious. Did you truly think nothing of it at the time?"

"At the time, Kallista, I believed she had decided to cruise up the Nile. This is hardly an earth-shattering course of action for someone who has spent years reading about the travels of others. Egypt led to Jerusalem, which led to Persia, which led to India, and so forth. I thought very little of it. Estella is a difficult person to know, and I had no reason to suspect anything was amiss."

"The profusion of newspaper photos I have seen strike the wrong chord with me," I said. "She had never before behaved in a way that suggested she craved attention, but we are to assume her travels changed this about her? I do not believe it. The pictures seem to me a way of proving she was where she claimed, but her face was not discernible in a single one of the photographs in your album other than the first, and that had been taken in a studio years before she left Paris. I am convinced that something has gone very much amiss."

We sat in a café near the place des Vosges to have a council of war after we had finished at Estella's house. Colin and Jeremy reported having found every room in perfect order. They had gone below stairs as well, and although the servants could not be described as overworked, neither were they at leisure. Their mistress's absence meant the cook did not have to prepare her meals, and that the laundress did not need to tend to any of her undergarments, but there were still the servants' meals, the bed linens and white goods throughout the house. Floors needed polishing, windows washing, and surfaces dusting. Because the house was not closed, the amount of work varied only slightly with Estella gone.

"So far as I can tell she kept no diary." Colin flipped through his notebook. "I found no correspondence to speak of. The steward told me he sends all her mail on to the solicitor, Pinard. Other than that, there is very little in the house that speaks to Miss Lamar's character."

"You saw her dolls, *non*?" Cécile asked.

"I nearly ran when Hargreaves opened the cupboard." Jeremy's face contorted in disgust. "Creepy things, if you ask me, all lined up on the floor like that around a little stool."

"Are they not in the nursery?" I asked.

"There were more than seventy on shelves in a room nearby," Colin said, "but we found a smaller grouping in a cupboard in the corridor on the top floor of the house. It appeared to have been fashioned into a hiding place for a small child."

"Estella must have kept it as it had been when she was a girl." I shrugged. "No reason to change it."

"She had a great affection for her dolls," Cécile said. "Her father gave them to her and she developed what I can only call an unnatural attachment to them. She confided in me that her mother told her the most wonderful, fantastical stories when she was young, and that she eventually started telling them to her dolls."

"Not entirely out of the ordinary, I imagine," Colin said.

"It would not have been had she abandoned the habit when she came of age, Monsieur Hargreaves, but Estella often had one or more of her dolls with her when I called on her. When she did, she explained that she had been in the middle of a story. At the time I assumed she was being facetious. Now I am not confident in that judgment."

"There can be no question that Estella is a strange lady," I said. "Let us take that as read. A person with childlike qualities is vulnerable to those who want to take advantage, and her fortune would make her ripe to be so targeted. I want to see Monsieur Pinard immediately. From what the servants have told us, he holds the purse strings. Let's see if he is controlling his client as well as her money."

Estella

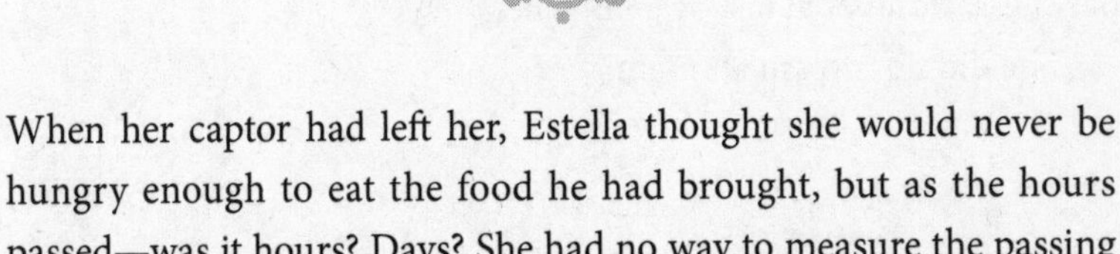

When her captor had left her, Estella thought she would never be hungry enough to eat the food he had brought, but as the hours passed—was it hours? Days? She had no way to measure the passing of time—her stomach, despite the fear and anxiety consuming the rest of her, began to rumble. She lined the food up next to her on the slab, evaluating her bounty. The grapes had seen better days, but the cheese did not look bad. She broke off a corner of it and tore a piece of the baguette. He had left her no knife—wise man—so she was forced to attack the pâté with the crust of the bread. It worked surprisingly well.

He had brought the wine already opened, the cork crammed back into the bottle's neck, so that she would have no need for a corkscrew. She had no glass, so was forced to guzzle directly from the bottle, an act that she found strangely appealing, so unlike anything she had been allowed to do in her regular life. The wine was atrocious, but it made her muscles relax and the sensation was so pleasant that she drank more than she perhaps ought to have. Her lids grew heavy, but she did not know whether to credit this to the libation or the hour. She wrapped the remaining cheese in its paper, popped a grape into her mouth—the fruit was not so bad as she had feared, but Estella acknowledged this, too, might be due to the effect of the wine—and made a neat pile of her provisions on the floor away from the slab.

She wanted to sleep, but even the wine could not disguise the intense discomfort one feels when reclining on bare stone. She had bunched her cloak into a ball, fashioning a sort of pillow from it. Her heavy petticoats provided a certain amount of padding, but nowhere near enough to make her position one that could be even generously described as comfortable. Eventually she was drowsy enough to decide it wise to blow out the candles and then, plunged once again into darkness, slumber at last overcame her.

She did not dream all night.

9

Monsieur Pinard's offices in the rue de Courcelles, just south of Parc Monceau, conveyed luxury the moment one entered them. Fine art hung on walls paneled in sumptuous wood, silk Persian carpets blanketed parquet floors, and the chairs were covered with butter-soft morocco leather. Estella might not have had a taste for Worth, but Monsieur Pinard inhabited another league entirely. His clothes were of the finest fabric and could only be described as violently fashionable. Colin and I had come to his office alone, leaving Cécile and Jeremy at the café. Four was too large a party for this part of our work. The solicitor did not keep us waiting long, despite our lack of appointment.

"I do hope you are not here because Mademoiselle Lamar caused a commotion in London." He sat behind an ebony desk after we refused the coffee he offered. "It would be very unlike her. She has proved herself a great adventurer, but has not once fallen afoul of the authorities in any of the countries she has visited. So please, Monsieur Hargreaves, do explain what my client has done to draw the attention of an agent of the British Crown."

"You believe Estella Lamar is, or has recently been, in London?" Colin asked.

"Your presence here suggests just that. I cannot give you details, as I am not in possession of them. I know little beyond what her invoices tell me. In this case, I remember very well a large one from the House of Worth for a masquerade costume intended for the Devonshire House ball."

"Mademoiselle Lamar did not appear at the ball," I said. The solicitor shrugged.

"This is hardly my concern."

"You should, perhaps, take better notice." Colin rose from his seat, placed his hands on the edge of Monsieur Pinard's desk, and leaned hard on them. "So far as we can tell, your client has not been in London at any time in the recent past. A woman came to the ball in the costume Mademoiselle Lamar commissioned from Worth. This woman identified herself as your client to the Duke and Duchess of Devonshire as well as to the rest of London society. When confronted by a lady who recognized the fraud, the woman fled, only to be found murdered some hours later."

"*Mon Dieu.*" Now Monsieur Pinard became serious. He tapped his hand on the desk. "You are quite certain Mademoiselle is not in the house in Belgravia?"

"She has not been there in more than two decades," I said. "Does this surprise you?"

"To own the truth, I would be more surprised if she were there. She has developed a taste for things considerably more exotic. The last letter I had from her indicated that she is planning to start for China by the end of the month."

"What exactly is your arrangement with Miss Lamar?" Colin asked.

"I was the executor of her parents' estate, and have handled her financial interests since their deaths. Mademoiselle Lamar showed little interest in the details of her fortune, beyond a brief period—that amounted to nothing—in which she flirted with the idea of investing in industry. I pay her bills, manage her investments, and, since she has been away, ensure that her houses are well run in her absence. If you have been to Belgravia, I assume you are aware that she wants everything left as if she were there."

"Yes," I said. "Is that not rather a wanton waste of money? We were in place des Vosges before coming to you. That is not an inexpensive house to run."

"Mademoiselle Lamar can well afford it. My job is not to judge her eccentricities. If she began to spend at an unsustainable rate, I would do my best to remedy the situation, but she has never approached that, even with her three houses."

"The third is a villa in the south?" Colin asked.

"*Oui,* but so far as I know Mademoiselle Lamar has not visited it since losing her parents. I make an annual trip there and to London to check on things. Her staff are very loyal, but one must make sure they are doing what they ought." He clasped his hands together on the desk and smiled. "I am painfully aware that this situation is most extraordinary. Servants running empty houses. An heiress traveling the world in the company of no one but a companion and foreign natives and all but refusing to return home. There is no denying the strangeness of all of it, but Mademoiselle Lamar is a grown woman in possession of a large fortune, and she has the unfettered right to spend it however she sees fit. My job is to do what she directs—I am employed by her, not vice versa."

"You are not concerned about her in the least?" I asked.

"This business of the costume and the murdered woman is unsettling, I allow you that." He paused, turned away from us in his chair, and looked out the windows behind his desk. "The only reasonable explanation is that Mademoiselle Lamar had decided to buy the costume for this other woman. Is it possible they met abroad?" He faced us again.

"Almost certainly not," Colin said. He had resumed his seat, but was staring at Monsieur Pinard with great intensity. "She was a midwife and a failed actress and would have had neither the means nor the opportunity to travel."

"It is quite a mystery then. Perhaps someone at the House of Worth could offer you assistance? If the costume were made for someone other than Mademoiselle Lamar, they would have had to know in order to make it fit the wearer, would they not?"

"Could we please see your copy of the invoice?" I asked.

"This is no problem." He pulled a thick folder from one of the side drawers in his desk, rustled through the papers in it, and produced the invoice in question. "You may take it with you if you like. I will also give you a note, explaining that you are working with me on a matter concerning Mademoiselle Lamar, so there will be no difficulties."

"Thank you." Colin's tone was all politeness, but I recognized a tension in it as well. "We will also need to go over all your records concerning Miss Lamar."

The solicitor threw his hands in the air. "I am most sorry, Monsieur Hargreaves, but I cannot allow that. My client's finances are confidential, and unless she directly orders me to share her private information with you, I am bound by ethics to deny your request."

I could see it was time for me to intervene. "Monsieur Pinard, no one could doubt either your keen sense of ethics or your devotion to your client." I smiled at him, forcing my eyes to linger on his. "I am most concerned about Mademoiselle Lamar. This murder, though it did not directly impact her, at least not so far as we know, is connected to her in some way, and she may be in a great deal of danger. Surely you will help me. I need you so very much. Without you, how can we protect Estella?"

He smiled while I spoke, which I took as a positive sign, and he fidgeted almost indiscernibly—I spotted it—before he replied. "Lady Emily, you are most passionate in your plea, and I am tempted more than you can know. I care deeply about Mademoiselle Lamar, but unless you can prove to me that she is in danger, I am afraid I cannot comply, no matter how charming you may be."

My face flushed hot. I was mortified to have so misjudged the situation—but who would not have made the same mistake? I had believed all Frenchmen susceptible to a friendly flirtation.

"My wife's worries stem from more than general concern, Monsieur Pinard. As you had no way of knowing that, you of course misunderstood her. Are you acquainted with Cécile du Lac, your client's closest friend from her years in Paris?"

"I do not know her personally, but am aware of her relationship to Mademoiselle Lamar."

"Madame du Lac is convinced something terrible has happened to her friend. As I explained, I am an agent of the British Crown. My wife is an investigator in her own right, and she is here not only to support my role, but also to further her own work. Madame du Lac has charged her with locating Estella Lamar."

I could have kissed Colin on the spot for having made something very nearly sensible come out of my blunder. "Forgive me if I was unclear before, Monsieur Pinard," I said. "Madame du Lac has no doubt that her friend is in the most perilous situation. Like you, I am bound by the confidential nature of the services I provide, and cannot disclose everything my client knows. I would never want to do something of which Mademoiselle Lamar would not approve. How long do you think it would take for you to receive a response from a telegram to her? Perhaps you could send one, and if she doesn't reply in a timely fashion, you would be willing to reconsider your position? If there is nothing wrong, she is bound to answer straightaway, either granting or denying you permission to give us what we have asked."

Confusion clouded the solicitor's face. "If Mademoiselle Lamar were easy to reach, Madame du Lac could confirm for herself that there is no problem. My client is not traveling in accessible locations. One cannot send a wire to the jungles of Siam."

"Do they have jungles in Siam?" I asked, sitting up straighter. "I have never traveled there myself."

"I am no expert on the geography. All I can tell you is that I cannot reliably communicate with Mademoiselle Lamar. She sends directions when she sees fit. She is not obligated to keep me abreast of her every whim."

"So if something were to go dreadfully wrong with her, you might not know in time to offer even the slightest assistance?" I asked.

"One could look at it that way, Lady Emily, but my job is not to offer assistance. It is not to rescue my client if she chooses to put herself in dangerous situations. As I have already said, I manage her finances and her properties, and unless someone in a position of authority requires me to share Mademoiselle Lamar's private information, I will not do so." He rose from his seat. "If you will be so good as to excuse me, I have a great deal of work to do."

"My deepest apologies for having bungled that. I thought a little flirting would distract him enough to say yes to whatever we wanted." Upon leaving Monsieur Pinard's office, Colin and I walked the short distance to Parc Monceau, and had settled on a comfortable bench to discuss our situation.

"It was not an altogether ridiculous strategy, although even a Frenchman, Emily, is bound to hesitate at flirting when the lady's husband is sitting two feet away."

"You know full well that is not true! I have seen, any number of times—"

"Do not excite yourself."

I sighed and slumped as much as my corset would allow. "Monsieur Pinard does not seem to have the slightest concern for Estella's well-being."

"He is correct when he says that is not his job. What matters at the moment, however, is that he had believed Estella to have been in London for the ball. His copy of the invoice from Worth gave no information about where the costume was to be delivered or mentioned anything to suggest it had been intended for someone other than Estella. We will find out more when we go to Worth."

"Do you not find everything about Monsieur Pinard suspect? I can hardly abide the sight of him. He is smug and so very ostentatious in the manner he displays his wealth. Did you see the size of the gold links on his watch chain? I should not be surprised at all if he is stealing from Estella."

Colin took my hand, raised it to his lips, and kissed it. "Your rampant imagination is getting the better of you. I had hoped he might give up his records, but knew it would be unlikely. Do try to remember that despite the fiction I wove for Monsieur Pinard, we are not here on Estella's behalf. We are here to investigate the death of Mary Darby."

"Which is intricately bound to Estella Lamar."

"It may be, or it may not. Until we know more, we must focus on Mary."

"I hope you know how deeply I am concerned with finding justice for her," I said. "No one deserves to suffer such a fate, and we know what a good and decent woman she was. Magwitch was in Paris less than a week ago. Is there any hope of determining what he was doing?"

"There would be more hope if we had the slightest clue as to his identity." Colin rose from the bench and pulled me up beside him. "Perhaps one of the Messieurs Worth will be able to enlighten us."

Cécile and Jeremy had kept the carriage with them, so we hired a cab to take us to the House of Worth. Of Charles Frederick Worth's two sons, who had taken over the business after their father's death, I was better acquainted with Jean-Philippe than Gaston-Lucien, and so asked to see the former.

"Lady Emily! This is an unexpected pleasure. I did not know you were coming to Paris, did I?" A look of concern crossed Jean-Philippe's narrow face as he kissed my hand.

"No, Monsieur Worth, this visit was spontaneous and, more's the pity, does not include time for me to peruse your new offerings. I have some questions for you that are best posed in private."

He led us through the ground-floor showroom, filled with a delicious concoction of gorgeous sample gowns, hats, parasols, and other accessories, and then took us upstairs to his office, which provided a study in contrast to Monsieur Pinard's orderly surroundings. Fabric samples, spools of decorative trim, and sketches of designs covered the desk and three tables. A dress form stood in the corner, draped with a shimmering silk voile so lovely I could not resist inspecting it.

Jean-Philippe picked up the fabric and draped it over my shoulders. "This would be stunning on you, Lady Emily. The color suits your complexion. I have only a few bolts of it—it is an extremely limited production. We will speak of it after you have asked me your questions." Colin passed him the invoice from Monsieur Pinard and explained our general purpose. "Ah, yes, I do remember this. I had worried you might be cross with us, Lady Emily, for creating a costume for the Devonshire House ball with so many similarities to your own. The color was different, though, and Mademoiselle Lamar had very unique ideas about what she wanted from her headdress."

"Do not trouble yourself with worry, Monsieur Worth. No one commented on the similarities, so as far as I am concerned, they did not exist. Did you speak with Mademoiselle Lamar about the design?"

"We corresponded by telegram. She had not previously been a client of ours, but explained that she has been abroad a great deal and was unable to come in even for a fitting. I nearly refused to work with her, as I had grave doubts that she could be satisfied with a costume made without us so much as seeing, let alone measuring, her, but she had her seamstress send me detailed information. It turned out that Mademoiselle Lamar matches almost precisely in size one of the models I already employ, so I agreed to the commission."

"Unfortunately, Monsieur Worth, your client did not wear the costume. It is unlikely she even knew of its existence," I said. "So far as anyone knows, she is in Siam. The address to which the gown was delivered belonged to a Mrs. Mary Darby, who wore it to the ball while pretending to be Mademoiselle Lamar."

"How very strange."

"Even worse, Mrs. Darby turned up murdered some hours after she left the ball."

"Did the killer believe he had attacked Mademoiselle Lamar?" Mr. Worth asked.

"I had contemplated the same question," Colin said. "The only person at the ball who could reliably claim to be able to recognize Miss Lamar spotted the fraud at once, so unless someone hired an assassin and failed to give this individual any means of recognizing his target, I must believe Mrs. Darby was the intended victim. We suspect someone—a man—hired Mrs. Darby to play a part at the ball, and hope that you would be willing to share with us any and all correspondence you had concerning Miss Lamar's costume. There may lie within your records something to point us toward the identity of the villain."

Mr. Worth shot to his feet. "Consider it done. I am most distressed to have participated, even without knowing, in any sort of fraud. You are certain Mademoiselle Lamar did not order the gown? I seem to recall that her telegrams did arrive from some far-flung location, although I do not think it was Siam."

Within a quarter of an hour, he had gathered for us a packet of information that included all the sketches and notes for the costume, the initial letter and subsequent telegrams from his client, his replies, the company's copy of the invoice, and even the canceled cheque that had paid the bill.

"Did anyone ever come into the shop regarding this order?" Colin said.

"I do not believe so. There is no record of such an occurrence, and we would have made note had she, or anyone else, made a personal visit. Please take as much time as you require going through all this. I must return downstairs as a client will be arriving to see me. If you require anything else, do not hesitate to let me or my brother know."

We started with the letter. There was no envelope, so we could not determine the location from which it had been posted, but Estella—if it was Estella who had written it—stated quite plainly that she was writing from Bombay, where she had broken her journey en route to London. She requested that the House of Worth design a costume for the Devonshire House ball, and that it be classical in design so that she might represent the goddess Diana.

"So you see she was Roman, not Greek. I much prefer the original."

"Do you suggest Artemis was the original goddess of the moon?" My husband looked at me with a puzzled expression. "I am quite certain the ancient Egyptians would have something to say on the matter."

"I believe the Egyptians worshipped a god of the moon, possibly Khonsu, but it is not my area of expertise. Regardless, I stand by my statement that Artemis is a superior choice to Diana." I returned my attention to the letter. Estella had authorized a budget of up to £5000—an astronomical sum, even for someone of her wealth—and listed a hotel in Constantinople as the next place at which she could be reached. She also promised to have her regular dressmaker send detailed measurements as soon as possible. Next, we studied the dressmaker's note. The woman's name and details matched those given to us by Estella's maid. Beyond that, the correspondence consisted of telegrams: Mr. Worth agreeing to the commission and asking for clarification on some of Mademoiselle Lamar's requirements, and so forth. The specifics of these were not important. More interesting were the locations from which Estella's subsequent telegrams had been sent.

The first came from the hotel in Constantinople she had mentioned, the next from Athens, then two from Rome, one from Sines, in Portugal, and a final one from London, confirming the receipt of the costume. I copied down the precise details of each, including dates. I tapped my pencil against my chin.

"There is something decidedly off about all of this. If these wires are to be believed, Estella managed to travel all the way from Bombay to Constantinople in little more than a fortnight. Is that even theoretically possible?"

Colin considered the question. "She could have taken a ship from Bombay to Suez, through the canal, and on to Port Said. From there, she could have gone anywhere. I am not certain as to the amount of time required for the journey, but my question is this: why, if London were her ultimate goal, would she have gone first to Constantinople?"

I picked up where he stopped. "And then on to Athens, Rome, and Portugal? The dates place her in London only four days before the ball. The initial letter was mailed only a few weeks after the duchess had sent her invitations and the gossips had started discussing the event in earnest. The newspapers had reported it almost at once, and had even followed the stories of some of the costumes being designed for the evening. To be in London on time, Estella would have had to move with extreme speed. She would not have been able to dally across the Continent. Furthermore, given the timetable before her, it makes no sense at all that she would have done anything in Port Said other than board a ship headed directly to London."

"I disagree with you there, Emily. It would have been more efficient to go to Marseille and get the train. Boats are much slower."

"I concede the point. Regardless, this itinerary doesn't fit. She could not have gone from Port Said to Constantinople to Athens, then to Rome and Portugal, and then to London, in the span of ten days."

"Agreed, but do remember that, so far as we know, she never made it to London—she may never have so much as intended to make the trip."

"Her intentions are not relevant at the moment. One person could not have sent all of these wires from each of these locations in the allotted time. I am beginning to suspect that Mary Darby is not the only person to have posed as Estella Lamar."

Estella

When Estella woke up in her prison, her entire body ached. Her muscles were tense, her right hip felt bruised—no doubt a side effect from sleeping on a stone slab—and her head pounded. She fumbled for her matches, lit two candles, and cringed when she saw the nearly empty bottle of wine on the floor. That it so repulsed her confirmed her suspicion that she had consumed far too much of it before she had fallen asleep. She drank nearly an entire flask of water and picked at the stale remains of her baguette, wondering when her captor would return. Surely it would not take long for him to get the funds he required.

A dark thought began to fester in her mind. What if he had no intention of returning for her? The promise of so obviously corrupt a man could hardly be sincere, and she had no reason to believe his insistence that he had no desire to bring her to harm. She swallowed hard and blinked, wanting to hold at bay the tears she could feel once again pooling in her eyes. How foolish to have agreed to write the cheque! He would never come back, and she would die here, alone and forgot, with no one to miss her, and all because she had stupidly done exactly what a maniac kidnapper had demanded of her.

She cried for a good long time and then stopped. If he had meant to starve her, why had he brought food in the first place? She had not left her house with a candle and matches in her reticule; he had placed them there, so that she would not be left alone in the dark, and had brought more candles with the food. No, this line of thinking was too optimistic. He had needed her to go along with his plan, and cajoling her gently, with sustenance and light offered as incentive, would have been easier than any sort of physical confrontation. Or was it? He could have left her alone in the dark, refused her all comforts—such as they were—and told her she would never again eat or drink or breathe fresh air until she signed the cheque. Estella pressed her palms against her temples. She had no way of knowing what this man would do.

She huddled into a corner, sitting on the floor, and pulled her cloak around her against the chilly damp of her room. After what seemed like an eternity, she fell asleep again, almost without realizing it. When she awoke, the two candles she had lit had burned themselves out. She rose stiffly from the ground and felt her way back to the slab. This time, she lit four of the wax tapers, and picked at the grapes she had rejected before, wondering how much time had passed since he had grabbed her in the street and how much longer she would have to wait for him to open the door in the ceiling.

Hunger gnawed at her again. Had she slept for another full night? Her addled mind could tell her nothing. She ate the cheese and the rest of the baguette, fruitlessly contemplating whether it was possible for one to measure time by careful analysis of the progression of staleness in bread. Whatever the number of hours that had passed, they were enough that the wine no longer repulsed her, and she emptied the rest of the bottle. Soon enough, fatigue again overcame her. She curled up on her improvised pillow, blew out the candles, and fell fast asleep.

When the creak of the trapdoor startled her from the depths of a dream, she jumped, but did not bother to light any candles. He had a lamp with him, dangling from his hand as he made his way down the ladder. "Did I wake you? I shouldn't have thought to find you asleep at this hour."

"How am I to know what time it is? How long have you been away?"

"You saw me yesterday." He opened his satchel and she could see it was full of food.

"More food? You cannot mean to keep me down here longer! Surely you have your money by now. Please, you must let me go!"

"There has been a slight complication. Evidently I removed from your desk a cheque from your father's account, not your own. The bank could not honor it."

"That is not my fault."

"You must tell me where to find your cheques. I will go to your house tonight, retrieve one, and bring it to you in the morning."

"Why would I continue to help you?"

He grasped her firmly on both shoulders. "Do not make me revisit this, Mademoiselle Lamar. You have no choice, do you remember? You will tell me what I need to know, and we will carry out our plan from there."

"It is not our plan, it is yours."

"I have brought you sliced ham, apples, and another baguette. I see you finished the wine. I had not anticipated that and will have to refresh your supply tomorrow."

"Why should you wait until tomorrow? Bring it to me after you have collected the cheque."

"I cannot risk being seen coming in and out of here at all hours of the day and night. It would do you well to stop behaving as if you are the one in control of this situation!" He slumped against the edge of the slab. "Forgive me. I have no right to be angry with you. If you only could understand the sadistic nature of the men with whom I am involved, you would do what I wish without question."

"Had you explained to me your predicament rather than attempting to trick me into a worthless investment, I might have given you the money and expected nothing in return."

"Mademoiselle Lamar, you have misunderstood me. Dr. Maynard's Formula was no con. It is an excellent product and I am confident that had you invested, we would have reaped enormous rewards. I never intended to make off with your money, only to divert a certain amount of it to paying my debt. The rest would have funded our enterprise."

"It hardly matters now." Estella picked up the baguette and examined it, wrinkling her nose. "Brioche would be nice. And if you are coming with wine before you plan to release me, you could at least bring me something to read. It is maddening sitting down here with nothing to do but worry that you have no intention of returning and are going to leave me to die—" A sob escaped from her throat and her captor's heart caught in his.

"You cannot think I would do such a thing!"

"You have drugged me, kidnapped me, and flung me into some awful sort of prison. How could I not expect the worst?"

"I swear to you, Mademoiselle Lamar, I have been nothing but honest when expressing my intentions to you, at least since the time I brought you here. I would never have taken such radical action had I not been forced into such a desperate situation."

Estella opened her mouth to say that he had no one but himself to blame for his current situation, but reckoned that goading him was unlikely to result in a positive outcome. "How long until you have your money?"

"I shall take the cheque to my bank the moment I leave you tomorrow. With any luck, they will verify your funds and give me my payment by the following morning."

"Could you not take it to my bank instead of yours? Then there would be no delay for verification."

"That is an excellent suggestion. I shall do just that."

"Brioche," Estella said. "Please remember brioche as well as a clock of some sort. I must be able to know how much time is passing. And you must leave the lamp with me. Candles are cumbersome."

Estella and her captor had struck their first bargain. All things considered, she slept exceptionally well that night.

10

After we left Worth, Colin and I called on Estella's seamstress, a stooped gray woman whose arthritic hands had forced her to stop sewing five years earlier. She remembered very little about the clothes she had made for Estella's travels abroad, other than that the man who brought the trunks—brand-new and purchased from Galeries Lafayette, the most exclusive department store in Paris—had chipped the paint on her doorjamb with the largest of them when he had carried them into her shop. Mademoiselle Lamar, she explained, had only the barest interest in clothing, and wanted nothing beyond the most basic garments, often refusing even to come in for a fitting. So far as she knew, a maid was called on to perform any alterations required. She showed us the message she had received by telegram requesting the forwarding of her measurements to the House of Worth and assuring the dressmaker that her figure had not changed in the slightest in the intervening years. I pressed the woman on this—whose measurements do not change at all in more than a decade?—but she only shrugged with superb Gallic nonchalance, saying she had no reason to doubt Mademoiselle Lamar, and that she had complied with the request. Other than that solitary telegram, sent from Bombay, she had had no word from Mademoiselle Lamar since she had left Paris so many years ago.

Colin and I stopped in a shop near the Sorbonne, purchasing a large map of Europe and Asia as well as a box of colored pencils. Back at Cécile's, we set up a war room in her library, conveniently connected by a narrow passageway to the bedroom in which we were staying. Colin spread the map on a table and circled every city we had a record of Estella having visited, while I wrote the name of each as well as the dates associated with her stay on small pieces of paper and then laid them out in chronological order.

"We have had no sign of Magwitch in Paris." Colin, having finished his task, poured a whisky for himself and Jeremy. Cécile sipped champagne. Port was ordinarily my preferred libation, but today I chose tea, wanting my head as clear as possible. "It may be best to return to London. We are no closer to understanding why Mary Darby had disguised herself as Estella Lamar. Her role, such as it was, might have had nothing to do with her murder."

"You cannot believe she was a victim of random violence!" I exclaimed. "The circumstances scream otherwise. Magwitch mistook me for her at the ball, and he was angry that I did not meet what he described as his very specific requirements, which suggests he had not yet met Mary in person. He had hired her without having seen her, but must have done his best to select an individual he thought could reasonably pass for Estella. Mary had dark hair, was of unremarkable height, and so far as I can tell from pictures, possessed a figure more or less similar to Estella's, so it is not difficult to see that he would have found me a disappointment in more ways than simply my age. From a distance, or in a photograph that obscured the details of her features, Mary could have convinced strangers that she was Estella, just as all the other Estellas have done in the past."

"Emily, this idea that there are dozens of ladies across the globe pretending—"

"I realize how ridiculous it sounds, but consider the evidence.

Estella Lamar could not have sent the telegrams to Worth, at least not all of them. Someone else is posing as her."

"Why?" Colin asked. "It may be that Estella is having a laugh. We all agree she takes eccentricity to new heights. It does not tell us that she was involved with Mary Darby's murder."

"If I discovered a chap impersonating me in a manner of which I did not approve, I'd be sorely tempted to murder him," Jeremy said. "Mary Darby caused a scene when she was exposed as a fraud, and that may have angered Estella."

"You cannot suspect Estella is our villain." Cécile placed her champagne flute on a Sèvres-porcelain-topped table. "If anything, she is a victim of this man."

"We have no evidence that Estella is doing anything but happily traversing the world," Colin said. "We can connect Magwitch to Mary, but we know neither why he hired her nor what, if any, Estella's involvement in the scheme may be."

"I intend to find that out." I refilled my teacup and added a splash of milk. An idea was tugging at me. "Cécile, do you remember Mr. Bennett who owns the *Herald*? We dined at his house one of the first times I was in Paris with you."

Years ago, when I was still a tiny baby, or perhaps even before my birth, Mr. Bennett had sent Henry Morton Stanley to Africa in an attempt to find the explorer Dr. David Livingstone, who had not been heard from in years. I had not given this incident much consideration when I met Mr. Bennett, but soon thereafter, while investigating the death of my first husband, Philip, Viscount Ashton, the story inspired me to hope—wrongly—that Philip, whom I believed to have died in Africa, was still alive. This had been my first foray into detection, and after uncovering the truth about Philip (and having taken the false step of briefly believing that Colin had murdered him—we all make mistakes), I found I had an affinity for the work, and had continued ever since.

"Yes, a rather bellicose gentleman and very pleased with himself. I have avoided him whenever possible."

"He wasn't so bad, at least not to us." In general, I found myself drawn to eccentric personalities, but Mr. Bennett had a habit of courting scandal like no one else I had ever met. The sequence of events that had led to the breaking off of his engagement some two decades previous—rumored to have caused his abandonment of his native America for Europe—is of such a nature to render it impossible to describe in polite company. His legendary temper brought him notoriety, and his playboy lifestyle sealed his reputation. "His archives at the *Herald* are bound to be a treasure trove of information about Estella's travels. I am convinced that if we are able to piece together what she is really doing, we will be able to determine why Magwitch hired Mary Darby to play her."

Colin did not attempt to dissuade me. It was too late in the day to embark on the scheme, so I set off the following morning, Jeremy in tow. My husband had an appointment set to consult with his French counterparts about how to best demand access to Monsieur Pinard's records. Cécile, not interested in seeing Mr. Bennett, begged off joining me, but called for the carriage to take Jeremy and me to Neuilly-sur-Seine, a town more like an offshoot of Paris than an actual suburb, just to the north of the Bois de Boulogne.

Mr. Bennett came out to us in reception the instant his clerk had alerted him of our arrival. "I remember you as Lady Ashton, the fetching young widow. What a crushing disappointment to bachelors everywhere that you have married again." He bent over my hand and kissed it. "I presume this is your husband."

Jeremy grinned and shook the American's hand. "Alas, I am not, although I did my bloody best to convince her to accept me. Jeremy Sheffield, Duke of Bainbridge."

"He did nothing of the sort. The duke is the worst sort of tease. I apologize for descending upon you without notice, Mr. Bennett, but it is a matter of some urgency. Are you at all acquainted with Mademoiselle Estella Lamar?"

"I am more indebted to her than you can know. The photographs of her adventures never fail to sell papers, and she provides them as well, giving me a result with almost no effort. She is a publisher's dream."

"You don't send photographers to follow her travels?" I asked.

"Heavens, no. Can you imagine what that would cost?"

"Of course. I did not mean specially to follow her, but I know the *Herald* has correspondents across the globe, and I would imagine photographers as well."

"We do, but given that Miss Lamar is so very good about documenting her movements on her own, I have never felt the need to chase after her. She is not news, after all, just a bit of excitement to entice readers to buy the paper. People like the idea of a lady explorer. I've been trying to get Gertrude Bell to write for me ever since I read her *Persian Papers*." Miss Bell and I were nearly of an age. I had never met her, but had envied from afar her studies at Oxford, where she had received a first in history, and I knew her to have recently set off on a trip around the world. "Miss Lamar is much easier to contend with. I can rely on the fact that every few months I will receive a photograph of her in a spectacular location."

"She sends them herself?" I asked.

"No, one of her companions manages that and includes a brief note of explanation so that we can caption the picture properly and write a small piece of our own."

"Do you recall the companion's name?"

He did not. He seated us in his office, and after quick consultation with his clerk, returned with a file. "Here is your name: Miss Lizzie Hexam," he said. I perked up, as would any well-read individual.

"It is critical that I gather as much information as possible about Miss Lamar. She may be in danger following a murder that recently occurred in London."

"Mary Darby?" Mr. Bennett asked.

"How did you know?"

"The *Times* offered very poor coverage, but the description of the dead woman's clothing shouted to me that she had been a guest at the Devonshire House ball."

"They did not say she was in costume," I said.

"No, but current fashion does not favor moon-shaped headdresses. I drew the obvious conclusion. I assume Devonshire wants the whole thing hushed up?"

"He does not want to be attached to any scandal, but has done nothing to impede the investigation of the crime."

"Not everyone has your temperament, Bennett." Jeremy, who had taken a seat in the corner of Mr. Bennett's office rather than in front of the desk, stretched his legs in front of him. "It's what makes society so very tedious. Devonshire should have put himself right in the middle of things, demanding justice and vowing to hunt the murderer to the edges of the earth."

"The earth is round, Jeremy," I said.

"Have they proved that?"

I glared at him.

"Mary Darby, so far as I can tell, had no business being at that ball," Mr. Bennett said. "Tell me why she was there and I shall give you full access to all my archives. Better still, I shall have my clerk pull everything for you, thereby sparing you what I promise would be an extremely long and dusty task."

"I avoid dust at all costs. Tell him whatever you must, Emily."

"Mrs. Darby presented herself to the gathering as Estella Lamar. I would prefer that you keep that tidbit to yourself for the moment." I hoped he did not miss the seriousness in my tone.

Mr. Bennett looked thoughtful. "I can promise to remain silent for now, so long as you give me an exclusive when the business is finished.

I'm tired of the *Times* always getting the inside line on your investigations."

"If you did not know I was married again, how do you know about my investigations?"

He grinned. "Oh, I knew, Lady Emily, but I never like to show all my cards." He sent us on our way with assurances that he would have everything to do with Estella Lamar sent to me at Cécile's as quickly as possible, giving me the file he had consulted in search of Miss Hexam's name. "To whet your appetite," he said. I devoured the contents of it in the carriage, smug with satisfaction.

"Colin cannot claim there is anything but the strongest connection between Estella and Magwitch now." I poked Jeremy, who had fallen asleep across from me.

"Right. Quite right. Just as you said."

"Have you even the slightest idea what I said?"

"None. Not a bit, I'm afraid."

"This file alone proves that Magwitch is involved somehow with Estella, or at least very strongly suggests it. I knew it the moment Mr. Bennett gave us Lizzie Hexam's name."

"I can't say I'm acquainted with Miss Hexam."

"Miss Hexam doesn't exit. She is a character in another of Mr. Dickens's novels, *Our Mutual Friend.* I think he chose Dickens because of *Great Expectations.*"

"I do not follow you, Em. Never could stand Dickens. Too many words."

"Jeremy, I am not entirely convinced you even know how to read." He picked up his hat off the bench beside him and placed it on his head, tilting it forward to cover his eyes.

"Why *Great Expectations*?"

"Because Estella is the name of the most important female character. You really ought to read it. Pip only has a chance at winning her affections—that is, at least he believes he has a chance—because of the anonymous monetary assistance given to him by Abel Magwitch."

Jeremy lifted the hat, just for a moment, so that I could see his eyes. "Same as the Magwitch bloke from the photograph."

"Yes. Magwitch is his *nom de guerre*."

"Must be blasted aggravating having to keep track of more than one name. So who is Pip?"

"He's the protagonist. As a young boy he—"

"No, no, not in the novel. I shall promise to read it if you can promise I shan't be bored. Who is Pip in our story? We've got our Estella and our Magwitch. Who's *our* Pip?"

His question struck me like a blow. Why had it not occurred to me that someone—I was not sure yet whether villain or hero—had machinated this entire situation based on the work of Mr. Dickens? "Jeremy, you may have just had your very first flash of brilliance."

I did not believe the key to our investigation was *Great Expectations* alone. Lizzie Hexam appeared in another novel altogether. What if the other players in our plot had chosen their *noms de guerre* to reflect qualities they shared with Mr. Dickens's characters? Abel Magwitch was an escaped convict who is dedicated to bettering the life of young Pip. It took no imagination to see that our Mr. Magwitch was a criminal, but I could not determine what might be the streak of good in him. Who was his Pip? Lizzie Hexam, a nauseating paragon of good in *Our Mutual Friend,* made an obvious candidate for Estella's companion.

Most curious, though, was Estella herself. Mademoiselle Lamar had no *nom de guerre*. Were the others so named because of the roles they played around a lady who could be compared to the cold and unhappy girl in *Great Expectations,* trained by the calculating Miss

Havisham to have no heart? Estella, who described herself as "bent and broken, but—I hope—into a better shape."

"I do not claim this theory ought to shape the remainder of our investigation," I said, when Jeremy and I had joined up again with Colin and Cécile, "but it deserves the strongest consideration."

Colin nodded. "There may be something to it. Well done, Bainbridge. I admit I did not think you had it in you."

"Cool your excitement, Hargreaves. I did nothing more than make a casual query about Pip. Our darling Em is the one who deserves credit for the rest."

A messenger from Mr. Bennett arrived with a large case full of files long after we had finished dinner; the newspaperman had not exaggerated when he claimed to be saving us from time-consuming work. I set myself to the task of reading and cataloging them as I had already done with the ones drawn from Cécile's album, and did not fall into bed until well after two o'clock in the morning. When I rose again, it was nearly noon, and I found myself the only member of our party at home. I pulled on a dressing gown and went into the library, going over the timeline I had constructed based on all our information before turning my attention to the photographs of Estella we had compiled. Twice servants came to offer me refreshments, but I refused, not wanting to be distracted until I had finished taking notes on everything I observed in the pictures. That done, I returned to my bedroom, rang for Meg, and allowed her to dress me.

Neither my husband nor my friends had left word as to where they had gone, and I decided a change of scene would clear my mind and better allow me to consider the facts of the case. I left the house and made the (extremely) short walk to Café de Flore, taking a table in the glassed-in front section to the right of the door. I had found, over many previous visits, this spot, located just before the curve in the banquette that ran the length of the wall, to be the preeminent one in all of Paris to sit without purpose and be endlessly entertained by the parade of passersby on the pavement outside. Today, I may have had a purpose, but I saw no harm in allowing myself a bit of fun as well. I ordered a *chocolat chaud* and alternated between studying the pages of my notebook and evaluating the current Parisian fashions on display beyond the window.

Not long after I had arrived, a gentleman sat at a table quite near mine, taking a seat that faced away from the window. This odd choice did not escape my notice. His hair, auburn but streaked with silver at the temples, was pomaded, as was his rather splendid handlebar mustache—I call it splendid as an example of its kind; as a rule I do not approve of mustaches—and his suit, though old-fashioned, had been cut from a wool of decent quality. A simple walking stick with a curved handle hung awkwardly over the back of his chair. His boots, which I could see better once he crossed his legs, were sturdy, their soles bearing evidence of having recently been in close proximity to a great deal of mud. Most important was that it quickly became evident that he was taking rather too much interest in my person.

A waiter brought my *chocolat,* and I poured it from its silver-plated pot into a china cup, stirring with a little spoon while avoiding my neighbor's stare. The irony was that he seemed to be making a very great effort at subtlety. He would look down at his table—whatever he had ordered had not yet appeared—as if studying the surface with the seriousness of the most dedicated man of science. Darwin and his finches would have flung themselves off the side of the *Beagle* had they known of the existence of such a man! After approximately thirty seconds of this, he would slowly raise his eyes until they met mine, at which point he would cough and abruptly turn away. Subterfuge could not be listed among his talents.

When at last a pot of tea arrived for him, he applied himself to it with keen attention. I abandoned my *chocolat,* left some coins on the table, and removed myself from the premises before he looked again in my direction. Ever so slightly unnerved, I made my way back toward Cécile's, but before long felt the uncanny prickling on the base of my skull that, without fail, signals that I am being watched. Crossing the narrow street that ran along Les Deux Magots and the wider one that came next—the one in which Cécile's house stood—I turned left toward the church of Saint-Germain-des-Prés. This was the oldest church in Paris, burial place of the Merovingian kings, and, most important to me now, conveniently situated almost directly across from my friend's house. A crowd of tourists covered much of the pavement, so I had no trouble diving into their midst so that I might succeed both in hiding and turning around to confirm my suspicions of having been tailed. There, standing on the opposite corner, was the auburn-haired man. I could no longer in good conscience refer to him as a gentleman.

His presence caused me a dilemma. I did not want to continue on to Cécile's, as I had no desire to alert him to that location as one at which he should expect to find me, but neither did I want to wander the streets of Paris in an attempt to lose him. I considered entering the church, but rejected the idea, deciding it would be simple enough for him to follow me inside and perhaps corner me. There had been a time when I might have stomped over and confronted him, but the days of my impetuous youth were behind me. My husband would never forgive me if I put myself in danger, and in the midst of a murder investigation one could never take for granted one's safety. The square tower of the church loomed over me. Looking up at it had been a mistake. My boot slipped on the cobblestones and I wrenched my ankle. The man had crossed the street and was now standing only thirty feet away from me. I ducked behind a portly German who was lecturing his equally portly offspring about the differences between Gothic and Romanesque architecture, putting them squarely between my adversary and myself. Then, as there were no better options readily at hand, I slipped into the church.

Inside, Saint-Germain-des-Prés could have been mistaken for the slightly shabby sister of Sainte-Chapelle. Its painted columns were not so bright, its stained glass not quite so spectacular, but the hint of gloominess seemed to bathe Saint-Germain in an air of medieval authenticity. I pressed myself against the side of a column away from the door, and considered my next course of action. It came to me in a flash.

A meandering queue of devout elderly Parisian ladies, many with rosaries in their hands, led to the odd-shaped box that I recognized as a confessional, the means of that strange Roman sacrament long since banished from the Church of England. "*Pardonnez-moi.*" I shoved my way to the front of the queue. "*Mon âme mortelle est en jeu.*" I considered myself more or less fluent in French, but had never included the sacred in my studies of the language, so did the best I could in the circumstances, and hoped that the ready-to-be-forgiven queuing up could recognize my mortal soul was in dire straits. A few of the ladies raised their eyebrows, but for the most part, they hardly took notice of my intrusion. Never before had I reaped the benefit of the French inability to queue in an orderly fashion. My actions never would have been tolerated in London.

Now at the head of the queue, I had only to wait my turn to enter the box. My heart was racing. I turned around in time to see the auburn-haired man step into the church. I had to act. I pulled open the door to the confessional and stuck my head inside. "*Allez vite, s'il vous plaît. Je suis désespérée!*"

I will not soon forget the shocked expression on the face of the woman whom I had interrupted. Flabbergasted, she sputtered for a moment, then, as if she recognized the true state of my emergency—although mistaking it for one spiritual rather than physical—she crossed herself and vacated the space. I shut the door. A moment passed, and I heard rustling on the other side of the grille that separated me from the priest who was to hear my sins and absolve me.

"Bonjour, Père," I began. *"Mon français n'est pas bien . . ."*

"That is no impediment, my child," came the voice from beyond. "We can speak in your language. How long has it been since your last confession?"

"Oh, you speak English? How very lovely. I . . . I have never made a confession before. I'm afraid I'm Anglican."

"Yet you have come to Saint-Germain-des-Prés in search of solace. What does that tell you?"

My stomach tied itself in knots. How could I lie to a priest? "The truth is, Father, I am in need of saving, but not in the way you think. A man was following me, and I was terrified—" A slight exaggeration, perhaps, but one that I think could be forgiven in the circumstances. "I knew I would be safe here."

"Did he follow you into the church?"

"He did."

"And this is why you disregarded the line?"

I squirmed on the hard, narrow bench, taking slim comfort in the fact that he could not see me. "Yes, Father."

"I will help you, madame, but only if you first promise to make a good confession."

"I—I—" I sighed. "All right." I described for him the auburn-haired man, and he assured me he would personally see to his departure from the building. The priest's door scraped as he opened it and again when he pushed it closed.

"Alors!" His voice echoed against the stone walls. *"Faîtes attention! L'église est fermée. Partez!"*

A low grumble filled the space, but the persistent sound of shuffling feet told me the faithful and the tourists were following the priest's directions. Any moment now he would return. What on earth was I supposed to say then?

Estella

X

Once again, Estella was asleep when her captor made his descent down the ladder. This time, the sound of the trapdoor hardly disturbed her; instead, it was the light from his lantern that roused her. "You're becoming something of a sloth." He held the light out in front of him, illuminating her huddled form.

She shielded her eyes from the brightness. "What else is there for me to do?"

"Plenty now." When he smiled, his face split in a manner reminiscent of a toad. He was broad, but tall enough to prevent the overall impression of him from veering entirely to the amphibian. "I have two books, a travel clock, and brioche, as well as another bottle of wine, plenty of water, two croissants, some ham and cheese, and, of course, the new cheque."

"Of course. You will want me to sign posthaste."

"If you would be so kind."

She saw no use in delay.

While she bent over her pen, he removed the varied detritus from her cell—including dealing with the chamber pot—and then spread a worn tablecloth over the stone slab. "I thought this would brighten things a bit for you."

"Flowers brighten things. Table linens that might be mistaken for rags . . . oh . . . it doesn't matter." She flung the cheque at him. He picked it up off the floor and placed the clock in the center of the tablecloth.

"I shall leave the rest to you. Do please try to forgive me, Mademoiselle Lamar. I promise this terrible situation is almost over."

"Morning or evening?" Estella picked up the clock, which read six forty-five.

"Evening." He looked around. "That should do until tomorrow, I think."

"Please come as quickly as you can. It is difficult being here." Her voice was strained and small and cut to the core of her captor's soul. If only there had been some other way out of this mess! He bade her good night and made his way up the ladder.

Estella set the food out on the tablecloth, begrudgingly admitting to herself that the linen, shabby though it was, was preferable to bare stone. She took a swig of water and looked at the books he had left with her. The first, *A Tale of Two Cities,* by someone called Charles Dickens, put her off even before she had finished the first sentence: *It was the best of times, it was the worst of times.* In her current predicament, she abhorred the implication that the worst might also be the best. She found the second book, a thick volume, much more appealing: *Narrative of the Operations and Recent Discoveries within the Pyramids, Temples, Tombs, and Excavations in Egypt and Nubia,* written by Giovanni Battista Belzoni. *As I made my discoveries alone, I have been anxious to write my book by myself, though in so doing, the reader will consider me, and with great propriety, guilty of temerity . . .*

This struck just the right chord with Estella. She had read about Egypt before—accounts from the Napoleonic explorations in a beautifully illustrated volume given to her by Cécile—but this man, this Giovanni Battista Belzoni, had explored Egypt's mysteries alone, just as she now was alone. He would provide her the perfect solace. Temerity indeed! This was a man she could admire. She broke a brioche in two, placed between the halves a slice of ham and a chunk of cheese and nibbled at it as she started to read. By the time she became aware of a nagging sensation of thirst, she looked at the clock to discover that it was already past nine. Morning would descend upon her in no time if she kept reading.

Estella rejected the apples, not wanting to eat them whole—only a savage would eat fruit not cut up—but made another little sandwich out of brioche, ham, and cheese. She tugged the cork out of the wine and set the bottle next to her, so that she could reach it with ease, not having to remove her eyes from her book. The next time she checked, it was after midnight. She kept reading, and soon it was nearly three in the morning. Her lids heavy, her eyes so tired she could hardly decipher the words on the page, she wrapped up her food, turned off the lantern, and curled up on the slab, clutching the book close to her.

She woke with a start, but not because her captor had returned. The trapdoor remained closed, and darkness bathed her. She lit the lantern; it was nearly eleven o'clock. Surely he would not be much longer. Anxiety returned, unsettling her stomach and her nerves, tension taking stiff hold in her neck and her shoulders. She rubbed them aimlessly, and considered her remaining food, regretting that she had not eaten the croissants while they were fresh. She tore the end off one and was pleased to find it still good. She placed them both, along with a flask of water, on the slab, then hopped up next to them and opened her book.

The trapdoor still remained in place at five o'clock and Estella's soul was becoming as frayed as her sad tablecloth. She could no longer read and had taken to pacing the length of her cell. He must not be coming for her. He would have the money by now—the banks were already closed. She clutched at her chest, fear pounding through her veins. He had left her here to die. The stone walls seemed to close in around her. Her hands flew to her throat. She could hardly breathe. Sobbing, she sank to the floor and remained there until she slipped into a stupor. She stared at the lantern's flickering flame. When she moved again, it was nearly seven o'clock in the evening.

Now it was time to accept her fate. Death had started its inevitable march. She cleared away her food and drink, smoothed the tablecloth, and pulled her cloak around her shoulders. Taking with her the copy of Belzoni's magnificent book, she climbed onto the slab, arranged her skirts and the cloak carefully, and held the book on her chest. Confident that arrangement of her limbs, at least, was as serene as the most beautiful medieval effigy, she closed her eyes. The lamp, still on the floor, continued to burn. She thought she might as well have light for a while longer.

When she heard the heaving of the trapdoor's hinges, her heart nearly stopped. She had been prepared for a prolonged death, but could his plans be more gruesome than that? She remained as still as possible, holding the book tight against her, and squeezed her eyes shut. She could hear him struggling with something and then the sound of something hitting the floor with a dull thud.

"Apologies for the disturbance, Mademoiselle Lamar, but we have a problem."

11

All things considered, the priest let me off lightly. He steered me deftly through the Ten Commandments—I did not fail to notice what could only be described as a sigh of relief when I assured him I had not violated the fifth and can only say in my defense that while I would have expected that implied judgment stemming from my having cut the queue had I been in England, to find it in one of Gallic sensibilities was a surprise—and assured me the penance he assigned was next to nothing. I was not, however, released without a stern lecture on my attitude about the fourth commandment. Obviously, the holy man had never met my mother.

When I was ready to leave the church, he exited in advance of me, and searched the place Saint-Germain-des-Prés for the auburn-haired man. Assuring me the miscreant was nowhere in sight, he insisted on ushering me across the street and to Cécile's house. He refused my friend's offer of refreshment, reminded her that he looked forward to seeing her at Sunday mass, and wished me all the best. I thanked him profusely for his assistance.

Colin paced as I recounted my story. "It is a stroke of luck that his hair color makes him easy to spot."

"The mustache is a sight to behold." Jeremy handed me a glass of port and I did not refuse it. People of quality might insist that it was a sin—venial, perhaps, but a sin nonetheless—to take port before dinner, but I felt the circumstances justified my choice of beverage. "He certainly stands out in a crowd."

"That works to our benefit."

"Monsieur Hargreaves, you must stop pacing. I am growing dizzy watching you."

Colin honored Cécile's request, but did not sit. He leaned against the wall, crossing his feet at his ankles and his arms across his broad chest. Brutus tugged at the hem of his trousers, wanting to play. Colin removed the little creature and, as Caesar already occupied Cécile's, dropped him onto my lap. "My contacts here in Paris have written up the necessary authorizations to give us access to Monsieur Pinard's records. Scotland Yard report having identified a deposit of £10 into Mary Darby's bank account from one belonging to Mademoiselle Lamar—"

"Our connection!"

"Yes, Emily. Our connection. I am afraid, Cécile, this suggests your friend may be embroiled in something most troubling."

"Do you believe her to be in danger?"

"That is impossible to know at the moment," Colin replied. "I hope Monsieur Pinard's records will elucidate the matter. That Mademoiselle Lamar is involved cannot be denied. Cécile has studied every letter purported to have been penned by Estella that is currently in our possession. Each of them—the one to Worth, the ones the servants have received, and even a handful sent to Mr. Bennett—appear to match what Cécile recognizes as her friend's handwriting. It is not a scientific conclusion and we must still bear in mind that all of these documents could be forgeries."

"My own analysis of the photos sent by Mr. Bennett is equally unsatisfying. Estella's face is obscured in every single one of them."

I consulted my notebook. "They are always taken in front of a well-known monument—the Taj Mahal, the pyramids at Giza, the Acropolis—and show Estella from a distance, which renders her features all but unrecognizable. Her hair is always dark enough, her figure of the right proportions, but none of them constitute what could be described as a reliable record."

"Other than having found a most excellent cravat at a charming shop in the rue de Rivoli, I was not useful in the least today." Jeremy slouched in his chair. "I warn you to expect much the same tomorrow."

"That will not be allowed." I tore a page from my notebook and handed it to him. "This is a list of all the people cited as living in Paris who were quoted in Mr. Bennett's articles about Estella. They each purport to have seen her abroad. Find out their addresses, call on them, and determine exactly what they know about her."

"I shall accompany you, Bainbridge," Cécile said. "Between the two of us, there is not a house in the city to which we will not be able to gain admission."

By the time dinner was announced, we had our strategies for the following day mapped in detail, and were welcoming the prospect of an evening spent in the genial company of our friends. We dined well—Cécile would stand for nothing less—and took port and cigars in the library, where I presented Jeremy with a copy of *Great Expectations*. I should not have been surprised Cécile owned an English edition; she deplored reading in translation. Jeremy made an admirable show of reading it, at least until he nodded off over the book. When at last we retired to bed, I was anticipating a pleasant interlude with my husband, and on this count Colin never disappointed. I felt as if I had been asleep for only a few minutes when I started at the sound of tapping on our bedroom door.

Colin, in a swift movement—the man moves with graceful ease even when half asleep—leapt from the bed and slid into his dressing gown. "Our servants at home know better than to disturb us in the middle of the night. A little earlier and this intrusion would have caused quite a scene."

On the other side of the door stood one of Cécile's footmen, his white wig askew on his head and his livery jacket pulled over his nightclothes. "Delivery for Lady Emily, sir. Urgent, I imagine, or it wouldn't have been left at this hour."

Colin nodded his thanks and took from the man a package of indeterminate shape. He closed the door, deposited it on a table, and flipped on the lights. I had remained abed, the blankets pulled up to my chin, and now reached for my own dressing gown. Standing beside my husband, I started to open the parcel. Colin looked at me as if about to issue a caution, then raised his hands as if helpless. "I suppose you may as well."

I had identified the contents almost the moment I had approached the table. The long shape, coupled with the loosely wrapped tissue paper, gave away the game. "Flowers." White lilies spilled out of the paper when I tore it. I wrinkled my nose. "We shall be overwhelmed by the scent." I gathered them up, ready to fling them from the nearest window—although knowing I would regret the action not only for having discarded what might be a clue, but also for the mess that would greet the gardener in the morning—and saw an envelope beneath them. I slit it open and pulled out a small card with a simple typewritten message:

I KNOW WHERE TO FIND YOU.

With a sigh, I dropped it onto the table, gathered up the flowers, wrapped them back in their paper, and placed them in the corridor outside our door. "I was not so clever as I hoped." I closed the door behind me. "He must have hidden, waiting for me to leave the church, and probably had no difficulty eluding the priest."

"It would have been impossible to prevent. You succeeded at protecting yourself and not allowing him to confront you when you were alone. There was nothing else to be done in the circumstances."

We summoned the sleepy servant, who told us that neither he, nor anyone else in the house, had caught sight of the person who had left the mysterious package. The first—and only—indication of his arrival had been the bell from the front door that awakened the footman. By the time he opened the door, there was no one there. The parcel had been left on the stoop.

"I did not delay, but had to dress in some fashion before going downstairs. You saw for yourself, Monsieur Hargreaves, that I had not dallied over my toilette." He was emphatic on this point. "I am most sorry for not having been quicker. Had I arrived more rapidly, I might have seen something."

"Do not trouble yourself with such thoughts," Colin said. "It is almost certain that the individual carrying the flowers deposited them, rang the bell, and fled immediately. He did not want to be seen."

The footman had collected the flowers from where I had placed them in the corridor and I reached to take them from him. "What time is it?" I asked.

"After three in the morning," my husband replied.

"These are quite fresh. I wonder what time deliveries to the markets begin."

"There are no markets open right now, Emily."

"I am well aware of that, but it is conceivable that suppliers may have already started gathering their wares." Colin took the flowers from me, returned them to the footman, whom he dismissed, and, once our door was closed again, guided me back to bed, first discarding what he referred to as my redundant dressing gown. "If we are forced to be awake at this hour, we are not going to spend our time discussing flower merchants."

It was all very well for Colin to dismiss my questions about the source of the flowers. He may even have been correct in his—very firmly expressed—belief that it would be impossible for us to track their origin. His subsequent attentions to my person left me quite incapable of arguing with him, a fact I was quick to point out the following morning over breakfast.

"Are you issuing a complaint?" His dark eyes danced over a cup of coffee.

I raised an eyebrow. "I see that you have been forced to reject tea in favor of something stronger. Are you not well rested after last night?"

"So no complaint?"

I wished Cécile were awake so that I might more easily change the subject, but was saved from having to reply to this undignified question by Jeremy's arrival. "Hargreaves! You look almost as bad as I. What a comforting sight." He heaped eggs onto a plate and topped them with three croissants. "I hardly slept what with all the noise."

"Noise?" I asked, blushing.

"I thought it must be feral cats at first, but then I realized I have not the slightest idea what feral cats sound like. Then I thought Cécile had an admirer trying to attract her attention from beneath her window." He took a large bite of eggs and chewed thoroughly, swallowing before he continued. "When I remembered that, unlike mine, her bedroom faces the back of the house, that explanation failed me as well. In the end I was forced to drag myself from my bed and look out my own window."

"What did you find?" Colin held up his cup to the footman

who had appeared with a fresh pot of coffee. "An admirer of your own?"

"I assure you, Hargreaves, no lady of my acquaintance would deign to place herself beneath my window and more's the pity for it. No, what I saw was a flower man in his delivery wagon making a clatter that ought to be illegal at that time of night."

"Did he have auburn hair?" I asked. "What time was this?"

"I don't know what time it was—surely you do not expect me to be consulting timepieces in the middle of the night? And you cannot mean to suggest that the gentleman you described having seen in Café de Flore doubles as merchant? Even I can identify that as farfetched, Em. No, it was not he. Well, at least not so far as I could tell. It was dark and I didn't get a good look at him. By the time I got to the window, he was driving away."

"So much for stealth." So far as I was concerned, this lack of finesse confirmed his identity as the auburn-haired man. He had exhibited the same qualities in Café de Flore. I shared these thoughts with Colin and Jeremy. My husband did not dismiss them, although Jeremy only just managed not to roll his eyes.

"Was his suit ill-fitting?" he asked.

"It was not. He had every appearance of a gentleman. Although he could not be described as fashionable, his clothes were well made, but the mud on his boots nagged at me. Perhaps they revealed the residue of his employment."

"Gentlemen are not employed." Jeremy wiped his lips with a napkin. "Flower merchants do not spend their afternoons in cafés. There is an order to things, Em."

"Although it pains me to do so, Emily, I am afraid I must support Bainbridge's beliefs on this matter. Had he got a look at the man's face we might be in an altogether different situation."

"I shan't argue with either of you. Regardless of the identity of the driver of the wagon, I hope you can agree that it is reasonable to surmise that the auburn-haired man—we really must find a better way to refer to him, but I am not yet certain that he is Magwitch—is behind the delivery."

"Yes." Colin nodded. "That much is evident."

"Was anything written on the side of the wagon?" I asked.

Jeremy produced, with a flourish, a scrap of paper from his pocket. "I knew you would ask, Em. *Swiveller.*"

"*The Old Curiosity Shop.*" Colin set down his coffee. "Dick Swiveller, I believe, though I can't say I remember anything else about him."

"I never much liked the book," I said, "but I do recall that Mr. Swiveller was something of a hero. Good, at least."

"Perhaps we should rename the auburn-haired man after the author," Jeremy suggested. "We could call him Charlie."

"There is no need to further confuse the situation," Colin said. "Bainbridge, leave the social calls to Cécile today. She can handle them without you. Instead find out whatever you can about Swiveller."

"How am I to do that?"

"Make inquiries at flower shops. Either Swiveller is a supplier or a florist with his own shop. It should not be difficult to determine which."

"And if I locate an address, am I to go there on my own?" Jeremy pushed away from the table. "I may joke otherwise, but I am here to assist, Hargreaves. Nonetheless, I am well aware that my lack of experience may prove an impediment. How should I proceed if I find Swiveller?"

Colin sat, silent, for a moment. I could only assume he was in a state of shock at having heard Jeremy speak with such measured reason and intelligence. My husband, capable of adapting to nearly any situation, quickly reacquired the ability to speak. "You impress me, Bainbridge. If you find them, you might pay the shop a visit, but only to buy flowers. Do not risk asking any questions that might suggest you suspect there to be a connection between Swiveller and anything to do with our current case."

"Perhaps it would be best if I limited my investigations to the outside of the premises."

"An excellent idea." Colin rose to his feet. "Emily, are you finished? Monsieur Pinard is expecting us."

The solicitor greeted us cordially, offering his apologies both for having denied our previous request to examine his records, and for the general awkwardness of our visit. The latter made me blush, and the rising color of my cheeks attracted his notice. "You are a lovely creature," he said to me, sotto voce, as he led us into a meeting room next to his office. More evidence of the abject failure of my ill-timed attempt at flirtation. I hoped he would not prove a pest.

"I have pulled everything together for you and thought this room would give you ample space to spread out as you see fit. Mademoiselle Lamar was in Portugal when she authorized the payment that caught Scotland Yard's attention. Here is the telegram."

The text, as is typical of messages conveyed through wires, was brief:

PLEASE PAY £10 TO MRS. MARY DARBY, LONDON.

It went on to include Mrs. Darby's account details. "There is no explanation at all?" I was disappointed.

"Mademoiselle Lamar does not often provide me with details."

Monsieur Pinard gave a half-smile. "I shall be in my office if you have any other questions."

Colin and I divided the work before us, splitting equally Monsieur Pinard's ledgers. My eyes started to swim after several hours spent combing through the narrow rows of figures, but it was not in vain. First, we found exorbitant monthly payments made to Swiveller, our marauding nighttime florist. The amounts were so large that I popped into Monsieur Pinard's office to inquire about them.

"*Oui,* it seems to be more than it ought. I had the same reaction initially, but it is for all three of Mademoiselle Lamar's houses."

"Swiveller supplies her in London? How can that be?"

"I am not interested in the details, Lady Emily. Perhaps he has a shop there as well."

"And one in the south, conveniently located to the villa?"

The solicitor shrugged. "I have no interest in arguing with Mademoiselle Lamar about her choice of florist. When considering the size of her three establishments, the amounts billed are what would be expected."

I returned to the antechamber and resumed my study of the ledgers, and soon had identified another oddity.

"Are you drawing the same conclusion as I?" I asked Colin.

"That is difficult to say, Emily. What is your conclusion?"

"There are multiple entries for the equivalent of about £10 in various local currencies, paid out always to women. It is a not insignificant sum—as much as many servants earn in a year. Enough, certainly, to buy discretion. I have cross-referenced them with the chronology I put together from our various sources, and can say with confidence that they correspond perfectly to the locations Estella Lamar was supposedly visiting at the time of the payments."

"Hardly surprising that she would have made payments in the places she was."

"Yes, but always the same amount? And always made to a woman?" I pushed my notebook across the table to him. I had made a neat list of the transactions in question. "We know Mary Darby was pretending to be Estella. Is it not reasonable to conclude these other women had been hired to do the same?"

He studied my notes and consulted the ledgers in front of him. "Well spotted, Emily. I can see a similar pattern in my half. If these women were hired to perform similarly to Mrs. Darby, what does it mean for Mademoiselle Lamar?"

"I have very great concerns in that regard. I am afraid that we shall have to face delivering the worst sort of news to Cécile."

Estella

xi

Upon his return, her captor had called to her through the open trapdoor, but Estella remained perfectly still. She did not want to disturb her carefully choreographed pose as living effigy. *A problem*, he had said. Her lips quivered.

"Are you awake down there?" he called.

She heard his boots on the rungs of the ladder and then on the floor.

"Mademoiselle! Are you unwell?"

This brought her to her feet and in an instant the dread and the fear and the ache of pain in her chest were replaced by simple anger. "Unwell? You have the audacity to inquire after my well-being when you have locked me up in a prison and left me to die? I suppose you have come to do your worst, and I, sir, am ready to face the end."

"You cannot—I—surely—did you think?" He sputtered on like this incoherently for some time and gradually Estella came to accept that he had no immediate plans to kill her. "The bank would not cash the cheque. Having only just had one submitted for an identical amount against your late father's account raised their suspicions. They will not release the funds until you respond confirming the transaction. They have sent a letter to your house."

"A letter I shall never receive."

"I thought, perhaps, you could write a reply nonetheless." He produced a sheet of paper and an envelope, and laid them both on the slab along with a pen and ink. "I am so very sorry, mademoiselle, but they assured me that once they had your authorization in hand, they would honor the cheque. Of course, today is Friday, so that cannot be until Monday at the earliest."

"Monday?"

"It is dreadful, I know, and I cannot begin to apologize for the additional delay. In an attempt to make things more comfortable for you, I have procured further supplies." He opened the large bundle he had dropped through the trapdoor onto the floor. Inside were two rather attractive Oriental carpets made from the softest wool, a pillow, blankets, and a featherbed. He also had with him two additional lamps, a picnic basket full of culinary delights—more wine, four different cheeses, pâté, baguettes, brioche, pain au chocolat, and a raspberry tart—as well as another soft package that he handed to her. "You will want to open that yourself."

She tore the paper and found a flannel facecloth, soap, a linen nightgown, and an assortment of undergarments, stockings, and shirtwaists. "The shopgirl assured me this was what you would require. I told her my sister was visiting and that her trunks had gone missing at the station. There is more." He disappeared up the ladder and returned with two large wooden buckets, one full of water, the other empty. "I thought you could use these to wash."

"Thank you." Estella could hardly believe she had spoken the words. What thanks did this wretched man deserve? He had kidnapped her! She should never thank him for managing to provide her with these basic supplies. The very idea outraged her.

"I know it does not go far in making up for what I have done to you, and I shall never be able to forgive myself. I hope that you can at least gain a small measure of satisfaction that you—even if unwillingly—will shortly have saved my life."

Estella made no reply.

"Would you like more books? The Dickens is one of my favorites. I was so pleased to find the French edition."

"How are you paying for all of this?" she asked.

His countenance darkened. "On credit. I shall pay the bills with a bit of the money from your cheque."

"So you admit to having asked for more than you owed?"

"Not much, I swear, Mademoiselle Lamar. I knew I had to get food and supplies for you. I should have told you as much, but I thought it awkward in the situation."

"Awkward?" Estella frowned. "Yes, I suppose that is one way of describing having to pay for one's own kidnapping."

"Is there anything else you require? I will get you whatever you want."

Except freedom, she thought. She looked around her. The carpets had gone a long way to improving the space, and the bedding would vastly improve her sleep. "There is one thing." Her eyes grew very wide as she spoke, and her voice jumped an octave. "I should like one of my dolls."

"Your dolls?"

"Bettina is my favorite, but you would not know how to find her in the nursery. I could try to explain—"

"It might be quite risky for me to search your house for a doll," he interrupted. "Fetching the cheque was much easier as it was on the ground floor. I imagine the nursery is not quite so accessible. What sort of doll is she? I could find you a similar one in the shops."

"She has the loveliest green eyes, just like my own, and a pretty porcelain face. I don't mind what color her dress is, so long as it is trimmed with lace."

As she spoke, a feeling of dread came over him. There was something about Mademoiselle Lamar that was not quite cricket. He had not noticed it before, but seeing her speak about this doll—the very idea that in her current situation she would choose to request a doll of all things—unsettled him. He wanted this business concluded in as rapid a fashion as possible.

First, though, he had to buy a doll.

12

When Colin and I, blurry eyed, left Monsieur Pinard's office, Jeremy was waiting for us. He was leaning against the building, his hat pulled low, an umbrella hooked over his arm, and a copy of *Le Figaro* in his hand. "I did not know you could read French." I gently tapped his shoulder with the ferrule of my parasol. "What other secrets are you hiding?"

"Fluent French is essential for leading a truly debauched life, Em. You ought to know that." He folded the paper. "Sorry to hover about waiting for you like this, but I found myself unaccountably excited by what I learned about our mysterious florist."

"Do tell!"

He offered me his arm—Colin shook his head and smiled, so I knew he would not object to my taking it—and we started to walk. "We must sit somewhere so I can recount the entire story with every thrilling detail." At this, I began to worry he was being facetious, but the flash in his eyes and the vigorous spring in his step as he all but dragged me along the block could only be indicative of earnest sincerity. Being in Paris, we had to walk no more than fifty feet before reaching an amiable-looking café, where, once seated, Jeremy ordered coffees for all of us.

"But I don't care for coffee," I said. "You know that."

"You will require the fortification, I promise you." The mere fact that he was considering coffee a fortifier rather than a stimulant was very nearly shocking enough for me to go along with his plan, but I stopped the waiter and told him to bring me *chocolat* instead.

"Please do not prolong our anticipation." I folded my hands neatly in my lap and gave Jeremy an encouraging nod.

"You will want your notebook at the ready, Em." Truly, he was warming to his subject to an alarming degree. "I visited six florists in succession, and though I can say with confidence that there is a rage in Paris for freesia at the moment, I was unable to learn a thing about Swiveller. No one in any of the shops showed even the slightest recognition when I mentioned the name. The bloke in the sixth shop suggested I go to the Marché aux Fleurs on the Île de la Cité—do you know it?"

"On the place Louis-Lépine near Notre-Dame?" I asked.

"The very one. I have always before operated under what I now believe to be a delusion that markets are open only during the earliest hours of the morning, but this most helpful florist assured me that the Marché is open all day—every day. Can you believe it? Evidently there is a bird market there as well on Sundays, so consider yourself warned if you want to peruse orchids untroubled by the competing songs of an unholy variety of species."

"So you went to the market?" Colin asked.

"Just so. Once there, I queried at stall after stall, but no one could tell me anything about Swiveller until, at last, I came to a rather fetching young lady who was manning her father's stand. She told me Swiveller isn't a regular florist, but a company that serves a small number of private—and wealthy—individuals. Monsieur Swiveller, as she referred to the proprietor, has a reputation in certain circles for exquisite taste and utter discretion. I took that to mean that one might trust him to keep straight which orders were meant for one's wife and which for one's mistress."

"Did you get an address?" Colin asked.

"Eventually, yes, but it is not at all what you think," Jeremy said. "First, she sent me to a drafty old covered ground in a part of town so nasty one could hardly believe it belongs to Paris. If it does, the map ought to be redrawn to exclude it. Inside is where growers from the country bring their blooms to sell to city florists."

"And you found Swiveller there?" I asked.

"No. He is neither a wholesaler nor a grower, Em, but I was able, after quite a bit of persuasion and the exchange of not a few francs, to learn which supplier he uses."

"Was the supplier there?" Colin asked.

"Alas, no. By this point in the day it was late enough that many of them were long gone, but I do have his name and he will be there early tomorrow morning should you wish to speak with him. While I was gathering this information, another of the flower growers approached me and said that he had supplied Swiveller only a few weeks ago as a favor to Swiveller's usual supplier, who had been unable to fill his order because of some sort of agrarian tragedy. Do not ask for the details—they are unimportant as well as deadly dull."

Jeremy stopped abruptly, a grim and serious look on his face, as the waiter approached with our hot drinks. It was as if he suspected the man might be obsessed with flower suppliers and hence have some sort of otherwise inexplicable desire to overhear our conversation. Only once the waiter had scurried off did Jeremy continue.

"This substitute supplier could not give me the address of Swiveller's establishment, but he knew the way there, and offered to take me, so we settled on a price and set off at once."

"You paid him?" Colin asked.

"*Bien sûr.* I assumed it to be standard practice in detective work. Was I in error?" He did not wait for a reply before continuing. "We went in his wagon—diabolically uncomfortable; I'm not sure my bones will recover any time soon—to a building a distance considerably south of the Luxembourg Gardens. Lovely place, those gardens. I always liked them when I was a boy. We must go there and sail a little boat in the little pond."

"Jeremy!"

"Yes, Em, I shall continue, but understand that you do owe me one boat rental before we leave Paris." He took a swig of his coffee and returned to his narrative. "Swiveller's building is beyond the entrance to the Catacombs—we have a history with catacombs, Em, and really ought to visit them—so far away from them one begins to wonder if one is still in the city."

"Swiveller owns an entire building?" Colin asked. Jeremy, who had been a picture of intelligent efficiency when we first sat down, had gradually taken on his usual posture, and was now slouching with an air of perfectly studied ennui. My husband's question must have reminded him of the importance of his story, for he shot up, arrow straight.

"Not at all. I was confused at first because I saw no shop front—the building by all appearances was strictly residential. My flower grower friend explained that he had met Swiveller out front, each of them with their wagons. He had assumed he would unload his bounty into a shop or a warehouse or some sort of place in which Swiveller's employees would then arrange the flowers, but Swiveller only wanted them transferred to his own wagon. The grower apologized, saying he would have happily met in a more convenient location so that Swiveller would not have to unload the wagon before setting to work—he admitted to me that he had hoped that he might be able to get a regular share of Swiveller's business—and asked where it was Monsieur Swiveller had his establishment. Swiveller gestured to the building and said he works out of a room in his apartment, with no employees to help."

"That is an unusual arrangement," Colin said.

"It certainly is. No concierge in a Parisian apartment building is going to tolerate someone running a business from what is meant to be a home." Jeremy swirled more cream into his coffee and stirred. "Any ordinary mortal, myself included, lives in fear of all Parisian concierges, so you can imagine well how I hesitated before disturbing Swiveller's. I waited until the flower man had made his way off, buzzed for entrance to the building, and was growled at by a lady who could not have been taller than three feet or younger than a hundred and ten. I told her I was an old friend of Swiveller's and that he was expecting me."

"Jeremy! You were meant to keep yourself firmly out of danger."

"I had a plan, Em. If admitted to his apartment, I was going to order flowers to be sent to a lady of my acquaintance who would not object to the attention. It never came to that, though, because the concierge told me—quite rudely—that there was no person of such a name in the building. She would not give me the names of anyone in the building and somehow, despite her size, managed to remove me rather forcibly from the premises. Here is the address of the building as well as details of the flower suppliers."

"Well done, Bainbridge," Colin said. "I am most impressed. You are not nearly so useless as you advertise."

"I do hope you will keep that tidbit between us. My reputation would suffer immeasurably if word got out."

Cécile's rate of success that afternoon could only be described as mixed. On the one hand, she had not located a single individual who could with any plausibility say he or she had directly spoken to Estella during her travels. A handful of them insisted they had seen her, but none of them could count themselves among her acquaintances in Paris or elsewhere, and, as such, were not in a position to recognize her. On the other hand, Cécile had identified among them three young ladies whom she believed to possess an aptitude for drawing. She was already arranging for them to advance their studies.

"I am most skeptical of this Swiveller," she said. "Even a man with three mistresses and a jealous wife would have no need for a private florist—I have never even heard of such a thing. It is nonsensical. Furthermore, if such a company did exist, why would Estella have needed it? She abhorred romantic assignations and certainly did not require discretion regarding the arrangement of flowers in her homes."

"Quite right, Cécile," I said. "I have been considering Estella and her travels. Ordinarily when a person of her position in society is abroad, she would make contact with the ambassadors in the places she visited. I have been meaning to call on Sir Edmund since we arrived in Paris; I haven't seen him since he was posted in Athens."

"Not everyone is so conscientious as you, my dear, in keeping up with the diplomatic community." I suspected my husband of no small degree of sarcasm, but thought it best ignored.

"It is wise, when traveling abroad, to check in with one's embassy," Cécile said.

"I shall telegraph to inquire with the ambassadors in the pertinent locations," I said. "Do you know, Cécile, if the Lamar family was personally acquainted with any of them?"

"It is highly unlikely."

"Do you think we ought to visit Estella's villa?" I asked.

"Please allow me to assist with that," Jeremy said. "All this work has left me exhausted. I could take the train down to Marseille, hop over to the villa to investigate, and then spend a few days on the Côte d'Azur to restore my strength. You wouldn't miss me here."

"I would miss you terribly, Bainbridge," Cécile said. "You must not think of abandoning me."

"You wouldn't miss me at all so long as you had Hargreaves to look at."

"A palpable hit, but you cannot blame me. I am only human."

My husband ignored both of them. "I sent a telegram this morning to the steward at the villa. His reply matches up neatly with what we have seen for ourselves here and in London. I do not think there is any cause to travel south."

Jeremy scowled.

"We have not yet shared with you the final oddity about Swiveller's business," I said. "M. Pinard has no address recorded for it. The invoices he receives instruct payment to be remitted to *poste restante*—general delivery. We have asked him to post today a cheque for Estella's current balance. The post office will receive it tomorrow. We will take shifts in turn watching the counter. As soon as anyone turns up to collect Swiveller's mail, we will leap upon him. I speak figuratively, of course."

"Bainbridge and I will take shifts. You and Cécile are not leaping on anyone, literally or metaphorically."

I knew better than to argue with his position. I might not like it, but it was reasonable. "Cécile and I will find another way to occupy ourselves."

Leaving our friends, Colin and I called at the post office on the rue du Louvre, the destination for general delivery mail. The postmaster there was as unhelpful as might have been suspected, but he did agree—begrudgingly, and only because of Colin's credentials, which now included a letter from the Sûreté, France's equivalent to Scotland Yard—to allow the gentlemen to sit, out of sight, and observe all collections of *poste restante*. We had no way of knowing how regularly Swiveller collected his post, but the large amount that was currently waiting for him at the post office suggested it would be soon. Jeremy was to take the first turn. Colin insisted upon this because he thought it unlikely that Swiveller would appear before he expected the large payment on behalf of Estella to have arrived. While Jeremy was inside, Colin would watch from an outside table at a café across the street, ready to assist, if necessary, in the pursuit of our man.

Cécile wanted to send Jeremy, who would not be comfortably ensconced in a café, off with a picnic basket, but Colin would not allow it—much to Jeremy's chagrin—so she limited herself to giving him a small sandwich, but made no effort to hide the fact that she did not consider this adequate. The look on Jeremy's face showed his agreement on the matter. The gentlemen had been gone for a few hours when a footman arrived with the morning mail. I had a letter from Nanny, whom I had instructed to send regular updates on the boys, and one from my mother. Nanny assured me her charges were all thriving. My mother scolded me for fleeing London in the middle of the season. Truth be told, having no interest in sporting with my intelligence, I did not read to the end of her letter.

Cécile's stack of mail was considerably more substantial. She attacked it in her usual fashion, ripping open invitations and either casting them aside with great zeal or placing them in a neat pile on her writing desk. Bills had a pile of their own, and this was more unruly than the one for rejected invitations. Personal correspondence she liked to save for last, so I was surprised when, only a few minutes after she had taken the mail from the footman, she waved a letter in front of me.

"Estella has written," she said, "and evidently from Paris."

Ma chère Cécile,

I have returned to Paris, but only for a short—and I hope anonymous—visit. I understand you have been seeking information about me, and I plead with you to not continue this maudlin pursuit. You, better than anyone, understand the difficulties I have faced in my life. I may have chosen a path that is difficult for my few friends to accept, but please, you must do just that. I have discovered my true self outside of France, and have returned only because a personal situation requires it. I wish to see no one, even you, my dear friend, as I know that any time in your company would make leaving again all the more difficult.

Let me assure you that I am quite well, happier, in fact, than I ever hoped to be. Should we never meet again, know that your friendship was instrumental in giving me the courage to pursue this new life of mine, and for that I will always be grateful.

The planning of my next trip is well under way, and I hope to leave before the end of the week. You will approve of my destination, I hope: I shall be touring coffee plantations in the Côte d'Ivoire. Should I discover any of particular note, I shall send you a sample of their beans.

I am your most devoted friend,

Estella Lamar

Estella

"She is not so fine as Bettina, but she will do." Estella bent over the doll her captor had brought her, scrutinizing every detail of it. "I should like her to have a better dress. Perhaps you could bring me a bit of emerald-green silk and some sewing supplies? Although I imagine you don't want me to have scissors."

"You will be home again before there would be time to make her a new gown." He looked uneasy, shifting his weight back and forth from the balls of his feet to his heels. "Do you require anything else? I will come back tomorrow with fresh water."

"You have already brought me enough to last a week. Leave me in peace tomorrow. What time should I expect you to fetch me on Monday?"

"I shall be at the bank when it opens. Assuming I encounter no difficulties, I should be finished with all of my business by mid-afternoon, but it would be best if I did not come for you until after dark."

"Yes, you wouldn't want to be caught red-handed with me."

"That is not my concern," he said. "No one believes you are missing."

"I want to take the Belzoni book and my doll with me when I go home."

"That will not prove problematic. You are abandoning the Dickens?"

"It does not appeal to me." Estella wrinkled her nose.

"I do wish you would give it another try. Perhaps you could take it with you as a gift of sorts from me."

"Am I not the one who paid for it?"

He stared down at his boots. "I am most thoroughly ashamed of myself."

"Get yourself gone," she said, "and leave me in peace until Monday. If you are fortunate, I shall allow you to keep the copy of Monsieur Dickens's wretched book for yourself."

He mumbled thanks and wished her well—as well as could be expected in the circumstances—and climbed the ladder. Once the trapdoor had snapped shut, Estella organized her new supply of food, folded the featherbed so that she might use it as a cushion on which to sit, and turned her attention to Belzoni, munching on a strawberry macaron as she read. The explorer's words thrilled her, and as she was currently enclosed in a small, stone space, much like, she imagined, the tombs of the Egyptian pharaohs—although those were much more prettily decorated—it took almost no effort to imagine herself at Belzoni's side. Why go to all the trouble to travel to Egypt when one could re-create the proper atmosphere here with the most facile labor? Even her bumbling kidnapper had been able to accomplish it. She reached into the little bakery box and pulled out another macaron. *Pistachio,* she thought, and bit into it thoughtfully as she considered the challenges facing Belzoni as he embarked on the task of moving an enormous sculpture of Ramses II.

She read until seven o'clock, when she had planned to stop to organize her dinner, such as it was. He had left her, among other things, a small quiche Lorraine, and had suggested it would make a nice evening meal, but the box of macarons had disappeared, and along with it her appetite. She had no desire for dinner; all she wanted to do was keep reading. Estella looked around her little room and realized that she did not have to dine if she did not want to. There were no servants to consult, no friends to please, no parents to disappoint. She need not consider anyone's wishes or feelings but her own.

Feeling rather triumphant, she flipped shut the lid of the picnic basket, fluffed the featherbed and returned to her book. When at last she grew tired—she did not bother to check the time—she prepared her bed on the slab, extinguished her lamp, and curled up to sleep. For the first time in as long as she could remember, Estella was looking forward to morning.

13

Estella Lamar was in Paris. Cécile assured me the handwriting could be no one's but her friend's, and the postmark on the envelope had been stamped in the French capital. We bathed in elation for a moment before returning to our senses. "What does this mean?" I read the letter over and over. "Why, if Estella does not wish to see you, would she bother to write, especially if she only plans to be in town until the end of the week? Doing so only serves to confirm that she is here, and is unlikely to deter you from calling on her. Her servants will have told her we were at her house—*seeking information*, which she considers a *maudlin pursuit*—but she offers little if any contrition for the worry she has caused."

Cécile took the letter from me. "It is very like Estella—I have told you she always did whatever she pleased—yet there is something about it that rings false to me. She is so very heavy-handed in the manner in which she sings the praises of this new life, and the way in which she refers to the Côte d'Ivoire feels like an attempt at dangling before me a location in order to satisfy my curiosity while simultaneously ensuring I will not come dashing off in search of her. Estella knows better than to think I would come dashing after her. That she is suggesting I might speaks to the possibility of her being in a situation that would merit such radical action on my part."

"I have already formulated a plan. Let's go to her house at once."

I instructed Cécile's driver to leave us off in the rue Saint-Antoine, so that we might walk the last block to place des Vosges. I had no intention of descending upon Estella's house, instead wanting to watch, hidden from view by a well-placed tree, to see what sort of activity was afoot. Not a single visitor came in or out of the house. No curtain so much as fluttered. A little before eleven o'clock, a maid opened the door, crossed the threshold, and swept the arcaded entranceway.

"Now I am certain something is amiss," Cécile said. "No one has their maids sweeping out front at this time of the day. That should be finished before seven in the morning. If Estella were in residence, she would tolerate nothing less."

"Do you think she would care quite so violently?"

"My dear Kallista, there are some standards so basic one could not ignore them and still consider oneself French."

Who was I to argue with this sort of reasoning? Cécile did raise a valid objection. No one wanted her stoop to be swept in the middle of the day; it should be done early, to remove whatever detritus may have accumulated overnight. We left the shade of our tree and made our way round to the back of the house and watched the service entrance, where a butcher's wagon was just pulling away. I made mental note of the name and address painted on its side and then dragged Cécile back to her waiting carriage in rue Saint-Antoine.

"Aren't we going to call and demand to see Estella?" she asked.

"Not yet."

As the astute reader will have already surmised, I ordered the driver to the butcher's, where I queried the owner about the delivery he had recently sent to the Lamar residence. "I am more embarrassed than I can say." I spoke to him in a low, conspiratorial voice. "Mademoiselle Lamar is to dine with me tomorrow—she is only just back in Paris, you know—and I want to make sure I do not serve her whatever she is having her own chef prepare tonight. Would you be so kind as to check what meat she ordered from you?"

"Mademoiselle Lamar, you say? I do not believe there has been any significant change to her standing order." He riffled through a stack of papers. "We only delivered soup bones and a bit of mutton today—that's what the servants always have. I wasn't aware the mistress of the house had returned. I would have sent over something special if I had."

We thanked him and went back to the carriage. "It is just as I suspected. Estella is not home."

"How can you be sure, Kallista?"

"Her chef would have ordered something more than that if she were. I cannot decide if we should return to place des Vosges. It is possible the house is being watched."

"By whom?" Cécile asked.

"The auburn-haired man, of course." The coachman, standing patiently beside my door, was waiting for directions to pass on to the driver. "I think we must risk it."

This time, once back in the square, we marched straight to Estella's front door. The servant who answered it recognized us, let us in, and asked if we wanted to see the steward.

"I was rather hoping to speak to Mademoiselle Lamar." I studied with great interest his reaction to my request. He cocked his head to one side, looking confused.

"I am most sorry, Lady Emily, Mademoiselle Lamar is still away."

"Are you quite certain? I saw her just this morning in the Luxembourg Gardens."

"You did? Will you excuse me, madame? I will fetch the steward."

It did not appear that the young man was feigning his disbelief, particularly as it mingled with a flash of fear, just the sort of thing one would expect from the members of one's staff if, while the mistress of the house was away, they were slacking in their duties—as evidenced in the maid so belatedly tending to the entrance of the house—and they now realize they are about to be caught. While we waited for the steward, I pressed my ear to each of the doors to the rooms facing the entrance hall, but heard no signs of habitation behind any of them.

"Lady Emily, Madame du Lac, do forgive me if I have kept you waiting. The footman tells me you have only just seen Mademoiselle Lamar. Did she inform you of her plans? Are we to expect her imminent arrival?"

His reaction, too, appeared in all ways genuine, but I knew better than to trust anyone blindly. "I was under the impression she hoped to be in later today, was that not right, Cécile?" Cécile glowered at me, but nodded her agreement. "Would you be so good as to escort us to her bedroom? We brought with us a few treats for her toilette that we would like to leave. A little surprise, to welcome her home."

That he did not balk at this request supported my belief in the veracity of his words. He led us up the stairs and opened Estella's door for us. "Do you require anything further from me? If not, I shall leave you to your task and start readying the house for Mademoiselle Lamar's arrival."

I dismissed him, feeling a pang of guilt for sending him into such a tizzy. Cécile was more upset than I.

"You will give the poor man a digestive disorder, Kallista! It is too bad of you—is it not obvious that Estella is not here and has had no contact with her staff?"

"It is obvious *now*." I was quickly rummaging through Estella's wardrobe and drawers, trying my best to remember what Colin had said he had seen in them the other day. So far as I could tell, there was nothing new, and there certainly were no trunks, valises, or anything strewn about that would point to the recent return of a weary traveler. The servants were telling the truth. "I did not mean to torment the poor man, Cécile, but it is essential that we act with extreme care. Someone—be it Estella or another person—wants us to believe that Estella is here when clearly she is not. Now, if Estella were behind this, I would have expected to find her in residence, but hiding from us. The servants will come to no harm by having been scared into doing their duties to whatever standard they believe their mistress requires. Are they not meant to be doing that regardless?"

Cécile shrugged. *"C'est bien."*

"It would be unkind, though, to let them continue in this delusion. Perhaps we should tell them the truth. Unless you think it possible Estella *is* hiding somewhere in the house?"

Cécile pursed her lips and tilted her head. "I think we should conduct a thorough search before we make any rash decisions about the servants. Estella's letter was sent from Paris. If she is not in her house, where is she?"

We stepped into the corridor, greeted by the sounds of bustling servants below us on the ground floor, and examined each of the rooms on the first and then second floors. The third floor was reserved for the servants, but I felt we could not exclude it from our examination of the house. If Estella were hiding, it would be as good a place as any. She was not there. Returning to the ground floor, we made our way through each of the rooms. Nothing had changed in any of them from our previous visit other than the flowers—the malodorous lilies had been replaced with arrangements featuring enormous blue hydrangeas.

Nothing further remained to be explored except the rooms below stairs. After finishing with those, and feeling confident Estella was not in the house—even the most cunning individual would be hard-pressed to leave no sign at all of her return after so many years—I asked one of the maids scurrying about with mops and buckets to summon the steward for me. When he appeared, beads of perspiration dotting his face, I requested that he sit down with us in the salon with tapestries. He did, and I explained to him what little we knew.

"This is most alarming, Lady Emily." He wiped his brow with the back of his hand. "I am relieved that Mademoiselle Lamar is not about to appear and find us so very behind in our duties. I assure you, we have not been lax—"

I interrupted him. "We have seen the state of the house. Its condition is excellent. If Mademoiselle Lamar did appear unannounced, she would not be much disappointed. I should take better care to see that the area around the front door is swept earlier in the day. Other than that, she could hardly complain."

"But where is Mademoiselle Lamar? You say she is in Paris—why is she not here?"

"We do not know that, and I was hoping that perhaps you would be able to illuminate us. Have you had any word from her at all?"

"No, nothing since her last letter from Siam, and I already gave that to you."

"Have you noticed anyone prowling around the house at night?"

"No, madame, nothing has been out of the ordinary. The place des Vosges is not an area ripe with burglars, if that is what you are suggesting."

"All areas can be vulnerable. Do, please, have everyone on the staff on their guard."

"Of course. Anything I can do to help."

"I would like to know more about the florist who delivers here.

You have been using him from the time Mademoiselle Lamar set off on her travels?" I asked.

"I do not remember specifically, but that sounds correct."

"Does Monsieur Swiveller deliver his arrangements himself?"

"I believe he has a delivery boy."

"Would you recognize the lad?" Cécile asked.

"Hardly. He rarely, if ever, sends the same one twice."

"What day does he come?"

"Wednesday, in the morning. You have just missed him."

"Could you contact Monsieur Swiveller and ask him to bring another arrangement?" Cécile asked.

"No, that would most likely alert him to a problem," I said. "I am going to come here next Tuesday night, and sleep in Estella's room. When the flower delivery boy arrives on Wednesday, no matter how early, I want him stopped so that I may speak to him."

"I do not know, Lady Emily, that Mademoiselle—"

"This is of critical importance. I have already communicated to you the possibility that Mademoiselle Lamar is in a great deal of danger. If she comes to harm, and you have impeded my investigation, you will be nearly as guilty as the miscreant at whose hands she suffers." I realized I was exaggerating, but sometimes one must paint a picture brighter than reality in order to persuade others to cooperate with one's schemes. If it turned out that Estella was cozied up at Hôtel Meurice with a dashing Bedouin she had collected on her travels, she might be furious that I had invaded her home, but she could hardly fault my motives. If she did, I was ready to face her ire.

The steward, having borne the brunt of my ever-increasing intensity, agreed to do whatever I thought best. I was grateful to him, but made a mental note to speak in the strongest terms to Davis on my return to England. I would not want him, no matter what anyone said, to ever let my own home be invaded.

That Estella was at Hôtel Meurice—with or without a dashing Bedouin—was a distinct possibility. Le Meurice, a favorite of mine, provided the exquisite service and accommodation favored by the most genteel of travelers, and I was pleased to see my old friend Monsieur Beaulieu still managing the hotel. He greeted me warmly as soon as the desk clerk had alerted him to our arrival in the lobby. I explained the situation to him, in tones both hushed and urgent, and asked if Estella Lamar was currently a guest.

"You are well aware, Lady Emily, that the privacy of those who stay with us is of primary concern, yet if you truly believe Mademoiselle Lamar to be in danger—you say your husband is working with the Sûreté?"

This was, perhaps, not strictly true. Colin worked alone, or with me, but the Sûreté had given him a letter authorizing his credentials in France. Surely that was virtually the same as him working in conjunction with them? "Yes. If he were here he could show you their letter, but he is currently occupied with another, more dangerous aspect, of the case. He felt certain I would be safe consulting with you." I felt a little flattery and a concession to Monsieur Beaulieu's sensibilities concerning ladies and detective work would be expedient.

Monsieur Beaulieu stroked his beard and nodded. "I can tell you that, although I myself would not be able to recognize Mademoiselle Lamar, I do not believe her to be staying with us. I would have taken note of her name."

"It is likely she would have given another name at registration. Might I take a peek at the book on the desk?" He hesitated, but I can be extremely persuasive when necessary, and before long he had agreed to my request. As I paged through the register, I was reminded of the first time I had stayed at Le Meurice. Colin had arranged rooms for me—this was before I had the slightest clue I was in love with him—when I was newly out of deep mourning for my first husband. I wished I could ask Monsieur Beaulieu to pull out the old volume with my signature in it. This, however, was not the time for sentimental pleasures.

Cécile and I considered each and every name entered into the book in the course of the past three weeks. There were no Dickensian names, nothing that appeared to be Estella's handwriting, and, obviously, perhaps, no Lamar. "Do any of these names seem suspect to you?" I asked my friend.

"A great number of them are what I would consider unfortunate—I give you Daffyth Kentwell-Hennebry—"

"That doesn't strike me as all that bad."

"Because you are English, Kallista."

"The Baroness von Hohensteinbauergrunewald is much worse."

"Hohensteinbauergrunewald?" Cécile asked. "I know that name. I am almost certain I came across it a few years back when reading a rather sensational account of an archaeological controversy of some sort in Egypt that led to murder. Is she still here? I would very much like to make her acquaintance."

"Only you, Cécile, could claim familiarity with the name von Hohensteinbauergrunewald. Unfortunately, the baroness checked out three days ago, so we will not be able to meet her."

Cécile shrugged. "Such a pity. She sounded more ridiculous than the average baroness and I have no doubt would have been most entertaining for a short while. As to your earlier question, Kallista, none of these names strike me as works of fiction. More importantly, none sounds like something Estella would choose to adopt."

"I quite agree."

We thanked Monsieur Beaulieu for his assistance, assured him we would be back to dine in the hotel's excellent restaurant before we left Paris, and stepped onto the arcaded pavement that ran along the rue de Rivoli. We could not search every hotel in Paris, and decided to walk back to Cécile's house. We dismissed the carriage and, crossing the street, entered the Jardin des Tuileries. "When I was a girl, the Tuileries Palace still stood here," Cécile said. "The view from the Champs-Élysées was destroyed when they burned it during the Commune. It was a tragedy of useless destruction, but those were terrible days of much violence. We are far better off now, but what a century it has been."

"They didn't pull it down immediately after it had burned, did—" My question went unfinished, as at that moment Cécile fell to the ground, pushed down by a man who seemed to have appeared out of nowhere. He barely broke his stride after the assault, continuing to run perpendicular to the direction we had been walking. I bent over to check my friend was not badly hurt, gathered my skirts, and then ran after the depraved villain.

Estella

xiii

Estella rose at precisely eleven forty-seven, and found it one of the most pleasing things she had ever done in her life. Eleven forty-seven! Nurse had never allowed such sloth, and it was only rarely that her mother tolerated sleeping beyond eight o'clock, and then, only if one had been out nearly all night at a ball. Estella stretched, reaching her arms toward the top of her stone room, and then bent at her waist until her fingertips skimmed the floor. The movement felt good, particularly as last night was the first time she had been without a corset since her captor had thrown her into this place. She considered the pile of discarded clothing she had left in a heap on the floor after she had dropped over her head the soft linen nightgown he had brought for her, and decided that she did not want to get dressed.

That her room was chilly could not be denied. She picked up her cloak, but it had suffered under hard use for too many days and nights as blanket, pillow, and sheet, and had taken on a not very appealing odor. She pulled on the loose robe that matched her nightgown and then wrapped a blanket around her shoulders before sitting on the floor—now soft with her new carpets—in front of the picnic basket. It was time for breakfast.

Estella wished there were more macarons. She would have to ask him for some, she thought, before remembering that would not be necessary. The next time he came, he would be ready to release her. She had brioche, but no jam to go with it—he was loath to give her any sort of cutlery, even a spoon—so she decided on pain au chocolat instead. On biting into it, she realized she wanted the quiche she had rejected the night before, skipping dinner having left her hungrier than she usually felt at breakfast. She abandoned the pain au chocolat and picked up a piece of the quiche, glad that he had thought to cut it into slices. There was no decorous way to attack a whole quiche in the absence of utensils.

Sated after three pieces, Estella washed her hands with the soap and water she had already made such good use of the previous night—bathing had never before seemed such a luxury—and picked up her book. This caused her to frown, as she realized she had fewer than a hundred pages left to read. She would be finished this very afternoon and left with only that miserable tome of Monsieur Dickens. There was nothing to be done about it. She devoured the rest of Belzoni in a greedy gulp. It was four o'clock now. Too soon for dinner. More macarons would have been perfect. She finished the pain au chocolat and paced around the room for a while before picking up *A Tale of Two Cities. The best of times and the worst of times,* she thought, remembering the line that had so offended her when she first read it.

She opened the cover of the book and started again. The featherbed nestled her comfortably as she sat on the slab, leaning back against the wall. She had thick, warm, and, best of all, clean socks on her feet. No one could bother her. Perhaps Monsieur Dickens was not so foolish as Estella had originally thought.

14

I may have a reputation for dressing finely, and I admit freely and wholly without embarrassment to having a weakness for beautiful clothes. As I have said on many a previous occasion, I have never believed that an appreciation for high fashion precludes possession of common sense. I might allow my maid to lace me tightly into a stunning Worth evening gown, but when in the midst of an investigation, I choose clothing that will not hinder my work. My stays were never pulled too tight, my skirts were never too narrow, and, perhaps most important, my boots were sturdy and comfortable.

Cécile's assailant had not counted on that last point. I flew after him with the speed of Hermes, the pale dust of the Tuileries' paths rising like smoke in my wake. I am well aware that this may be considered something of a mixed metaphor, but believe I may be forgiven the faux pas. It is what I thought in the moment, and one can hardly be expected to summon eloquence when apprehending the vicious attacker of one's dearest friend.

He had not expected me to follow him. If he had, I am certain he would not have made the mistake of slowing his pace so measurably as he approached the gate at the edge of the park. Feeling almost triumphant as I grew close, I decided that I would fling myself against him with all my weight, screaming for help all the while. I had no doubt that, once the miscreant was on the ground, any number of gentlemen would step up to assist me. They could hold him in place while I summoned the police.

But I had made a grievous error of my own. He had slowed down specifically because he did know I was following him. When I was very nearly upon him, without stopping, he flung over his head a sheaf of papers that scattered over me. They broke my pace and disoriented me—there must have been hundreds of them, each the size of the page of a novel—and when I regained my composure, he was gone.

Furious that I had allowed myself to be so easily thrown off course, I stomped through the papers and out of the gardens. He had exited back into the rue de Rivoli, and would have had no difficulty disappearing into the throngs of tourists there. I felt a tug on my arm—a policeman—who, upon having assured himself that I was unharmed, began to scold me for having caused a scene, not to mention a grievous mess in le Jardin. I brushed past him, knowing he would follow me, and returned to Cécile, who was now back on her feet and being propped up by an extremely handsome gentleman. On my way to her, I stooped over to collect a handful of the papers the villain had thrown. They had already blown all over, littering the park in a most indecorous fashion. I could understand the displeasure of the policeman. Printed in thick block letters on each sheet were two short sentences:

LAISSEZ ESTELLA SEUL. DÉSOBÉISSEZ À CET AVERTISSEMENT À VOS RISQUES ET PÉRILS.

"Did he elude you, Kallista?" Cécile was doing her best to remove from her walking dress the fine layer of dust that had clung to it after her fall. Her efforts did not accomplish a great deal; the navy blue was all but covered with white.

I thrust a bunch of the papers at my friend. "It was the auburn-haired man. I did not have to see his face to confirm as much."

The policeman was beginning to growl again. "Monsieur, you must not be so horrible. It is not my friend who caused this mess," Cécile said. "It was a diabolical criminal." The officer listened carefully to her story, nodding and making sympathetic noises when she reached the part in which she had been flung to the ground.

"Are you injured, madame?" he asked.

"Only my pride, but I am greatly concerned that you have let this man escape."

"Madame, I was not on hand—"

"One ought to be able to take a turn in a public park without suffering at the hands of a maniac. I am not interested in any excuses as to where you or any of your colleagues were at the time of the incident. I merely want your assurance that it will not happen again."

"Madame, I—"

Cécile raised a hand. "I am not interested. Are we quite finished here?" I had gathered up as many of the papers as I could, and told her I thought it best that we return home. The handsome gentleman who had leapt to Cécile's side offered to escort us. His carriage, he said, was waiting near the Pont Royal, just outside the gardens.

"Absolutely not." I looped my arm through Cécile's and pulled until she had no choice but to move. She hobbled along, fighting me all the way to the river. Although the Pont Royal was nearer to us than the Pont Solférino, I elected to walk the longer distance, as I had no intention of putting us near the gentleman's carriage. A glance behind us told me he had not followed us, but I did not trust that his driver had not been instructed to intercept us.

"You cannot think Monsieur Aguillon is in league with the auburn-haired man!"

"Monsieur Aguillon? He had time to introduce himself in the midst of all the commotion, did he?"

"Marcel, as I hope to soon be calling him," Cécile said. We were on the bridge now, and she tugged hard on my arm to force me to stop walking. "Enough, Kallista!"

"So I am to believe it was a happy coincidence that landed Monsieur Aguillon so conveniently at your side following the attack?"

Cécile shrugged. "With a face so handsome as that, his criminal connections, whatever they may be, are of little interest to me."

"Don't be absurd. What would have happened if I hadn't returned with the police? He might have been deliberately lurking, waiting, so that he could spirit you away while I was distracted."

"It is a risk I am willing to take." She put her arm through mine again, congenially, and patted me with her other hand as we started to walk again, crossing the bridge. "You are kind to worry about me, Kallista, but when a lady reaches a certain age, she finds that her standards become more fluid than they once were. Monsieur Aguillon is very nearly as handsome as your own Monsieur Hargreaves. Do you really expect me to fling him aside on the grounds that he may possibly have a connection to someone we may possibly believe to be engaged in what may possibly be a criminal activity?"

"Yes. That is precisely what I expect."

"You are so very young, *ma chère amie.* When Monsieur Aguillon calls—and I assure you he will—I have every intention of receiving him."

"You are impossible, and I am not so very young. I was only recently lamenting the demise of my impetuous youth."

"No matter how rapidly you age, Kallista, you will always be younger than I." We had crossed the river and continued along the rue de Solférino until we reached boulevard Saint-Germain, where we turned left toward Cécile's house. Soon after, I noticed a printer's shop, and an idea struck me. A bell tingled from the door as I pushed it open, and before long a wiry man with a fine example of an aquiline nose stepped from the back room to greet us as he wiped his hands on the long, ink-spattered apron tied around his waist.

"Bonjour, mesdames."

We returned his greeting. "I was hoping you might be able to assist me." I smoothed one of the pages I had collected from the ground in the park and pushed it across the counter to him. "Is there, so far as you know, any means of identifying who printed this?"

He picked up the leaf, studied it, and then held it up to the light. "There is a watermark on the paper, but I am afraid it identifies it as one of the most commonly used brands in France. The typesetting, however, is more unique. It may look to you like any other serif font, but it is more special than that." He flipped the paper around so that we could see the words right side up. "This typeface is designed to have only capital letters—you see that all the letters are capital, but the ones we would expect to see capitalized, such as the first in each sentence, are larger than those that follow. Other than that, what is most strange is that although the words are written in French, the spacing has followed English rules."

"Could you explain?" I asked.

"In France, we leave a single space before and after most punctuation marks. In England, there are generally no spaces before punctuation, and one inserts a double space between sentences. You see here that there is no space before either period, but a double space after the first one. No Frenchman would set type in this manner unless specifically directed by his customer, and even then, would argue strongly against it."

"Bien sûr," Cécile said.

"Is the typeface itself common?" I asked.

"Not so much. I have seen it before, but it is not one I use."

"Have you any suggestions as to how we might locate the printer?"

"It would be very difficult," he said. "There would be no way to know except by asking shop by shop."

"How many printers are there in Paris?"

"Hundreds, madame."

We thanked him for his time and continued on our way. "This confirms what I already suspected—the auburn-haired man is English. He would have insisted that his flyer be punctuated correctly."

"Or incorrectly, given that he is in Paris and writing in French," Cécile said.

"Touché. This will make an excellent assignment for Jeremy to tackle once he has finished at the post office."

"You cannot expect the poor man to go to every printer in Paris! That would be too cruel."

"I am never cruel, Cécile. We believe Swiveller's lair is in the neighborhood around the Catacombs. He can focus his search accordingly. It does him good to be of use."

"What are you going to do, Kallista, when at last he does marry? I suspect you will miss his attentions more than you think."

"Ridiculous. Jeremy will marry, but not for ages, and I can assure you when the glorious day at last comes, I will be more delighted even than his own mother."

Cécile arched her eyebrows. "Skeptical does not begin to describe me."

We called in at Café de Flore on our way home, on the chance that the auburn-haired man had returned there. He had not, but this did not detract from my enjoyment of a superb *chocolat*. When at last we returned to Cécile's—I confess we lingered over our beverages for more than an hour—Colin and Jeremy were already there. Cécile made a dramatic entrance in her dusty dress, sending both gentlemen shooting to their feet the instant they saw her, alarm etched on their faces.

She raised a weary hand to her forehead and begged them to forgive her—she was enjoying every second of this performance—she would tell them everything once she had bathed and changed into more suitable attire. I was not party to this anticipatory delay, and, once she had retired upstairs, I gave them the whole story, unabridged, presenting them each with one of the printed sheets.

"A warning! How terribly exciting." Jeremy dropped the paper next to him on the settee where he was sitting. "I do think, Hargreaves, this calls for whisky?" Colin agreed, and Jeremy poured for them both. "Port, Em?" I saw no reason to deny myself the comfort of a spot of my favorite libation.

"What of your own travails?" I asked as he handed me a glass of the tawny liquid.

"Nothing yet," Colin said, "but we expected little else today. I suspect that all the excitement in the park may keep him from collecting his post tomorrow—that would be wise if he has any inkling that we are onto him—but we will watch all the same."

"I suppose you can't spare Jeremy, then?" I asked, and described for them my strategy concerning the printers. "Neither Cécile nor I would make a good second should you require assistance in stopping the wretch if he manages to leave the post office. I proved that much by letting him get away this afternoon."

"I am glad you got no further than you did," Colin said. "The effort was admirable, my dear. I am most impressed."

"I suppose Cécile and I could deal with the printers—"

"But you thought it sounded tedious and that is why you wanted to put me on the case," Jeremy interrupted.

"Am I so obvious? Darling Jeremy, after seeing how well you did with the florists, I can hardly be blamed. I think, when we are in the neighborhood investigating printers, Cécile and I should inquire with Swiveller's concierge as to the availability of apartments in her building."

"Absolutely not." Colin set his empty whisky glass onto the side table next to him with such force I feared it would shatter. "If he were there, he would recognize either of you. We cannot take the risk."

"A fair point." I sighed. "We shall limit ourselves to the printers."

Cécile returned, wearing a frothy tea gown, and crossed directly to the *rafraîchissoir,* where, with a deftness one would not expect from a lady undertaking the task, she opened a bottle of Moët et Chandon. "I had a revelation while I was in the bath. If Estella is indeed in Paris, and for only a short while, it is likely that she will visit the graves of her parents. She was always devoted to them and had a habit of bringing a fresh wreath to them every week. Tomorrow, Kallista and I will go to the cemetery and watch for her."

"Won't she see us and run away?" I asked.

"Parisian cemeteries are not like English ones. There will be plenty of places for us to hide."

As I was not particularly eager to trudge through a far-off neighborhood interviewing printers, I agreed to her plan. The truth was, I expected us to make little progress in the case until either the auburn-haired man collected his mail or until I, next week, was able to speak to Swiveller's delivery boy. In the meantime, an outing to the cemetery sounded like an excellent diversion.

Estella

A wonderful fact to reflect upon, that every human creature is constituted to be that profound secret and mystery to every other. A solemn consideration, when I enter a great city by night, that every one of those darkly clustered houses encloses its own secret; that every room in every one of them encloses its own secret; that every beating heart in the hundreds of thousands of breasts there, is, in some of its imaginings, a secret to the heart nearest it!

Estella, now three chapters in, was thoroughly enjoying Monsieur Dickens's *A Tale of Two Cities*. She paused at this passage, reading it over and over, delighting in the thought that she, hidden away here in her little room in the cellar of some house—it must be a cellar, she had decided, for where else would a person build walls of stone for a room accessible only by trapdoor?—she herself was a secret enclosed.

She glanced at her clock. Six forty-five in the evening. She should think about dinner soon. The quiche might be too old now, and she did not want to risk any sort of digestive disturbance. She limited herself to bread and cheese and a small fruit tart. When she had finished eating, she returned to her book, and fell asleep with it still in her hands.

The next morning, Sunday—nearly the last of her imprisonment!—she awoke and was pleased when she saw the time. It was only seven-thirty. As much as she was looking forward to going home, she wanted to take advantage of these last hours on her own. She had relished staying in her nightgown all day yesterday, but today, she was going to dress. She lathered her soap, wrapping it in a flannel and dipping it into the bucket she used for her toilette. Soon she was clean and dressed in her old skirt, but with new undergarments and a fresh shirtwaist. She couldn't manage her corset well without assistance, but was able to button the blouse even in the absence of her constricting stays. Her skirt would not fasten all the way, but who would see her to notice? She even put on her boots, but after several days of not having worn them, they felt stiff and uncomfortable, and she wondered how she had ever been able to stand them. She flung them into the corner of the room where she had already heaped her dirty clothes.

As the day progressed, Estella grew melancholy. She did not eat anything for luncheon, and did not even bother to open the wine her captor had left. Water kept her thirst at bay, but there was an ache building deep inside her that she could neither identify nor satisfy. She returned to her book, weeping when poor Lucie was reunited with the father she had believed to be dead, and soon found herself so caught up in the story that the ache had all but disappeared. She read, on and on, until hunger began to gnaw at her, and she reached for the last of her cheese and a piece of now stale baguette. The bread was so hard she could barely tear it, but she managed, and found it wasn't so bad as she would have thought. At ten-eighteen her eyelids started to feel heavy. For the last time, she fluffed up her featherbed, changed into her nightgown, and settled down to sleep on her stone slab.

15

Paris's Père-Lachaise bore almost no resemblance to any cemetery I had visited before, although I could see that it had originally been intended to conjure up visions of the ancient tombs lining Rome's Appian Way. Far in the northeast of the city, the Cimetière de l'Est—its official name—had been constructed at the end of the previous century in an attempt to provide burial sites outside what were then the limits of the city. France, post-Revolution, was secular to its core—at least in theory—but the builders gave their grounds a Jesuitical nickname. The historical Père de la Chaise, confessor of King Louis XIV, had once acquired for his order the land on which the cemetery now stood to serve as a resort for the priests. When contemplating the luxurious holidays they must have enjoyed, one can hardly argue with the country's desire for secularity.

Secular though their government may be, the Parisians are a devout lot, largely followers of the Roman church, and once the Cimetière de l'Est had been dubbed Père-Lachaise, the citizens began to accept that it was a respectable, hallowed place. There are few people more conscious than the Parisians of tradition and the importance of doing things in a manner suited to reflect their station, and the organizers initially had a great difficulty convincing members of the best families that they ought to choose this new cemetery as their final resting place. In an effort to manipulate attitudes, they began exhuming bodies of famous Frenchmen and reburying them in Père-Lachaise. Before long, high society was clamoring to rest in the same location as Abélard and Heloïse, Molière and La Fontaine, Louise de Lorraine—the widow of Henri III—and Caron de Beaumarchais, who had written *The Marriage of Figaro*.

Cécile's driver left us directly in front of a steep set of stairs that, from the street, appeared to lead to the top of a high wall. In fact, the cemetery's ground, on a hill, began above street level. Once inside, I felt as if I had entered another world, a true city of the dead, with long, narrow avenues crossing long, narrow streets, lined on both sides by tombs that looked almost like narrow houses. Cécile's late and unlamented husband was buried here, and although she had never been fond of the man, she did very much appreciate the fortune he had left her, and she always credited him with having taught her how to shoot. Thus, she had brought with her a simple wreath to lay on his grave—or so I had thought before I understood the nature of things at Père-Lachaise.

We hiked what felt like a mile up a hill, then turned left and then right. There were some slab graves, but mostly tombs, and I assumed the bodies were buried, so to speak, inside the walls of these structures, but I quickly realized my mistake when, thirty yards down a narrow street, Cécile stopped and put her hand on the door of one of the tombs.

"You're not going to open it?" I gasped.

"Why on earth not? The dreadful man is buried here. Where else would you have me leave his wreath?" The door swung open and revealed what to all appearances was a small and extremely narrow chapel, with an altar, a stained-glass window above it, and hooks attached on both sides of the walls running perpendicular to it. Cécile stepped inside, hung the wreath on one of the hooks, and frowned. She raised a gloved hand to one of the names carved on the wall and ran her fingers over it. "I suppose I ought to do this more often, and perhaps I would, if he had ever in his life given me cause to miss him."

I stepped away from the iron door to give Cécile some privacy. The bodies of the dearly departed, I realized, were buried below these tombs. It was obvious when I thought about it, but I had assumed a raised tomb meant a raised grave. Most of the little houses above the graves were slightly wider and slightly longer than a coffin. The depth of the grave—or graves—below determined how many members of a family might be stacked, one on top of another. The condition of the tombs varied wildly. Some were beautifully tended: the doors gleaming, the stained glass polished, and fresh flowers arranged on the little altars. I could see all this through the windows in many of the doors. Others, however, were in a sorry state of disrepair, their doors hanging off the hinges, dust, dirt, and dead leaves accumulating on their floors, the dry remains of long-forgot flowers crumbling inside.

Cécile did not remain inside her husband's tomb for long. She closed the door behind her and found me peeking into one of the more derelict tombs. "When one purchases a plot here, one is given a concession *à perpétuité*—they are to have the plot forever—so long as they tend to the grave. Ones like this"—she shrugged—"will eventually have their occupants exhumed to the Catacombs, and the space will be sold to another family."

"How awful." The door was already partly open. I pulled it the rest of the way, its rusty hinges groaning. Inside, the stained glass was broken, large pieces of it missing. I brushed aside an enormous spider's web with my parasol and looked at the carving on the wall:

ICI REPOSE

MME V GIFFART

NÉE FLORETTE DAUVILLIER

DÉCÉDÉE LE 9 MARS 1822

À L'ÂGE DE 23 ANS

"So young to die." I used my handkerchief to brush the dust of her inscription. "I wonder if she fell ill, or if it was childbirth, and why is no one taking care—"

"You already fall victim to Père-Lachaise, Kallista. It is impossible to come and not wonder about the stories of all the people resting here. There is no time for it now. We must hurry to the Lamar family tomb."

My heart ached as I closed the door as far as it would go. Perhaps Florette had never had children, and her husband had remarried after her death. His new wife might not have wanted him tending to the grave of her predecessor, the woman up to whose memory she could never live. Or Florette's husband could have died as well—with her, during an epidemic—I turned back, wanting to look at the other names on the walls, but Cécile took me firmly by the arm. "Another day, Kallista, you can return and study the dead." We started back down the hill. "There is Molière—look quickly as we pass—it is easy to get confused on these roads and we don't have time to get lost."

The playwright rested in a large stone sepulcher held above the ground by four thick columns. His having been one of the bodies moved in an attempt to lure others to the cemetery, I wondered what he would have made of his new digs. Cécile was dragging me along too quickly for me to give much consideration to the question. We cut across another avenue—each was named, and there were signposts at every intersection—and soon were in front of the Lamar family tomb. Although it could not really have been, it seemed even narrower than some of the others. A large stone cross jutted up from the front of its steeply peaked roof, below which, on the structure's façade, was a small Gothic window above an ornate ironwork door. Everything about the tomb was pristine. The door was locked, but we could see inside through its window.

"There is a wreath there," I said, careful not to press my nose against the glass and leave a mark. "It looks fresh."

"We have missed her." Cécile shrugged. "It was worth trying, but who knows when she came here. It may have been immediately upon her arrival in the city."

"How do we know it's her wreath? Didn't she have siblings?"

"Half siblings, who were so displeased by the distribution of their father's estate that I would fall over dead with shock if any of them ever came to his grave, let alone tend to it."

I sighed. "I do hope my dawdling didn't ruin us."

"You didn't really dawdle for long, Kallista. For all we know, she came even before we suspected she was back in Paris."

"This does seem to confirm she is here, somewhere. In Paris, that is."

"Oui," Cécile said. "Come, I will show you my favorite tomb—"

"We ought to start on the printers," I interrupted.

"It will not take long." She led me to an imposing monument rising high above all those around it. Like Molière, this person did not have one of the little houses. Perhaps the famous among the dead preferred something more spectacular, more likely to draw the eye of every passerby. This sepulcher was topped by decorations of hideous winged skulls. A carving on a side panel depicted ordinary people cowering at the sight of demons and a grotesque flying skeleton.

"Robertson," I read off the tomb. "Étienne-Gaspard. I do not recognize the name." Beneath the dates of his birth and death were three words:

PHYSIQUE

FANTASMAGORIE

AEROSTATS

"Monsieur Robertson was a magnificent magician," Cécile explained. "He could conjure spirits in front of an audience—there was a scientific explanation, *bien sûr,* but who is interested in such a thing?—and his show was once banned when a royalist asked him to summon the ghost of the dead king. This was not long enough after the Revolution, you see."

"They forced him to stop?"

"What else could they do? Have the king's spirit floating about Paris unattended? I have often wondered whether his head had been returned to his body after death. At any rate, those who believe in the black arts insist that if one is to come here, after dark on a moonless night, one will see the skulls on Monsieur Robertson's tomb dancing."

"You can't possibly believe that." I certainly didn't, but neither could I deny the goose bumps prickling up my neck.

"I have never been tempted to scale the walls after the cemetery is closed. Dancing skulls, to me, are not enough of an enticement to merit the effort."

"It is a dreadful thought. Let us leave the black arts behind us and enter a more pedestrian world: that of the printer."

The trek from the far northeastern corner of the city back south of the Jardin du Luxembourg, into the Fourteenth Arrondissement, past the entrance to the Catacombs—I had had enough of the dead for one day—in the general direction of the Parc Montsouris, took long enough for Cécile to have a little snooze in the carriage. The printer we had visited in Saint-Germain-des-Prés had given us the address of a shop he knew in the neighborhood, and I planned to start our search there. The proprietor showed no signs of recognition when he looked at the samples I had brought with me of the pages the auburn-haired man had flung in the Tuileries, but he was quick to point out that he would never have made such an outrageous error in typesetting. He referred, of course, to the English manner in which the punctuation had been handled. The man was genial and kind, and made a list for us of his colleagues in the area. Fortunately for us, there were not too terribly many. If we were efficient, we would be able to speak with all of them before the afternoon was over.

What followed was a series of visits that went much like our first. Every printer balked at the terrible way the punctuation had been butchered. No printer claimed the work as his own. At three o'clock Cécile insisted that we needed a break, so we took a table in a café across from the entrance to the Catacombs, where a line of tourists, fueled by morbid curiosity, waited to exchange a few coins for permission to descend below the ground.

We had missed luncheon, so I took the opportunity to order a *croque-monsieur,* while Cécile chose an omelette aux fines herbes. We shared a small carafe of house wine. The warmth of the sun had lured us to sit outside, which made watching the progress of the Catacomb visitors impossible to avoid.

"I object in the strongest of terms to the parade of individuals marching through that disgusting place." This statement took me aback. So far as I knew, Cécile had no concerns about tourism in any other catacombs. She had toured them in Rome (I believe as part of a romantic rendezvous) and had pressed me for details of my own visit to the ones in Vienna (when I had refused Jeremy's request to entomb his bones there).

"What is so awful about these in particular, other than the piles of moldering bones?"

"These skeletons come from all the old cemeteries of Paris, dug up in the last century and moved to what used to be part of *les carrières*—limestone mines. I cannot recall the details, only that when houses started sinking into the ground, the tunnels were rediscovered and repurposed. The bones of six million people—*six million*—are heaped up in the most grotesque arrangements: skulls one on top of another, femurs packed tight, sometimes combined to form repulsive little decorative shapes. Hearts, even. There is no dignity in it. None at all. It is one thing to choose to be interred in catacombs. It is another entirely to have your remains dug up and flung into a pit during what is meant to be a modern and enlightened age. The entire endeavor was rampantly unscrupulous."

I was trying to remember the story of the catacombs in Rome. So far as I could recall, the Christians had used them for burials, and they were decorated to honor the dead—no skulls forming precious patterns like hearts—and hence were deliberately chosen by the people who had lost their loved ones. The Paris Catacombs, it seemed, removed the humanity from its occupants. It reminded me a little of the derelict tombs in Père-Lachaise. There, too, no one was left to care about what happened to the mortal remains of individuals who, no doubt, had once been dearly loved.

Cécile divided the rest of the wine between us. "I do not like things that are morbid."

"How can you say that when you have only just shown me the tomb of Étienne-Gaspard Robertson—surely that, and the accompanying stories—could be considered nothing but morbid."

"There is a difference, Kallista, between morbidly entertaining and morbidly depressing."

I considered her point. "I understand what you—"

During the course of our meal, I had kept an eye on the tourists, as they were amusing to watch. Children tugged at their nurses' hands—I wondered what their parents would have to say about the day's outing—lovers looked at each other with mooning expressions, and an unaccountably large number of young gentlemen were all but chomping at the bit to gain entrance. Two of them caught my attention when they began balancing on the rail that ran around the garden that stood in the center of the circle where the queue had formed. One of them was about to fall, but what brought me in that instant to my feet was something else altogether.

The auburn-haired man was walking in the street on the other side of the queue.

Estella

XV

Morning light!

Not sunlight, but the beam from Estella's lamp. She had not slept well, a curious combination of anxiety and sadness disturbing her slumber all night, but was determined not to light the lamp until morning. This proved difficult, as reading the clock's hands in the thick darkness of her room was well nigh impossible. When at last Estella struck a match, it was nearly nine o'clock. The lamp, now shining bright, illuminated the space around her with its warm golden glow. It was time to ready herself to leave.

There was no need to rush. Her captor would not arrive until late afternoon—he would have to collect his money from the bank and then pay off the notorious usurers with whom he had entangled himself. Estella got dressed, tugging at her corset until it was tight enough that the clothes she had been wearing when he had abducted her would fit. That done, she completed her toilette, smoothed her doll's hair—she had not yet bestowed upon her a name—and sat down on the slab, the doll on her lap. She studied the porcelain face, the green eyes that opened and closed, and the ringlets of dark hair that spilled from beneath a green velvet cap. Lucie. She would call her Lucie, after the girl in Monsieur Dickens's novel.

That decided, she collected the bits of food that still remained, the empty water flasks, and the full bottle of wine, and packed them back into the picnic basket. None of the food appealed to her. She wanted macarons. She tidied up her clothing, folding her nightdress and robe, along with the new items her captor had brought for her, and bundled them all up. She did not want to take them home with her, but also did not want to leave her little room a mess. Her boots, which she had carelessly discarded, she lined up against the wall, near to where the ladder would be lowered this afternoon. Satisfied with her work, she opened her book, but it did not fall open to the page she had marked, instead to one she had read before:

> *Sadly, sadly, the sun rose; it rose upon no sadder sight than the man of good abilities and good emotions, incapable of their directed exercise, incapable of his own help and his own happiness, sensible of the blight on him, and resigning himself to let it eat him away.*

Estella sighed when she read this passage and touched the words, feeling the ink beneath her fingers. She said the words aloud, repeating them again and again, feeling a kinship to the man of good abilities and good emotions. Like him, she was incapable of her own help and her own happiness, but she would not—could not!—let it eat her away.

She slammed the book shut, jumped down from the stone slab and walked the perimeter of her room. For the first time, the sound of her clock ticking plagued her, as if it were mocking her, counting down the rapidly diminishing number of seconds before she would be thrust back into the world. Tick! Tock! Tick! Tock! Estella was convinced the sound was growing louder, and she covered her ears against it, but to no avail. She picked up the clock and shook it, then raised her arm to fling it, with all her might, against the wall.

But then she stopped and reconsidered.

There was another way.

16

He was there—that villainous soul—just beyond my reach. Almost without thinking, I moved forward, ready to pursue him. Cécile grabbed me by the wrist. "We cannot risk alerting him to our presence."

She was right, but I was not about to let him disappear once again. Our waiter stood only a few steps away, taking an order at another table. I crossed to him, thrust at him a handful of coins, more than enough to cover our bill, and then took Cécile by the hand. "We shall follow at a reasonable and safe distance, taking every precaution against him seeing us."

We used the queue outside the Catacombs to block our initial approach, slouching to avoid detection as we made our way around the circle. I kept a close watch on our prey, who was headed south on the avenue d'Orléans. We kept on the opposite side of the street from him, taking great care to hide ourselves by staying behind individuals of, shall we say, greater girth than that possessed by either Cécile or myself. This proved problematic only once, after Cécile had taken on the idea that she would be even less visible if she adopted a (ridiculous) hunched-over position. Ambling along in this awkward pose, she bumped into the large person meant to be shielding her. This substantial individual, a lady clothed in an unattractive gown of burnt orange—a shade wholly at odds with the bright rouge painted onto her cheeks and lips—shrieked when she felt Cécile slam into her, and turned around, swinging her parasol as if it was a weapon she felt confident would be effective, but possessed no idea of how to wield.

Cécile, abandoning the posture that had caused the trouble, made a quick apology and shoved past the woman. The auburn-haired man was nearly a block ahead of us as we approached the église Saint-Pierre-de-Montrouge. The church, an excellent example of the Romanesque revival of our current century, rose beside us, its bell startling me when it clanged to life. At rue Beaunier, the man turned left, and following him on this smaller street proved more of a challenge, but, fortunately, a challenge we were able to meet, thanks to a few obliging doorways against which we pressed ourselves. The road ended at the avenue Reille, which he crossed and then turned immediately left, shortly thereafter making a quick right into a small, cobbled street, lined with unremarkable houses, that led directly into the Parc Montsouris.

"Someone ought to pull all these houses down," Cécile said. "This location lends itself to something rather more charming, don't you think? Perhaps I should hire an architect—"

I shushed her, paused outside the entrance to the park, and then poked my head through the gate. The auburn-haired man was almost out of my sight. Following him through the park proved significantly more difficult than it had in the street. Although the grounds were full of trees and hedges, the paths cut through them were not so crowded as one would hope when in the midst of a clandestine operation. He traversed the park while we kept a fair distance behind, using our parasols to block our faces whenever we feared he might turn around and see us. I breathed a sigh of relief when I saw the gates on the opposite edge. He crossed out of one of them and back into the street.

From there, he took a circuitous route to a modest apartment building, whose address I recognized at once as the one Jeremy had identified as Swiveller's. We hung back as he opened the door with a key and entered the building. I studied the windows after he had disappeared inside, hoping that the flutter of a curtain or the raising of a sash might alert us to the location of his particular apartment. Alas, it was not to be.

Cécile—not surprisingly—spotted a café down the street. We could not risk taking a table outside. The object of our attention might spot us, either from his window or if he left his abode and walked past. We found a spot, just inside, that afforded us a reasonable view of the entrance to the building, while shielding us from prying eyes. With *chocolat* (for me) and coffee (for Cécile) to strengthen our resolve, we sat and waited.

"What exactly are we waiting for?" Cécile was on her third cup of coffee and beginning to show signs of agitation.

"We want him to leave the building. If he does, and if we can determine that his destination is one from which he does not intend to quickly return, we can speak to the concierge."

"Monsieur Hargreaves was most adamant that we ought not—"

"We will be risking nothing if we are certain he will not return and find us in the building. This is an opportunity, Cécile, of which we must take full advantage."

"Yes, but won't the concierge tell him we—"

"I will not be dissuaded." Cécile knew when my resolve was implacable. She said nothing else to stop me. An hour and half later, the man emerged from his home or place of work or whatever it was, a gaily wrapped parcel in his hand. I cautioned Cécile to remain where she was and followed him. He had not gone far before he boarded a double-decker *impériale,* one of the omnibuses that provided transport throughout the city.

Unable to conceal my excitement when I returned to Cécile at the café, I all but dragged her from her seat. "The way is clear!"

While she agreed that all signs suggested he was unlikely to return home with great expedience, she pointed out that this also suggested we could take the little time required to pay our bill. I did not display a great deal of patience while she handled the transaction, although it almost certainly had not taken so long as it felt it did. While I waited, I realized we needed a strategy, and I came up what I still believe to have been a reasonable one.

At the auburn-haired man's building, we rang for the concierge. Cécile, speaking German, shouted at the tiny woman who appeared at the door, demanding that she be taken to her niece at once. The concierge let this torrent of words descend upon her with little, if any notice. When Cécile paused for breath, the concierge spoke.

"I have no idea who your niece is, madame." Her words, though spoken in French, indicated that she understood German. I had chosen the language as a ruse so that if the concierge mentioned us to the auburn-haired man, she would describe us as residents of that land.

Cécile continued in German, explaining that the young woman had been spirited away from her, by a profligate fortune hunter, while they had been touring the cathedral of Notre-Dame. It was, she said, the third time they had encountered the auburn-haired gentleman, and her niece had grown unaccountably fond of him.

The concierge shrugged. "I still, Frau Hohensteinbauergrunewald"—Cécile, fond of the name, had adopted it as her *nom de guerre*—"have not the slightest idea as to the identity of your niece. As such, it is impossible for me to tell you whether or not she is here. Furthermore, I do not keep track of everyone who comes in and out of this building. I am a busy woman."

This could be nothing other than a test. I realized it the moment I looked at Cécile's face and recognized the considerable effort she was expending to keep her eyebrows from shooting up to the top of her forehead. There are few, if any, species more surly and less helpful than that of the Parisian concierge, but there was no Parisian better capable than Cécile of handling the moods and prejudices of even the most odious of the breed, and I knew every French bone in her body ached to arch her brows and bend over the little woman, shouting that she knew full well any decent concierge not only kept track of every person crossing the threshold of her building, but also every detail of every person, information that, once in a while, could lead to a great deal of—shall we say—little gifts, intended to offer as incentives for keeping that information private. Instead, she sniffed the air, a look of disgust on her face, and wrinkled her nose. "Was that a cat that just brushed past me?"

"*Mon Dieu!*" The little woman sprang to life, pushing past Cécile toward the street. "Did you see which way he went?"

"I have no interest in feline creatures." Cécile's voice dripped with contempt.

"I am excessively fond of them," I said, my German not so good as Cécile's—it had always proved the most difficult language for me—but passable enough in the circumstances. "He darted straight into the street, but I would not worry if I were you. Cats always find their way home." I hoped these words of encouragement would make her unlikely to suspect this all was a ruse to get her out of the building.

"My niece!" Cécile thundered after the concierge. "Where is the wretched man's apartment?"

"He is not home, so I don't know why it matters. *Quatrième étage. L'ascenseur ne marche pas.*" Of course the lift was not working, and of course he was on the fourth floor. The delight on the concierge's face as she communicated this to us was evident. The door slammed behind her as she went off in pursuit of the cat—a cat that I could plainly hear meowing from inside her owner's loge.

We mounted the winding staircase. Its stone steps were well worn, the iron railing, though ornate and no doubt lovely in its prime, was now a bit rickety, and the black paint covering it was peeling off in large chunks. "How did you know she had a cat?" I asked as we passed the second floor. "I did not hear it until after she had set off in search of it."

"Kallista, all concierges in Paris have cats. It is practically a requirement of the job, coming just after a bad disposition and a dedication to nosiness."

As we reached the top of the fourth flight of stairs, breathless, I pulled out of my reticule a small set of tools Colin had purchased for me, and taught me how to use, some years earlier. "Do you think this is a good idea, Kallista?" Cécile looked nervously down the stairs as I began to work on the door's lock.

"If we see the concierge again, we can tell her we slid a note under the door. No one will ever know we were inside. Unless—" The door flew open and I saw no point in completing my thought. The apartment was modestly furnished, with objects that spoke to bourgeois tastes without a matching budget. Everything was a little shabbier than one would want. The carpet in the sitting room was almost threadbare in the center, and in the dining room only three chairs were placed around a table that would easily have seated twelve. There was a small kitchen and a single bedroom as well, and Cécile took to searching those while I perused the bookcase in the sitting room. Not surprisingly, it contained a set of the works of Mr. Dickens, in English. Only one novel was missing: *David Copperfield.* I had no doubt the copy we had found in Mr. Magwitch's room at the George would be a perfect match for the rest of the set.

Many people cannot resist the urge to write their names in their books. *David Copperfield* had not been so marred, but I checked the volumes here, to no avail. Alongside the Dickens was a bible—the King James translation—two issues of *Mercure de France,* a literary magazine, and a well-worn English translation of a thick book about the exploration of Egypt written by Giovanni Battista Belzoni, the former circus strongman turned archaeologist whose techniques could be generously described as barbarous. I recognized the walking stick balanced in the corner near the door as the one I had seen hanging on the back of the auburn-haired man's chair in Café de Flore, and a chill went down my spine at the thought of having invaded the notorious criminal's private space.

Perhaps it was an exaggeration to consider him a notorious criminal, but to my mind, it was a fitting description. A cursory search of the rest of the apartment provided little illumination of its owner. He had three suits (counting the one he was wearing when he left the building), only one spare pair of boots, and nothing of any value other than his small collection of books. His kitchen, not surprisingly, showed no signs of ever having been used. He would not know how to cook, and did not appear to have the money to hire even a single servant. He would have made a habit of dining out in those sad little haunts frequented by bachelors of limited means. I could not muster any sympathy for him.

Cécile, who had finished with what she considered to be her part of the task, was now following close behind me. "I think we ought to go now, Kallista. We cannot risk him returning to find us here. Or, for that matter, the concierge."

"The concierge is not going to go up all those steps, but what would it matter if she did? She knew this was our destination. She sent us here." I looked around the apartment one more time, and then went back to the wardrobe in the bedroom, checking the contents of the pockets in the overcoat that hung inside. In one, I found a ticket for the boat train from London to Paris—when he had returned after leaving the George, no doubt. When I let the coat fall back into place, I saw that the bottom hem had got caught on something. I knelt down. I had already noticed the spare blankets folded and stored in the back of the wardrobe, but they did not come up high enough to impede the coat. I reached behind them, and felt something cold and hard.

"Cécile, I am most alarmed." I pulled out a doll, her face, hands, and boots made from fine porcelain. Her eyes, that opened and closed, were emerald green, as was her silk dress, trimmed with lace. My friend, who had been looking out the window, watching, I suppose, for the auburn-haired man, turned and blanched when she saw what I held.

"Mon Dieu!" She clutched at her throat and collapsed. I rushed to her side, and found that she had not fainted—I would not have expected her to—but the shock had, she explained, made jelly of her knees. "He has killed Estella, has he not?"

"I have the gravest concerns," I said. Cécile's upset was evident. She blinked away tears and lifted her chin, virtuously doing her best to banish all outward signs of emotion. For a moment, I could have believed her to be English. I, on the other hand, had grown angry on her behalf, and the feeling emboldened me. "I have had enough of this man." I ripped a blank sheet from my notebook and scrawled on it a single sentence before leaving it in the center of the dining room table:

I KNOW WHERE TO FIND YOU, TOO.

Estella

XVI

Estella was ready for her captor when he arrived. She was sitting, fully dressed, on the stone slab, *A Tale of Two Cities* on her lap. He smiled when he saw her, and she could read the relief evident on his face. "It is all taken care of now. My debt is paid, and I wish there were some way, my dear Mademoiselle Lamar, that I might be able to express the deep, deep thanks I owe you. I have brought what I hope is a rather spectacular picnic by way of celebrating. I will be leaving Paris tonight, but before I depart, I will deliver to your house the letter explaining how you may be rescued. I thought that in order to reassure you, I would leave the trapdoor open when I go. Obviously, I will have to pull up the ladder—"

"You do owe me thanks, that is true, and there is something I require from you in return," Estella said, wringing her hands. "I find myself, after so many days in captivity, quite terrified at the prospect of returning to my ordinary life. I realize this sounds peculiar, but to repay me for what you have done, I want you to let me stay here, just for a few more days, so that I might be able to reenter the world better prepared."

"You want to stay here?"

"Just for a few days—a week at the most. Surely this will not prove inconvenient to you."

"I have already booked passage—"

"That can be canceled. Picking a different ship is much less inconvenient than having been kidnapped, is it not?" Estella asked.

"Well, I—"

"That is all we need say on the subject." She looked through the contents of the new picnic basket. "You have done very well, but there are a few more things I require. You do have a writing instrument, I hope?" Incapable of coherent response, he gave her a pencil. She tore a blank page out from the back of *A Tale of Two Cities*. "I shall make you a list. First, I must have macarons from Ladurée. Rose and strawberry are my favorites, but I would like a nice assortment, and a new box each day. Second, apples, but I will need cutlery to be able to eat them as a civilized person does. Now that you are doing me a favor, and allowing me to stay rather than keeping me here against my will, you can let me have a knife and fork. I promise not to stab you. And books I am in desperate need of more." She continued on in this manner, giving him specific instructions explaining everything she was writing.

"Mademoiselle, this isn't right. How can I keep you—"

"Only for a few days. Come see me tomorrow with everything on my list. What time is convenient? I want to know when to expect you."

"Six-thirty generally works well." His voice was hesitant, confused, and his eyes clouded. Estella found she enjoyed this. It was, after all, his turn.

"I shall be nearly ready for dinner by then." She took the list back from him and scrawled a few more items on it. "You do have enough money left for all this?"

"Yes, that is not a problem, mademoiselle."

"I suspected the buffer you included for yourself in the cheque you had me write was on the generous side. Still, I do not want to put you out. You might decide to leave me down here if I do. Why don't you return to my house and fetch my entire supply of cheques? That will make things much simpler."

"Mademoiselle Lamar, it would be an honor to pay for whatever you need out of my own funds—"

"They are more my funds than yours, so let's follow my directions now, shall we? Run along and leave me to my picnic. I shall look forward to seeing you tomorrow." She pointed to the list. "Do not forget the books."

17

Colin and Jeremy had not yet arrived back at Cécile's when we returned from our adventures at Mr. Swiveller's residence. This gave me time to consider the best approach to explaining to my husband why I had decided to go to the apartment despite his insistence that I keep away—and then I remembered, he had not said to avoid the apartment altogether. He had merely balked at my idea of applying to the concierge for information about the availability of lodging in the building. Cécile and I could not be accused of having done that.

Colin did not much appreciate this technical detail, but he admitted that as we had done an admirable job avoiding danger, he had no cause to be angry. "You made sound decisions, Emily, and have given us reasonable confirmation that the auburn-haired man, Magwitch, and Swiveller are one and the same. That is an important advance in our case."

"Not to mention that besides being useful, you had a far better time than we did." Jeremy dropped his head against the back of his chair and sighed. "I am going mad with boredom in that post office."

"Is there any merit in continuing to wait for Swiveller there?" I asked. "Surely the train ticket and the doll, along with the supplier having identified the building as Swiveller's place of business, is enough for us to abandon the mail and grab him the next time we can catch him at the apartment?"

"I do not believe he will return there. Your note will have alarmed him, Emily—"

"I had to do something—"

"I understand your anger, and I do not mean to suggest that you have set us back by having written it. You have, however, put him on notice, and he is likely afraid of being caught. This may serve to our benefit, in the manner of flushing him out. We must take extreme caution to ensure neither you nor Cécile is vulnerable to him. Monsieur Pinard's cheque is going to lure him, eventually, to the post office. Do remember that we have no evidence that anything has happened to Estella—"

"But the doll!" Cécile exclaimed. "No bachelor would have such a thing."

"He may have a niece of whom he is extremely fond," Colin said.

"It is possible," I agreed. "But is it likely? I have the deepest suspicions concerning Mr. Swiveller. We know someone has been lying as to Estella's whereabouts, but we do not know what would have motivated the action. When I look at the route she supposedly took from Siam to London, it is as if a person with no knowledge of travel whatsoever had a quick look at a world map and plotted what he—or she—thought seemed to be a reasonable path."

"Estella had almost no experience traveling before her parents died," Cécile said.

"So it could be she who is behind all this. We believe she is currently in Paris—"

"I am certain she was at Père-Lachaise either today or yesterday," Cécile said.

"Anyone could have put that wreath in the tomb," Colin said.

"No." I thought back carefully over our visit to the cemetery.

"The Lamar tomb was locked, was it not? Your husband's wasn't, Cécile—is it usual to lock them?"

"Some people do, others feel the precaution unnecessary."

"Perhaps Estella's steward has a key to the tomb," Jeremy said. "Then she wouldn't have to bother with it at all. Or the florist—why wouldn't she send her man there directly?"

"Estella was devoted to her parents," I said. "She would not have considered taking a wreath to their grave an inconvenience."

"Be that as it may, Bainbridge raises an interesting point. The only piece of firm evidence we have to suggest Mademoiselle Lamar is in Paris is the letter she sent Cécile. We know the handwriting is correct—at least so far as we can tell—and we know it was mailed from Paris. What we do not know is when it was written."

I nodded. "An interesting point. Estella—or someone else—has likely staged any number of communications, in the form of letters, telegrams, and photographs in the newspaper. Swiveller-Magwitch could have arranged every one of these things, but he could not write the letters."

"He might have forced Estella to write a stack of them before killing her." Cécile's voice was flat.

"Estella Lamar has been away from Paris for many, many years," Colin said. "It stretches credulity to suggest that this man—or someone else—has been embezzling money by using, for all that time, letters written under duress."

"I have studied further the notes I took at Monsieur Pinard's," I said. "The payments to Swiveller are the only ones the attorney has made on his client's behalf that seem wildly out of line. The rest of the expenses for the household are ordinary enough. No one in their right mind would spend so much on flowers, even for three houses, and I do not recall seeing a single blossom at Estella's house in Belgravia. Part of Swiveller's money may go for flowers here, but Swiveller's apartment does not suggest he is keeping the rest. Perhaps Monsieur Pinard has a vested interest in paying Swiveller's bills without question."

"Pinard?" Colin's brow crinkled. "He is a well-respected, successful solicitor who does not appear to be living above his means. Furthermore, he could not have killed Mary Darby. He was dining with the American ambassador and a large party the night of the murder. I have confirmed his alibi. Let us do be careful to remember that Mary Darby's death is our primary concern."

"Monsieur Pinard may have been in Paris, but that does not preclude the possibility of his having hired Mr. Swiveller to do the job for him."

Colin threw his hands in the air. "Theoretically possible, of course, but we would need more evidence—no, not more, *some*."

"If neither the solicitor nor this wretched Swiveller isn't keeping the money, where does it go?" Jeremy asked.

Our lively discussion did not continue, being interrupted by a footman who entered and handed me a small parcel. Almost before my hands were on it, Colin had raced from the room. I heard the front door slam behind him and knew he was doing his best to catch the delivery boy. I tugged at the string wrapping the box until I loosened the knot enough to remove it, and opened the lid, recoiling at what I saw: a fine linen handkerchief, edged with Belgian lace, soaked in a dark, sticky substance that could only be blood. A folded sheet of paper, also damp with blood, had typed on it only a single word:

STOP

Cécile gasped, and Jeremy held her firmly by the shoulders. "This does not mean a thing," he said. "That blood could be anyone's."

"I think we must assume it is not just anyone's," I said.

"I do not know what it means, other than that we have no choice but to obey. How can we continue this investigation if, by doing so, we are putting Estella at risk?"

"Cécile, darling, if Estella is in the hands of some madman, the only chance she has to escape from his clutches is for us to continue our work. We have to find her." My friend, visibly shattered, did not wait for Colin to return before retiring upstairs for a bath. I promised to come to her with any news.

Jeremy and I sat together on a settee, the box and its foul contents on a table in front of us. "Do you think she is alive?" he asked.

"I believe she is, and I would stake my life on a bet that Estella Lamar is not booked on a passage to the Ivory Coast or anywhere else. If she is in Paris, and she is alive, why would Swiveller, or whoever is benefiting from her money, want her dead?"

"Why would he have kept her alive this long?" Colin had just returned, and was breathing heavily from his chase. He poured a glass of whisky before he sat down and raised it to the identical one already in Jeremy's hand. "I caught the boy. He was paid in advance with a gold coin and given strict instructions to deliver the box and flee."

"Paid in advance," I said. "What a disappointment."

"Risky as well," Jeremy said.

"Not really." Colin picked up the box containing the bloody handkerchief. "He scared the boy into thinking he would come to great harm if he didn't complete the task as directed, and said he would be watching from afar."

"Was the boy able to describe him?" I asked.

"Yes. It is our old friend, the auburn-haired man. His prominent mustaches make identifying him rather simple—and that is something of which he surely is aware." He held the box up to me. "I presume we are meant to believe this blood is Estella's?"

"I can't imagine what else we would think," I said. "Let us return to Swiveller's apartment at once. I realize he is unlikely to be there, but surely with our accumulated evidence, we can justify using your credentials to make that horrible concierge at least give us the man's real name. French bureaucracy does not allow for taking an apartment using a *nom de guerre*."

"You are quite right, Emily, the French are notoriously strict about such matters. If you only knew what one must do to obtain a bank account here. It is a good plan. I shall set off at once."

I rose to his side. "I shall accompany you."

"No, Cécile is upset and you should remain with her. Bainbridge, can I trust you to guard the ladies?"

"We do not require guarding," I said.

"I will derive considerably more pleasure from watching them than from watching the post office," Jeremy said.

Colin gave him a wry look. "Perhaps it would be better for you to come with me, Bainbridge, on the off chance our friend, if I may call him that, is still in residence."

"You think I can't handle the ladies?"

"I'm more afraid that you'll be too adept at the task." Colin glowered, but the amusement in his dark eyes belied the expression. "You, Emily, take care of Cécile."

He gave me no further instructions—a wise decision, as I have never taken well to direction—and left with Jeremy. I went upstairs to Cécile, who was still submerged in her tub, and spoke to her through the bathroom door. "I cannot think of a single reason that Estella, regardless of where she is in the world, would want Mary Darby dead. There can be no doubt that Swiveller killed her—and most likely because she did not succeed in the job for which he had hired her, playing Estella. Swiveller does not live like a criminal mastermind, but more like an ill-used henchman, so we must deduce that he is acting on behalf of someone else, and who else could that be but Monsieur Pinard?"

I heard the sound of dripping water. "I am coming out, Kallista. It was wrong—and cowardly—of me to say we should heed this awful man's warning. Let us go see Monsieur Pinard. I have realized also that we made a grave error at Swiveller's today. We did not search the attic room that would be assigned to his apartment for a servant. He could have any number of things stashed up there, including Estella."

I had forgot that Parisian apartments generally included space for, at the very least, a maid, and Colin was unlikely to think of it, either. "We must go there at once and catch up with the gentlemen. Monsieur Pinard can wait until we are finished there."

Cécile dressed in near record time, and soon we were in the carriage. When we reached the building, we had to ring repeatedly before the concierge shuffled to the door. "Back so soon, Frau Hohensteinbauergrunewald? Two gentlemen have already been here. Am I to presume they, too, are in search of your niece?" My friend did not dignify this inane question with a response. She shoved past the woman and stomped up the stairs, ignoring the piercing shrieks demanding that she stop. I followed, avoiding eye contact as I passed.

From the fourth-floor landing, I could see that the door to Swiveller's apartment stood open. I called out to my husband as we crossed the threshold, but he did not answer. Inside, there was no sign either of him or of Jeremy. The scene that greeted me set my heart racing. The dining chairs had been overturned, the lamp in the sitting room lay shattered on the floor, and there was a hole crashed through the front window that could only be described as head-shaped. Blood stained the shards beneath it on the carpet. Cécile gripped my hand. "Come, let us see what is in the bedroom."

That room, as well as the kitchen, appeared in every way wholly undisturbed. Whatever action had transpired, it had been limited to the sitting and dining rooms. My lips quivered. "We should check the attic room first and then go back to the concierge."

"I will go up," Cécile said. "There is no need for two of us—"

"No." I pulled myself up to my full height. "I am coming with you, no matter what is to be found." I followed my friend through the back door off the kitchen and up a narrow set of stairs that wound up to the eaves. Cécile found the room whose number matched the one on Swiveller's apartment, and rapped on the door. There was no answer. She turned the handle.

"It is locked."

I had the set of picks in my reticule, but did not want to waste time using them. I flung myself against the door, confident that the force of the strike would break it down. My aspirations, however, fell somewhat short of reality. I picked myself up from the floor where I had fallen after bouncing off the door, retrieved my tools, and picked the lock with shaking hands. I closed my eyes as I pushed on the door, terrified of what I might see.

A sigh escaped Cécile's lips. *"Mon Dieu."*

I forced my eyes open. The light from the corridor spilled into the small room. The bloodied bodies of neither Colin nor Jeremy were inside, only a desk heaped with voluminous amounts of paper, a filing cabinet, and an enormous rat, chewing on an unidentified but unarguably motley object. That the rodent did not scurry off the moment we entered the room suggested it was all too familiar with humans, so I stamped on the floor as hard as I could. He looked up at me with his beady eyes and slunk into a hole in the knotty wood of the floor. The room, unlike the corridor, did not have electric lights, but there was an old-fashioned oil lamp on the desk, and a box of matches next to it. I entered the room and struck a match. Once illuminated, the lamp's light spread over the surface of the desk, but not much beyond.

A cursory glance at the papers sent a shiver through me. There were notes about hotels in Bombay and Constantinople and more other places than I could count, as well as contact details for Mary Darby. I picked up the paper that listed her address and her banking details. "He killed her. There can be no doubting that now. As for Estella . . . I am afraid, Cécile, that we need to try to find Colin and Jeremy before we peruse these papers in detail. The blood on the glass downstairs—"

"I understand." Without having to be asked, Cécile started to gather up the papers in her arms, carrying as much as she could. We could not take everything. The filing cabinet was locked, and I did not want to waste time on it when the most precious— But I could not think of that now. We carried the papers down to the concierge's loge.

The Parisian part of Cécile—to be fair, that was all of her—could no longer tolerate dealing with the concierge as she had up until now. She abandoned her pretense of being German as she shoved the collected papers at the woman and spoke in a tone that would have chilled the blood of the most vicious reprobate. "You will guard these papers with your life. Hide them in your little hovel and give them to no one but us when we return. Where did the gentlemen go?"

"They were drunk and disgusting." The concierge sneered. "Monsieur Jones's friend could barely hold himself upright. It was a spectacle I hope never to see repeated in this building."

"What about the other man?" I asked.

"Monsieur Jones was holding him up. Was I not clear enough for you?"

"And the third man?" Truly, this woman was infuriating. I felt a most inappropriate urge to fling her on the floor and stomp on her until she told me what I needed to know.

"There were only the two of them. I told you as much when you stormed into the building. *Two gentlemen,* I said. I will keep these papers, but if you have not collected them by noon tomorrow—"

"You will keep them as long as I see fit," Cécile growled. "Now. Which direction did they go when they left the building? Do not pretend you didn't look."

"I never said they left the building, did I?" The concierge scowled. A large brindled cat peeked his head out the door, looked dissatisfied with what he saw, and retreated inside.

"They are not upstairs," I said. "We were just there."

She shrugged. "If you hadn't been so rude when you came, I might have told you not to bother with the stairs. It's your husband, isn't it? Can't hold his drink, can he, though I suppose you're used to that. They're in the courtyard, no doubt hoping the night air would sober them up."

Wasting no time, we darted through the foyer and out the back door to what, if well tended, would have been a lovely garden instead of an overgrown mess. There was a wrought-iron table and four chairs on paving stones, but no sign of Colin or Jeremy. Eyewitness testimony is notoriously unreliable, even when the witness in question is trying his best to tell the truth, but I found it hard to believe the concierge could be so very wrong. We went back to confront her.

"They are not in the courtyard, and they are not upstairs, which means they must have left the building."

The concierge narrowed her eyes. "They did not leave the building."

She was impossible. "You must not have noticed them, which is odd considering that their alleged drunkenness supposedly disturbed you so very much. Please try to remember—they came down the steps, and they—"

"And they went into the courtyard. That is all." She stepped back into her loge and slammed the door. Either she was lying, confused, or had not been paying attention. Cécile and I went back into the street, crossed it, and stood looking at Mr. Jones's building, unsure of where to go next. I hesitated, then started to walk east. Before we had covered fifty yards, I heard a familiar voice, moaning.

"Em? Is that you, Em?"

Jeremy, blood drying on his forehead, was lying in the dark, hidden from the pavement by a large planter containing an immaculately trimmed shrub. He moaned again and reached up to me. "What happened to you?" I dropped to my knees next to him.

"It doesn't matter now," he said. "You must find Hargreaves. He has Hargreaves."

Estella

Estella could not remember when she had passed so many pleasant days in a row. Her captor—but she must not call him that any longer—Monsieur Jones had proved a reliable supplier, well able to follow directions. He came with macarons every day before seven o'clock, along with whatever else she had instructed him to bring. Today, she had even had hot coffee, as he had carried it directly to her after it had been made in a nearby café. She had finished reading Jean-François Champollion's *Monuments de l'Égypte et de la Nubie,* an account of that explorer's journey through the land of the pharaohs, a place to which Estella was becoming more and more attached. Monsieur Jones had brought more Dickens as well, but she had not yet perused any of that.

She had hung tapestries on her stone walls—not the best quality, but it was proving a tad difficult to get Monsieur Jones to spend her money freely—and she now had a chair, as well as plates and cups and cutlery. "You should join me for a glass of wine," she said as he descended the ladder.

"Mademoiselle Lamar, it has been three days now. You are going to have to leave soon. Shall we make a plan? I am of the opinion that you might feel more comfortable if you knew what, precisely, you wanted to do once you have left this—"

"Prison? Were you going to say prison, Monsieur Jones? An apt description, but one that no longer fits quite so neatly as it once did."

"I have come to the conclusion that it might be better if I plan to take you home myself. I do believe I can trust you not to alert the police, can I not? You are fragile after this experience, and there is no one to blame for that but me. I cannot in good conscience leave you down here waiting to be rescued."

"I have very little interest in going home," Estella said.

"Well, I can take you wherever you want. You have a house in the south, is that correct?"

"It is as boring as the one here. I long for adventure, Monsieur Jones." She waved her two books about Egypt in front of him. "Messieurs Belzoni and Champollion have lit inside me a fire."

"You would like to go to Egypt?" He balked at first, but then considered the idea. It was not the worst he had ever heard.

"First, I must read more, so that I might plan a suitable itinerary."

Monsieur Jones nodded. "I shall gather all the information I can about ships and hotels and guides. Is there anything else?"

"At the moment, no, unless you would care to join me for wine?"

He refused the offer, and took from her the list she now gave him daily. "No macarons this time?"

"Three days, apparently, is what it takes for me to grow tired of them. I am asking for chocolates instead, and I should like coq au vin for dinner tomorrow."

"Very well." He disappeared up the ladder. Estella opened the notebook he had brought her the day before yesterday and sat, not on the chair, but on the slab, so that she might have both of her Egyptian tomes by her side as she started to write:

ALEXANDRIA

She drew a line under the name of the city and then wrote:

WE WILL BEGIN HERE.

18

He has Hargreaves.

I kept hearing Jeremy's words over and over in my head and could barely manage to focus. All of the world had narrowed for me, and there was nothing but a long, dark tunnel, at the end of which I was destined to find my husband, gravely injured, if not dead—

I felt a sharp slap on my cheek. "Forgive me, Kallista, but you were insensible." I shook the pain away and nodded to indicate there were no hard feelings; Cécile had, after all, forced me to regain my much-needed composure.

"What happened?" I asked Jeremy. "No, first, how badly are you hurt?"

"There is no cause for concern regarding my health, and, unfortunately, there is very little more I can tell you. When we arrived at the building, Hargreaves instructed me to stay outside and watch for our cursed villain. If I saw him, I was to shout and raise an alarm. Hargreaves went inside, and I presume was able to gain access to the apartment, as he did not return again in short order. Furthermore, from my post I could see the light go on in the front room on the fourth floor. I saw Hargreaves in the window and saluted him from here. A moment later, I felt a large crash of pain in my skull, accompanied by what I can only describe as a decidedly sickening thud. Everything went black as I fell to the ground, and I remember nothing else."

Jones—for there could be no doubt as to the identity of Jeremy's assailant—must have spotted my friend watching the building and panicked. But what had happened to Colin? "He must have found Colin inside and somehow managed to—"

Still squatting next to Jeremy, I rose to my feet, wanting to scream, but as I am a rational person, I knew this would accomplish nothing. "We know they were both in the apartment. We know they fought—the state of the rooms and the broken window make that much clear. One of them was injured, and the other more or less dragged him downstairs and past the concierge, who assumed they were drunk."

Cécile had pulled Jeremy up from the ground, and the two of them stood in front of me, silent. I started nodding, too quickly, as the words spilled from my mouth. "If Colin had vanquished his opponent, he would have incapacitated him and come for you, Jeremy, which means that we must operate on the assumption that it is Colin who was dragged down the stairs." Tears were smarting in my eyes.

Jeremy took my hand, stood directly in front of me, and tipped my chin up until I was looking him directly in the eye. "We are going to the police, Em, and I promise they will find him. You know he would never let himself come to any serious harm, because then you would be left on your own and wholly incapable of fending off my advances. We all know Hargreaves would never stand for that."

I sniffed. Cécile put her arm around my shoulders. "He is right. Monsieur Hargreaves would never leave you to suffer that sort of indignation. Nonetheless, we may as well arrange for his rescue sooner rather than later, so let us go at once to the police."

Reason was beginning to return to me. "We do need them, I agree with you both there, but we cannot leave it all to them. Cécile, can you manage summoning them on your own? I want to search the building again. The concierge, unreliable though she might be, was adamant that they didn't leave the courtyard." Neither of them was prepared to argue with me, and Cécile set off at once.

The blue tinge of twilight engulfed us as Jeremy and I returned to the house. We had to bang on the door repeatedly—the concierge ignored the bell—and did not gain entry until Jeremy, blood still oozing from his forehead, rapped on the concierge's window. "I say, good woman, I am the Duke of Bainbridge, come to collect my friend, who I believe has caused something of a commotion this evening. Would you be so kind as to let me in?"

She opened the door, but only six inches, and stuck her thin nose through the gap. "I've had quite enough of this lady." She glared at me.

"And I have had quite enough of you." For the second time, I flung myself against a door, this time meeting with more success. My action sent the concierge flying across the foyer, where she landed in an inglorious heap. I paid her little attention as I stormed past her, back into the courtyard. "Where can they be?"

"Not here," Jeremy said, pressing his handkerchief to the gash on his head to stop the bleeding. There was only the single entrance to the building's outdoor space, and nothing but windows on the walls. After thoroughly searching every inch of it, I rushed back into the foyer and stormed through the open door of the concierge's loge. Cécile was inside with the woman.

"The police are on their way," Cécile said. "I telephoned them from the café."

I thanked her and then stood in front of the concierge. "Did you see them go into the courtyard? Actually see them? Or did you merely assume that is where they went?"

"I heard them on the stairs. It was quite a commotion. I was sitting here in my chair"—she spat the words—"and you can observe well enough for yourself that had they left the building, they would have passed directly in front of me." The chair was situated so that she had a clear view of the entrance.

Feeling as if I were going mad, I returned to the foyer and then the sensation of madness gave way to that of revelation. Next to the elevator, on the opposite side from the stairs, around a small corner so that it was just out of sight, stood an iron door, almost medieval in its design, which looked better suited to a castle dungeon than an apartment building. I had not noticed it before. Jeremy, a step behind me, took me by the arm.

"Allow me," he said, and swung open the portal. Narrow stone stairs descended into the dark, which meant we had to return to the concierge for candles (fortunately for us, Cécile had the woman now well under her thumb) before beginning our descent. The room at the bottom was dank and dusty and full of a motley collection of boxes and trunks that looked as if they had been abandoned in some earlier century. Though we listened carefully, we heard no sound but that of our own breath. I raised my candle above my head and went to the center, where I stood and turned slowly and methodically, looking for anything that might provide a clue as to my husband's fate.

The dust of the floor was disturbed, suggesting that ours were not the only feet to have recently trod on it, but there was no clear path marked in it. Once I had made a complete rotation without noticing anything else amiss, I closed my eyes to focus my attention—all the while ignoring the pounding in my chest—and then opened them to repeat the endeavor. This time, I did not stay in the middle, but walked the perimeter, and noticed a stack of boxes that had fallen over. I kicked them aside, only to find a heavy trunk directly in front of me, more boxes piled on top of it. A handprint stood out in the dust on the dark leather of the trunk. Jeremy lifted the boxes off the trunk, the pile reaching above the top of his head, but he managed, with my assistance, to deposit them on the floor without dropping them. Our candles struggled against the unrelieved darkness as we turned back to the trunk. Now that the boxes were gone, we could see the outline of a door on the wall behind it.

Jeremy bent to move the trunk, but I was too impatient to wait for that. I reached over him and pushed against the door, finding, fortunately, that it swung in the opposite direction from the trunk and was unhindered by its proximity to the luggage. We scrambled over the top and entered into a tunnel whose Stygian darkness swallowed us. Terrified, but bent on finding Colin, we followed it as it meandered beneath the city.

I had read about the network of tunnels beneath the city, and knew how extensive it was, but until now I had not appreciated just how extensive. After walking for what felt like miles, the passage twisting and turning, we reached a junction. "Which way?" I asked. I closed my eyes and struggled to hear anything that might indicate the path Colin and his attacker had taken, but could hear nothing except the occasional rustle of rodents. I sighed. "The only thing to do is try one direction, and if we find nothing, come back and go the other. I do not think it would be wise to investigate separately."

"Absolutely not," Jeremy agreed.

"We should make some sort of mark so that we can find our way back." The mere act of entertaining the possibility of getting lost made me feel as if the walls, carved out of the city's bedrock, were pressing in against us. I reached down for a rock and struck it against the wall of the passage that led back to the entrance, but it did not leave a mark, so I tore a strip of fabric from my petticoat, rent it into three pieces, and laid them along the edge of the wall.

"I always thought, Em, that I'd feel rather a different sensation if I ever saw you removing your petticoat." I appreciated his attempt at humor even as he slumped against the side of the passage, his face alarmingly pale.

"Right or left?" I asked. He made no reply. I took his hand in mine and pulled him to the right.

Right proved wrong. After traversing a distance of approximately seventy-five yards, we reached a dead end, and were forced to retrace our steps. This time, we meandered for a goodly distance, and I was beginning to feel extremely disoriented. Panic pushed against my chest. Jeremy, recognizing this, squeezed my hand, and we continued on, our candles doing their best to fight the smothering darkness. At the next junction, there were three paths from which to choose. I ripped my petticoat again, and again used strips of fabric to mark the way from which we had come.

"Let's make a practice of always choosing the passage the farthest on the left to begin," I said. There was no reason for this decision, but I felt it incumbent on me to attempt as organized and controlled an assault on these tunnels as possible. If we did, eventually, get confused and lost, having followed a rational and consistent system would prove helpful. This time, my first guess was a good one, and we did not reach a dead end, but as we continued along the narrow path, I worried that either of the two we had not taken might have been a better choice. We went back to the junction, and explored the other two, both of which went only a short distance before ending. From this, I drew the conclusion that we could reasonably assume there to be one main route through the tunnels, with shorter, subsidiary ones splitting off. So long as we did not reach a dead end, we were headed—headed where? And headed to what?

Our candles flickered and I blew mine out, not wanting to have no light waiting for us in reserve. The passage turned and then ended sharply at a staircase cut into the rock. We descended it, and at the bottom, met with a horrible sight. Bones—human bones, mostly femurs—covered the floor, almost a foot deep. "We must be at the Catacombs," I said.

"I don't think we should walk over them." Jeremy winced and sat on a step.

"I'm afraid we must." I took his candle and bent over, illuminating the pathetic remains beneath us to reveal a channel of sorts that crossed through the bones, as if they had been pushed apart. "Someone else has already made his way through here." Gingerly, I stepped into the pile, doing my best to disturb the bones as little as possible, and tasting bile every time I heard one crunch beneath my feet.

I still had the candle, and Jeremy was just behind me. The passageway widened and then grew suddenly narrow before ending at another set of steps. We descended, thankful for the absence of bones on them. At the bottom of these steps was a large, circular room. Femurs, stacked one on top of another, their ends pointing to the center of the chamber, lined the walls, and in front of their eerie display were more bones, these crushed and fragmented. We followed a passage out of this room, which snaked around for a while, the ceilings considerably lower, until we saw letters carved on the wall: *Chemin du Port Mahon*. Beyond this, someone had made elaborate carvings in the stone walls. The scene looked like a medieval citadel with no detail forgot. I stopped, just for a moment, in front of a depiction of an ornate building over which the words *Quartier de Cazerne* had been carved, and stood very still.

"Did you hear that?" I whispered. Jeremy shook his head and silently raised a finger to his lips. "There—again." It was unmistakable this time. This was not the rustle of a small animal, this was something much larger, and it sounded as if it—he?—were moving rocks. We crept in the direction of the noise, exiting the room with its carved walls and entering an extremely narrow passageway that went down two steps before turning hard to the right. From here, no fewer than five tunnels presented themselves to us. The noise grew louder, and became clearer. It was not someone moving rocks; it was someone moving something against them. I raised my candle and stepped into the passage from which it came, following twists and turns until I saw my husband, his chiseled features bruised and battered, his wrists and ankles bound. His arms had been wrenched behind his back, and he was methodically rubbing the rope around his wrists against a bit of the wall that jutted out enough to create a hard edge.

"Colin!" I fell upon him at once, covering his face with kisses before removing from my reticule the penknife I always carried with me. My hands were shaking so much I did not trust myself to free him from his bonds without further injuring his dear person, so I gave the knife to Jeremy, who made neat work of it. Colin's wrists were bloody and raw, and he winced as the rope fell to the ground.

"Did you see him?" he asked.

"No," I replied. "What happened?"

"He found me in his rooms and we fought. I had the advantage, but he managed to throw himself across the room and make his way into his bedroom. He bolted the door behind him. I was ready for him when he opened it, only a few minutes later, but now our struggle was not so evenhanded. He had soaked a rag with chloroform—the bottle must have been in his bedroom—and held it over my face long enough to incapacitate me. I have vague memories of being dragged through darkness, but not much else. I take it we are in the Catacombs?"

I replied in the affirmative and helped him to his feet. Jones, no doubt, had long since made his escape. "I do not think he meant you serious harm," I said. "We are not so far from the main route through the path taken by tourists that your struggles would have gone unnoticed."

"There are only tours of the Catacombs twice a month, Em," Jeremy said.

"And one of them was yesterday," I said. "Thank heavens you were not left down here for a fortnight. This Jones is not quite so clever as he thinks. It was a grave error to take you someplace so easily located from his own residence." I wanted to keep the mood light. "Now then, let's make our way back. Cécile will be beside herself with worry and will not enjoy having to manage the police by herself."

We retraced our steps back past the carved citadel, the cavern of bones, and up the stairs. Colin nodded his approval when he saw the shreds of my petticoat marking our way. "Good thinking, my dear." We lit my reserved candle long before we reached the cellar, and when, at last, we came to the still-open door, our return was greeted by a gaggle of disgruntled-looking policemen.

"Worthless," Cécile said. "They are all worthless." One uniformed officer helped me over the trunk that blocked the door. "I couldn't even persuade them to move that, let alone go after you."

A rough voice called down from the top of the stairs. "You had better hope you have not damaged anything! I will not tolerate the destruction of property!" I am not ashamed to say that Colin had to physically prevent me from doing bodily harm to the infuriating concierge. She is fortunate he was there to protect her.

Estella

xviii

The train to Marseille would take almost no time, and from there, one had only to catch a steamer to Alexandria, from where—Estella consulted the guidebook Monsieur Jones had brought to her the day before—they would travel by train to Cairo. She would have to hire a companion and order some suitable traveling clothes, but neither of those tasks would prove problematic. She began a letter to her dressmaker, but found herself so distracted by the thought of the Great Pyramids at Giza that she could not focus on writing an orderly set of directions for the woman.

Putting aside her missive, she opened Monsieur Belzoni's book, and spent a blissful four hours making a list of every site he mentioned that she intended to visit, pausing frequently to consult her other Egyptian books, and adding sketches to the margins of her list. The sketches, and her inability to satisfactorily reproduce the complicated hieroglyphic signs, frustrated her. Tomorrow she would ask Monsieur Jones if he could get his hands on a copy of Monsieur Champollion's *Grammaire Égyptienne,* which was referred to her in travel book as including a list of all the signs. She wondered if it might include instructions on how to draw them.

"I would not trouble myself with such a task now," Monsieur

Jones said the next evening. She had persuaded him to have a glass of wine. "I will, of course, find the *Grammaire* for you, and you can dedicate yourself to the study of it on the boat to Alexandria."

"That is an excellent idea." Estella drained her glass and refilled it. "I am beginning to think, Monsieur Jones, that you ought to accompany me on my journey."

"I could not—"

"Do not reject the idea out of hand. I was rather fond of you before you flung me in here, and you have taken good enough care of me for these past days—weeks?—how long have I been away?"

"It is a approaching a fortnight now, mademoiselle."

"I will hire a companion, of course, as it would not be proper to travel, unaccompanied, with a man. I am of the opinion that your presence could prove most useful. You are capable of handling baggage, I imagine?" He mumbled some sort of incoherent reply. "I will take you on as a member of my staff."

"If you require the services of a companion, mademoiselle, you will want to interview candidates. Would you like me to place an advertisement for you? You could arrange to meet applicants at your house starting at the end of the week."

"I shall do that as soon as I have finalized our itinerary. May I count on you to make one of the party?"

"I could hardly deny you anything, Mademoiselle Lamar, after what I have done to you."

"Very good," Estella said. "Tomorrow I will give you a letter to post to my dressmaker. I will need you to buy new trunks for me—ones from Galeries Lafayette will do nicely—have them delivered to her so she can pack the clothes directly into them and send them to the train station. If all goes smoothly, we could be steaming across the Mediterranean in only a few weeks. I have never before so looked forward to anything in my life."

Monsieur Jones smiled. "I am most glad to hear it. If there is nothing else . . ." He started for the ladder.

"One more thing, Monsieur Jones. I would like another doll, please. One with blond hair this time, I think, and dressed in a traveling costume. Would that be too much trouble?"

"It will be my pleasure."

19

The clock struck midnight long before we arrived back at Cécile's. Both Colin's and Jeremy's injuries appeared superficial, but—despite their protestations—I required them to submit to the examination of a physician. The police, after very firm direction from us, agreed to make as comprehensive as possible a search of the Catacombs, but not until the following morning. If I had not suspected Mr. Jones had long since made his getaway, I would have demanded they start immediately, but given the battered condition of our gentlemen, I agreed that a period of a few hours of rest would be advisable.

As for myself, no matter how I tried, I could not lure Morpheus to me that night, and I abandoned the pursuit once the golden pink streaks of sunrise began to pierce the dark sky. I took care to dress quietly, and obviously did not call for Meg at such an early hour. After splashing cold water onto my face in the bathroom attached to our room (Cécile viewed en suite baths as essential to civilized life), I slipped into the corridor and down to the first floor. No one else in the household was yet awake. I pulled open the curtains in the grand front sitting room and looked out the window. The street was quiet, only a few lonely pedestrians and a dissatisfied-looking cat on the pavement.

The room was still a mess from the commotion caused by our arrival. Head wounds, even when they are not serious, bleed profusely, and Jeremy had left a dark red smear on the golden upholstery of the chaise longue onto which he had collapsed before making his way upstairs. A trail of smut and gritty dirt had followed him, Colin, and me from the Catacombs, and Cécile, seeing no use in more people losing sleep, had ordered the servants to leave it until morning. I tiptoed around the worst of it, not wanting to spread it further. A policeman, following my orders, had deposited on a table the large stack of papers we had taken from the attic of Mr. Jones's apartment. I scooped them up and took them to what Cécile called the *petit bureau,* a cozy room tucked almost underneath the curving staircase. Paintings of Venice flanked the dark gray marble mantelpiece.

To start, I sorted through the papers, dividing them into stacks surrounding me on the red silk settee that matched the walls. There were scores of travel itineraries—Estella's, as her name was written on all of them, along with that of her companion, Miss Hexam—dating back for at least five years. I unrolled a crushed world map, larger than the one we had marked up in the library, that was covered with smudged red scrawls, made with a wax pencil, the sort one used for marking porcelain. The similarities between it and our own attempt at tracking Estella's voyages were not inconsiderable. This one, however, included more stops and lines that I could only presume were intended to mark the path of her journey. There were lists of hotels, names of individuals—many I recognized as having received payments of £10 from Monsieur Pinard—and more train and boat timetables than I knew existed on the earth.

Then, in the midst of all these papers, I found a slim softbound notebook, filled with handwriting now familiar to me: Estella's. I started at the first page:

ALEXANDRIA

WE WILL BEGIN HERE.

What followed were detailed plans for a trip from the city of the great Alexander (I could not remember if he had ever actually visited there, or if it was merely one of the many named in his honor) to Cairo, and on from there, to Giza, up the Nile and to the Valley of the Kings. Estella had recorded the opening times of various monuments, and had filled the margins of the book with sketches, most of them the sights she had seen in the ancient land of the pharaohs. After the first few pages, which were primarily dedicated to travel details, the book began to take on the form of a diary, recording her adventures. It was written in a style similar to most travel memoirs, self-indulgent and grandiose, but there was a charming naïveté to Estella's narration. As well as frequent references to Miss Hexam (who proved a most excellent companion), there were many to someone called Hettie. Hettie was frequently described as being dragged from place to place, was never recorded as having a thought or idea of her own, and, after Estella discussed putting her on a high shelf after she had been intolerably surly on a day when the sun had been particularly strong, I came to the obvious conclusion that she must be one of Estella's dolls.

Mr. Jones was mentioned, but only frequently in the first quarter of the volume. She called him an excellent man and a stalwart supporter, and so far as I could tell, he had accompanied her at least so far as Cairo. I skimmed through the remaining pages, which ended abruptly with the announcement of Estella's intention to depart for India and also of her intention to send Mr. Jones home. There was no hint in her tone, no veiled suggestion, that she had grown disaffected with the man; she did not explain her decision. As I closed the book, I could not help but wonder the circumstances in which a young lady—for Estella would not have been so old as I when she wrote these pages—would decide to give her diary, full of tender and personal feelings and observations, over to the care of a young man? Nothing she had written suggested she harbored romantic feelings for him. Quite the contrary, she appeared to treat him—appropriately—like a valued servant, and because of this, finding the book among his things did not sit well with me. Mr. Jones should never have been in possession of it.

Evidently, Mr. Jones had returned to Paris, not England—which I surmised to be his true home—and continued to keep close tabs on his former employer. I consulted my own notebook to check the date on which Monsieur Pinard had started to write cheques to Swiveller, our erstwhile florist. The payments had begun only a few weeks after Estella's initial departure from France. Perhaps I had leaped to a hasty conclusion when I had decided that Mr. Jones and Swiveller were one and the same. Thinking about it, I did not recall seeing Mr. Jones listed anywhere, ever, in Monsieur Pinard's ledgers, but surely Estella had been paying him while he had been with her in Egypt? Nothing about Mr. Jones's situation suggested he could afford to travel abroad. I would have to check the solicitor's records again. If Estella had never paid him, it could be that his situation had changed, but had he been a gentleman of means when they met, she would not have written about him in the manner she had. I laid the diary aside and continued to make my way through the remaining papers. Among them was a brittle envelope, stuffed with five thin sheets of paper, each containing directions for telegrams. The first read:

NOT STAYING AT SHEPHEARD'S IN CAIRO BUT
CAN RECEIVE MAIL THERE UNTIL THE BOAT SAILS.
DESPAIR NOT IF I DON'T REPLY!

It was addressed to Monsieur Pinard at his office and written in Estella's handwriting. The other four messages were equally innocuous, and I could not imagine why Mr. Jones would have saved them. Unless—an idea gripped me. What if Mr. Jones had harbored romantic notions about his employer? He had served her admirably, but when she learned of his affections and inclinations, she could have done nothing but reject him. Stung, he stole her diary—hoping, no doubt, to find some tender reference to himself—and fled the country. He might have remained in touch with Miss Hexam, although she, too, was most likely of too high a station to entertain him as anything beyond a servant. Through her, he could have tracked Estella's every move, growing more and more obsessed with her as the years passed.

That could not explain why he would have such detailed records of her travels. Miss Hexam—I had already decided she was reliable, though boring—would never have agreed to reveal her employer's plans to someone who had been dismissed from service, and there was no one other than she or Estella who could have kept him so well informed of their arrangements. I tapped a finger against my lip. Perhaps *dismissed* was too strong a word, or even the wrong word altogether. What if Mr. Jones had been sent back to Paris to organize the details of Mademoiselle Lamar's travels? No, that would be better and more easily done wherever she was.

Then it struck me—what if Mr. Jones, after proving himself through loyal service, returned to Paris to keep an eye on Monsieur Pinard? What if Estella had come to doubt the character of the gentleman charged with overseeing her finances? This struck me as an excellent plot for a novel, but I had to admit it unlikely in reality. Mr. Jones would have had neither influence over Monsieur Pinard nor the ability to interfere with the solicitor's actions. There was one other possibility: Monsieur Pinard could have been the one employing Mr. Jones from the beginning, sending his loyal man with Estella, ordering him to keep her away from Paris until he had figured out a way to make her fortune his own. What might Mr. Jones have done in Egypt when Estella had threatened to send him away?

A chill ran down my spine. I rose from the table and paced the room, pausing to look out the window again. Vehicles had already started to fill the boulevard to my south, but none of the traffic turned into Cécile's street. A solitary man crossed the pavement in front of Saint-Germain-des-Prés, and for a moment I could have sworn it was Mr. Hopwood, husband of the unhinged woman whose baby Mary Darby had not been able to save. I blinked to better focus my eyes, but when I looked again, he was gone. Surely, he would have no reason to be in Paris?

I went back to my work. There was no question that Mr. Jones—wretched, horrible man though he was—could be accused of living off the spoils of Estella's fortune. The state of his rooms testified to that. Cécile and I, before the turn of events last night, had been prepared to call on Monsieur Pinard, and I was still convinced the solicitor was using Estella very ill. Could he, in fact, be Swiveller? Jeremy had asked his florist contact to describe the man, but he only remembered him as of moderate height. He had mentioned neither auburn hair nor handlebar mustaches, so it was not unreasonable to surmise that someone other than Mr. Jones had played the part. I frowned. How long did it take to grow handlebar mustaches?

So plagued was I by this question, that I had started for my bedroom. Much though I wanted Colin to sleep, I needed his assistance, and I knew he would not be pleased if I left him to his slumber when there was work to be done. As if in anticipation of my needs, he was already descending to me as I mounted the stairs. The bruises on his face had bloomed overnight to alarming effect, and I placed a hand on his cheek, gently, so as not to cause him further pain.

"My darling love, you are a fright. Does it hurt very much?" A kiss was my answer, and both the vigor and thoroughness attached to the action laid to rest any concerns I had about his physical condition.

"It looks far worse than it feels. You are up early. Is there tea?"

I had been so intent on my work that I had not taken any notice of the fact that the servants were now all up, tending quietly to their duties, until now, when the sight of the footman in the front hall reminded me that we were not alone. We requested a pot of the genial beverage and drank it while I recounted for Colin all that I had learned.

"I do not think I will find any sign of Swiveller-Magwitch-Jones in the Catacombs," he said, "but I will have to look."

"You are not in any condition to be trekking through those tunnels—"

"I am perfectly able to do it. Another call on Pinard is worthwhile." He sifted through the papers in front of him. "I am in agreement with your analysis of these for the most part, but must remind you to keep Mary Darby front and center. If Jones killed her—and I believe he did—it indicates a great deal rides on his ability to make the world think Estella Lamar is alive and well."

"You are of the opinion she is not?"

He brought the edges of the papers into a perfect line. "It becomes harder and harder to believe anything else. And if she is dead—"

"He likely killed her in Egypt. I could book us onto the next steamer—"

"We are not going to Egypt."

I sighed. "If Estella is dead, what about the letter Cécile has only just had from her?"

"I have already pointed out that we cannot determine when that was written, and now that we know Jones had the diary, we also know he could have used that to study and copy her handwriting."

"I have an idea—it is not much, but may prove useful, if only to occupy me while you descend into the Catacombs," I said.

"I know you would rather accompany me—"

"I have had enough of those tunnels, and am fully aware that the police are unlikely to welcome me as a member of their search party."

After having seen Colin off, I checked on Jeremy, whose reaction to waking up and finding me in his bedchamber proved at once that his injuries were not grave, although he did his best to insist he would never have attempted to embrace me if his mind hadn't been addled by Mr. Jones's blow to his head. Upon hearing that my husband had already left to meet the police, he ordered me out of his room so that he might dress and follow. I tried to dissuade him, arguing that he ought to rest, but he would hear none of it.

"Such a commotion coming from in here!" Cécile stood in the doorway, a wicked smile on her face. "But not the sort I would have expected from you, Bainbridge. It is a crushing disappointment to find you *en déshabillé* and engaged in so decidedly an unromantic disagreement."

Jeremy looked as if he might throw something at her, so I determined it would be best for us to leave him alone. Cécile and I had a leisurely breakfast and still managed to leave the house before him, and I can only conclude that mortification kept him upstairs until he knew we had departed. Monsieur Pinard greeted us warmly—an act for which I credit Cécile, as the solicitor made no attempt to hide his admiration for her—and did not balk at my request to revisit his records. Cécile and I had agreed in advance that I would deal with the ledger books while she interrogated Monsieur Pinard.

My search revealed, as I had expected, no mention of Mr. Jones. More surprising was that not a single payment had been recorded for

Miss Hexam, either. I suppose it was not impossible that Miss Hexam—or whatever her real name was—could be a lady of independent means, but if that were the case, one would expect her to be traveling as an equal of Estella's, and the diary made clear that this was not the case. More likely, the arrangement to which she and Estella had agreed was that Estella would pay all travel expenses and had given her any nominal payment beyond that in local currency, from her own supply.

I also checked the entries reflecting Estella's payments to her solicitor. Monsieur Pinard billed her at a shockingly low rate—making me all the more suspicious that he was collecting Swiveller's money. This reminded me of the cheque still waiting at the post office. How foolish of us to have been so convinced the auburn-haired man would be the one to collect it! If Monsieur Pinard was Swiveller—

Cécile interrupted my thought. "Are you finished, Kallista?"

"Yes, I think I have gleaned all that I can out of these." I closed the ledger books. We thanked Monsieur Pinard—he lingered obscenely over Cécile's hand—and took our leave.

"That man is no criminal mastermind." Cécile stepped into the waiting carriage. "He is barely capable of engaging in a little illicit flirting."

"He seemed most capable of that," I said. "He could hardly pry his eyes away from you."

"I don't mean that sort of flirting, Kallista. I asked him everything you wanted me to, and his answers do not even bear repeating. So I took a different tack, and began to query him about doing business with me. I have a large fortune, after all, and explained to him that I would be most agreeable to hiring a solicitor able to manage things for me in certain advantageous ways."

"Ways one might consider unethical?"

"Precisely. He did not categorically refuse."

"So he did flirt with the idea?"

"*Oui,* in a way, but he handled it all so very badly that it was clear he had not the slightest idea how to go about it. I believe him incapable of taking on the role of Swiveller."

I had no wish to deny Cécile the feeling of success she was so clearly enjoying, but was not confident that this single conversation was enough to absolve Monsieur Pinard of all suspicion. The carriage having arrived at our next destination, we alighted and stepped into one of my favorite stores in Paris. Neal's Library, on the rue de Rivoli, was an English-language bookshop with a charming reading room and a select assortment of English stationery. I had brought with me the letter Estella had ostensibly mailed from Paris and pulled it out to show the paper to the clerk at the counter.

"Could you tell me something about this envelope?" I asked. "It is so beautifully lined."

"*Ah, oui, madame!* It is one of my favorites. We sell full boxes of the envelopes with writing sheets to match. If you would follow me—" He took us to a shelf on which the stationery was displayed.

"Is it a new design?" I asked.

"We have had it for nearly a month now. It is meant, I believe, to honor the celebration of your queen?"

"I suspected as much." I smiled and told him I would like to purchase a box. It seemed a small price to pay for such an important revelation. The transaction complete, Cécile dismissed the carriage and we walked to the place de la Concorde and crossed the river.

"How, Kallista, were you able to know how to find Estella's stationery?"

"If you look closely at the pattern lining the envelope, it is made up of little diamonds. I had seen similar designs on any number of things in London in the approach to the queen's Diamond Jubilee. Mr. Jones is British, so I thought it reasonable that he would shop somewhere like Neal's—his books, after all, are all in English. Neal's will not be the only place in Paris one could buy that stationery—it's a common brand—but I wanted to confirm that the paper, at least, is not something Estella could have used years ago."

"So this proves the letter was only recently penned?"

"Yes, but it does not prove that Estella wrote it." I told Cécile what Colin suspected after seeing the diary—that Mr. Jones could have used it to study her handwriting. "I have very grave concerns about your friend. Would you expect her to frequent an English stationers?"

"Non."

Dire forebodings consumed my thoughts. Colin and his associates might not find evidence of Mr. Jones in the Catacombs, but what if they stumbled upon something far worse? He had left my husband there to die. What if he had done the same with Estella? I went over every detail of the case again and again, but could not conjure up a single piece of evidence to suggest Estella had ever returned to Paris. Yet something nagged at me, and I could not let the suspicion go. We needed someone capable of verifying, once and for all, whether Estella had written the letter herself.

Estella

Hettie was a beautiful doll, quite as lovely as any her father had ever given her. Monsieur Jones had outdone himself! And he had brought Estella fabric—a good, sturdy wool in a practical navy that very nearly matched one of her own new outfits—so that she could sew an appropriate travel costume for Hettie, and now that she had completed that, there was nothing to further delay the trip. Despite Monsieur Jones's repeated admonishments, she had declined to interview Miss Hexam in person. Every detail of the lady's experience and references confirmed to Estella that she would make a perfect companion. The letters the two ladies had exchanged were enough to persuade Estella to hire her with no compunction. Monsieur Jones needed to come to terms with the fact that he was no longer in charge.

Estella smiled when she considered how very different her circumstances were now to those when, not so long ago, she had feared Monsieur Jones, and thought of him only as her captor. Now, he was something else: her liberator, and this made her consider him with the warmest of emotions. He was more loyal to her than any of the servants in her parents' numerous houses had been, and she intended to reward him generously for his efforts.

The only thing lacking was a fresh supply of books about Egypt.

Monsieur Jones insisted she had exhausted the entire supply of Parisian shops, and that it was time to rely on her own observations of the country. The steamer would leave Marseille in three days. Estella smiled every time she thought about it.

20

The bulky person manning the desk at the front of the offices of the Sûreté stared at me blankly when I introduced myself. He appeared equally unimpressed when I told him the identity of my husband. When I explained to him that I was here on behalf of a French citizen who may have come to an inglorious end, he covered his mouth with his hand. It was an inelegant gesture that did little to hide his muffled laughter. Sensitive to the signs of outrage, which were currently boiling in the deep recesses of my chest, I thought it best to speak to his superior, hoping that gentleman would prove less useless.

Monsieur Valapart emerged from behind a closed door and greeted us before offering us tea and ushering us into his office. He apologized for his underling's treatment. "Molestre has no manners with ladies. I pray you will not hold his lack of breeding against the entire Sûreté?" His charming smile made it impossible to answer his question in any way but the affirmative.

After barraging Monsieur Valapart with a brief series of questions, I determined that he was reasonably familiar with Colin's work on the Mary Darby case, including the search of the Catacombs currently in progress. I explained to him our theories about the connection to Estella Lamar, and as he listened, his face, lined with age and wisdom, grew serious.

"We have had no reports of anything amiss with Mademoiselle Lamar. My understanding is that she is currently in London."

"You keep track of her?" I asked.

"I read the papers."

"The papers did not say she was in London. Their last accounting of her, I believe, was in Siam."

"And so it may be. Her solicitor, Monsieur Pinard, has been in touch, only this morning. He is concerned about you, Lady Emily. He feels you are violating the privacy of his client and mentioned, during the course of our conversation, that Mademoiselle Lamar was recently in London. Perhaps I misunderstood."

"Monsieur Pinard knows full well that we have no reason to believe Mademoiselle Lamar was recently in London. We do, however, suspect that she may be in Paris, but it is possible that the letter she sent to her dear friend, Madame du Lac, is a forgery." I passed to him the document in question. "I am aware of the superior reputation of the Sûreté, and I know that my own country's Scotland Yard was modeled after your excellent organization. As a result, you will hardly be surprised that I would turn to you for advice concerning handwriting experts. Surely you have one you could recommend?"

"The science is not so reliable as I would like, Lady Emily, but I can send you to Monsieur Nalot, a man we consult on occasion." He scrawled a note, sealed it, and handed it to me. "This will serve as a letter of introduction. His address is on the front."

We continued to chat with him briefly—I quizzed him to see if he would reveal anything else he knew about the case, he inquired after Colin's injuries from the previous night—and we thanked him for his time. He insisted on walking us out, and hailed a cab for us.

"A pleasant enough man," Cécile said as the cab pulled away from the curb. "I notice, though, that he was careful to tell us nothing we did not already know."

"I expected nothing else. Interesting that Monsieur Pinard is cross enough to report me to the Sûreté. At least, however, Monsieur Valapart has given us Monsieur Nalot. Let us hope the introduction proves fruitful." We had to stop in at Cécile's to collect the diary before continuing on to the handwriting man's premises. This enabled us to switch from the cab to the carriage which we had earlier dismissed, thinking the afternoon would be good for nothing but a walk home after we had left Neal's Library.

When we called, Monsieur Nalot was home, in humble but well-kept rooms in a building just west of the Hôtel des Invalides. His clothing, which was tailored beautifully, told me he was not without a decent income, but that he chose to spend it on something other than furnishings. He scrutinized Monsieur Valapart's letter, going so far as to study it with a magnifying glass, while he kept us standing just inside his door, but in the end he must have determined it to be legitimate as he invited us to sit.

"These are the documents in question." I handed him the diary and the letter, as well as two other letters purported to have been written by Estella after the commencement of her travels.

"Can you confirm Mademoiselle Lamar penned this diary?" he asked.

Anticipating this question, I had insisted that we make a stop at Estella's house on our way, where I collected a number of letters she had written to her mother before that woman's death, as well as a stack of canceled cheques from the years before she left France, each bearing her signature.

Monsieur Nalot spread all of these out on the ledge at the bottom of a long slanted desk above which hung a bright electric light. "Handwriting is something to which we give very little consideration, once we have left the schoolroom. We use it almost constantly, but rarely think about it. When we are writing, we are more conscious of the words we choose than the manner in which we form their letters. As a result, it is difficult for us to fully understand what it is, precisely, that makes our own handwriting unique—and I assure you that every individual's is unique. When you consider the challenges faced by a forger, this lack of active knowledge comes firmly into play. It is extremely difficult for anyone to wholly rid his writing of the unique characteristics that identify it."

"Yet some forgers manage to do just that," I said.

"Yes, certainly, but it is rare. Extremely rare. A forgery may deceive you or even the police, but to an expert—like myself—the differences are often easily discernible."

"I brought this as well." I passed him a sample of the papers we had collected from Mr. Jones's attic. "I cannot be absolutely certain they were penned by the man we suspect of forgery, but it is likely they are in his handwriting."

"This is quite a gift! It will make my work much easier." He started with the letters to Estella's mother, making notes on a large sheet of paper, sometimes drawing large examples of letters. He seemed particularly interested in her capital *E*s and her lowercase *y*s and *d*s. Next he studied the diary, followed by the more recent letters. He made what seemed only a cursory study of Mr. Jones's papers. When at last, more than an hour later, he looked up from his table, he rubbed his eyes and offered us cognac, which we refused. "If you do not mind, I will indulge. I find that in small amounts it combats the strain to my eyes that my work inflicts."

I did not like to rush him, but was frantic to hear his results. "Have we given you enough to make a conclusion possible?"

"What I have done, Lady Emily, is only a very brief analysis, but it is enough for me to say with confidence that the same individual who wrote the letters to Estella's mother wrote the diary, as well as the letter to Madame du Lac. It is not, however, the same person who wrote what you identify as having belonged to Monsieur Jones. The other two letters—the ones describing Estella's travels—appear to have been written in a hurry, but exhibit all the same characteristics of Estella's other papers. If you look here"—he held open the diary for us—"you can see the way she forms the loops of her *y*s. They are identical in the letters." He detailed for us other defining characteristics, and then showed us how Mr. Jones's method of forming letters differed.

"So you are quite certain that Estella wrote all of these?" I asked.

"There can be no question, so long as you are confident she signed the cheques and wrote the letters to her mother."

Of that we had no doubt. Which could only mean one thing: Estella was in Paris, and very much alive, at least when she had written the letter. We thanked Monsieur Nalot, and I inquired whether I could consult him in the future should the need arise. He agreed to this with a pleasant smile, and I told him I hoped we would meet again, as I was fascinated by his skills. I wondered if I might even be able to persuade him to offer me lessons in his art. We could not linger at present, though. Back in the carriage, we directed the driver to take us to the Catacombs, where I knew if we could not readily find Colin and Jeremy, we would at least learn from the officer guarding the entrance where we should seek them.

Estella may have been alive to write the letter, but I had great concerns about her present state.

Cécile was blissfully unconcerned. "This proves it, Kallista. Estella is a strange woman. I would not be surprised to find that she, herself, is Swiveller."

"Don't be naïve, Cécile. Estella would have no reason to be Swiveller. She has control of her own finances and does not need to pay herself in order to access her funds. We now know that she wrote the letter. The diary tells us she was in Egypt, and that Mr. Jones was with her. Mr. Jones, the same man who tried to kill my husband, knocked Jeremy unconscious and murdered Mary Darby. Can you truly believe this individual, who has so much information about Estella's travels, is not involved at all in her disappearance?"

"Estella disappeared, if it can even be called that, of her own accord. I have no doubt I will receive a letter from her soon after she reaches the Côte d'Ivoire."

I did not share my friend's confidence. By the time we reached the Catacombs, Colin and Jeremy were standing outside the entrance, speaking to several police officers. All of them were covered with the dust and grime one would expect for them to have attracted during their underground search.

"Did you find anything of note?" I asked, picking a cobweb out of Colin's hair and pulling him away from the group before relating to him everything I had learned in the course of the day.

"No evidence of Jones and no signs of anything amiss in the parts of the ossuary open to the public. We spent hours searching farther afield, focusing on the passages nearest to the apartment. There is plenty of evidence in those of habitation even, and the police tell me they are aware of groups of people who meet underground for various purposes."

"To practice the black arts, no doubt."

Colin raised an eyebrow and answered in a flat tone. "No doubt. Regardless, I saw nothing to suggest that Estella has been there. I gather that is what you fear?"

"Precisely."

He brushed some of the dust off his jacket sleeves and squinted.

"I agree, Emily, that something is amiss, but I cannot yet identify what it is."

"Can we search again tomorrow—and I do mean *we*—there may be something you missed."

"The network of tunnels beneath the city is so extensive it would take weeks to search. I think we had better apply ourselves to further examination of Jones's documents."

"Cécile and I did not get all of them. There was a filing cabinet—"

He bowed and swept his hand in front of his body to indicate that I should start walking. "The carriage awaits, dear lady. I have already sent the police with the contents of the cabinet to Cécile's, thinking you would be there to receive it. I did not realize you had other plans for the day."

"I still think—"

"I am happy to order a continued search of the tunnels, my dear, but there is no reason for you—"

"I may notice something none of you did."

"You often do, but right now it makes much better sense for you to apply yourself to the contents of Jones's cabinet." I knew he was trying to prevent me from the horror of finding Estella's body, and I appreciated the gesture even though I considered it unnecessary. He walked me to the carriage, in front of which Cécile and Jeremy were still standing. Once he had helped both of us ladies into it, he closed the door.

"You gentlemen are not going to accompany us?" Cécile asked while I frowned.

"No," he replied. "I am following the most excellent advice of my wife and am going to take another stroll through the Catacombs, this time keeping in mind a different objective."

"Does he agree with you that Estella may be in trouble?" Cécile asked as the carriage pulled away.

"He is humoring me. Think nothing of it." I saw no benefit in persuading her to worry.

The police had removed not only the contents of Mr. Jones's cabinet, but the cabinet itself, to Cécile's entrance hall. A footman, his face twisted in apology, said he had not known where else to put it. "I was afraid, madame, that its filth would leave a mark on any carpet." A ring of dusty dirt surrounded it on the marble floor. The footman barked an order to the maid who was already coming down the steps. "This is the third time she will have swept around it. The object, madame, sheds dirt like the most disagreeable sort of cat leaves deposits of fur." As if on cue, Caesar and Brutus bounded—so far as their short legs allowed for bounding—to their owner and yapped at the hem of her skirt.

"You have done all that is possible." She shooed away the maid and scooped up the little dogs. "There is no point in continuing until we have finished with the wretched thing."

I asked the footman to bring us chairs and a narrow table, and we set to it. We did not need to fiddle with the lock; I presume the police had seen to that. Of the four drawers, two were filled with older versions of what we had found on Mr. Jones's desk: itineraries, notes about hotels, railway timetables. The other two were of more interest.

The first initially appeared to have nothing at all to do with Estella. The front section contained papers detailing plans for something called Dr. Maynard's Patented Formula—a substance that, so far as I could tell, differed not from hundreds of its kind, worthless liquids of indeterminate color and bitter taste that had no effect whatsoever on the complaints they claimed to treat. Six bottles of the stuff took up the back of the drawer, their exuberant labels claiming myriad health benefits.

I paged through the documents, not expecting to find much of interest, but was taken aback when I came across a drawing of the label, done as a sample, on a single sheet of large paper. In the center was a large pyramid, much like those found at Giza, entwined with vines that ended, on either side, with a burst of floral blossom. Across the bottom of the page was Estella's signature, and the word *approved*. "Have you ever heard of this?" I held one of the bottles up to Cécile. She shook her head. "It seems that Estella was in business with Mr. Jones. At least she was consulted as to the design of the label."

"I do remember this," Cécile said. "She mentioned it in passing once, some months before she left Paris, when she had been casting about for something in which to invest. I told her at the time it was an awful idea, and she never brought it up again."

"It must be how she met Mr. Jones. Perhaps she thought he would make a better porter than a salesman and convinced him to abandon the stuff in favor of world travel." The last drawer, the bottom one, held a mishmash of receipts, most of no consequence, but among them were four that merited further consideration, from Au Nain Bleu, a name I recognized because I had intended to procure for my boys little presents from this well-known toy shop. Each of the receipts was for the purchase of a doll, and each was dated after Estella had supposedly left Egypt. None of the descriptions of the dolls matched the one currently residing in Mr. Jones's wardrobe.

"I cannot believe he bought these for anyone but Estella?"

"He could have sent them to her abroad."

"Theoretically possible, yes, but my instinct tells me he did not. He has her, I am convinced of it."

"In the Catacombs, you think?" Cécile asked. I very much appreciated my friend not pointing out the general inadequacy of intuition in detective work. My husband would not have been so kind.

"Where else but the Catacombs?" Adopting my husband's habit, I started to pace. "The tunnels go on for miles, and Jones had ready access to them from his own cellar. He has kept her alive all this time in order to steal her money."

"But we had already determined, had we not, that he does not seem to be benefiting from her money?"

"Not so far as we can yet tell, but we have missed something fundamental about the character of Mr. Farrington Jones."

"Farrington?" Cécile looked down her nose, disgust writ on her face.

"That is what it says on his papers for Dr. Maynard's Formula. The doll receipts were written up for a Wilkins Micawber."

"I presume that to be a name from yet another of the novels of Monsieur Dickens?"

"*David Copperfield*. Mr. Micawber is a financial disaster, but exceptionally kind. One can only surmise that our Farrington considers himself in possession of similar qualities." The observant reader may have wondered whether I had forgot my—and Jeremy's—earlier theory regarding our villain and the works of Mr. Dickens. Rest assured, I had not. The addition of Mr. Micawber provided just the insight I needed into the character of Farrington Jones (a name worthy of Dickens himself). Mr. Jones viewed himself as a good man, but one embroiled in some sort of criminal activity. His finances were a mess. His purchase of the dolls—each was expensive in the extreme—could be taken as a generous gesture to Estella's obvious passion for the objects. What I could not decide was why he had not given her the doll we found in his wardrobe. Had she died in captivity before he could make the gift? I shuddered, picturing an eerie image of Estella clutching her four dolls in a dark tunnel of the Catacombs until death released them from her arms.

I could not let myself be distracted by such morbid thoughts. I took care as I combed through the rest of the documents in the drawer, going so far as to revisit the ones I had rejected as uninteresting before finding the doll receipts. I had not noticed it at first, but upon second study, I realized the significance of the papers that now lay in my lap. Mr. Jones had purchased a motley collection of items from a number of vendors: ammonia, scrubbing brushes, heavy work gloves, ribbon, wire, and a considerable quantity of mortar.

"Mortar?" Cécile blanched when I showed them to her. "You don't think he has walled her in?"

I did not answer her question, but I had a fair idea of where we would find Estella.

XX

Egypt was exactly—down to the most insignificant detail—how Estella imagined it. Limestone monuments gleamed. The waters of the Nile reflected the sunlight as dancing jewels. The natives adored her. The temperature was not so fierce as she had feared.

But that last should have come as no surprise.

Miss Hexam delighted her, anticipating her needs and reminding her of things that she should have Monsieur Jones collect. Miss Hexam preferred French food to Egyptian, and Estella agreed, although she suspected that if Monsieur Jones were left to his own devices, he would seek out the dark cafés frequented by the natives. Estella insisted on things she knew would cause no digestive disturbances—had she not done so from the beginning?—and never had cause to regret it.

Having run through all her Egyptian books, Estella followed Monsieur Jones's advice and read all of the works of Monsieur Dickens. She settled on *Bleak House* as her favorite, adoring Esther, and read over and over one passage:

> *I found every breath of air, and every scent, and every flower and leaf and blade of grass and every passing cloud, and everything*

in nature, more beautiful and wonderful to me than I had ever found it yet. This was my first gain from my illness. How little I had lost, when the wide world was so full of delight for me.

A shot of understanding coursed through Estella every time she read it. She knew what it was to find the world more enchanting than one had before thought possible. She knew what it was to be gone from it and then back—back to a place wholly different from what it had been before—back to a place that proved to her how little she had lost.

Estella bit into the last macaron in her box. She was going to read Belzoni again.

21

I sat beside Cécile in the carriage and held her hand the whole way back to the Catacombs. I reminded her that ammonia was often used to revive ladies from a faint, but she reminded me that in such cases, one used the solid form rather than the liquid.

"It is why, Kallista, they are called smelling salts, not smelling spirits."

Colin and Jeremy were not above ground when we arrived, but the officer stationed at the entrance—the police activity at the site had caused a crowd to gather, and he was meant to keep them back—let us down the narrow steps after supplying us with candles and matches. At the bottom of the stairway, we reached a sizable vestibule that led to a stone doorway, carved over which were the words *Arrête! C'est ici l'empire de la mort.* Were we not on so important an errand, I might indeed have given pause before entering the empire of death. We followed the sound of voices along tunnels lined from floor to ceiling with neat stacks of bones, and I found I agreed with Cécile's earlier judgment of the place. Here, the dead had lost their humanity. We reached two policemen, who at first mistook us for tourists who had somehow managed to finagle our way past the guard upstairs. A quick explanation led one of them to accompany us in search of my husband.

For more than half an hour we meandered through the subterranean maze, eventually turning in a direction not marked by the black arrows painted on the ceilings to guide the tourist route. The path became dirtier, littered with dust and chips of bones. Twenty more minutes and, at last, I heard Colin's voice in the distance.

"Emily! What are you doing here?" He came to me the moment we were within sight of him. I leaned close and explained my theory in a hushed voice. He nodded, and laid a gentle hand on my arm. "I am afraid you are most likely right. How is Cécile?"

"As you would imagine. Not altogether well, but she insisted on accompanying me. I could hardly deny her."

"Of course not."

"It will take us nearly an hour to get back out, so I think we had better set off without delay," I said.

"It will be quicker to leave through Jones's cellar. We are closer to that than to the public entrance."

"If only I had known."

"I don't think time will make any difference at this point, my dear." I bit my lips and wished I could believe otherwise.

Jeremy had already taken charge of Cécile, and kept close hold of her as we traversed the route to our chosen exit. She looked ill when we reached that passage I remembered all too well, the one with bones scattered all over, where there was no way forward but to wade through them. Jeremy, sensing her discomfort, picked her up and carried her across to the steps rising from the far end of the tunnel. When at last we emerged through the door in the cellar wall, the policemen on guard registered a great deal of shock at seeing us ladies. They took it in stride, however. We collected a shovel, hand trowel, and wooden bucket from a corner and made our way upstairs. The concierge did not even bother to scowl at us as we passed her window.

The only cabs to be seen at that moment were open victorias, which only seated two. Colin and I—my husband carrying the tools—stepped into the first we hailed. Jeremy and Cécile would follow. It took nearly forty minutes to reach our destination, and we arrived at the gates of Père-Lachaise just as the closing bell rang, warning those visitors inside that they had only half an hour in which to make their way to the front and leave. Jeremy and Cécile approached as Colin was finishing speaking with the custodian, who, after seeing the letter from the Sûreté, agreed to let us take as much time as necessary.

The cemetery shut at seven o'clock, but fortunately for us, the light would last much beyond that on this summer evening. Cécile led us to the Lamar tomb. I held her hand while Colin picked the lock. The man at the gate had sent one of his colleagues with us—not another custodian, but a gravedigger, who had rejected our motley collection of tools, giving preference to his own. He used a crowbar to lift one of the stones in the floor, revealing a dark, narrow crypt below. Colin pulled off his coat and stepped forward to assist him. The top of a coffin was visible approximately six feet below the floor. Together, the two men worked to wrench the lid off it.

"Emily, Cécile, please turn away." Colin's voice, full of force, was not to be ignored. We followed his directions without complaint. I could hear the hideous sound of wood straining and the creak of metal. "It is not she."

Despite myself, I turned around. "Are you certain?" I peered into the open grave. Inside were the remains of a gentleman, remnants of a gray beard still visible on his badly decayed face. "Monsieur Lamar?"

"Most likely. I do not think there is reason to believe he would have removed her father's coffin and put hers beneath. That would have been a complicated enough procedure to draw unwanted attention. Adding a single coffin on top of the rest would be much simpler."

I stepped away from the tomb, and crossed the narrow cobbled street, where I pressed my hands against the cool wall of another monument, supporting my weight as I bent forward and did my best not to be sick. The sound of banging indicated that they were now closing the coffin.

"Why did he not bury her with her parents?" Cécile was behind me, her voice choked. "It makes no sense."

"Perhaps he thought it would cause him to be discovered."

"So where is she?"

"We may never know, Cécile." Jeremy put an arm around her shoulder. "I am so very sorry."

I was about to add my condolences when I noticed a wreath on a nearby simple slab grave. The inscription had long since been eaten away by rain and erosion, and the stone itself was not in good shape. Yet someone had taken the time to leave a memento. A memento, that if I remembered correctly—

I crossed back to the Lamar tomb. The gravedigger had not yet replaced the heavy stone in the crypt, but from outside I could see the wreath we believed Estella had left. It was nearly identical to the one on the slab. A quick study of the rest of the street revealed similar wreaths on—or in—three more tombs, each of which had clearly fallen into disrepair. As I examined them, I pointed out to my friends the evidence of recent repairs. On one, the door's hinges had recently been oiled. On another, there were signs of fresh mortar having been applied where the stone must have crumbled.

"We cannot dig up grave after grave, Emily," Colin said.

"I am perfectly well aware of that, but we may be able to spot some sort of a sign. Don't you think that if he put her somewhere else, it would have been in a place he felt was appropriate? He bought her dolls, Colin. He must have had some warm feelings toward her, even if he did—"

"Yes, it is not uncommon for—" He stopped and looked at Cécile. "Madame du Lac, there is no need for you to stay here any longer. I assure you that Emily and I will—"

"I want to help," Cécile said. "I know better than any of you what a—*friend* does not seem the right word—person acquainted with Estella might deem appropriate."

We divided into pairs. Cécile and Jeremy would search the streets to the west of the avenue Principale, the wide drive that started at the main gate, while Colin and I would focus on the ones to the east. This gave us a larger area to cover, but we thought it best to give Cécile the less overwhelming task. The gravedigger stood, listening silently as we mapped out our strategy. Once Cécile and Jeremy had set off and gone almost out of sight, he approached my husband.

"There is a man, a very good man, who does much work restoring the deserted tombs in this cemetery. He is the one who places these wreaths for which you now search."

"Could you describe him?" Colin asked.

"His hair is of a ginger color and his mustaches—"

"Farrington Jones!" I did not need to hear any more to identify the wretched man.

"You are a friend of Monsieur Jones?" the gravedigger asked.

"You know him as Monsieur Jones?" I could feel the deepening furrows on my brow. I would have expected another *nom de guerre*.

"*Bien sûr*. He is a favorite here. He comes nearly every day, always with fresh flowers, and always to make repairs." This fully explained the items on Mr. Jones's receipts that had led me to the cemetery.

"Are there any places in particular on which he focuses?" Colin asked. The gravedigger shrugged.

"He works everywhere in the cemetery. He doesn't want anyone to lose his space, you see."

"Of course." I turned to Colin. "Cécile explained to me that if tombs become too derelict, the bodies are exhumed and the plots sold to someone else. Making repairs when there are no relations left to oversee them ensures that the bodies will remain where they were buried." I took out the map I had pulled from my Baedeker's guide before leaving Cécile's, and held it up to the gravedigger, asking him if there was anywhere in particular he thought we should focus on during our search. The grounds covered more than a hundred acres; without direction, we might never find Estella. Alas, the man only shrugged, and told us that he could offer no advice. He wished us luck, then sheepishly slunk off, explaining that his wife would not forgive him if he were late for dinner.

"What a pity Mr. Dickens isn't buried here. That would make things simpler." I studied the map, focusing on the names of the famous personages identified on it, but there were none that struck me as particularly meaningful to Estella. "I don't suppose you know the names of any famous doll makers?"

"I think it best that we work our way to the end of one street, go over to the next, and work our way back and forth, accordingly. Proceeding in an orderly fashion will in the end save time by allowing us to keep track of our progress."

I agreed, and his method worked well enough on the central streets that kept to the basic shape of a grid, but many of the others did not, instead forming loops and curves. These were at best confusing and at worst caused us to lose our way, as it was not always a simple task to follow them. Many times we were forced to double back in order to make sure we had not missed a single tomb. Colin kept to the one side of every street, I to the other, and we made notes about each grave upon which Mr. Jones had left a wreath, as well as ones that showed signs of recent restoration. After two hours of this, I was growing frustrated. The shadowy veils of dusk had started to cover the sky. Colin had brought with him two lanterns, and had given one to Jeremy and Cécile. As the sun slipped away, he lit ours, and our search became even less efficient, as we could no longer cover opposite sides of the street simultaneously.

We had fallen into confusion after following the Chemin du Dragon to its end, where it curved off in three separate directions, and we were soon circling section number 28, seemingly over and over. "We have passed the Hertford family vault at least three times," I said, indicating a stone tomb to our left, large enough to house myriad coffins. "A structure such as that wouldn't require a crypt, would it?"

"It would not require it, but if the family wanted a chapel aboveground . . . are you thinking what I am?"

"Yes. If Mr. Jones chose a large tomb, he might not have had to dig to dispose of Estella." This observation renewed our resolve, and we continued our quest with more vigor than before. We had agreed that when darkness fell, we would meet Jeremy and Cécile at the large chapel that stood on the top of a hill almost in the center of the cemetery. I did not like to stop our search, even for this, but I had no choice. With only one lantern between us, I could not continue without Colin.

Cécile, exhausted and drawn, begged off continuing. She could not face any more tombs. Jeremy wanted to go with Colin, leaving me to sit with Cécile, but my husband thought it best to not leave ladies unaccompanied, so we promised to come for them as soon as we had exhausted the secrets of the cemetery. We returned to section 28, neither of us feeling satisfied that we had finished exploring it. Halfway down a row of graves that stood so close together the effect was almost claustrophobic was one not so large as the Hertfords', but three times as wide as its narrow neighbors.

"It is not derelict," Colin said.

"Excellent care has been taken of it, but there are signs of repairs, especially on the corners. The mortar looks newer than the stone."

Godeau was carved over the door, which was locked. Holding the lamp up to it, I tried to peer inside, but could see nothing in the darkness.

"I think we should keep moving." Colin took the lantern from my hand and we stepped back onto the cobbled street.

"Wait." I pointed to a carving on the step below the door: a pyramid entwined by vines that ended with a flower on either side. It was identical to the image on the bottles of Dr. Maynard's Patented Formula I had retrieved from Mr. Jones's drawer. I explained this to Colin, who immediately set about picking the lock to the tomb.

"It is well oiled and clearly used regularly," he said, as it snapped open. He held the lantern above his head and we stepped inside.

There were no wreaths or flowers here, and the space, approximately ten feet wide, though large enough to have housed numerous coffins, contained none. It was a chapel, grander than those in some of the smaller tombs, having four stained-glass windows and a padded kneeler—its upholstery looked almost brand-new—in front of a marble altar.

"The last burial here was in 1838." I read the names of the Godeau family off the inscriptions on the wall. "He must have put her here. The careful maintenance would serve two purposes—it prevents the tomb from falling derelict and, hence, from being exhumed, and it assuages his guilt."

"If he feels any." Colin was examining the floor, looking for the spot in which he should apply the crowbar he had borrowed from the gravedigger. "The crypt below will be large enough that I may have to descend to inspect the coffins. I have a rope, but there is nothing to which we can safely secure it."

"You could use it to lower me—"

"My dear, I do not want you—"

"I cannot bear to wait even another hour to find out what happened to Estella. Please, Colin. If we tie it around my waist using a knot that—"

"I am well aware of the best way to approach such a task." His dark eyes met mine. "You are quite certain you want to attempt it?"

"There is no danger. The dead cannot hurt me."

He clasped my arm and continued to search the floor. "Here." He handed me the lantern and went to work with the crowbar, but found the tool unnecessary. The stone was false, nothing more than a theatrical prop attached to hinges. Colin lifted it with ease. The sight—and sounds—of what greeted us will haunt me until my dying day.

"You have kept me waiting longer than I would have liked, Monsieur Jones," a reedy voice called from below. "I do hope you have my macarons."

22

My feet stuck to the floor of the tomb as if the icy fingers of Death himself were gripping my ankles. Colin took the lantern from my hand and, lying flat on the ground, held it down into the crypt.

"What are you up to, Monsieur Jones? I do not like this, not one bit. You ought not come to me this late at night! What if I had been sleeping? As you're here you may as well lower the ladder and bring me my macarons. I have decided not to go to the Côte d'Ivoire, and Miss Hexam is quite in agreement. She thinks it a tedious sort of place where there are unlikely to be nice pâtisseries."

"Mademoiselle Lamar?" Colin called down to her. "We are here to rescue you. Monsieur Jones will not hurt you anymore."

Sounds of whimpers and scampering came from below. "Who are you? Go away. Bring me Monsieur Jones. You should not be here disturbing me."

I crouched over the trapdoor, observing that a sturdy stone ledge, which stood out two inches from the hole in the floor, supported it from below. "Mademoiselle, I come on behalf of Cécile du Lac, your dear friend, who has been searching for you. She is most worried—"

"I told her to leave me be! Go and fetch Monsieur Jones!"

Colin and I stepped away from the opening in the floor. "Did you see her?" I asked. "It's like Miss Havisham gone, well, more mad." Estella's hair, which reached almost to the floor, was a mass of untamed gray, her face more pale than that of a corpse, and she appeared to be able to move only with great difficulty. "What should we do?"

"We need a ladder. I have the keys from the custodian—no doubt we can find something of use among the gravediggers' supplies. They would need something to enable them to reach these crypts."

"We cannot leave her here. What if Mr. Jones is lurking outside? He is certain to kill her now that she has identified him to us."

"I agree. You take the lantern. I will stay outside and guard the door from nearby. We should tell her . . . something."

I went back to the little door. "Mademoiselle! We are going for help—"

"I want Monsieur Jones and my macarons, you young wretch. You have no business disturbing me in my home."

These words cut into me like none had before. Her home? "I shall look for Mr. Jones, mademoiselle. Do not disturb yourself. I am sure he will be along with your macarons shortly." This seemed to calm her. She was sitting in a chair, a thick blanket wrapped around her, and reached down to the floor—carpeted—on which lay a book. She lifted it to her lap and adjusted the lamp on the small table that stood next to her chair.

"Get yourself gone. I am trying to read."

Colin lowered the trapdoor. "Do you think you can find your way back to Bainbridge?"

"Yes. Need I remind you of my excellent sense of direction?" I thought a lighthearted comment best for the extremely unusual circumstances in which we now found ourselves. We stepped out of the tomb, and Colin embraced me, his arms firm and strong.

"Take care, my dear. We do not know where Jones may be lurking.

If anyone approaches you, scream like the devil himself has you. I will come at once." He kissed me, then handed me the lantern.

"I do not like leaving you here in the dark," I said.

"Do not trouble yourself. I look forward to another encounter with our villain. He did not fight fair the last time we met—I mean to level the balance when I see him again."

I followed the cobbled street, moving with deliberate care because the lantern illuminated only the space immediately around me. When I came to a street sign, I lifted the light. AVENUE TRANSVERSALE NO. 1. Somewhere, I had taken a wrong turn and wound up north of where I had intended. Remembering that each of the avenues Transverales in the cemetery ran perpendicular to the chapel, I headed east until I could turn to the south. This choice proved ill made as well, as I wound up—how, I could not imagine—once again on the Chemin du Dragon. It was time to consult my map.

I studied it, but to little use. The streets were so narrow, and I was certain they were not all on the map. Although I am assured that is not the case, anyone who has struggled to find her way through Père-Lachaise in broad daylight will understand all too well how difficult, nigh impossible, it is to do on a moonless night. I folded the map, returned it to my reticule, and was about to set off again when a sound startled me, a rustling of sorts, but there was no wind to blow leaves. I felt the uncomfortable prickle of being watched, but there was no sign of anyone in the vicinity. Could Mr. Jones be hiding in one of the nearby tombs? I steeled myself, ready to confront him, and relaxed only when the swoop of bats above my head made me realize their wings had been the source of the sound.

The tombs, with their peaked roofs and ornate decoration, had charmed me during the day, drawing me into the stories of their inhabitants, and the cemetery had seemed a romantic, wonderful place. Now, though, carved skulls and winged creatures danced in the moving light of my lantern, and the squeals of nocturnal animals—owls, rodents, and I know not what else—menaced me. I had begun to feel bats circling above me almost without ceasing, but whenever I looked up to see them, they were not there, and I suspected my mind was falling prey to the evil atmosphere that now seized Père-Lachaise.

When I found the avenue St. Morys, I breathed a sigh of relief, knowing that following this road south would take me directly to the chapel, and soon I reached it. My friends were no longer on the bench in front of the building, and I began to panic when I could not find them. I placed the lantern on the ground, not trusting my shaking hand to keep hold of it, and lowered myself to the bench, where I would—somehow—force myself to regain my composure and decide how to best proceed.

No sooner had I drawn a single deep breath than Jeremy came bounding toward me. "Em! Are you all right? Where is Hargreaves?"

"Where is Cécile?"

"She's in the chapel. This place is creepy in the dark, Em, and I could tell being outside and surrounded by tombs and death was taking a toll on her. The door to the building was unlocked, so I thought we might as well sit inside."

"We mustn't leave her alone." My concern was unnecessary. Cécile had already left the chapel and was upon us in an instant. "We have found Estella," I said. Cécile closed her eyes and sighed. As she lifted her handkerchief to her face, I reached for her hand. "She is not dead."

"*Non?* This is excellent news—"

"It is not quite that," I said. "It appears she has been living, all this time, in the crypt of a tomb." My friends stood, their faces slack with horror, as I described for them what Colin and I had found. "We must go at once and find a ladder." From the chapel, getting to the Garde-Partier, where we had met the custodian, was simple enough—all we had to do was cut over to the avenue Principale and walk in a straight line. I did my best to keep everyone's spirits up, suggesting that, once we had rescued Estella, we might as well take advantage of the moonless night to see if the skulls on Mr. Robertson's grave did, in fact, dance.

When we reached the main gates of the cemetery, Jeremy insisted that we summon the police before doing anything else. I did not want to leave Colin alone in the dark, vulnerable to Mr. Jones, but I could not argue that Jeremy's plan was a wise one. My husband had given me the gate key entrusted to him by the custodian, and we let ourselves out, crossed the boulevard de Ménilmontant, and shouted for help. We did not see a policeman, but a waiter at a café, who had come forward to see who was causing the commotion—and, he admitted later, to scold us for disturbing his customers if we were not in dire straits—agreed to call the police and have them meet us at the entrance to Père-Lachaise.

That done, we returned to the cemetery. "One of us needs to wait for the police," I said. "It cannot be me, for I alone know how to find Colin, and I will not delay getting back to him."

"I want to see Estella," Cécile said. "From everything you have said, Kallista, it is clear she is in a dangerous frame of mind. I am the only one among us known to her. I must try whatever I can to help her. Furthermore, Jeremy would never allow one of us to wait here, alone and unprotected."

"I don't much like the idea of the two of you setting off without me. If Jones—"

"From what Estella said, it does not sound like he made a habit of coming to her this late at night. I do not anticipate any problems." I did not feel entirely confident in this statement, but said it with force, and, as I have found on many other occasions, speaking in such a manner often persuades one's audience to believe one, regardless of the facts.

"Other than those problems one ordinarily expects to face in cemeteries in the middle of the night," Cécile said. The flash in her eyes told me she was back to herself. We opened the guard's house, and in a small back room found a ladder that, between the two of us, we could carry without too much difficulty. Before we left him, I showed Jeremy on the map where the tomb was in section 28, but I could not leave it with him in case Cécile and I lost our way. There was a large board with a plan of the cemetery near the entrance, and he said he would study it while he waited for the police.

The ladder made it impossible for us to move quickly. I had tied the lantern to a rung so that we could—more or less—see where we were going, and we started up the avenue Principale, I holding the front, Cécile in the back. This return trip was far less frightening than the one I had made by myself. Cécile, bolstered by the knowledge that her friend was alive, made little jokes and twice tried to scare me. Her efforts, much to her despair, failed. When we turned onto the street that held the Godeau tomb—carefully, as navigating narrow spaces with a lengthy ladder requires a certain degree of skill—we fell silent, listening for sounds of struggle. There were none. Soon I recognized my husband's footsteps on the cobbles. He untied the lantern and took the ladder from us.

Cécile rubbed her hands. "These gloves are entirely ruined. I see now, Kallista, why the undertaking of work in a cemetery requires something far heavier." She gave Colin a kiss on each cheek. "You have found my friend."

"Emily is the one who spotted the tomb."

"Any sign of Mr. Jones?" I asked.

"None, but I think we should operate on the assumption that he could appear at any moment. Let's not dawdle."

Back inside the stone structure, I opened the trapdoor in the floor and was immediately greeted by Estella's raspy voice.

"Monsieur Jones, is that you? I am being harassed by some young people—you must make them go away if you see them."

"Estella, *chérie,* it is Cécile. I have come to pay you a visit. Monsieur Jones assured me you would be most pleased to see me. May I come down?"

"Cécile, did you not receive my letter? I do not wish to be disturbed. My travels keep me so very busy, I have not time—"

"We have brought you information about the Côte d'Ivoire," I said. "Cécile made the acquaintance of a gentleman who has only just returned from there, and he would like to speak to Miss Hexam about her concerns about the lack of bakeries."

"Would he, now?" came the voice from below. "You may come down, Cécile, but only for a moment. My train leaves in the morning and I must be ready to get to the station."

Colin lowered the ladder into the crypt and held it steady while Cécile stepped onto it. I waited until she was halfway down to follow. Estella—and, one must presume, Mr. Jones—had fitted out the crypt with once-fine Persian rugs. Tapestries with medieval hunting scenes covered the stone walls. A bookcase at one end held at least a dozen dolls and a profusion of books. There were two lamps, casting a dim yellow light over everything. Against one wall stood a large stone sarcophagus with a flat, slablike top. It had been made up like a bed. I shuddered. The entire space smelled of damp and mildew and unwashed body.

Estella cowered in her chair, her breathing coming ragged and hard. "I do not like being disturbed like this. Why have you come, Cécile, when I asked you not to?"

If Cécile felt any horror at the sight of her friend, she did not show it. Estella flinched when she tried to take her hand. "Now I will have none of that, *chérie.*" Cécile picked up an ivory-backed hairbrush that, along with the rest of a dresser set, was on a trunk at the end of the room opposite the bookcase. "You cannot travel with your hair such a mess. What will Mademoiselle Hexam say when she returns?"

"Do you know Mademoiselle Hexam, Cécile? She did not tell me."

Cécile began to brush Estella's hair, getting out the worst of the knots and then braiding it and coiling the thick rope on top of her head, fastening it in place with pins she pulled from her own hair. The act had a calming effect on Estella, but it was short-lived, as a commotion from above signaled the arrival of Jeremy and the police. She knocked the brush out of Cécile's hand with a force I would not have expected, sending it flying across the crypt. "Who is that, now?" Her eyes were wild. With great effort she pushed herself out of the chair. Once on her feet, she started for the trunk. Her every movement was labored; her strength had wasted away from years of hardly using her limbs. She bent down over the trunk, removed the dresser set, and raised the lid, pulling out a shredded piece of dark blue velvet that looked as if it had once been a cloak. Cowering in a corner, she wrapped the tattered remains of the garment around her.

Cécile approached her, but Estella shrieked, begging her to stop and go away, all the while sobbing hysterically and clawing with bent fingers at the air around her. I climbed the ladder until my head was out of the trapdoor.

"She is not going to go gently. Even if she were not so upset, I do not think she is in possession of the strength necessary to climb the ladder."

"I will come down," Colin said.

"She will not like it."

"She has no choice."

I descended and he followed. The sight of him set Estella into another round of terrified shrieks. He crouched in front of her, speaking quietly, doing everything possible to try to ease her fears, but nothing worked. He did not flinch when she hit him, again and again, begging him to leave her be. At last, realizing she was not going to go willingly, and knowing that she could not remain in this sordid state, he gathered her up in his arms, with the intention of—somehow—carrying her up the ladder.

No sooner had he taken a single step than Estella, exhibiting that same maniacal strength as when she had flung the hairbrush, kicked and flayed, desperate to free herself from his arms. He held her with more strength, but did not approach the ladder. Instead, he lowered her onto her bed. Estella, now panting like a wounded animal, gathered herself up into a small ball, bringing her knees to her chest, and rocked forward and back, forward and back, muttering something I could not understand.

"Cécile, you stay with her. Your presence is the least upsetting. Emily, ascend with me." He climbed the ladder first, helping me when I reached the top. There was a long scratch on his left cheek.

"Good God, Hargreaves, what is going on down there?" Jeremy, along with two sturdy-looking policemen holding bright lanterns and wielding clubs, gathered around us.

"Removing her is going to prove something of a challenge," Colin said. "She is—"

"She does not want to go. I've tried more times than I can count." The voice, with a clipped English accent, came from the door of the tomb. We all turned as one and saw him—Farrington Jones, the auburn-haired man.

23

Colin started for Jones at once, but the auburn-haired man stepped forward, his hands raised in a position of surrender. "I am all too aware of my crimes, sir, and have no intention of running from you now. This is no time for discussion, however, as you see how disturbed Mademoiselle Lamar is. I have what you need—"

"Stop right there, Jones," Colin interrupted as the man reached for his coat pocket. Mr. Jones raised his hands again.

"There is chloroform and a clean handkerchief in my left pocket. Please remove it yourself. I understand that you cannot trust me."

I could hear my husband muttering under his breath something about understatements as he removed the items from Mr. Jones's coat. "Keep this with you always, do you?"

"Not ordinarily, no. Did you find my ladder or bring one of your own?"

Colin stood directly in front of him and glared at him, and then turned back to the hole in the floor and nodded at the policemen, who quickly bound Mr. Jones's wrists. "Bainbridge, come with me. I may require your assistance." The look on my husband's face pained me. I knew it went against every fiber of his being to restrain a lady against her will, but in the circumstances, what choice did we have? I did not watch from above as they administered the chloroform, but the bansheelike cries that came from Estella as she resisted shattered the night and reverberated horribly against the stone walls of the tomb. The silence that followed was almost as painful. Colin carried Estella up the ladder, Jeremy following close behind, helping him keep his balance with his awkward load.

Cécile emerged last from the crypt. "We must get her to a doctor at once." Her voice was calm and steady. "How long, Monsieur Jones, can one reasonably expect the effects of chloroform to last?"

Once Estella had been safely remanded to the excellent care of the staff of the Maison Municipale de Santé on the rue du Faubourg-Saint-Denis—the hospital upon which Cécile had insisted—we went to the station where the police had taken Mr. Jones. The physician treating Estella had told us that her physical difficulties were not great. She was not suffering from malnutrition, but the atrophy to her muscles from so many years spent without a great deal of movement would prove challenging, though not impossible, to overcome. Her mental situation, however, was very bleak.

The police led us into a sorry little room, empty except for a grubby table and some chairs—they had brought more in so that all of us could sit down. Mr. Jones was already seated, his wrists still bound.

"Mademoiselle Lamar—is she all right?"

"Are you concerned she will die and you will be facing two murder charges?" Colin asked.

"You do not understand, sir, not at all—"

I believed I did understand. "If you will allow me to speak . . ." No one objected, so I continued. "I presume you used chloroform when you took Mademoiselle Lamar?"

He hung his head. "I did. I am so ashamed—"

"Now is not the time for assuaging your conscience, Mr. Jones," I said. "You were after money? Do not answer, that much was evident the moment I found the records from your ill-fated business venture. Mademoiselle Lamar was, perhaps, not quite so wise as she thought when she refused to invest in Dr. Maynard's Formula. Ordinarily one does not expect businessmen to be twisted kidnappers."

"I never, ever intended for things to get so out of hand. It was only to be for a few days—just long enough for the cheque to clear—but then there were delays and when at last I was ready to free her, she was no longer willing to go."

"You cannot be foolish enough to think we would believe that," Cécile said.

"Does it matter?" Mr. Jones shifted in his chair, still unable to meet our eyes. "I thought it was a flawless plan. She had no family to speak of—her half siblings paid little enough attention to her—and it was so easy to take her. I owed a great deal of money, you see, to very unpleasant and violent men, and they were going to kill me. The scheme came to me when I was attending the funeral of a friend. Père-Lachaise does rather get one's imagination going, and when I saw how easy it was to enter long-abandoned tombs . . ."

"What you did is reprehensible," Jeremy said. I hushed him, for although I agreed with his sentiment, I wanted to hear the rest of Mr. Jones's story.

"How did you settle on the Godeau tomb in particular?" I asked.

"When I learned that tombs that have fallen into a state of disrepair could be more or less repossessed, I began to search the cemetery. The Godeaus' fit my every need. It was large enough to have a spacious crypt, so that Mademoiselle Lamar's stay would not be too unpleasant, I hoped. It was showing signs of dereliction, but not so much that it was in danger of being repurposed. No family members seemed to have visited in years, and I was able to discover that the only remaining son had long since moved to America. Confident that it was a safe place, I brought Mademoiselle Lamar there.

"All went well enough at first," he continued. "She was upset, as was to be expected, but she agreed to give me the money I required. There were two delays at the bank, though, and I did my best to make her more comfortable during them. I had already brought her books and carpets and fresh clothing—I can't remember what came precisely when—but with the second delay, she started asking for more specific things. Macarons from Ladurée. More books. A doll. When I had the money and my debt was paid, she had made herself so comfortable that she refused to leave. I tried to cajole her, but to no avail. She had been reading a number of books about Egypt, and expressed a great interest in the place."

"So you decided to pretend she was traveling?"

"No, Lady Emily, that was entirely Mademoiselle Lamar's idea. I expect your disbelief, but I was not made for this. I felt terrible from the moment I purchased the chloroform, and despaired when I could not persuade her to leave."

"Surely you were not going to remove her from the tomb yourself?" Colin asked. "She would have had you arrested on the spot."

"I had written a letter, detailing how she might be found, that I planned to deliver to her house immediately before I boarded a ship that would take me far away from France."

"So why didn't you deliver it, man?" Rage colored my husband's face. "Had you not done enough damage by taking her in the first place?"

Mr. Jones dropped his head onto the table. "Yes, that is what I should have done. But you saw, did you not, her reaction to being removed? At first, she asked me for just a few more days, saying she was unprepared and not ready to return home. She said I owed her at least that much, after what I had done. How could I argue? Then a few days became a few weeks. She had decided she wanted to go to Egypt—or so I believed—and convinced me that she did not want to make the plans from her house, as her solicitor would surely interfere. She demanded more books and travel information, all of which I brought her. I eventually persuaded her to let me put an advertisement for a companion in the paper—a lady could not travel alone—and I thought this would lure her out, as she would need to interview the candidates."

"Instead she chose a character from *Our Mutual Friend,"* I said.

"Yes. I had encouraged her to read Dickens—he has always been a favorite of mine—but when she told me that she and Miss Hexam had exchanged letters and that she could hire her without conducting an interview, I began to realize that something was very seriously wrong. Before then, I had let myself believe that she really would go to Egypt. Now it was clear she had no intention of leaving the crypt into which I had placed her."

"So why didn't you remove her?" Colin asked. "You obviously knew how."

"Guilt consumed me, Mr. Hargreaves. I had put her in this unspeakable place, and now she thanked me for it, telling me she had never been happier in her life. She had grown rather fond of me, and bossed me around like I was a favorite servant. I thought I might be able to use this fondness as leverage, telling her that I was likely to be sent to jail if she refused to come out—reminding her that her prolonged absence would not go unnoticed. That was when she took total control of the situation. She wrote to her solicitor, to her staff, to her siblings, telling them all she was leaving France. She ordered clothes from her dressmaker, and had me take trunks to the woman's establishment on the pretext that I was bringing them directly to the station."

"You should never have allowed any of this," Colin said.

"That is easy to say now, all these years later," Mr. Jones replied. "But at the time I felt that I had no choice but to do what she asked. I mailed her letters, sent telegrams as directed."

"But the telegrams came from far-flung places," I said. "How did you manage that?"

"That, too, was Mademoiselle Lamar's idea. I tried, again and again, to make her see that she could not remain out of sight forever—that if no one ever saw her, her friends would surely raise an alarm. To counter that, she ordered me to hire women to pose as her at locations throughout the world. It was much less difficult than you would think. For a few pounds, I could hire a would-be actress or a woman down on her luck to stand in front of the pyramids and be photographed for the newspaper. She would then send, from her location, the photograph and a letter Mademoiselle Lamar had written, to the papers. It became almost a sort of game for her. She delighted in seeing the pictures. It was almost as if she believed she was the one in them.

"She planned an entire trip to Egypt—did you know that?" he asked. "It was when I arrived one day, with supplies for her, and she greeted me, saying that Cairo far exceeded her expectations and inquiring whether I had fallen victim to sunburn, that I began to see how unraveled her mind had become."

"Yet you did not release her." I leaned forward across the table. "How could you let this continue, Mr. Jones?"

"She begged me to! Can you not understand? What I did for all of these years was exactly what she asked of me. I obeyed her every whim. I soothed her moods and met her demands. She wanted the life she had, and I was the only one who could help her to have it."

"This is sick," I said.

"I do not argue the point."

"It does seem, Mr. Jones, that your scheme—do not interrupt me, I know you will say it was her scheme—could have gone on indefinitely. But you hired Mary Darby to play her in London. Why did you take such a risk? Why have her appear in a location where someone might actually recognize her as a fraud?"

"I did not think it could happen. After so many years of our game, we had never once come close to being unmasked. I brought Mademoiselle Lamar the paper nearly every day, and she had read about the grand masquerade ball planned by the Duchess of Devonshire. She told me in no uncertain terms that she wanted to go."

"And you took this to mean she wanted a double to attend?" Colin asked.

"Sir, that *is* what she meant. I hired Mrs. Darby through my usual methods—I placed an ad. The details are unimportant."

"Why did you go to London?" I asked.

"It was a grave error on my part. I had thought that, as it is easy enough to slip over to London for a few days—"

"Leaving Mademoiselle Lamar alone and without fresh food or water—"

Mr. Jones interrupted my husband. "It was not like that. Mademoiselle Lamar periodically asked me to leave her alone, sometimes for almost a week. I have grown as attached to her as she has to me, and I found it increasingly difficult to stop myself from visiting her. I do worry, you know. On two separate occasions, I came back before the time she had requested, and it sent her into a spiral of panic and despair similar to what you witnessed tonight. When she asked me to give her five days, at just the time of the ball, I decided a little trip would do me good, and I wanted to meet Mary Darby. As you know, it proved disastrous."

"You thought I was Mary Darby," I said.

"Yes, and I reacted badly. Your costume was so like hers, and you completed the line of Homer as I had instructed her to do so that I might confirm her identity . . . and then when I did spot her, it was just when you, Madame du Lac, had exposed her as a fraud. The instructions Estella had written for her—the same ones she sent to all her ladies—said in no uncertain terms that she was to leave immediately if this happened. Instead of handling herself with dignity and grace, Mrs. Darby fled like a thief, and I went after her, terrified that she had laid us open to serious danger. Furthermore, she said she had been in Egypt, when I had told her in no uncertain terms that—"

"So you killed her." Colin stated it plainly, folding his arms, and glaring at Mr. Jones, down whose face tears now streamed. "You will gain no sympathy from me by false shows of regret."

"I regret more than you can ever know," he said. "I do not know what came over me. I was seized with terror, not only for myself, but for Mademoiselle Lamar. I knew what the exposure of our scheme would do to her already frayed nerves. I went after Mary Darby, and she must have seen my anger. She ran and ran. I could hardly keep up. When I reached her, I pulled the dagger from my costume, almost without knowing what I was doing, and stabbed her until she stopped screaming. I will never forgive myself."

"As well you shouldn't," Jeremy said.

"I returned to Paris and Mademoiselle Lamar, worried that I had attracted unwanted attention. When the lot of you began snooping around—"

"You did whatever you could to try to scare us off." I felt not a bit sorry for Mr. Jones. "And failed miserably. The handkerchief—"

"I soaked it in chicken's blood," he interrupted, his shoulders slumping. "I have betrayed Mademoiselle Lamar so terribly. She will never be able to forgive me. I promised she could live out all her days in her little home, and that I would take care of her until the end. If you only knew how happy she has been—"

"That is quite enough," Cécile said. "If she were happy, it was only as a means of coping with the hideous situation caused solely by you."

"You speak the truth, but she would not agree. And now, I am the one who shall be happy, happy in my punishment. Do you know what it has been to live with this? To get away with it? For all of these years, I have collected money from Mademoiselle Lamar, posing as a florist—but you figured out that much. I did not want it. I used it to get her whatever she desired and to restore the tombs of the forgot in Père-Lachaise. Some of it had to go for flowers, so that no one would doubt the bills, but the rest, every dime has plagued me. All I wanted was to pay my debt, and in doing so, I succeeded only in taking on a far greater one. And now, now I will have the punishment I have so long craved, but at the expense of Mademoiselle Lamar, who has been forced from her home, and thrust into a world she wanted only to reject—"

"You, Monsieur Jones, did nothing but take advantage of her vulnerability and then used it as an excuse to take the easiest route. You listened to the ravings of an unhinged mind and obeyed them instead of getting my friend the help she needed. Yes, you did betray her, but not by failing to further extend her captivity. I can no longer tolerate your presence." Cécile rose from her chair and turned to leave the room. Jeremy took her arm and led her away. I followed, but paused and looked back just as I reached the door.

"When we first met, you greeted me with a line from Homer, Mr. Jones. I shall leave you with another. 'Of all creatures that breathe and move upon the earth, nothing is bred that is weaker than man.'"

24

In the weeks that followed Mr. Jones's incarceration, Estella recovered enough to be released from the hospital. She refused, despite Cécile's admonitions, to stay with her friend. Instead, she called at the prison to see the man she called her dearest boy. She would not let us go in with her, but when she came out, she told us she had much admired his cell.

"It was so very charming," she said, as the carriage took us toward her house. "It reminded me of my first days in my little house and that put me onto an excellent plan."

Her so-called excellent plan was realized, some months later. Cécile's letter describing the end result gave me the most unpleasant chills. Estella had lined one of the rooms in her house with stone blocks, creating a perfect copy of the crypt in which she had been imprisoned. She had moved everything from the tomb—carpets, books, tapestries, et cetera—to her house, and once it was all in place, she went into it, and refused to come out. Her servants, who had no choice but to obey her orders, brought her food and water and tended to all her needs, but were instructed not to disturb her more than once a day. Even Monsieur Pinard, whom I had once suspected of evil intentions, tried to persuade her to come out, but she would not submit.

I passed Cécile's letter to my husband. "I cannot imagine she will live much longer." His prediction was off the mark—Estella would remain, entombed in her house, for nearly another seventeen years before she died—but we did not know that at the time. It was nearly Christmas now, and we had retreated to Anglemore Park, our estate in Derbyshire.

"This business has put me off the idea of a tomb altogether." Colin and I were sitting in front of a roaring fire in the library. I put down the volume of Greek lyric poetry which I had been reading. "I think, Emily, a funeral pyre, in the style of the ancients, would be much preferable."

"I don't think spectacles of that sort are permitted in England," I said.

"I shall have to die in Greece, then. I imagine the laws about such things are more lax there."

"Don't suggest I should fling myself on your flaming body. I do adore you, but not that much."

"You are far too sensible to consider such a thing."

"Quite, but I admit that Estella's plight has not put me off a nice tomb. We should leave something interesting for archaeologists to dig up after a thousand years."

"How did we ever get on such a morbid topic?" Colin asked. "Abandon it at once, my dear, as I have other, more immediate, plans that require you to be very much alive." I was about to insist that we retire upstairs so that I might abandon myself to his attentions when Davis opened the door.

"Sorry to disturb, madam. A telegram for you." He presented it to me on a silver tray, bowed, and left the room. I opened it and read it three times before looking up at my husband.

"Jeremy is engaged to be married."

"Bainbridge? Heaven help the girl. Who is she?"

"Amity Wells, a friend from Christabel Peabody's Cairo days. He invites us for New Year so that we might make her acquaintance."

"Must we?"

"We must." I smiled, glad that my friend had at last met his match. "I should reply without delay. He will be waiting—he's obviously agitated, or he would have sent a letter instead of a telegram." There may have been the slightest of pangs in my heart to have lost his affections, but if so, they were replaced almost at once by great joy. My husband removed the telegram from my hand, dropped it onto the floor, and scooped me up in his arms.

"I have grown tired of Estella Lamar, tombs, Bainbridge, telegrams, anything, in fact, that might distract me from giving you the very thorough seeing-to I have had in mind since I saw you this morning." He shifted me so that he could open the door. The sight of us startled the footman on duty in the Great Hall, but he managed to more or less maintain his composure. Colin nodded as we passed him and then carried me up the stairs.

Who could think of telegrams at a time like that?

AUTHOR'S NOTE

This novel was inspired by two pieces of research that I had done years ago. The first came when I was writing my second book, *A Poisoned Season*. While searching for information about the London season, I came across a magnificent cache of photographs, taken at a fancy dress ball given by the Duchess of Devonshire in 1897—six years too late for me at the time. I took copious notes, tracked down a copy of an out-of-print book written on the subject, and filed it all away. Seven years later, as I was mulling over the plot of *The Counterfeit Heiress*, I decided that the book had to open at a masquerade. I remembered the photographs, and, figuring they would now be useful, pulled out my book, only to realize that the ball, given on 2 July 1897, coincided perfectly with the time my novel was set. Kismet!

I have endeavored to describe the ball as accurately as possible, this made easier by the photographs of so many of the guests. The duchess hired Mr. Lafayette to record the event, and as he explained, "I created a temporary studio in the garden, with a powerful installation of electric light; and though it may sound immodest to say so, the appearance of 'a gay photographer' at such a function was considered highly original, and was openly spoken of as a feature of the historic occasion." These pictures (and the ones taken in his studio—many of the attendees chose to pose formally before or after the ball) would have been lost, had a collection of eighty thousand negatives not been discovered in a London attic in 1968. This astonishing archive of the Lafayette Studio from the nineteenth and early twentieth centuries was saved, but no one did anything with it until 1988, when they were divided between the Victoria and Albert Museum and the National Portrait Gallery, and subsequently made available to the public.

The ball was a spectacle that London would not soon forget. The elaborate costumes, many fashioned by the top dressmakers of the time, including the House of Worth, were exquisite. Jean Worth commented that the jewels sewn into one "kept several girls busy for almost a month." The queen herself did not attend, but the Prince and Princess of Wales led the royal party, and were seated to watch a series of processions, in which the guests marched by, divided into courts, as dictated by their costumes. First came the English Court, which included, among many others, Lady Tweedmouth dressed as Queen Elizabeth and Lady Edmonstone as Mary, Queen of Scots. The Austrian Court of Maria Theresa, the Russian Court of Catherine the Great, a group of Orientals (replete with the Queen of Sheba, a snake charmer, and any number of Cleopatras), then Italians, and, finally, those in allegorical costumes followed. The final person to parade by was Lady Wolverton, dressed as Britannia.

I based Emily's dress for the occasion on that worn by Lady Archibald Campbell. I did not, however, give her the lady's crescent-moon headdress glowing with electric light. That seemed better suited to Mary Darby's version of Artemis.

All this wonderful information about the ball did not become necessary until I had first settled on the basic story of the book, and that was inspired by Huguette Clark's obituary in the *New York*

Times on 24 May 2011. Miss Clark, who died at 104, was the youngest daughter of a copper baron, and heiress to a $300 million fortune. She was a child of her father's second marriage, and was unusually close to her mother. She collected dolls, was in possession of magnificent works of art, and was married, briefly, in 1928. Her former husband claimed the marriage was never consummated. When she died, she had been living in hospitals for more than twenty years, despite the fact that she had three homes, including a forty-two-room apartment on Manhattan's Fifth Avenue, and two estates, one in Connecticut and one in Santa Barbara, California. Each of these residences was fully staffed and in tip-top shape, ready for Miss Clark to arrive at any time, but she had not been in any of them in decades. It was this last detail that grabbed my attention. Three magnificent homes, and Miss Clark chose to live in hospitals. Yet despite that choice, she maintained all of her residences. Why?

Estella Lamar is not Huguette Clark, but I used Miss Clark's story as a stepping-off place for the character. A few weeks after I had finished writing the first draft of the book, I started reading more about Miss Clark, and learned that Au Nain Bleu, the shop I had chosen from a nineteenth-century Baedeker guide to Paris as Estella's preferred source for dolls, was also where Miss Clark had bought many of hers. More eerie was the information that, before she started living in hospitals, Miss Clark had retreated into a single room in her New York apartment, lit only by a single candle. Perhaps she was more like Estella than I had imagined.

The details concerning Père-Lachaise and the Paris Catacombs are all factual. Any mistakes are my own.

Finally, I must give credit to Barbara Mertz, writing as Elizabeth Peters, for one bit of *The Counterfeit Heiress*. Like many of my readers, I am a huge fan of the Amelia Peabody series, and while writing this novel, I decided to include an Amelia reference. The Baroness von Hohensteinbauergrunewald, whose name Emily and Cécile discuss at Le Meurice, is a character in the second Amelia book, *The Mummy Case.* Cécile, naturally, is aware of the baroness, having read the newspaper coverage of Amelia's numerous adventures in Egypt. The astute reader will also recognize my reference to the *Daily Yell.* Sadly, there is no redheaded reporter. If you are not familiar with Amelia's numerous adventures, you should remedy the situation at once; I promise you will be delighted.

Two days after I wrote that scene, Barbara Mertz passed away. I am quite confident her heart balanced perfectly with the feather of Maat, and that she was sped along to a most pleasant eternal life. Would Osiris stand for anything less? Amelia certainly would not.

AN INTERVIEW WITH THE AUTHOR

Stephanie Stewart-Howard:

What keeps you, and contemporary readers, so drawn to the Victorian era—it wasn't exactly all fairy-tale romance for women in 1890? I mean, there are the clothes and all, but . . .

Tasha Alexander:

The clothes are indeed fabulous, but you are quite right—it was far from all fairy-tale romance for women of the era. However, it was a time during which women were (finally) able to make significant strides toward suffrage, and that, combined with the political situation on the continent and in England, as well as the social mobility brought by the Industrial Revolution, gives it a depth and excitement not found in many other periods. The world is in turmoil, and on the verge of a war that will reshape civilization, but no one can see that in the 1890s, a fact I have always found rather poignant. The English aristocracy believed they—and the Empire—would go on forever, but in fact they were in the midst of a decline that would not be stopped. The luxurious trappings of the Gilded Age may have allowed them to ignore what they wanted to ignore, but it could not stave off the inevitable.

SSH:

Emily is a great character—you've kept her arc slow enough to have her proto-feminist enlightenment, and those of her significant other and friends, be believable. What do you feel you can and can't do with her to keep it that way?

TA:

Thank you! It is very important to me to keep her character realistic. For us, in the twenty-first century, it is easy to reject all the inconvenient parts of Victorian social mores. Why didn't women refuse to be treated as they were? Why on earth did so many people accept such a repressive society? To those brought up in the nineteenth century, the problems and limitations of their world were not quite so obvious, and it is essential that I keep in mind that Emily would not have rejected wholesale her entire upbringing overnight. When I first started to construct her character, I was interested in exploring the idea of social change, and what is necessary for it. The Victorian era is replete with wonderful iconoclasts, individuals who seem to have been born to fight for social justice. People like this are essential to change, but until a greater part of the population begins to agree with them, it is unlikely that the status quo will be threatened. With Emily, I wanted to explore what it would take for a young woman who is living quite comfortably—the current social mores give her more or less everything she thinks she would want—to begin to question the world around her. First, I wanted her to undergo an intellectual awakening, because that is essential to her further development. She needs to be able to think and observe and analyze. Next, she needed to start to see a broader view of the world, both through travel and by beginning to get to know people who are not of her class. Only then can she begin to recognize injustice and gather the courage to fight for change. Because it did take courage.

SSH:

This book deals with a Parisian heiress who's revealed to be an imposter. Obviously, in a pre-modern tech world, it's easier to fake an identity but can you tell us, without giving too much away, what it took to really pull something like this off 120 years ago?

TA:

So much easier without our current technology! Although, I suppose one could argue that there are ways (Photoshop, etc.) that it might be simpler in our world. In the nineteenth century, people did not have easy methods to communicate across long distances. Yes, one could send a telegram or a letter, but either could be forged. Also, because people did not have their photographs taken constantly, as we do now (thank you—or not—cell phones), it was harder to recognize individuals whom one had not seen for years and years. So if one resembled a person well enough, and one stayed away from anyone who knew said person well (or at all), it would be possible to pose as someone else.

SSH:

Were there actual cases of imposters pulling off something like this at the time? Do you have real-life inspirations for this book?

TA:

I came across many stories of imposters when I was researching my second book, *A Poisoned Season.* Most are about individuals who claimed to be a famous thought-to-be-dead child, e.g., the Dauphin of France after the revolution, the Little Princes in the Tower, etc. The more direct real life inspiration for this book, however, is Huguette Clark, an American heiress who died in New York City at 104 in 2011. There was no question of imposters here, but Miss Clark's life fascinated me. She had an immense fortune, but chose to live in a hospital room for two decades, leaving three empty homes, each furnished and staffed, as if waiting for her arrival.

SSH:

There's the cliché about life in the past having been "simpler"—do you really think it was, for the people who lived it?

Tasha:

I think we all like to believe that the past was simpler, and there are, no doubt, ways in which it was, but at the same time, there were just as many ways in which it was not. I, for one, am immensely grateful for the invention of dishwashers. That said, there is no question that the modern world makes it difficult to live in the moment and take pleasure in simple things without being distracted by cell phones, computers, etc., etc. We do, though, have the option of ignoring them or turning them off, so we really have no one to blame but ourselves. In the end, I think our lives are no more or less simple than those of people in the past. The complications are just different now.

SSH:

What are the things Emily puts up with in daily life that you honestly couldn't deal with?

TA:

This might sound crazy, because, yes, there are times I really do wish I could summon a butler to bring me tea, but I do not think I could live in a house with servants. You would never have privacy, and I would always feel bad about not helping them work. Of course, had I lived in the nineteenth century, neither of these concerns would ever have occurred to me, as I would have grown up accustomed to them.

SSH:

Cosplay, yes or no? Have you ever run into anyone dressed as one of your characters? And who do you want to dress up as?

TA:

Cosplay? Oh, heck, yes! Who wouldn't want to dress up? I only wish I had more opportunity to do it. I haven't ever run into someone dressed as one of my characters, but would love to. As for what I would dress as . . . there are too many. I have a Princess Leia costume for Halloween. I'd love a Regency day dress, a reconstruction of an 1890s Worth ball gown, a sari covered with jewels, a Roman pelpos with really fabulous pins, one of those gorgeous frothy turn-of-the century creations, a pioneer costume (back to my Little House days). I could go on and on. Haven't run into anyone dressed as one of my characters yet, but that would be amazing. . . .

Excerpted from an interview conducted by Stephanie Stewart-Howard on The Mary Sue.

1. Emily has constant obstacles thrown in her way because she is a woman. Are there any ways, however, that being a nineteenth-century woman works to her advantage?

2. Britain in 1897 was a society with enormous gaps between the wealthy and the poor. What would Mary Darby have thought when she saw the interior of Devonshire House?

3. How much more difficult would it be for any of us today to disappear in the way Estella did? Does modern technology limit us as much as it helps us?

4. Do you believe Jeremy's stated goal of being "the most useless man in England"? Why or why not?

5. Was the decision to move the bodies of the famous—Abélard and Héloïse, Molière, among others—to Père-Lachaise morally sound? What about the skeletons stacked in the Catacombs? Do we worry less about the moral implications of the treatment of human remains when we can't identify the individuals?

6. Are there ways in which Cécile, who has very rigid ideas about certain aspects of her life, and Estella are similar? Where is the line between charmingly eccentric and mad?

7. How morally culpable is Farrington Jones? He shouldn't have kidnapped Estella, but, in the end, did he actually make it possible for her to live the way she desired? Or, might she have lived a "normal" life if he'd never taken her?

8. Should Estella's servants have suspected something was amiss when they went so many years without seeing their mistress?

9. What do you think of Estella's decision to re-create the tomb in her house? Would she have preferred to stay in the original?

10. Estella's version of happiness is not one many others would share. Does that make it less valid?

Read on for an excerpt from
Tasha Alexander's next novel

THE ADVENTURESS

Available Now

1

"The English duke is dead."

The words, muffled and heavily accented, hardly reached me through the voluminous duvet that, while I slept, had somehow twisted around me with such violence that it now more closely resembled mummy wrappings than a blanket. Struggling against its bonds, I managed to extricate one hand before realizing my head was under a stack of pillows. I flung them aside and sat up, turning to discover my husband was no longer in the bed. The words came again, and this time vanquished in an instant all of the confusion clouding my mind after being awoken from a deep slumber.

"Monsieur, the duke, the English duke, he is dead."

"Jeremy?" I leapt from the bed, dragging the duvet with me (I had not been quite so successful in the removal of it from my person as I had hoped), and started for the narrow patch of light coming into our room from the door, held open by my husband, his dressing gown pulled around him. A chasm seemed to open inside me, as if my heart were splitting and filling me simultaneously with intolerable cold and heat. Jeremy Sheffield, Duke of Bainbridge, my dearest child-hood friend, who had tormented me in my youth not quite so much as I had tormented him, could not be dead. I tried to step forward, but my limbs would obey no commands.

"Is he in his suite?" my husband asked. The man standing in the corridor nodded. "I shall come at once."

He must have closed the door, but I have no memory of him having done so. I collapsed in an undignified heap, my legs no longer able to support me.

"Emily." Colin knelt at my side, scooped me into his arms, and deposited me back onto the bed. "I must see what has happened and will return as quickly as possible. Will you be all right?"

"Yes, of course." I rubbed my face. "No. No. I must come with you."

"I don't think you ought." His dark eyes locked onto mine, and I could see pain and worry and just a bit of frustration in them.

"I have to see him. I—"

"No." He squeezed my hand and slipped the dressing gown from his shoulders, finding and putting on the stiff boiled shirt he had discarded earlier in the evening with entirely no regard for its subsequent condition. After retrieving his trousers from the back of a chair and locating his shoes—one had disappeared under the bed—he shrugged into his tailcoat and walked to the door, pausing to turn back and look at me as he opened it. Had I not been so upset, I would have better appreciated the handsome dishevelment of his cobbled-together evening kit. "I am so terribly sorry, Emily."

The tears did not come before the door clicked shut behind him, but then my eyes produced a worthy monsoon. Sudden storms are short, however, and this was no time for succumbing to emotion. I splashed water on my face, pulled on my dressing gown—there could be no question of returning to my own previously discarded garments. Ladies' gowns are designed to require assistance, and while this may allow for a more beautifully designed bodice, it proves an immense frustration when one finds oneself on one's own.

Fortunately, no one saw me slip out of our room as there were not yet other guests meandering through the Hotel Britannia, the most fashionable place to stay on La Croisette in Cannes, and arguably on the whole of the Côte d'Azur. A clock near the curved marble staircase told me it was nearly half five in the morning. Anyone awake now would either be a servant or someone staggering in from a long evening probably spent playing baccarat at the Cercle Nautique. I climbed one flight to the top floor, where Jeremy had insisted on staying. The view, he said, was incomparable. His door was closed and locked, so I tapped on it, and a man I did not recognize opened it without delay.

"Madame, you would not wish—"

I pushed past him and went straight through the sitting room to the bedroom, where I saw my husband standing with two other men. On the bed was the prostrate form of a gentleman in evening kit.

I recognized the wiry man closest to the bed as the hotel doctor. He adjusted the tortoiseshell pince-nez on his long nose and placed his unopened bag on a bedside table. "We will need to further examine him, of course, but there is no question—"

"There is no question," I said, stepping forward with no regard for any of them, "because this is not the duke."

"Emily—" Colin reached for my arm, but I pulled away and moved to the opposite side of the bed, closer to the body, determined to confirm the identity of the man. It was harder to move him than I had anticipated, but I managed to roll him over and reveal his face, the eyes staring and vacant.

"Chauncey Neville." I was shaking rather violently now, and realized that I was barefoot and my teeth were chattering. "It is not Jeremy. Not Jeremy." Mr. Neville, a shy, soft-spoken gentleman from Cornwall, had always seemed an unlikely friend for Jeremy, but the two had been close since their days at school. We often joked that they tempered each other, Chauncey reeling in Jeremy when he got too out of hand, and Jeremy prodding Chauncey to embrace joviality. Shy though he was, Mr. Neville never proved awkward in social situations, but instead was kind and thoughtful, always on hand to support his friends in any of their schemes.

"Come, my dear," Colin said. "You will catch your death of cold. You know how chilly the seaside gets at night."

Any person who has had the privilege of forming even the barest sort of acquaintance with Colin Hargreaves knows he is not the sort of gentleman to make such trite remarks. Rather, he is the most trusted agent of the Crown, a particular favorite of Queen Victoria's, and the individual most frequently called upon by the palace to assist in delicate matters that threaten the state of our great empire. My eyes focused better on the room now, and I saw the manager of the hotel wringing his hands.

"Fear not, Monsieur Fortier, this is not the first body I have seen," I said. In fact, I had seen many. The work my husband and I shared—sometimes in official capacities, sometimes when we chose on our own to help those in need of assistance—had led us to reveal the identities of no fewer than nine cruel murderers. I was not a stranger to violent death. Whether my words soothed the concerned hotelier, I do not know. Colin removed me to our own suite of rooms before I could gauge the man's reaction. Regardless, the untimely demise of one of our party would dramatically alter what had been intended as celebratory holiday on the Côte d'Azur.

Nearly four months ago, at Christmas, I had received a telegram from Jeremy, announcing his engagement to Miss Amity Wells, an American heiress who had realized her parents' dearest hopes by catching an English duke. Miss Wells's mother, a veritable battle-axe of a woman, far better suited to roping steers on the range than moving in high society, insisted on throwing an engagement party to celebrate the match, but would not content herself with a ball in Mayfair. Instead, she had planned a trip to the south of France, where all the closest friends and family of the bride and groom would spend a fortnight culminating in a party she assured us would be more spectacular than any we had ever seen. England, she explained in a coarse whisper, was such a little island it could not possibly be expected to hold all her big ideas.

Colin and I had met mother and daughter over New Year at Jeremy's estate in Kent; the Wellses had cut short a trip to Egypt for the occasion. While Mrs. Wells could be described as a force of nature, one had to accept Amity as something akin to a dream. Her fresh-faced beauty, enviable figure, flair for fashion, and quick wit made her a favorite in London society. A favorite with the gentlemen, that is. I am sorry to say that my own fair sex proved far less generous with her, a reaction firmly footed in the lair of envy. I scorned this, knowing it to be unfair, but must acknowledge that my reaction to Miss Wells proved somewhat more complicated than I should have liked.

The estate of the Duke of Bainbridge lay adjacent to that of my own excellent father, and Jeremy and I had been inseparable as children. When it came time for him to leave for school, I cried for three days straight, and marked on my calendar when he would be home between terms, counting the weeks until I would see him again. By the time he had finished at Harrow and was leaving for Oxford, we no longer climbed trees together, instead finding great amusement in the knowledge that both our mothers longed to see us (and our families) united in marriage. Neither of us could think of anything more ridiculous, for although we adored each other, our temperaments and our interests could not have been more at odds. I had grown up studious and intellectual; Jeremy had championed the goal of being the most useless man in England. When his father died suddenly during his son's second year at university, everyone hoped the new duke would undergo a transformation à la Prince Hal and adopt a more solemn and appropriate demeanor. This served only to spur him into more questionable behavior.

Jeremy played the rake with consummate skill, but, at heart, his kindness and steadfast loyalty prevented him from ever becoming truly profligate. He claimed this to be his greatest disappointment. He took splendid care of his mother, refusing to let her be holed up in dowager quarters, and, knowing both what an asset she had been to his father and how much she had enjoyed helping to run the estate, insisted that she continue her work. He did as little as possible, squeaked through Oxford with a degree he claimed disgraced every Bainbridge ancestor, ran with a fast set, and, perhaps, drank too much on occasion, but he never got himself into irreparable trouble. Everyone in society fawned over him, particularly the legion of mothers who longed for the dashing, fun-loving duke (whose fortune was even more attractive than his bright blue eyes) to someday propose to one of their daughters.

Over the years, Jeremy's steadfast resistance to marriage became the stuff of legends. He did everything in his not inconsiderable powers to avoid it, including pretending to court my close friend Margaret Michaels, née Seward. Their deception was borne out of mutual need. Margaret, an American, had been sent to England much like Amity Wells, to catch a titled husband. She, however, had no interest in such things, wanting instead to study at Oxford. She and Jeremy spent a season pretending to be in and out of love. Eventually, when he threw her over (at her insistence, of course), she pled a broken heart and convinced her parents that they must not try to force her into marriage until she had quite forgot the duke. Jeremy let it be known (quietly) that he felt an English peer ought not marry an American, a sentiment lauded by the aforementioned legion of mothers. Their daughters vied for his attention with such implacable nerve that it began to make him quite unable to enjoy all the social functions in which he used to take such pleasure. Finding this condition unacceptable in the extreme, he decided to direct all of his affections toward me, his oldest friend.

At the time, I was a young widow, my first husband having been murdered only a few months after our wedding. Out of mourning and back in society, I had fallen in love with Colin Hargreaves, and even after I had accepted his proposal of marriage, Jeremy refused to stop pressing his own suit. Not, mind you, because he actually loved me, but because he knew I would go along with his scheme. He viewed my engagement as a gift from the Dear Lord himself. Society believed him to be heartbroken and devoted to a lady he could not have, and the legion of mothers could tolerate with relative equanimity waiting for him to recover from the blow my second marriage struck.

Colin accepted this arrangement with good humor, knowing full well Jeremy had never been a threat to our marital happiness. He also knew that one day, Jeremy would have to marry. He might play the profligate, but he would never leave his dukedom without an heir. Much as I enjoyed Jeremy's little game, I had rejoiced when I read his telegram and knew it was over. I longed to see my friend as happily settled as I.

Then I met Amity Wells.

I am, perhaps, not being entirely fair. She failed to make much of an impression at our first meeting, but balls do not provide much of an opportunity for deep conversation. Our trip to Cannes was to offer us that. Yet almost from the moment I stepped into La Croisette with her, I knew we could never be friends. And I feared Jeremy would never forgive me for that.

Amity
Twelve months earlier

India did not suit Amity. The oppressive heat reminded her too much of her grandparents' plantation house in Natchez, Louisiana, where she had spent more than one unhappy summer while her parents retreated from New York's Fifth Avenue to their mansion in Newport. This arrangement came at the insistence of her grandmother, Varina Beauregard Wells, who was as unhappy at the Confederate loss in the War between the States as she was that her Harvard-educated son had abandoned all his breeding and married a Yankee. She had always objected to sending him north for an education. The fortune he earned in copper tempered her displeasure, but she was not about to let her only granddaughter grow up with coarse northern manners. Her daughter-in-law made no effort to dissuade her. Learning to simper in that charming southern way could do nothing but enhance Amity's value on the Marriage Market, and Birdie Wells had every intention of seeing her daughter married to an English nobleman. So far as she was concerned, this outcome was nonnegotiable. Her husband had no interest in arguing with her regarding this or anything else about which she felt strongly.

"She must be a duchess, don't you think?" Birdie—Amity had

never been able to think of her mother as anything but Birdie—made a habit of talking about her daughter as if she were not there.

"I am sure you know best, dearie." Amity's father loved to indulge his wife, who was delightfully unlike the Southern belles his mother had traipsed before him, hoping he would take one of them as his bride. Their superficial charms were many, but none could compete with his Birdie, who spoke with a shocking degree of directness. The day they met she had looked him in the eyes and said, *You are less of a fool than I expected, Wells,* and he knew he had found his partner in life.

"I am doing this all for you, my dear. Vanderbilt's daughter caught a duke and we cannot tolerate falling beneath that family. I should be unable to take so much as a step out of the house. We have got to take her abroad without delay."

"I would never deny you something you want so badly, Birdie." Mr. Wells folded up his newspaper and left for his office, where, after finalizing a deal that nearly doubled the family's already enormous fortune, set about making plans for their trip. That he chose to start with India reflected his priorities. An old friend who had wrangled himself a plum position after the dissolution of the East India Company had invited him to visit, with the object of convincing him to invest in what he was certain would prove a most profitable arrangement. They would be in India by February, and stay until the following winter, when they would remove themselves to Egypt, and form all the acquaintances necessary to make an appropriate splash in London the following spring. Birdie would have preferred to start in London, but understood her husband too well to suggest an alternative to his itinerary.

Within hours of their arrival in Bombay, Amity was being heralded as the belle of ex-pat society. Invitations poured in, and the family found themselves in even greater demand than that to which they were accustomed in New York. Birdie's exuberant parties proved a great success with the British community, although Amity noticed more than a few ladies looking down their nose at her mother, especially when she insisted they ride camels to the site of one of her picnics. Regardless, Amity allowed herself to be escorted to countless events by a series of young men Birdie had vetted, but she took little pleasure in the company of any of them. She did not object to making a good marriage, but felt that she ought at least to be allowed to like her future husband. Her new friend, Miss Christabel Peabody, shared this view. Miss Peabody, a young lady whose British manners and affability were both approved of by Birdie, had traveled to India to visit her brother, who was serving there in the army. Within a fortnight of their introduction, she and Amity were inseparable.

"I do not think I shall ever adjust to being here," Amity said, as she and Christabel lounged in the courtyard of the villa Mr. Wells had taken for their stay. "The humidity is intolerable." She stretched out on a chaise longue and waved a large ostrich fan in front of her face.

"And it is not yet summer," Christabel said. "You will adore Simla, though. Everyone spends the summer there. The society is incomparable."

"Incomparable society in Simla?" A stocky man in uniform approached them, Birdie's housekeeper following behind, doing her best to announce the visitor. "Christabel, you are giving this young lady the wrong idea altogether."

"Captain Charles Peabody, Miss Wells!" The servant made a slight bow, her hands pressed together as if she were praying.

"Very good, thank you," Amity said.

"And Captain Jack Sheffield as well."

Amity thanked the housekeeper again and inspected the new arrivals. Christabel's brother, Captain Peabody, was a bit of a disappointment; Amity preferred her officers to cut rather more of a dashing figure in uniform. Fortunately for her, the gentleman with him filled the role admirably. Tall and lanky, Captain Sheffield moved with careless ease, and Amity was taken at once with his easy humor and self-deprecating ways.

"The society in Simla is the worst sort of colonial balderdash," Captain Peabody said. "If one is to be in India, one ought to *be* there, not set up some sorry version of England instead."

"Going native, Peabody?" Captain Sheffield's grin brightened the room.

"I take all my opinions from you, old boy, so you ought not criticize me."

"Quite right." Captain Sheffield tugged at the cuffs of his bright red jacket. "India is magnificent: exotic and mysterious. How many forts have you ladies visited thus far?"

"Forts?" Amity asked, pursing her perfect lips and raising her eyebrows. "Why should I have even the slightest interest in visiting forts? Unless you can promise me more officers as charming as the two of you?"

"Not that sort of fort, Miss Wells," Captain Sheffield said. "I speak of the ruins of ancient citadels, the towering walls and heavy gates that kept safe the maharajas and their jewels. You do know about the maharajas and their jewels?"

"What girl worth her salt wouldn't?" Amity smiled. "Daddy promised me emeralds while we are here."

"Good girl. Insist on rubies as well."

"Sheffield is a terrible influence," Captain Peabody said. "But you could not put yourselves in better hands should you want a guide to show you the area. I am afraid, Christabel, that I will not have quite so much liberty as I had hoped during your visit. Mother is furious, but I must do my duty."

"Of course, Charles. No one would expect less from you," Christabel said.

"I have brought my friend along as a peace offering. Mother has no interest in doing anything beyond taking tea with her old friends, and I do not wish to see you trapped doing only that. So far as she is concerned, she has already seen the best of India."

"She and father were here for nearly a decade."

"Yes, but she is very keen on you having a wander around, so long as it does not interfere with her routine. Sheffield is as good a bloke as I know. He will look after you well."

"I am still in the room, Peabody."

"Right. Well. I must be off. I shall leave the three of you to formulate a plan for your adventures."

From that day forth, Captain Sheffield spent every waking hour not required of him by the army with Amity and Christabel. Birdie initially balked at the young man. Captain Sheffield would never make an acceptable candidate for her daughter's husband—he was a dreaded younger son, and, hence, without title or fortune—but once she learned he was the brother of the Duke of Bainbridge, Britain's most desirable bachelor, her feelings warmed slightly. That is to say, she no longer did her best to discourage the acquaintance.

Amity, Christabel, and Jack—for none of them required formality of the others any longer—began to refer to themselves as The Three Musketeers. They traveled (chaperoned, of course, by Birdie) to the Golden Temple at Amritsar, where Amity threatened to become a Sikh, but only if she would be allowed to wear a turban and carry a dagger. The dagger, Jack assured her, was a requirement. They lamented the sorry state of the Lake Palace at Udaipur, where the damp had taken hold and ruined much of the fine interior.

"I shall make it my mission to return here and restore every corner of this place," Amity said.

"I have been laboring under the impression that India did not suit you," Jack said. "It would be impossible to count the number of times you have told me you would prefer to be in Paris or London—"

"Or the Alps," Christabel continued, crossing to her friends after she had finished photographing the remains of a frieze on one of the walls. Her brother had given her a camera for Christmas, and she had become something of an expert at using it. Carrying it on their trips often proved problematic, but they all agreed it was worth the aggravation when they saw her pictures. "Or Rome—"

"Stop, you wretched beasts! I repent," Amity said. "I repent wholly. The subcontinent has grown on me. When are we to see the tigers?"

Birdie categorically refused to allow a safari of any sort, tigers or not. This did not give Amity more than the slightest pause. She appealed to her father, who never could resist her, and he organized a hunting party for them. Christabel very nearly begged off coming, but was persuaded in the end, although she was convinced, up almost to the last moment, that it was a wretched idea.

"Come now, Bel," Amity said. "Think of us, camping in the wild, riding on elephants—"

"I do quite fancy riding on an elephant," Christabel said.

"I promise you will never regret it."

"Oh, Amity, I can never say no to you!"

"Why would you want to?" Amity smiled. They departed for the Rajastani hills the next morning.

MINOTAUR SIGNATURE EDITIONS

READ THEM ALL

ACCLAIMED TITLES—ONLY $9.99 EACH!

ENJOY FIRST-IN-SERIES AND "GATEWAY" BOOKS FROM BESTSELLING AND AWARD-WINNING AUTHORS.

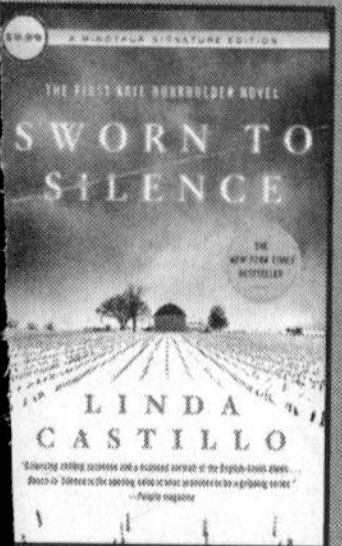

978-1-250-16163-5
ON SALE 9/5/17

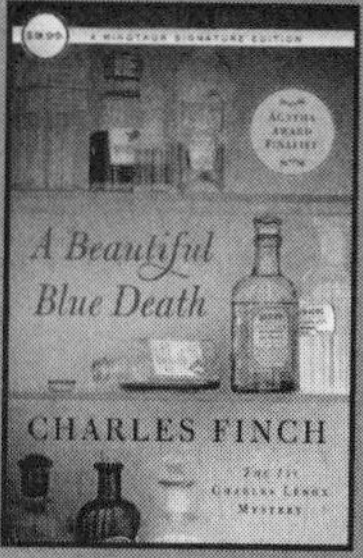

978-1-250-16164-2
ON SALE 9/5/17

978-1-250-16165-9
ON SALE 10/3/17

978-1-250-16166-6
ON SALE 10/3/17

978-1-250-16036-2
ON SALE 11/7/17

78-1-250-14468-3
ON SALE 11/7/17

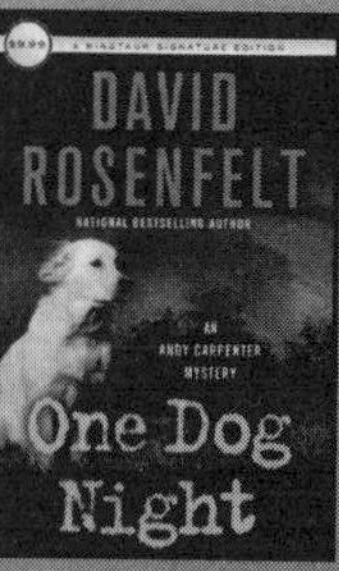

978-1-250-16035-5
ON SALE 12/5/17

978-1-250-16034-8
ON SALE 12/5/17

978-1-250-17515-1
ON SALE 3/6/18

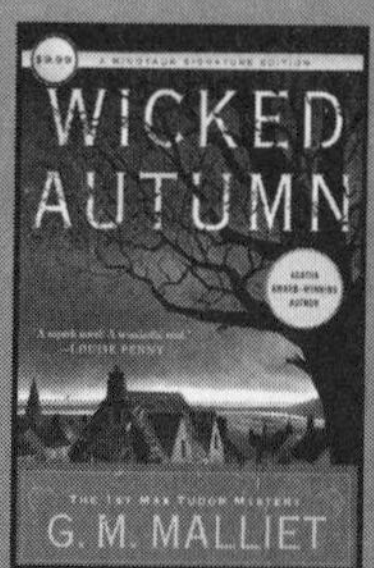

978-1-250-17505-2
ON SALE 3/6/18

BONUS MATERIAL INCLUDED:

W INTRODUCTIONS, READING GROUP QUESTIONS, AND TEASER EXCERPTS